Accomplished screenwriters and producers Michael Hjorth and Hans Rosenfeldt stormed the bestseller lists with the publication of *Sebastian Bergman* in their native Sweden in 2010. Rosenfeldt is the creator of the hit BBC4 series *The Bridge* and both authors contributed to the recent screenplay for the original Swedish series of *Wallander*.

SEBASTIAN BERGMAN

HJORTH ROSENFELDT

TRANSLATION BY MARLAINE DELARGY

TRAPDOOR

First published in Sweden in 2010 as *Det Fördolda* by Nordstedts
First published in Australia in 2012 by Pier 9, an imprint of Murdoch Books
First published in Great Britain in 2012 by Trapdoor

3 5 7 9 10 8 6 4

A CIP catalogue record for this book
is available from the British Library.

ISBN 978-1-84744-575-9

Typeset in Bembo by M Rules
Printed and bound in Great Britain by
Clays Ltd, St Ives plc

Papers used by Trapdoor are from well-managed forests
and other responsible sources.

MIX
Paper from
responsible sources
FSC® C104740

Trapdoor
An imprint of
Little, Brown Book Group
Carmelite House
50 Victoria Embankment
London EC4Y 0DZ

An Hachette UK Company
www.hachette.co.uk

www.littlebrown.co.uk

SEBASTIAN BERGMAN

The man was not a murderer.

He repeated this to himself as he dragged the dead boy down the slope: *I am not a murderer.*

Murderers are criminals. Murderers are evil. The darkness has swallowed up their souls, and for numerous reasons they have embraced the blackness and welcomed it, turned their backs on the light. He was not evil.

On the contrary.

Hadn't he recently provided clear proof of the absolute opposite? Hadn't he almost completely put aside his own feelings, his own wishes, restrained himself, all for the wellbeing of others? Turned the other cheek – that was what he had done. Didn't his presence here – in this bog in the middle of nowhere with the dead boy – provide still further proof that he wanted to do the right thing? *Had to do* the right thing? That he would never be found wanting again?

The man stopped and let out a long breath. Although the boy wasn't very old, he was heavy, muscular. Many hours spent at the gym. But there wasn't far to go. The man grabbed hold of the trouser legs, which had once been white but now looked almost black in the darkness. The boy had bled so profusely.

Yes, it was wrong to kill. The fifth commandment: *Thou shalt not kill.* But there were exceptions. In many places the Bible actually justified killing. There were those who deserved it. Wrong could be right. Nothing was an absolute given. And what if the reason behind the killing was not selfish? If the loss of one human life would save others? Give them a chance. Give them a life. In that case, surely, the act could not be classed as evil. If the intention was good.

The man stopped by the dark waters of the little pool. Normally it was several metres deep, but the recent rain had saturated the

1

ground, and now it was more like a small lake in the middle of the overgrown bog.

The man leaned forward and seized the shoulders of the boy's T-shirt. With considerable difficulty he managed to get the lifeless body into a half-standing position. For a moment he looked straight into the boy's eyes. What had been the boy's final thought? Had there even been time for a final thought? Did he realise he was going to die? Did he wonder why? Did he think about all the things he hadn't managed to do in his short life, or about those things he had actually done?

It didn't matter.

Why was he torturing himself like this – more than necessary?

He had no choice.

He couldn't let them down.

Not again.

And yet, he hesitated. No, they wouldn't understand. Wouldn't forgive. Wouldn't turn the other cheek, as he had done.

He gave the boy a push and the body fell into the water with a splash. The man gave a start, unprepared for the sound in the dark silence.

The boy's body sank down into the water and disappeared.

The man who was not a murderer walked back to his car, which was parked on the little forest track, and headed for home.

'Västerås police, Klara Lidman speaking.'

'I'd like to report my son missing.'

The woman sounded almost apologetic, as if she wasn't quite sure she had the right number, or she didn't really expect to be believed. Klara Lidman reached for her notepad, even though the conversation was being recorded.

'Could I have your name, please?'

'Eriksson, Lena Eriksson. My son's name is Roger. Roger Eriksson.'

'And how old is your son?'

'Sixteen. I haven't seen him since yesterday afternoon.'

Klara made a note of the age and realised she would have to pass this on for immediate action. If he really had disappeared, of course.

'What time yesterday afternoon?'

'He went off at five o'clock.'

Twenty-two hours ago. Twenty-two important hours when it came to a disappearance.

'Do you know where he went?'

'Yes, to see Lisa.'

'Who's Lisa?'

'His girlfriend. I called her today, but she said he left her at about ten o'clock last night.'

Klara crossed out 'twenty-two' and replaced it with 'seventeen'.

'So where did he go after that?'

'She didn't know. Home, she thought. But he hasn't been home. He hasn't been home all night. And now the whole day has almost gone.'

And you didn't ring until now, Klara thought. It struck her that the woman on the other end of the phone didn't sound particularly agitated. More subdued. Resigned.

'What's Lisa's surname?'

'Hansson.'

Klara made a note of the name.

'Does Roger have a mobile phone? Have you tried calling him?'

'Yes, but there's no reply.'

'And you have no idea where he might have gone? Could he have stayed over with friends, something like that?'

'No, he would have called me.'

Lena Eriksson paused briefly and Klara assumed that her voice was breaking, but when she heard the sucking intake of breath on the other end she realised that the woman was taking a long drag on a cigarette. She heard Lena blow out the smoke.

'He's just disappeared.'

The dream came every night. It gave him no peace.

Always the same dream, bringing with it the same fear. It irritated him. Drove him crazy. Sebastian Bergman was better than that. More than anyone, he knew what dreams meant. More than anyone, he ought to be able to rise above these febrile remnants of the past. But however prepared he was, however aware of the real significance of the dream, he still couldn't avoid being caught up in it. It was as if he was stuck between what he knew the dream meant and who he was, and he was unable to move between the two.

04:43.

Outside, it was starting to get light. Sebastian's mouth was dry. Had he cried out? Presumably not, since the woman by his side had not woken up. She was breathing quietly, and he could see a naked breast half covered by her long hair. Sebastian straightened his cramped fingers without giving it a thought – he was used to waking up with his right hand tightly clenched after the dream. Instead, he tried to remember the name of the person sleeping by his side.

Katarina? Karin?

She must have mentioned it at some point during the evening. *Kristina? Karolin?*

Not that it really mattered – he had no intention of seeing her again – but rooting around in his memory helped to chase away the last wisps of the dream which seemed to cling to all his senses.

The dream that had pursued him for more than five years. The same dream, the same images every night. The whole of his subconscious on edge, working through the one thing he couldn't cope with during the day.

Dealing with the guilt.

Sebastian slowly got out of bed, suppressing a yawn as he picked

4

up his clothes from the chair where he had dropped them several hours ago. As he dressed he gazed uninterestedly around the room: a bed; two white fitted wardrobes, one with a mirrored door; a simple white bedside table from IKEA with an alarm clock and a magazine on it; a small table with a photograph of the child she had on alternate weeks, and a few other bits and pieces next to the chair from which he had just picked up his clothes. Nondescript prints on the walls, which some skilled real estate agent had no doubt described as 'cappuccino coloured' but which were, in fact, dirty beige. The room was like the sex he had experienced in it: unimaginative and slightly boring, but it did the job. As usual. Unfortunately, the satisfaction didn't last very long.

Sebastian closed his eyes. This was always the most painful moment. The transition to reality. The emotional U-turn. He knew it so well. He concentrated on the woman in the bed, particularly her visible nipple. What was her name again?

He knew he had introduced himself when he bought the drinks, he always did. Never when he asked if the seat beside her was free, whether he could buy her a drink, what she would like. Always when he placed the glass in front of her.

'I'm Sebastian, by the way.'

And what had she replied? Something beginning with K – he was fairly sure of that. He fastened his belt. The buckle made a faint, metallic scraping noise.

'Are you leaving?' Her voice rough with sleep, her eyes searching for a clock.

'Yes.'

'I thought we were going to have breakfast together. What time is it?'

'Almost five.'

The woman propped herself up on one elbow. How old was she? Forty, maybe? She pushed a strand of hair off her face. Sleep was fading, gradually giving way to the realisation that the morning she had pictured was never going to happen. They would not be eating breakfast while reading the newspaper and chatting easily.

5

There would be no Sunday stroll. He didn't want to get to know her better, and he wouldn't call, whatever he might say.

She knew all that. So he simply said,

'Bye, then.'

Sebastian didn't make any attempt at a name. He was no longer even sure it began with K.

The street outside was silent in the dawn light. The suburb was sleeping and every sound seemed muted, as if no one wanted to wake it up. Even the traffic on Nynäsvägen, a short distance away, sounded respectfully subdued. Sebastian stopped by the sign at the crossroads: VARPAVÄGEN. Somewhere in Gubbängen. Quite a long way from home. Was the subway running at this hour of the morning? They had taken a cab last night. Stopped at a 7-Eleven to buy bread for toast, she remembered she didn't have any at home. Because he would be staying for breakfast, wouldn't he? They had bought bread and juice, he and ... It was so fucking annoying. What the hell was her name? Sebastian set off along the deserted street.

He had hurt her, whatever her name was.

In fourteen hours he would be going to Västerås to continue his work. Although that was different: he couldn't hurt the woman in Västerås any more.

It started to rain.

What a bloody awful morning.

In Gubbängen.

Everything was going to hell in a handcart. Inspector Thomas Haraldsson's shoes were letting in water, his radio was dead and he had lost the rest of his search party. The sun was shining straight in his face, which meant he had to screw up his eyes in order to avoid stumbling over the undergrowth and roots scattered unevenly across the marshy ground. He swore to himself and looked at his watch. In just two hours Jenny would be on her lunch break at the hospital. She would get in the car and drive home, hoping he would have made it. But there was no chance. He would still be in this fucking forest.

Haraldsson's left foot sank deeper. He could feel his socks sucking up the cold water. The air held the young, fleeting warmth of spring, but winter still had the water clutched in its icy grip. He shivered, managed to extract his foot and find solid ground.

He looked around. East should be that way. Weren't the National Service recruits over there? Or the Scouts? Then again, he could have travelled in a complete circle and totally lost his bearings as to where north might be. He spotted a small hill a short distance away and realised this meant dry ground, a patch of paradise in this sodden hell. He started to move in that direction. His foot sank once more. The right one this time. Fan-fucking-tastic.

It was all Hanser's fault.

He wouldn't be standing here soaked to the skin halfway up his legs if it weren't for the fact that Hanser wanted to give the impression that she was strong and capable of decisive action. And she certainly needed to, because at heart she was no real police officer. She was one of those law school graduates who sneak through and grab the top job without getting their hands dirty or, as in Haraldsson's case, their feet wet.

No: if Haraldsson had been in charge, this would have been

7

handled very differently. True, the kid had been missing since Friday and according to regulations the correct procedure was to widen the search area, particularly as someone had reported 'nocturnal activities' and 'lights in the forest' around Listakärr that particular weekend. But Haraldsson knew from experience that this was an exercise in futility. The kid was in Stockholm, laughing at his worried mother. He was sixteen. That was the kind of thing sixteen-year-old kids did. Laughed at their mothers.

Hanser.

The wetter Haraldsson got, the more he hated her. She was the worst thing that had ever happened to him. Young, attractive, successful, political: a representative of the modern police force.

She had got in his way. When she'd held her first meeting in Västerås, Haraldsson had realised that his career had screeched to a halt. He had applied for the job. She'd got it. She would be in charge for at least five years. *His* five years. The ladder leading upwards had been snatched away. Now his career had slowly begun to plateau instead, and it felt like only a matter of time before it started to slide downwards. It was almost symbolic that he was now standing, up to his knees in stinking mud, in a forest some ten kilometres from Västerås.

The text message he had received this morning said SNUGGLE LUNCH 2DAY in big letters. It meant that Jenny was coming home during her lunch break to have sex with him, then they would have sex once or twice more during the course of the evening. That was how their lives were these days. Jenny was undergoing treatment for their failure to conceive a child, and together with the doctor she had worked out a schedule that was supposed to optimise their chances. Today was one of those optimum days. Hence the text message. Haraldsson had mixed feelings. On the one hand he appreciated the fact that their sex life had increased by several hundred per cent of late, that Jenny always wanted him. At the same time, he couldn't escape the feeling that it wasn't really him she wanted: it was his sperm. If she hadn't been so desperate for a child, it would never have occurred to her to nip home at lunchtime for a quickie. There was something of the stud farm about the whole thing. As soon as an egg began its journey towards the womb, they were at it like rabbits. In between times, too, to be honest, just to be on the safe side. But never for pleasure these days, never for the closeness. What had happened to the passion? The desire? And now she would come home in her lunch break to an empty house. Perhaps he should have called her and asked if he should jerk off before he left and stick it in a jar in the fridge. Unfortunately he wasn't completely certain Jenny would think it was all that bad an idea.

It had started the previous Saturday.

A call had been put through to the Västerås police via the emergency number at about 15:00. A mother had reported her sixteen-year-old son missing. Since the call involved a minor, it was given top priority. Entirely in accordance with regulations.

Unfortunately the prioritised report was left lying around until Sunday, when a patrol was asked to follow it up. This resulted in a visit by two uniformed officers to the boy's mother at approximately 16:00. The officers took down the details once again, and their report was logged when they went off duty later that evening. At that point no action had been taken, apart from the fact that there were two neat, identical reports about the same disappearance. Both marked 'top priority'.

It was not until Monday morning, when Roger Eriksson had been missing for fifty-eight hours, that the duty officer noticed that no action had been taken. Unfortunately a union meeting about the National Police Board's proposals on new uniforms took up some considerable time, and it wasn't until after lunch on Monday that the case was passed on to Haraldsson. When he saw the date of receipt he thanked his lucky stars that the patrol had visited Lena Eriksson on the Sunday evening. There was no need for her to know that they had simply written another report. No, the investigation had got under way on Sunday, but had produced nothing so far. That was the version Haraldsson intended to stick to.

Haraldsson realised that he would need some fresh information, at least, before he spoke to Lena Eriksson, so he tried calling Lisa Hansson, Roger's girlfriend, but she was still in school.

He checked both Lena and Roger against official police records. There were a few incidents of shoplifting involving Roger, but the latest was about a year ago, and it was difficult to make any link with the disappearance. Nothing on the mother.

Haraldsson rang the local authority and found out that Roger attended Palmlövska High School.

Not good, he thought.

Palmlövska was an independent grammar school that also took boarders. It ranked among the top schools in the country as far as examination results were concerned. Its pupils were gifted and highly motivated, and had rich parents. Parents with contacts. They would be searching for a scapegoat to blame for the fact that the investigation hadn't been started immediately, and it wouldn't look good if the police had made no progress by the third day. Haraldsson decided to put everything else on the backburner. His career was already at a standstill, and it would be stupid to take any more risks.

So Haraldsson worked hard all that afternoon. He visited the school. Both Ragnar Groth, the head teacher, and Beatrice Strand, Roger's class teacher, expressed great concern and confusion when they heard that Roger was missing, but they were unable to help. Nothing had happened that they knew about, at any rate. Roger had behaved perfectly normally, had attended school as usual, had had an important Swedish exam on Friday afternoon, and, according to his classmates, had been in a good mood afterwards.

Haraldsson did, however, get hold of Lisa Hansson, the last person to have seen Roger on Friday evening. She was in a parallel class, and Haraldsson asked someone to point her out in the school cafeteria. She was a pretty girl, but fairly ordinary. Straight blonde hair, her fringe swept back with a plain hair slide. Blue eyes, no make-up. A white shirt buttoned almost to the top, worn beneath a waistcoat. Haraldsson immediately thought of the Free Church when he sat down opposite her. Or the girl in that series

The White Stone, which had been on TV when he was young. He asked her if she would like anything to eat or drink. She shook her head.

'Tell me about Friday, when Roger was at your house.'

Lisa looked at him and gave a slight shrug.

'He arrived at around half past five, we sat in my room and watched TV, and he went home around ten. Well, he said he was going home, anyway . . .'

Haraldsson nodded. Four and a half hours in her room. Two sixteen-year-olds. Watching TV. Nice try. Or maybe he was just damaged by the life he led. How long was it since he and Jenny had spent an evening watching TV? Without a quickie during the ads? Months.

'So nothing else happened? You didn't have an argument, fall out or anything?'

Lisa shook her head. She nibbled at an almost non-existent thumbnail. Haraldsson noticed that the cuticle was infected.

'Has he disappeared like this before?'

Lisa shook her head again.

'Not as far as I know, but we haven't been together very long. Haven't you spoken to his mother?' For a moment Haraldsson thought she was accusing him, but then he realised that of course that wasn't the case. Hanser's fault. She had made him doubt his own abilities.

'My colleagues have spoken to her, but we need to talk to everyone. Get an overview.' Haraldsson cleared his throat. 'How are things between Roger and his mother? Any problems?'

Lisa shrugged her shoulders once more. It occurred to Haraldsson that her repertoire was somewhat limited: shaking her head and shrugging her shoulders.

'Did they quarrel?'

'I suppose so. Sometimes. She didn't like the school.'

'This school?'

Lisa nodded in response.

'She thought it was stuck up.'

She's not bloody wrong there, thought Haraldsson.

'Does Roger's father live in town?'

'No. I don't know where he lives. I'm not sure if Roger knows either. He never mentions him.'

Interesting. Haraldsson made a note. Perhaps the son had taken off to look for his roots. To confront an absent father. Kept it secret from his mother. Stranger things had happened.

'What do you think has happened to him?'

Haraldsson's train of thought was interrupted. He looked at Lisa and realised for the first time that she was on the verge of tears.

'I don't know,' he said. 'But I expect he'll turn up. Maybe he's just gone to Stockholm for a while, or something. A little adventure. Something like that.'

'Why would he do that?'

Haraldsson looked at her questioning expression. The unvarnished, chewed nail in a mouth free of lipstick. No, little Miss Free Church probably wouldn't understand why, but Haraldsson was becoming more and more convinced that this disappearance was actually a case of the boy running away.

'Sometimes things just seem like a good idea at the time. I'm sure he'll turn up.' Haraldsson gave Lisa a reassuring smile, but he could tell from her expression that it wasn't working.

'I promise,' he added.

Before Haraldsson left he asked Lisa to make a list of Roger's friends and the people he hung out with. Lisa sat and thought for a long time, then wrote something down and handed him the piece of paper. Two names: Johan Strand and Erik Heverin. *A lonely boy*, Haraldsson thought. *Lonely boys run away.*

When he got in the car that Monday afternoon, Thomas Haraldsson felt quite pleased with the day in spite of everything. Admittedly the conversation with Johan Strand hadn't thrown up anything fresh. The last time Johan had seen Roger was at the end of school on Friday. As far as he knew, Roger was going round to

12

Lisa's that evening. He had no idea where Roger might have gone after that. Erik Heverin had been given an extended leave of absence from school. Six months in Florida. He'd already been gone for seven weeks. The boy's mother had taken up a consultancy post in the USA and the whole family had gone with her. *It's all right for some*, thought Haraldsson, trying to recall the exotic locations to which his own job had taken him. That seminar in Riga was the only thing he could come up with off the top of his head, but he'd had a stomach bug most of the time, and his overriding memory was of staring into a blue plastic bucket while his colleagues had an infuriatingly good time.

Still, Haraldsson was fairly satisfied. He had followed up several leads and, most importantly, he had found a possible conflict between mother and son, which indicated that soon this might no longer be a police matter. Hadn't the mother used the phrase 'went off' when she rang in? Indeed she had. Haraldsson remembered that he had reacted to this when he heard the tape. Her son didn't 'leave' or 'disappear' – he 'went off'. Didn't that suggest he'd left home in a strop? A slammed door, a faintly resigned mother. Haraldsson was becoming more and more convinced: the boy was in Stockholm, expanding his horizons.

However, just to be on the safe side, he thought he might swing by Lisa's house and knock on a few doors. The plan was to be noticed, to make sure a few people would recognise him just in case anyone started wondering how the investigation was going. Someone might even have seen Roger heading for the town centre and the station, with a bit of luck. Then he would go and see the mother, put a bit of pressure on to find out how much they really did quarrel. *Good plan*, he thought, and started the car.

His mobile phone rang. A quick look at the display screen sent a slight chill down his spine. *Hanser.*

'What the fuck does she want now?' Haraldsson muttered, switching off the engine. Should he ignore the call? Tempting, but maybe the boy had come back. Perhaps that was what Hanser wanted to tell him. That Haraldsson had been right all along. He answered the phone.

The conversation lasted only eighteen seconds, and consisted of six words on Hanser's part.

'Where are you?' were the first three.

'In the car,' Haraldsson replied truthfully. 'I've just spoken to some of the teachers and the girlfriend at the boy's school.'

To his immense chagrin, Haraldsson realised he was adopting a defensive position. His voice had become slightly submissive. A little higher than usual. For fuck's sake, he'd done absolutely everything he was supposed to do.

'Get here now.'

Haraldsson was about to explain where he was going and to ask what was so important, but he didn't have time to say anything before Hanser ended the call. Bloody Hanser. He started the car, turned it around and headed back to the station.

Hanser met him there. Those chilly eyes. That slightly too-perfect fall of blonde hair. That beautifully fitting, doubtless expensive suit. She had just had a call from an agitated Lena Eriksson, wanting to know what was going on, and now she was asking the same question: *What, exactly, was going on?*

Haraldsson quickly ran through the afternoon's activities, and managed to mention no less than four times that he had only been given the case after lunch that day. If she wanted to have a go at someone, she ought to start on the weekend duty team.

'I will,' Hanser said calmly. 'Why didn't you inform me if you knew that this hadn't been dealt with? This is exactly the kind of thing I need to know.'

Haraldsson was aware that things weren't working out the way he wanted. He stood there defending himself.

'This kind of thing happens. For God's sake, I can't come running to you every time there's a bit of a hitch. I mean, you've got more important things to think about.'

'More important than making sure we start searching for a

14

missing child straightaway?' She looked at him with an enquiring expression. Haraldsson stood there in silence. This wasn't going to plan. Not even a little bit.

That had been on Monday. Now he was standing in Listakärr in soaking wet socks. Hanser had gone in with all guns blazing, door-to-door enquiries and search teams which were being expanded every day. So far without success. Yesterday Haraldsson had bumped into the local chief superintendent at the station and casually pointed out that this wasn't going to be cheap. A significant number of officers working long hours, searching for a kid who was having fun in the big city. Haraldsson couldn't quite interpret the reaction of his superior officer, but when Roger came back from his little excursion, the chief would remember what Haraldsson had said. He would see how much money Hanser had wasted. Haraldsson smiled when he thought about that. Procedure was one thing, a police officer's intuition was something else entirely. That was something which couldn't be taught.

Haraldsson stopped. Halfway to the hill. One foot had sunk again. Right down this time. He pulled it out. No shoe. He just had time to see the mud hungrily closing around his size 43 as the sock on his left foot sucked up a good deal more cold water.

Enough.

That was it.

The final straw.

Down on his knees, hand into the mud, out with his shoe. And then he was going home. The rest of them could carry on running around in their bloody search teams. He had a wife to impregnate.

A cab ride and 380 kronor later, Sebastian was standing outside his apartment on Grev Magnigatan in Östermalm. He had been intending to get rid of it for a long time – the place was expensive and luxurious, perfectly suited to a successful author and lecturer with an academic background and a wide social network. All the things he no longer was and no longer had. But the very thought of clearing the place out, packing and sorting through all the stuff he'd collected over the years, was just too much for him. Instead he had chosen to shut off large areas of the apartment, using only the kitchen, the guest bedroom and the smaller bathroom. The rest could remain unused. Waiting for . . . well, something or other.

Sebastian glanced at his permanently unmade bed but decided to have a shower instead. A long, hot shower. The intimacy of last night was gone. Had he been wrong to rush away like that? Could she have given him anything if he'd stayed a few more hours? There would have been more sex, no doubt. And breakfast. Toast and juice. But then? The definitive farewell was unavoidable. It could never have ended any other way. So it was best not to spin things out. Still. He missed that interlude of togetherness that had lifted his spirits for a little while. He already felt heavy and empty again.

How much sleep had he had last night? Two hours? Two and a half? He looked in the mirror. His eyes seemed more tired than usual, and he realised he ought to do something about his hair fairly soon. Maybe get it cut really short this time. No, that would remind him too much of how he had been before. And before was not now. No, but he could trim his beard, tidy up his hair, maybe even get a few streaks put in. He smiled at himself, his most charming smile. *Unbelievable, but it still works,* he thought.

Suddenly Sebastian felt immensely weary. The U-turn was complete. The emptiness was back. He looked at the clock. Perhaps he should go and lie down for a while, after all. He knew that the dream would come back, but right now he was too tired to care. He knew his companion so well that sometimes, on the few occasions he slept without being woken by it, he actually missed it.

It hadn't been like that at first. When the dream tormented him for months, Sebastian grew so tired of the constant waking, tired of the nonstop dance around fear and the difficulty in breathing he started having a strong nightcap before going to bed. The number one problem solver for white middle-aged men with an academic background and a complicated emotional life. For a while he managed to avoid the dream completely, but all too soon his

16

subconscious found a way past the barrier of alcohol, so the night-caps got bigger and were consumed earlier and earlier in the afternoon in order to achieve the effect. Eventually Sebastian realised that he had lost the battle. He gave up immediately.

He thought he would live through the pain instead.

Let it take its time.

Heal.

That didn't work either. After another period of waking up over and over again, he began to self-medicate. Something he had promised himself he would never do. But it wasn't always possible to keep your promises – Sebastian knew this better than most from his own experience – particularly when you are faced with the really big questions. When that happens, you have to be more flexible. He rang up a few less-than-scrupulous former patients and dusted off his prescription pad. The deal was simple: a 50/50 split.

The authorities got in touch, of course, wondering about the quantity of drugs he was suddenly prescribing. Sebastian managed to explain it away with a few well-fabricated lies about 'restarting his practice', and an 'intensive introductory phase' with 'patients in a state of flux', although he did increase the number of patients so what he was up to wouldn't be quite so obvious.

To begin with he stuck mostly to Propavan, Prozac and Digesic, but the effects were annoying short-lived, and instead he began to investigate Dolcontin and other morphine-based substances.

The medical authority was the least of his problems, as it turned out. He could deal with that. The effects of his experimentation were another matter. The dream disappeared, admittedly, but so did his appetite, most of his lectures and his libido – an entirely new and terrifying experience for Sebastian.

The worst thing of all, though, was the chronic drowsiness. It was as if he could no longer manage complete thoughts: they were snipped off halfway through. It was possible to conduct a simple everyday conversation, with a certain amount of effort, but a discussion or a longer argument were completely out of reach. As for analysis and conclusions – no chance.

For Sebastian, whose whole existence was predicated on the awareness of his intellect, the very basis of his self-image the illusion of his own razor-sharp mind, it was terrible. Living an anaesthetised life – yes, it numbed the pain, but it deadened so much more: life itself, until he could no longer feel the edge. That was where he drew the line. He knew he had to make a choice: to live with the fear but retain the ability to think, or to choose a dull, blunted life with half-formed thoughts. He realised he would probably hate his existence whatever he did, so he chose the fear and stopped the self-medication immediately.

Since then he had touched neither alcohol nor drugs.

He didn't even take a painkiller if he had a headache.

But he dreamed.

Every night.

Why was he thinking about this, he wondered as he contemplated himself in the bathroom mirror. Why now? The dream had been a part of his life for many years. He had studied it, analysed it. Discussed it with his therapist. He had accepted it. Learned to live with it.

So why now?

It's Västerås, he thought as he hung up the towel and left the bathroom, completely naked. It's all because of Västerås.

Västerås and his mother. But today he would close that chapter of his life.

For ever.

Today might just be a good day.

This was the best day Joakim had experienced for ages as he stood in the forest outside Listakärr, and it got even better when he was one of the three chosen to receive direct instructions from the police officer who had come to tell them where to go and what to do. Scouts was usually pretty boring, but suddenly it had turned into a real adventure. Joakim stole a glance at the police officer standing in front of him, particularly at his gun, and decided he was going to be a policeman one day. A uniform and a gun. Like the Scouts, but with a serious upgrade. And God knows it was much needed. To be honest, Joakim didn't think going to Scouts was exactly the most interesting thing in the world. Not any more. He had just turned fourteen, and the activity that had been his hobby since he was six was beginning to lose its attraction. The spell had been broken. The outdoor life, survival, animals, nature. It wasn't that he thought it was uncool, even if all the other boys in his class thought so. No – he just felt as if he was over it now. Thanks, it was cool while it lasted, but now it was time for something else. Something real.

Perhaps Tommy, their leader, knew that.

Perhaps that was why he had gone up to the police and the soldiers and asked what was going on when they got to Listakärr.

Perhaps that was why he had offered the services of himself and the group.

Whatever the reason, the police officer – whose name was Haraldsson – had thought things over and after a certain amount of hesitation had come to the conclusion that it couldn't do any harm to have nine more pairs of eyes in the forest. They could have their own little sector to stomp around in. The police officer had asked Tommy to split them into groups of three, to choose a leader for each group and to send the leaders to him for instructions. Joakim felt as if he'd won the lottery. He was in a group with Emma and Alice, the prettiest girls in the troop. And he was chosen as leader.

Joakim went back to the girls, who were waiting for him. Haraldsson had been wonderfully monosyllabic and firm, just like the detectives in the Martin Beck series. Joakim felt incredibly important. He could already picture the way the rest of this fantastic day would pan out. He would find the missing boy, seriously injured. The boy would look up at Joakim with that pleading expression only the dying can achieve. He would be too weak to talk, but his eyes would say it all. Joakim would pick him up and carry him towards the others, just like in a film. The others would catch sight of him, smile at him, applaud, cheer and everything would be absolutely perfect.

19

Back in the group Joakim organised his team so that he had Emma on his left and Alice on the other side. Haraldsson had given strict orders to keep the chain together, and Joakim looked seriously at the girls and told them how important it was to stick together. Time to step up to the mark. After what felt like an eternity, Haraldsson signalled to them, and the search party began to move at last.

Joakim soon noticed that it was very difficult to keep a chain together, even though it consisted of only three groups with three people in each. Particularly as they moved deeper into the forest and the boggy ground forced them to take a detour away from the marked route, time and time again. One group found it difficult to keep up, the other didn't slow down at all and soon disappeared behind the hillocks. Just as Haraldsson had said. Joakim was even more impressed by him. He seemed to know everything. Joakim smiled at the girls and made them repeat Haraldsson's final words.

'If you find anything, you shout "Found!"'

Emma nodded crossly.

'You've said that like a thousand times.'

Joakim did not allow himself to be put off by her response. With the sun in his eyes he trudged on, trying to maintain the distance and the alignment, even though it was becoming more and more difficult. And he could no longer see Lasse's group, which had been slightly to the left of them just now.

After half an hour Emma wanted a rest. Joakim tried to make her understand that they couldn't just stop. They might fall behind and lose the others.

'What others?' Alice said, smiling.

Joakim realised they hadn't seen the others for a while now.

'It sounds as if they're behind us.'

They fell silent, listened a little more carefully. Faint sounds in the distance. Someone shouting.

'No, we'll keep going,' said Joakim, although deep down he felt Alice was probably right. They had been moving too fast. Or in the wrong direction.

'In that case, you're on your own,' Emma replied, her expression furious. For a second Joakim felt that he was losing his grip on the team, and that Emma was slipping through his fingers. And she had actually looked at him appreciatively in the last half-hour. Joakim was suddenly dripping in sweat, and it wasn't only because his underwear was too warm. He had driven them on to impress her, couldn't she see that? And now she was acting as if it was all his fault.

'Are you hungry?' Alice interrupted Joakim's train of thought. She had taken a packet of wraps out of her backpack.

'No,' he answered a little too quickly, before realising that he was indeed hungry. He walked off and clambered up onto a hillock so that it would look as if he had a plan. Emma gratefully accepted a soft wrap, completely ignoring Joakim's attempts to appear important. Joakim decided he needed to change tack. He took a deep breath, allowing the fresh forest air to fill his lungs. The sky had clouded over, the sun had disappeared, and with it the promise of a perfect day. He went back to the girls. Decided to soften his tone.

'Actually, I would like a sandwich if you've got one left,' he said as pleasantly as he could.

'Sure,' Alice replied, digging out a wrap for him. She smiled at him, and Joakim could see that this was a better strategy.

'I wonder where we are,' Emma said, pulling a small map out of her pocket. They gathered around it, trying to work out where they were. It was quite difficult: the terrain had no real distinguishing features, just hillocks, forest and boggy ground giving way to one another. But they knew where they had started from, after all, and roughly in which direction they had been moving.

'We've been heading north almost all the time, so we should be in this area,' Emma suggested. Joakim nodded; he was impressed. Emma was smart.

'Shall we carry on, or wait for the others?' Alice wondered.

'I think we should carry on,' Joakim replied quickly, then added, 'unless you'd rather wait?'

He looked at the girls – Emma with her bright blue eyes and her soft face, Alice with her slightly more angular features. They were both gorgeous, he thought, suddenly wishing that they would suggest waiting for the others. And that the others would take a long, long time to come.

'I suppose we might just as well carry on. If we're here, it's not far from where we were supposed to meet up anyway,' said Emma, pointing at the map.

'Yes, but you're right, the others are behind us, so maybe we ought to wait for them,' Joakim ventured.

'I thought you wanted to get there first. I mean, you took off like a bat out of hell,' said Alice. The girls laughed, and Joakim realised it was good to laugh with pretty girls. He gave Alice a playful little shove.

'You weren't exactly hanging about yourself.'

They started chasing each other. They ran between the pools of water, randomly at first, but after Emma stumbled into one the aim was to get the others as wet as possible. It was a brilliant break from the slightly boring search, and just what Joakim needed. He ran after Emma and briefly grabbed her arm. She tore herself free and tried to run away from him, but her left foot caught on a protruding tree root and she lost her balance. For a second it looked as though she would stay on her feet, but the area around the pool was slippery with mud and she fell in, the water reaching her waist.

Joakim laughed, but Emma was screaming. He fell silent and moved towards her. She screamed even louder. *Odd*, thought Joakim. *It isn't that bad, surely. Just a bit of water.* Then he saw the pale white body sticking up just a short distance away from Emma. It was as if it had been lying beneath the surface, waiting for its victim. That was the end of innocence and their childish game. There was nothing left now but dizziness and blind panic. Emma threw up; Alice started sobbing. Joakim stood there frozen in time, staring at the image that would be with him for the rest of his life.

Haraldsson was in bed, dozing. Jenny was lying next to him, the soles of her feet on the mattress, a pillow underneath her bottom. She hadn't wanted to drag things out.

'Best if we get it over with, then we can do it again before I have to get back.'

Get it over with. Is there a bigger turn-off in any language? Haraldsson doubted it. But there you go, they'd got it over with and Haraldsson was dozing. Someone somewhere was playing Abba's 'Ring Ring'.

'That's your phone.' Jenny poked him in the side. Haraldsson woke up, well aware that he wasn't supposed to be in bed with his wife. He grabbed his trousers off the floor and dug out his mobile. Hanser. Obviously. He took a deep breath and answered.

Five words this time.

'Where the fuck are you?'

Hanser rang off crossly. *Sprained his ankle.* No chance. She had a good mind to drive to the hospital, or at least send a car there just to prove that the bastard was lying. But she didn't have time. She was suddenly responsible for a murder investigation. It hadn't exactly helped that the person responsible for the team working around Listakärr hadn't been on site, or that he had agreed to use under-age Scouts in the search party. Minors for whom she would now need to arrange counselling, since one of them had fallen into a pool of water and brought a corpse up with her when she got to her feet.

Hanser shook her head. Everything to do with this disappearance had gone wrong. *Everything.* No more mistakes. From now on they had to start getting it right. Being professional. She looked at the phone, which was still in her hand. An idea was born. It was a big step to take. Too early, many people would think. It might possibly undermine her leadership. But she had long ago promised herself that she would never be afraid of uncomfortable decisions. There was too much at stake.

A boy was dead.

Murdered.

It was time to work with the best.

*

23

'There's a call for you,' said Vanja, poking her head around Torkel Höglund's door. His office, like most things about Torkel, was lean and simple. Nothing fussy, nothing expensive, hardly even anything personal. With its furniture sourced from a central storage depot somewhere, the room gave the impression that it was occupied by a junior-school head teacher in some cash-strapped small town, rather than by one of the most senior police officers in Sweden. Some of his colleagues found it strange that the person responsible for the National CID murder squad, known as Riksmord, had no desire to show the world how far he had come. Others interpreted it differently, concluding that his success had not gone to his head. The truth was simpler: Torkel never had any time. His job was demanding. He was always travelling around the country, and he wasn't the kind of man who wanted to spend his spare time beautifying an office he rarely used.

'It's Västerås,' said Vanja, sitting down opposite him. 'The murdered sixteen-year-old boy.'

Torkel watched Vanja settle down. Clearly he wouldn't be taking this call in private. He nodded and picked up the receiver. Since his second divorce it felt as if phone calls were about nothing but sudden death. It was more than three years since anyone wondered if he'd be home on time for dinner, or anything else gloriously trivial.

He recognised the name: Kerstin Hanser, who headed up the team at police HQ in Västerås. He had got to know her on a course a few years ago. A good person and undoubtedly a good boss, he had thought at the time, and he remembered feeling pleased when he read about her new post. Now her voice sounded stressed and strained.

'I need help. I've decided to ask for Riksmord, and I'd really appreciate it if you could come. Might that be possible?' Her tone was almost pleading.

For a second Torkel considered ducking the question. He and his team had just returned from an unpleasant investigation in Linköping, but he realised that if Kerstin Hanser had phoned him, it was because she really needed help.

24

'We got this one wrong from the start. There's a risk the whole thing might blow up in our faces, so I really do need your help,' she said, as if she had picked up on his hesitation.

'What's it about?'

'A sixteen-year-old. Missing for a week. Found dead. Murdered. Brutally.'

'If you email me all the material I'll take a look at it,' Torkel replied, looking at Vanja, who had moved to the other phone and picked it up.

'Billy, can you come to Torkel's office? We've got a job,' she said before hanging up. It was as if she already knew what Torkel's response would be in the end. She always did, apparently. Torkel felt proud and slightly annoyed at the same time. Vanja Lithner was his closest ally on the team. She had only just turned thirty, but in spite of her tender age she had developed into a fine murder investigator in the two years she had worked with him – he found her almost irritatingly good. If only he had been as good when he was her age. He smiled at her as he ended the conversation with Kerstin Hanser.

'I'm still the boss here,' he began.

'I know, I'm just getting the team together so that you can hear what we think. Then it's your decision, as always,' she said with a glint in her eye.

'Oh yes, as if I had a choice once you get your teeth into something,' he replied, getting to his feet. 'I might as well start packing – we're off to Västerås.'

Billy Rosén was driving the van up the E18. Too fast as usual. Torkel had stopped commenting on it long ago. Instead he concentrated on the material about the murdered boy, Roger Eriksson. The report was rather short and sparse, and Thomas Haraldsson, the investigating officer, didn't seem to be the kind of man who overexerted himself. They would probably have to start all over again.

Torkel knew that this was exactly the kind of case the tabloids loved to get hold of. It didn't help that the preliminary cause of death – established where the body was found – indicated an extremely violent assault, with countless stab wounds to the heart and lungs. But that wasn't what bothered Torkel the most. It was the short final sentence in the report, a statement made by the pathologist at the scene.

A preliminary examination indicates that most of the heart is missing.

Torkel looked out of the window at the trees flying by. Someone had removed the heart. He hoped for everyone's sake that the boy hadn't been a fan of hard rock, or too much of a dedicated World of Warcraft player. If so, the speculation in the press would be completely crazy.

Crazier than usual, he corrected himself.

Vanja looked up from her folder. She had probably just seen the same sentence.

'Perhaps we ought to bring Ursula in as well,' she said, reading his mind as usual. Torkel gave a brief nod. Billy glanced over his shoulder.

'Do we have an address?'

Torkel gave it to him and Billy quickly entered it into the GPS. Torkel didn't really like Billy doing other things while he was driving, but at least he slowed down while he was keying in their destination. Which was something.

'Another thirty minutes.' Billy put his foot down and the big van responded. 'We may do it in twenty, depending on traffic.'

'Thirty is fine. I always find it so unpleasant when we break the sound barrier.'

Billy knew exactly what Torkel thought of his driving, but he just smiled at his boss in the rear-view mirror. Good road, good car, good driver. Why not take full advantage? He increased his speed even more.

Torkel picked up his phone and called Ursula.

The train left Stockholm's Central Station at 16:07. Sebastian settled down in first class. He leaned back in his seat and closed his eyes as they left the city.

In the past he had never been able to stay awake on trains. But now, even though his body was telling him how welcome an hour's sleep would be, he couldn't find the necessary peace of mind.

Instead he took out the letter from the funeral director, opened it and read it. He already knew what it said. One of his mother's former colleagues had called and told him she had passed away. It had been quiet and dignified, she said. *Quiet and dignified* – his mother's life in a nutshell. There was nothing positive in this response, at least not if your name was Sebastian Bergman. No, for him life was a battle from the first moment to the last. Those who were quiet and dignified had no place in his world. *Dead and boring* – that's what he usually called them. People who lived with one foot in the grave. He was no longer quite so sure. How would his life have turned out if he had been quiet and dignified?

Better, presumably.

Less painful.

At least, that's what Stefan Hammarström, Sebastian's therapist, had tried to get him to believe. They had discussed the matter at a recent session, when Sebastian mentioned that his mother had died.

'How dangerous can it be to be like other people?' Stefan had asked when Sebastian made it clear what he thought about 'quiet and dignified'.

'Extremely dangerous,' Sebastian had replied. 'Lethal, in fact. Evidently.'

They had then spent almost an hour discussing mankind's genetic predisposition for danger. It was a subject Sebastian loved.

He had realised how important danger could be as a driving force, partly through his own life, partly because of his research into serial killers. He explained to his therapist that there are two real motivators for a serial killer: fantasy and danger. The fantasy is the engine humming away: a constant presence, but simply idling.

Most people have fantasies. Dark, sexual, brutal, always affirming our own ego, always destroying whatever or whomever might be standing in our way. In our fantasies we are powerful. Very few people actually live out their fantasies. Those who do have found the key.

The danger.

The danger of being caught.

The danger of doing the unmentionable.

The adrenaline and the endorphins released at that moment provided the turbo charge – the fuel, the explosion – that made the engine function at the peak of its capacity. That was why thrill-seekers sought new thrills, why serial killers became serial killers. It's difficult to go back to idling once you've revved the engine. Felt the power. Discovered what it is that makes you feel alive. *The danger.*

'Is it really danger you're talking about? Isn't it excitement?' Stefan leaned forward as Sebastian fell silent.

'Is this a language lesson?'

'No, this is you giving a lecture.' Stefan poured a glass of water from a carafe on the table beside him and passed it to Sebastian. 'Didn't you used to get paid for doing that, instead of paying out yourself?'

'I'm paying you to listen. To whatever I say.'

Stefan smiled and shook his head.

'No, you know why you're paying me. You need help, and these small digressions mean we have less time to discuss what we should really be talking about.'

Sebastian didn't reply. Didn't change his expression one iota. He liked Stefan. No bullshit.

'So let's get back to your mother. When's the funeral?'

'It's already taken place.'

'Were you there?'

'No.'

'Why not?'

'Because I thought it should be a ceremony for people who actually liked her.'

Stefan had looked at him in silence for a few seconds.

'There you are, you see – we've got lots to talk about.'

Outside the swaying carriage lay an attractive landscape. The train forged ahead through the fresh green meadows and forests north-west of Stockholm. It was just possible to catch a glimpse of Lake Mälaren in all its sparkling glory through the trees. For any other passenger this might have stirred thoughts of life's possibilities. For Sebastian, exactly the opposite was true. He saw no possibilities in the beauty around him. He turned his gaze up to the ceiling. All his life he had been running away from his parents. His father, against whom he had battled ever since his youth, and his mother, quiet and dignified but never on his side. *Never on his side.* That was how he felt.

Sebastian's eyes filled with tears for a moment. This was something that had developed in recent years. Tears. *Strange*, he thought, *that I should have to discover something as simple as tears at my age.*

Emotional.

Irrational.

Everything he had never wanted to be. He went back to the only thing he knew that was capable of numbing his emotions: women. Another promise Sebastian had broken. He had kept to the straight and narrow from the moment he met Lily and had vowed to remain faithful to her. But with the excoriating dream that haunted him at night and the empty, meaningless days, he could see no other way out. The hunt for fresh conquests and the few short hours with different women filled his life, and his thoughts managed to overcome the feeling of powerlessness – for a while, at least. As a man, a lover, a predator, constantly on the hunt for new women, he was able to function. This was a skill he had retained in spite of everything. This both pleased and frightened him. The fact that he was everything he was. A lonely man who filled his time with the young and old, students, colleagues, married or unmarried. He didn't discriminate against anyone. For him there was just one rule: she was going to be his. She would prove that he wasn't worthless, that he was alive. He knew exactly how destructive his behaviour was, but he welcomed it and pushed away the knowledge that one day he would probably have to find a way out.

He started to look around the carriage. It was half full. A brunette a short distance away caught his eye. Around forty, greyish-blue blouse, expensive gold earrings. *Not bad*, he thought. She was reading a book. Perfect – women in their forties reading a book only notched up a three on the difficulty scale, in his experience. It depended to a certain extent on what they were reading, but even so . . . He got up and walked over to her seat.

'I'm just going to the buffet car – can I get you anything?'

The woman looked up from her book with an enquiring expression. Unsure if he was speaking to her. Evidently he was, as she realised when she met his gaze.

'No, thanks, I'm fine.' She went back to her book.

'Are you sure? Not even a cup of coffee?'

'No, thank you.' She didn't even look up.

'Tea? Hot chocolate?' This time she took her eyes off the book, looking up at Sebastian with a certain amount of irritation. Sebastian gave her his smile, which was practically patented.

'You can even get wine these days, but maybe it's too early?'

The woman didn't reply.

'Perhaps you're wondering why I'm asking,' Sebastian went on. 'I have no choice. I feel it's my duty to save you from that book. I've read it. You'll thank me one day.' The woman looked up and met his eyes. Sebastian smiled. The woman smiled back.

'A cup of coffee would be nice. Black, no sugar.'

'Coming up.' Another quick smile, which grew wider as Sebastian made his way along the carriage. Perhaps the trip to Västerås wouldn't be so bad after all.

Västerås police station was buzzing with activity. Kerstin Hanser glanced at the clock, her expression slightly stressed. She had to go. God knows she didn't want to. She could easily come up with a hundred and one things she would rather do than go to the mortuary to meet Lena Eriksson. But it had to be done. Even though they were 100 per cent certain that the boy they had found was Roger Eriksson, his mother still wanted to see him. Hanser had advised against it, but Lena Eriksson insisted. She wanted to see her son.

It hadn't happened earlier in the day because Lena had put it off twice. Hanser didn't know why. Nor did she care. She would have preferred it not to happen at all. Not with her in attendance, at any rate. This was the part of the job she hated the most, and she wasn't all that good at it either. She tried to avoid the situation as often as possible, but it seemed as if people expected her to cope better because she was a woman. They imagined it would be easier for her to find the right words. That the relatives, the bereaved, would feel more comfortable with her presence, simply on the basis of her gender. Hanser thought this was nonsense. She never knew what to say. She could express her deepest condolences, perhaps put an arm around them, provide a shoulder to cry on, give them the number of someone to talk to, assure them over and over again that the police would do all they could to catch the person who had caused them so much suffering. She could certainly do all that, but mostly it was a matter of just standing there. Anyone could do that.

Hanser didn't even remember who had been there from the police when she and her husband had identified Niklas. It had been a man. A man who had just stood there.

She could, in fact, send someone else with Lena. She probably would have done, if the investigation thus far had looked slightly different. As it was, she couldn't take any risks. The press were everywhere. It seemed that they already knew that the heart was missing. It was only a matter of time before they found out the boy had been gone for almost three days before the police started looking for him. Then there were the traumatised Scouts in the forest and Haraldsson's 'badly sprained ankle'. From here on, though, there would be absolutely nothing to criticise in this investigation. She would make sure of that. She would work with the best and quickly put this terrible case behind her. That was the plan.

The telephone rang.

Reception.

The Riksmord team was asking for her. Hanser glanced at the clock on the wall. They were early. Everything was happening at once. She must go and welcome them, there was no question about that. Lena Eriksson would just have to wait a few minutes. It couldn't be helped. Hanser tucked in her blouse, straightened up and headed for the stairs leading down to the main entrance. She stopped at the locked door separating reception from the inner areas of the station. Through the tiny leaded squares in the glass she could see Torkel Höglund strolling around calmly, his hands behind his back. A man and a woman were sitting on the green sofas by the window overlooking the street. They were both younger than Hanser. Torkel's colleagues, she guessed as she pressed the keypad and pushed the door open. Torkel turned as he heard the click of the lock, and smiled when he saw her.

Suddenly Hanser felt a little unsure of herself. What was the right thing to do? A hug or a warm handshake? They had been on a few courses together, had lunch now and again, met in corridors.

Hanser had no need to wonder. Torkel walked up to her and gave her a friendly hug. Then he turned to the others, who had got up from the sofa, and introduced them. Kerstin Hanser welcomed them.

'I must apologise, but I'm in a bit of a rush. I'm on my way to the mortuary.'

'The boy?'

'Yes.'

Hanser turned to the receptionist.

'Haraldsson?'

'He should be on his way. I called him straight after I'd spoken to you.'

Hanser nodded. Another glance at the clock. She couldn't be too late. She looked quickly at Vanja and Billy, but turned to Torkel when she spoke.

'Haraldsson has been leading the investigation up to now.'

'Yes, I saw his name in the material we were sent.'

Hanser was slightly taken aback. Was there a hint of condescension in Torkel's voice? If so, his expression gave nothing away.

Where was Haraldsson this time? Hanser was about to get out her mobile when the lock of the door she had just come through clicked and Haraldsson walked into reception, limping badly. He deliberately took his time to reach the new arrivals and then shook hands.

'What have you done?' Torkel nodded at Haraldsson's right foot.

'I sprained it when I was leading the search party looking for the boy. That's why I wasn't there when they found him.' The final remark was directed at Hanser, with a brief glance.

She didn't believe him, he knew that. So it was important to remember the limp over the next few days. She wouldn't contact the hospital, surely? And if she did, they wouldn't tell her whether he'd been there or not, would they? That must come under some kind of patient confidentiality agreement. Employers aren't allowed to look at their employees' notes. Or are they? He'd better check with the union. Haraldsson was so lost in his own thoughts that for a moment he had stopped listening to his boss. Now he became aware that she was looking at him, her expression serious.

'Torkel and his team are taking over the investigation.'

'From you?' Haraldsson looked genuinely surprised. He hadn't expected this. Things were looking up. This was a team of real police officers, just like him. Obviously they would appreciate his work more than the desk-bound lawyer who was his boss.

'No, the ultimate responsibility remains mine, but Riksmord

will be leading the operational side of the investigation, starting from now.'

'Working with me?'

Hanser sighed to herself and said a silent prayer that a crime wave wouldn't suddenly sweep through Västerås. They wouldn't stand a chance.

Vanja gave Billy an amused look. Torkel listened to the conversation, his face expressionless. To degrade or humiliate the local force was the worst way to start the collaboration. Torkel had never been much of a one for marking his territory. There were better ways to get the best out of everyone.

'No, they will be responsible for the investigation. You are being relieved of that duty.'

'But of course we would prefer to work in association with you,' Torkel interrupted, looking seriously at Haraldsson. 'You have unique insights into the case which could turn out to be critical for our continued success.'

Vanja looked at Torkel with admiration. Personally she had already consigned Haraldsson to her HC file: a Hopeless Case who would be allowed to have his say then be sidelined as far away from the investigation as possible.

'So I'll be working with you?'

'You will be working in association with us.'

'What does that mean?'

'We'll see. To begin with you could tell us about everything that has happened so far, and we'll take it from there.' Torkel placed a hand on Haraldsson's shoulder and steered him gently towards the door.

'See you later,' Torkel said over his shoulder to Hanser. Billy went over to the sofas to collect their bags; Vanja stayed where she was. She could have sworn the former leader of the investigation had taken those first steps with Torkel without limping.

Lena Eriksson pushed another Läkerol pastille into her mouth as she sat in the little waiting room. She had stolen the box from work. Yesterday. They were on the shelf right next to the till. Eucalyptus. Not her favourite, but she had just taken the nearest one and slipped it in her pocket when they were shutting the shop.

Yesterday.

When she had been convinced her son was still alive. When she had unquestioningly believed the policeman she had spoken to, the one who told her all the indications were that Roger had gone off of his own free will. To Stockholm, perhaps. Or somewhere else. A little teenage adventure.

Yesterday.

Not just another day, but another world entirely. When hope was still alive.

Today her son was gone for ever.

Murdered.

Found in a pool.

Without a heart.

Lena had not left the apartment all day after she had been given the news. She was supposed to have met the police officer earlier on, but she had phoned and postponed it. Twice. She couldn't get up. For a while she was afraid she would never find the strength to get to her feet again. So she sat there. In her armchair. In the living room where they had spent less and less time together, she and her son. She tried to remember the last time they had sat there together.

Watched a film.

Eaten.

Talked.

Lived.

She couldn't remember. It must have been just after Roger started at that bloody school. After only a few weeks with those stuck-up kids, he had changed. For the last year they had been living more or less separate lives.

The tabloids kept on ringing her, but she didn't want to speak to anyone. Not yet. In the end she unplugged the landline and switched off her mobile phone. Then they turned up on her doorstep, shouting through the letter box, leaving messages on the mat in the hallway. But she never opened the door. She didn't get up out of her armchair.

She felt absolutely terrible. The coffee she had drunk when she arrived was moving up and down in her throat like a lift. Had she eaten anything since yesterday? Probably not. But she had drunk plenty. Alcohol. She didn't usually do that. Hadn't done it for months. She was extremely moderate, which nobody who met her would believe. Her home-bleached hair with the dark roots. Her weight. The chipped nail polish at the end of her stubby fingers, festooned with rings. The piercings. Her fondness for velour track-suit bottoms and oversized T-shirts. Most people quickly formed an opinion of Lena when they met her. Most of their preconceptions were confirmed, to be fair. Desperately short of money. Left school at fifteen. Got pregnant when she was seventeen.

Single mother.

Low-paid job.

But alcohol or drug abuse? Never.

Today, though, she had been drinking. Just to silence that little voice at the back of her mind which had made its presence felt as soon as she was given the news about Roger, and had grown in strength as the day went on. The little voice that refused to go away.

Lena was starting to get a headache. She needed some fresh air. And a cigarette. She got up, picked up her handbag and headed for the exit. Her worn heels echoed desolately on the stone floor. She was almost there when she saw a woman of about forty-five dressed in a suit, rushing in through the revolving doors. The woman marched purposefully towards her.

'Lena Eriksson? Kerstin Hanser, Västerås police. Sorry I'm late.'

They travelled down in the lift in silence. Hanser opened the door when they reached the basement and allowed Lena to step out in front of her. They went along the corridor until they were met by a bald man wearing glasses and a white coat. He led them into a smaller room where a trolley stood alone in the middle of the floor, lit by a fluorescent tube. Beneath the white sheet the contours of a body were visible.

Hanser and Lena walked up to the trolley and the bald man moved slowly around to the other side. He met Hanser's eyes and she nodded. He turned the sheet down carefully, exposing Roger Eriksson's face and neck as far as the collarbone. Lena gazed down steadily at the trolley as Hanser took a respectful step back. She heard neither a sharp intake of breath nor a muffled cry from the woman by her side. No sobbing; no hand raised to the mouth in a reflex movement. Nothing.

It had struck Hanser as soon as they met in the waiting room. Lena's eyes were not red and swollen from crying. She didn't look grief stricken or as if she was just holding herself together. She seemed almost calm. But Hanser had picked up a whiff of alcohol in the lift, overlaid with eucalyptus, and guessed that this was the reason for the lack of emotion. That and the shock.

Lena stood motionless, looking down at her son. What had she been expecting? Nothing, really. She hadn't dared to think about what he would look like. Hadn't been able to imagine how she would feel, standing there. What would the time in the water have done to him? He was slightly swollen, definitely. As if he'd had some kind of allergic reaction, but otherwise she thought he looked just the way he always did. The dark hair; the pale skin; the black, prominent eyebrows; a hint of stubble on his upper lip. Eyes closed. Lifeless. *Of course.*

'I thought he would look as if he was asleep.'

Hanser remained silent. Lena turned her head towards her, as if seeking confirmation that she wasn't wrong.

'He doesn't look as if he's asleep.'

'No.'

'I've seen him asleep so many times. Especially when he was little. I mean, he's not moving. His eyes are closed, but . . . '

Lena didn't finish the sentence. Instead she reached out and touched Roger. Cold. Dead. She let her hand rest on his cheek.

'I lost my son when he was fourteen.'

Lena still had her hand on the boy's cheek, but she turned her head slightly in Hanser's direction.

'Oh?'

'Yes . . .'

Silence again. Why had she said that? Hanser had never mentioned it to anyone else in a similar situation. But there was something about the woman by the trolley. Hanser had the feeling that Lena wasn't allowing herself to grieve. Couldn't grieve. Perhaps she didn't even want to. So it was meant as a consolation. An outstretched hand to show that Hanser understood what Lena must be going through.

'Was he murdered too?'

'No.'

Hanser suddenly felt stupid. As if her comment was meant as some kind of comparison when it came to suffering. *Look, I've lost someone too, so there you go.* But Lena didn't appear to give it another thought. She turned back and looked at her own son once more.

So many years when he had been the only thing she had to be proud of.

Or so many years when he had been the only thing she had.

Finished.

Is this your fault? the little voice in her head began to ask. Lena withdrew her hand and took a step back. The headache was relentless.

'I think I'd like to go now.'

Hanser nodded. The bald man turned up the sheet as both women headed for the door. Lena took a packet of cigarettes out of her bag.

'Is there someone you can call? Perhaps you shouldn't be alone.'

'But I am. I am alone now.'

Lena left the room.

Hanser just stood there.

Exactly as she had known she would end up doing.

The conference room in Västerås police station was the most modern in the building. The pale birch-wood furniture was only

38

a few weeks old. Eight chairs around an oval table. The new wall-paper on three walls was in a discreet, relaxing shade of green, and the fourth wall was a combined whiteboard and screen. In the corner nearest the door the latest technology was linked to a projector on the ceiling. In the middle of the conference table a console controlled everything in the room. As soon as he set foot on the grey fitted carpet Torkel had decided that this would be the team's base.

He gathered up the papers on the varnished surface of the table in front of him and emptied his bottle of water. The meeting to review the progress of the investigation so far had gone more or less as he'd expected. There were really only two occasions during Haraldsson's account when something surprising had come up.

The first was when they were going through the investigation chronologically. Vanja looked up from her papers and asked, 'What did you do on the Sunday?'

'The investigation got under way in earnest, but led nowhere.'

The answer came with some speed. Practised speed. Unconvincing speed. Torkel made a note of it, and knew that Vanja had done the same. She was the closest thing to a human lie detector Torkel had ever encountered. He looked at her with a certain amount of anticipation as she gazed at Haraldsson for a long time then glanced back at her papers. Haraldsson let out a long breath. They were on the same side, sure, but there was no need for his colleagues to know that there might have been the odd mistake in the initial stages. They had to focus on the future now. He was therefore slightly irritated – and a little worried – when Vanja waved her pen once more. Billy smiled. He was also well aware that Vanja had picked up something in Haraldsson's voice that didn't ring true. She had no intention of letting it go. She never did. Billy leaned back in his comfortable chair and folded his arms. This would be fun.

'When you say "got under way",' Vanja went on, her tone somewhat sharper, 'what did you actually do? I can't find any interviews, neither with the mother nor anyone else, no reports from door-to-door enquiries, nobody putting together a time line from the Friday.' She looked up and stared straight at Haraldsson. 'So what exactly did you do?'

Haraldsson shuffled uncomfortably in his seat. Why the fuck did he have to sit here defending other people's mistakes?

'I wasn't on duty that weekend. I didn't pick up the case until the Monday.'

'So what happened on the Sunday?'

Haraldsson glanced at the two men in the room, as if seeking support for his view that looking backwards wasn't particularly helpful. No support was forthcoming. Both of them were gazing expectantly at him.

'As I understand it, uniformed officers went to see the mother.'

'And did what?'

'Took down information about the boy's disappearance.'

'What information? Where is it?'

Vanja didn't take her eyes off him. Haraldsson realised they weren't going to get anywhere until they found out everything that had happened. So he told them. The truth. Afterwards there was a different kind of silence in the room. A silence that Haraldsson at least interpreted as the kind that might arise when a group of people is busy digesting what might well be the finest example of incompetence they've ever heard. Eventually Billy spoke.

'So the only thing that happened on the Sunday was that some-one wrote another report about the same disappearance?'

'Well, yes, technically.'

'Okay, so the boy disappeared on Friday at twenty-two hundred hours. When did you actually start looking for him?'

'On the Monday. After lunch. When the report was passed on to me. Well, we didn't actually start looking then, but we did speak to his girlfriend, the school, witnesses ...'

The room fell silent once more. Experience told them that in all probability the boy was already dead by then, but if not – if he'd been held captive somewhere ... *Three days! Good God!* Torkel leaned forward, gazing at Haraldsson with earnest curiosity.

'So why didn't you tell us this when we asked what happened on the Sunday?'

'It's never pleasant to admit that mistakes have been made.'

'But it wasn't your mistake. You didn't pick up the case until the Monday. The only mistake you've made is not telling us. We're a team. We can't afford to be anything less than honest with each other.'

Haraldsson nodded. He suddenly felt as if he were seven years old and had been sent to the headmaster for silly behaviour in the playground.

During the remainder of the briefing he told them everything (apart from the lunchtime quickie with Jenny and the fake visit to Casualty), which meant they didn't finish until after nine o'clock.

Torkel thanked him. Billy was stretching and yawning and Vanja had started to pack away when the second surprise of the evening came.

'Just one more thing.' Haraldsson took a small but effective pause. 'We haven't found the boy's jacket or watch.' Torkel, Vanja and Billy all straightened up. This was interesting. Haraldsson could see Vanja fishing for her folder in her bag.

'I didn't put it in the report – you never know who gets to read them, where a piece of information like that might end up.'

Vanja nodded to herself. Clever – it was precisely that kind of detail they didn't want leaked to the press. It would be worth its weight in gold in an interrogation. Perhaps Haraldsson wasn't completely hopeless after all, even if most of the indications were to the contrary.

'So he was robbed?' Billy said.

'I don't think so. He still had his wallet, with almost 300 kronor in it. And his mobile in his trouser pocket.'

Everyone in the team considered the fact that someone – presumably the murderer – had taken selected items from the victim. That meant something. That and the missing heart.

'The jacket was Diesel,' Haraldsson went on. 'Green. I've got pictures of the relevant style on my desk. The watch was a ... '

Haraldsson consulted his notes. 'A Tonino Lamborghini Pilot. Same applies – I've got pictures.'

Afterwards Torkel sat alone in the windowless room, trying to think of a reason not to go to the hotel. Should he start drawing up the time line on the whiteboard? Put up the map? The pictures? Go through what Haraldsson had told them again? Then again, Billy would do all that much more quickly and efficiently tomorrow morning, probably before anyone else had even arrived at the station.

He could go out for something to eat. But he wasn't that hungry – not enough to sit alone in a restaurant. He could ask Vanja to keep him company, of course, but she was going to spend the evening reading up on the case in her hotel room. He knew that. Extremely ambitious and conscientious, Vanja. She probably wouldn't say no if he asked her to join him for dinner, but it wasn't what she wanted, and she would feel slightly stressed all evening. Torkel dismissed the idea.

Billy? Torkel thought Billy had many excellent qualities, and his knowledge of computers and technology made him an invaluable member of the team, but Torkel couldn't remember ever having dinner together, just the two of them. The conversation didn't flow as easily with Billy. Billy just loved a night in a hotel. There wasn't a single TV program on any channel showing between ten o'clock at night and two in the morning that Billy hadn't seen, and he liked to chat about them. TV, films, music, games, computers, new phones, foreign magazines that he read online. When he was with Billy, Torkel felt like a dinosaur.

He sighed. It would be a walk and a sandwich and a beer in his room, with the TV for company. He consoled himself with the thought that Ursula would be coming tomorrow. Then he would have a companion for dinner.

Torkel switched off the lights and left the conference room. Last to leave as usual, he thought as he walked through the empty office. Hardly surprising that his wife had had enough.

It was dark by the time Sebastian paid the cab driver and got out of the car. The driver also got out, opened the boot, lifted out Sebastian's bag and wished him a nice evening. A nice evening in his parents' house? *Well, there's always a first time*, Sebastian thought. And the fact that both of his parents were dead certainly increased the chances significantly.

Sebastian crossed the road. The cab, which had turned around in the neighbours' drive, passed behind him. He stood by the low white wooden fence that needed painting and noticed that the mailbox was overflowing. Didn't some kind of central notification go out when someone died, stopping all the mail? Evidently not.

On his arrival in Västerås several hours earlier, Sebastian had gone to the funeral director's office to pick up the house key. Apparently one of his mother's oldest friends had organised the funeral when he'd refused to have anything to do with it. Berit Holmberg. Sebastian couldn't remember ever having heard the name. The funeral director had offered to show him some kind of album of the ceremony, which had allegedly been very beautiful, atmospheric and well attended. Sebastian had declined.

He had gone to a restaurant afterwards. Spent a long time over a good meal. Lingered over coffee, reading a book. He had fingered the card the woman on the train had given him, but decided to wait. Tomorrow or the following day he would ring her. Interested but not desperate – that was always the best approach. He had gone for a stroll. Thought about seeing a film but decided against it. There was nothing he found appealing. Eventually he had been unable to put off the real purpose of his visit any longer and hailed a cab.

Now he was standing in the street staring at the house he had left the day after his nineteenth birthday. Well-tended flowerbeds lined both sides of the stone garden path. At the moment they consisted mainly of low, neatly pruned conifers, but soon the perennials would be in flower. His mother had loved her garden and had cared for it tenderly. In the backyard there were fruit trees and a vegetable patch. The stone path led to a two-storey house. Sebastian had been ten years old when they moved in; it had just been built. Even in the faint light of the street lamps Sebastian could see that it really needed some attention now. Lumps of plaster had fallen off the facade, the paint on the window frames was flaking and in two places the roof was a shade darker. Missing tiles, probably. Sebastian overcame his sheer physical reluctance to go inside and walked the few steps to the front door.

He unlocked it and stepped into the hallway. It smelled musty. Stuffy. He dropped his bag and remained standing in the archway leading to the rest of the house. Just on the other side were a dining table and chairs, and further to the right the living room opened out. Sebastian noticed that a wall had been knocked down, and that the ground floor was now what was known as 'open plan'. He moved a little further inside. He recognised only a fraction of the furniture. A bureau that had belonged to his grandfather was familiar, and some of the paintings on the walls, but the wallpaper behind them was new to him. So was the flooring. How long was it since he had been here? Sebastian refused to think of this house as 'home'. He had moved out when he was nineteen, but he had visited after that. Nurtured a vain hope that he and his parents might be reconciled when they were all grown up. But no. He remembered visiting the week after he turned twenty-five. Was that the last time? Almost thirty years ago. It wasn't surprising that he hardly recognised a thing.

There was a closed door in one wall of the living room. When Sebastian lived there it had been a guest room. Rarely used. His parents had a wide circle of acquaintances, but they were almost all from the town itself. He opened the door. One wall was covered in bookshelves, and where there used to be a bed there was now a desk. With a typewriter and an old-fashioned calculator with a roll of paper on it. Sebastian closed the door. Presumably the entire house was full of shit like that. What was he going to do with it all?

He went into the kitchen. New cupboards, new table, same old car dealer's floor made of vinyl. He opened the door of the fridge. Full. All rotten. He picked up a carton of milk from the door. Opened. *Best before 8 March*. International Women's Day. Even though he knew what to expect, Sebastian stuck his nose in the opening. Pulling a face, he put the carton back and took out a can of beer that was next to a bag containing something he guessed might once have been cheese, but which now resembled a successful research project in a laboratory specialising in mould.

Opening the beer with one hand, he went back into the living room. On the way he switched on the main light. The bulbs were uplighters beneath an edging strip all the way around the room, providing an even, pleasant light. A tasteful detail that felt almost modern. Sebastian caught himself feeling reluctantly impressed.

He sat down on one of the armchairs and put his feet on the low coffee table without removing his shoes. Then he took a swig of the beer and leaned his head back. He absorbed the silence. The total silence. You couldn't even hear any traffic. The house was almost at the end of a cul-de-sac, and the nearest main road was hundreds of metres away. Sebastian spotted the piano. He took another swig of his beer, put the can down on the table, stood up and went over to the black, shining instrument.

Absentmindedly he pressed one of the white keys. A dull, slightly out of tune A broke the silence.

Sebastian had started playing the piano when he was six. Stopped when he was nine. At that point his private teacher had taken his father to one side after a lesson during which Sebastian had virtually refused to touch the keys at all, and had told Herr Bergman that it was a waste of her time and his money for her to turn up once a week and try to teach a pupil who was so lacking in motivation and, she was absolutely certain, any kind of musical ability. Which was incorrect. Sebastian did not lack musical ability. Nor had he refused to play as some kind of rebellion against his father; that came many years later. He had simply thought it was indescribably boring. Pointless. He couldn't get involved in something that he found so uninteresting. Not then.

Not since then.

Not now. There was no limit to the amount of time and energy he had once been able to devote to those things that interested and fascinated him, but if they didn't ... Putting up with something, tolerating it – these were concepts unknown to Sebastian Bergman.

Slowly he leaned forward and scrutinised the photographs on the lid of the piano. His parents' wedding photo in the centre; two pictures of his maternal and paternal grandparents on either side. A picture of Sebastian when he left school, and one in which he was perhaps eight or nine years old, posing in his team uniform in front of a set of goalposts. His foot resting on the ball as he gazed into the camera, his expression serious, certain of victory. Then a photo of his parents together, with a coach in the background. On holiday somewhere in Europe. His mother looked about sixty-five in this picture. Twenty years ago, then. Even though it had been a very deliberate choice, Sebastian was struck by how little he knew about his parents' lives after he had left them. He didn't even know what his mother had died of.

Then he caught sight of the photograph right at the back. He picked it up. It was the third picture of him. He was sitting on his new moped in front of the garage. Sebastian's mother had been very fond of that picture. He had a theory that it was because it was one of the few pictures from his teenage years – perhaps the only one – in which he looked genuinely happy. But it wasn't the picture of him sitting on his Puch Dakota that had captured his interest: it was a newspaper cutting tucked into the frame. The picture showed Lily in her white hospital gown, holding a tiny sleeping baby in her arms. Beneath the picture it said *Eine Tochter* and a date, 11 August 2000. And, below that, his and Lily's names. Sebastian removed the cutting and examined it carefully.

He remembered when he had taken the picture, and suddenly

he could almost smell the hospital and hear the sounds they both made. Lily had smiled at him. Sabine had been asleep.

'Where the hell did you get this?'

Sebastian stood there with the cutting in his hand. He was totally unprepared for this. There wasn't supposed to be anything in this house to remind him of it. But here he stood, with the picture of the two of them in his hand. They didn't belong here. They belonged to a different world. His two worlds, his two circles of hell. Each difficult enough to handle on its own, but together . . . They weren't supposed to have anything to do with one another. He clenched his right hand into a tight fist, over and over again, without even being aware of it. *Fuck her!* Even though she was dead, his mother could still get to him. Sebastian could feel his breathing growing more laboured. *Fuck her! Fuck this entire house!* What was he going to do with all the *crap* in here?

He carefully folded up the newspaper cutting, tucked it into his inside pocket and walked back into the kitchen. He opened the door of the cleaning cupboard and *bingo* – the telephone directory was on the shelf, exactly where it had always been. He took it over to the armchair and looked up real estate agents in the Yellow Pages. He started with A. Not surprisingly, no one answered. The first three firms carried a message about office opening hours and suggested he might like to call back, but the fourth ended with 'If you would like to leave a message after the tone, we will call you back.'

Sebastian waited.

'My name is Sebastian Bergman. I want to sell a house and all the contents. I don't know how this works, but I really want to get it sorted so that I can leave this fucking town as soon as possible. I couldn't give a toss about the money. You can take whatever percentage you want, just as long as it goes through quickly. If you're interested give me a call.'

Sebastian left his mobile number and hung up, then he leaned back in the armchair. He felt immensely tired. He closed his eyes, and in the silence he could hear his own heart beating.

It was too quiet.

He was lonely.

His hand moved up to the breast pocket of his shirt, which contained the card the woman on the train had given him. What time was it? Too late. If he called her now he might as well start the conversation by asking if she fancied a shag. That wouldn't work on her. He knew that. He would just lose what he had achieved so far, and have to start again with minus points. He wasn't that interested in her. He took a deep breath and allowed the air to escape slowly in a long exhalation. Again. With each breath he could feel the tiredness strengthening its grip on him. He wouldn't ring anyone. He wouldn't do anything.

He wanted to sleep.

He was going to sleep.

Until the dream woke him.

Torkel was having breakfast in the hotel dining room. Billy had already gone to the station to set up their office, and he hadn't seen any sign of Vanja yet. Outside the window the residents of Västerås were hurrying to work on this overcast spring day. Torkel glanced through the morning papers, both national and local. They all carried stories about the murder. There was less in the nationals; they were mainly giving an update. The only new information they had, apart from the fact that Riksmord had arrived, was that it could be some kind of ritual murder, according to sources close to the police, since the victim's heart was missing. Torkel sighed. If the morning papers were speculating about ritual murder, what on earth would the evening tabloids make of it? Satanism? Organ theft? Cannibalism? Perhaps they would find some German 'expert' who would inform their readers that it was not at all impossible that a disturbed individual suffering from certain delusions might eat another person's heart in order to absorb some of that person's strength. There would be a reference to the Incas or some other long-extinct tribe linked in people's minds with human sacrifice. And then there would be the web survey:

Could you imagine eating another person?
☐   *Yes, we're animals after all.*
☐   *Yes, but only if it was a question of my own survival.*
☐   *No, I would rather die.*

Torkel shook his head. He would just have to put up with it. He was turning into what Billy called a GOM – a Grumpy Old Man. Even though he surrounded himself with younger people all day, he was aware that more and more frequently he was slipping into a way of thinking that might suggest he felt things were better in the past. Nothing was better in the past. Apart from his private life, but then that didn't exactly have any bearing on the rest of the world. He just had to make the best of things. Torkel really didn't want to turn into one of those tired old police officers who complained cynically about the times they were living in, while sinking deeper and deeper into their armchairs with a glass of whisky in their hand and Puccini on the stereo. Time to pull himself together. His mobile buzzed. A text message. From Ursula. He pressed *Read*. She had arrived and gone straight to the scene where the body was found. Could they meet there? Torkel emptied his coffee cup and left the dining room.

Ursula Andersson was standing at the edge of the little pool. With her knitted woollen jumper tucked into dark green waterproof trousers that came up to her chest, she looked more like an angler, or someone about to clean up an oil spill on some beach, than one of the sharpest police officers in the country.

'Welcome to Västerås.'

Ursula turned and saw Torkel nod to Haraldsson before ducking under the police tape cordoning off most of the hollow.

'Nice trousers.'

Ursula smiled at him.

'Thank you very much.'

'Have you been in?'. Torkel nodded towards the pool.

'I've measured the depth and taken a few samples of the water. Where are the others?'

'Billy's sorting things out at the station, and Vanja was going to speak to the girlfriend. As far as we know, she was the last person to see the boy alive.' Torkel came over and stopped by the edge of the pool. 'How's it going?'

'No chance of any footprints. A whole crowd of people have been tramping around here. The kids who found the body, police, ambulance crew, people out for a walk in the forest.' Ursula crouched down and pointed to a shapeless dent in the muddy ground. Torkel squatted down beside her.

'Besides which, any traces are deep and sunken. It's too muddy and waterlogged.' Ursula made a sweeping gesture with her hand. 'A week ago it was even wetter, apparently. Most of the hollow was under water.' She stood up and glanced over in Haraldsson's direction, leaning slightly closer to Torkel.

'What's the name of that guy over there?' She nodded towards Haraldsson, and Torkel looked over his shoulder, even though he knew perfectly well whom Ursula meant.

'Haraldsson. He was in charge of the investigation until we got here.'

'I know. He told me at least three times on the way here. What's he like?'

'He needs to work on the first impression he makes, but I think he's . . . okay.'

Ursula turned towards Haraldsson.

'Could you come over here for a moment?'

Haraldsson ducked under the tape and limped over to Ursula and Torkel.

'Have you dragged the pool?' Ursula asked.

Haraldsson nodded. 'Twice. Nothing.'

Ursula nodded to herself. She hadn't expected a murder weapon. Not here. She turned away and gazed around the area once more. Everything fitted.

'Go on,' said Torkel, who knew from past experience that Ursula could see a great deal more than the sodden forest bog in front of them.

'He didn't die here. According to the preliminary autopsy report, the stab wounds were so deep that there were marks on the skin left by the handle of the knife. That indicates that the body was lying on a hard, unyielding surface. If you stab someone who's lying in water, the body will sink down, away from you.' Ursula gestured towards her feet. 'If we assume it was even more wet and muddy last weekend, it would have been almost impossible to thrust the knife in right up to the handle. In the softer parts of the body, anyway.'

Torkel looked at her with admiration. Even though they had

worked together for many years, he was still impressed by her knowledge and her ability to draw conclusions. He thanked his lucky stars that she had sought him out just a few days after he had been put in charge of Riksmord. She had simply been standing there one morning, seventeen years ago. Waiting for him outside his office. She hadn't booked an appointment with him, but said it would take five minutes maximum. He had let her in.

She was working at SKL, the national forensic laboratory. She had begun her career as a police officer, but before long she had begun to specialise in crime-scene investigation, and subsequently in technical evidence and forensics. That was how she had ended up in Linköping. At SKL. Not that she wasn't happy there, she had explained in her five minutes, except she missed the hunt. That was how she had put it. *The hunt*. It was all very well standing in a lab wearing a white coat, securing DNA evidence and test firing weapons, but it was an entirely different matter to be able to analyse evidence on the spot, then to track down the quarry as part of a team before arresting him or her. That gave her a kick and a sense of satisfaction a matching DNA sample could never provide. Could Torkel understand that? He could. Ursula had nodded. *There you go*. She had looked at her watch. Four minutes and forty-eight seconds. She had spent the last twelve seconds giving him her number and leaving the room.

Torkel had asked around and no one had anything but praise for Ursula, although what finally made him make a swift decision was the head of SKL, who virtually threatened him with physical retribution if he so much as looked in Ursula's direction. Torkel did more than that: he gave her the job that same afternoon.

'So the body was just dumped here.'

'Probably. If we assume that the murderer chose this spot, that he knew the pool, then he has local knowledge and would have parked his car as close as possible. Up there.'

She pointed to a slope some thirty metres away, perhaps two metres high and quite steep. As if responding to an invisible signal, they set off, Haraldsson limping along behind.

'How are things with Mikael?'

Ursula gave a start and glanced at Torkel.

'Fine, why do you ask?'

'Well, it's only a few days since you got home. He didn't get to keep you there for long.'

'It's the job. He understands. He's used to it.'

'Good.'

'Besides, he's going to some trade fair in Malmö.'

They had reached the slope. Ursula looked back at the pool. The perpetrator should have made his way down somewhere around here. The three of them began to examine the incline. After a minute or so Ursula stopped. Took a step back. Looked at either side for comparison purposes, sat down to get the view from the side. But she was certain. The vegetation was slightly flattened. A lot of it had sprung back up, but there were signs that something had been dragged along. She crouched down. A couple of branches had been snapped off a spindly shrub, and on the whitish-yellow broken surface there was a discolouration that could be blood. Ursula took a small evidence bag out of her case, carefully snipped off the branch and put it in the bag.

'I think I've found the spot where he came down. Could you two carry on up?'

Torkel waved to Haraldsson, and they continued to the top of the slope. When they reached the narrow dirt track, Torkel looked around. Their own cars were parked a short distance away.

'Where does this go?'

'Down into town – this is the way we came.'

'And in the other direction?'

'It twists and turns a bit, but after a while you come out on the main road.'

Torkel looked down the slope, where Ursula was crawling around on all fours, eagerly turning over every single leaf. If that was where the body had been dragged down, it was possible it had been hauled out of the boot or back door of a car just above. There was no reason for the murderer not to take the shortest route, so to speak. The dirt track was compacted and hard, with no chance of tyre marks. Torkel looked over at the cars they had arrived in. They had been parked to one side so that they wouldn't take up as much room on the narrow track. Was it possible . . . ?

He went and stood exactly above the narrow area in which Ursula was working. *If the boot was here . . .* Torkel pictured the car parked in front of him. That would mean that any tyre tracks would be a metre or so further on. He moved carefully into the ditch. He was pleased to find that it was considerably softer underfoot than the track itself, but it wasn't as muddy as down in the hollow. He began gently moving undergrowth and branches to one side, and got a result almost immediately.

Deep tyre tracks.

Torkel smiled.

This was getting off to a good start.

'You haven't changed your mind?'

The woman asking the question placed a cup of steaming hot tea on the table and pulled out the chair opposite Vanja, who shook her head.

'No, thanks, it's fine.' The woman sat down and started stirring her drink. Breakfast was laid out on the table. Milk and plain yoghurt stood beside boxes of muesli and oats. A basket made of woven birch bark contained slices of soft wholemeal bread and two kinds of crispbread. Butter, cheese, ham, sliced gherkins and a packet of spreadable liver pâté completed the array. The table contrasted sharply with the rest of the kitchen, which looked as if it had come out of a catalogue. Not exactly the latest trends, but the tidiness was exceptional. No dishes by the sink, no crumbs on the worktops, empty and clean. The black cooker hob was spotless, as were the cupboard doors. Vanja could swear that if she got up and ran her finger over the herb and spice rack above, she wouldn't find the slightest film of grease. Judging by what little Vanja had seen, the zero tolerance approach to mess applied to the rest of the house as well.

There was, however, one item that stood out. Vanja tried but couldn't tear her eyes away from the object adorning the wall behind the woman drinking tea. It was a large framed picture made of beads that depicted Jesus with his arms outstretched, his white robe hanging down. A golden yellow halo blazed around his head, and the black-bearded face with its intense bright blue eyes was looking upwards at an angle. Above his head the words 'I am the Truth, the Way and the Light' were picked out in red beads. The woman opposite Vanja followed her gaze.

'Lisa made that when she had chickenpox. She was eleven. She had a bit of help, of course.'

'It's lovely,' said Vanja. *And slightly scary*, she added to herself. The woman, who had introduced herself as Ann-Charlotte when she opened the door and let Vanja in, nodded contentedly at the praise and took a small sip of her tea. She put down the cup.

'Yes, she's very talented, is our Lisa. There are over five thousand beads in that picture! Isn't that fantastic?'

Ann-Charlotte reached for a crispbread and began to butter it. Vanja couldn't help wondering how they knew that. Had they counted the beads? She was about to ask when Ann-Charlotte replaced the butter knife and looked at her, her brow furrowed with concern.

'It's terrible, what's happened. To Roger. We prayed for him the whole week he was missing.'

And much good it did, thought Vanja, making noises that she hoped indicated agreement and sympathy, while at the same time casting a slightly exaggerated glance at the clock. A gesture that Ann-Charlotte seemed to understand.

'I'm sure Lisa will be down at any moment. If we'd known you were coming, then ...' Ann-Charlotte spread her hands apologetically.

'It's fine. I'm grateful for the opportunity to speak to her.'

'No problem. Anything we can do to help. How's his mother? Lena, isn't it? She must be absolutely devastated.'

'I haven't met her,' said Vanja. 'But I'm sure you're right. Was Roger her only child?'

Ann-Charlotte nodded and suddenly looked even more worried, as if most of the world's troubles had just landed on her shoulders.

'They haven't had an easy time of it. Things have been a bit difficult financially for a while, as I understand it, and then there was all that trouble at Roger's previous school. Although things seemed to be working out for him recently. And then this happens.'

'What kind of trouble at his previous school?' Vanja said.

'He was bullied,' she heard from the doorway.

Both Vanja and Ann-Charlotte turned. Lisa was standing there. Her straight hair hung down over her shoulders, still wet but neatly brushed, the fringe swept up with a plain slide. She was dressed in a white shirt buttoned right to the top, with a plain knitted waistcoat over it. Around her neck she wore a gold cross, with the chain looped over one side of her collar. Her skirt ended just above the knees, and she wore opaque tights. Vanja thought of the girl in some '70s TV series that had been repeated when she was little. Not least because of the girl's serious, slightly sullen expression. She got up and held out her hand to the girl, who came into the kitchen and pulled out a chair at the end of the table.

'Hello, Lisa – my name is Vanja Lithner. I'm a police officer.'

'I've already spoken to the police,' replied Lisa as she took Vanja's outstretched hand, squeezed it briefly and bent her knees in a small curtsey. Then she sat down. Ann-Charlotte got up and fetched a teacup from one of the cupboards.

'I know,' Vanja went on. 'But I work in a different department, and I'd really appreciate it if you wouldn't mind speaking to me as well, even if I ask the same questions.'

Lisa shrugged her shoulders and reached for the box of muesli. She shook a considerable pile into the bowl in front of her.

'When you say Roger was bullied at his previous school, do you know who was bullying him?'

Lisa shrugged her shoulders again.

'Everybody, I think. He didn't have any friends there, anyway. He didn't really like talking about it. He was just glad he'd left there and come to our school instead.' Lisa reached for the yoghurt and covered the muesli with a thick layer. Ann-Charlotte placed a cup of tea in front of her daughter.

'Roger was a wonderful boy. Calm. Sensitive. Mature for his age. I just can't understand how anyone could . . . ' Ann-Charlotte didn't finish the sentence. She sat down again. Vanja opened her notebook and jotted down 'previous school – bullying'. Then she turned to Lisa, who was shovelling a spoonful of yoghurt and muesli into her mouth.

'If we could just go back to the Friday when he went missing. Can you tell me what you did – if anything in particular happened when Roger was here – everything you can remember, however ordinary or insignificant it might seem.'

Lisa took her time; she finished chewing and swallowed before answering Vanja, her gaze steady.

'I've already done that. With the other police officer.'

'Yes, but as I said, I need to hear it as well. What time did he get here?'

'Some time after five. Half past, maybe.' Lisa looked to her mother for help.

'Closer to half past,' Ann-Charlotte supplied. 'Erik and I had to be somewhere at six, and we were just on our way out when Roger arrived.' Vanja nodded and made a note.

'And what did you do while he was here?'

'We were in my room. We did a bit of homework that had to be in on Monday, then we made some tea and watched *Let's Dance*. He left shortly before ten.'

'Did he say where he was going then?'

Lisa shrugged her shoulders once more.

'Home, he said. He wanted to know who got voted off the show, and they don't tell you until after the news and the adverts.'

'And who did get voted off?'

Vanja saw the spoon pause on its way to Lisa's mouth with another load of yoghurt and muesli. Not for long. It was almost imperceptible, but still: the hesitation was there. Vanja had only been making small talk, a way of breaking the atmosphere of an interrogation. But the question had taken Lisa by surprise, Vanja was sure of it. Lisa carried on eating.

'I dode – doe –'

'Don't speak with your mouth full,' Ann-Charlotte interrupted. Lisa fell silent. She chewed mechanically, her gaze fixed on Vanja the whole time. Was she buying time? Why didn't she answer before she shoved the spoon in her mouth? Vanja waited. Lisa chewed. And swallowed.

'I don't know. I didn't watch after the news.'

'What dances did they do? Do you remember that?' Lisa's expression darkened. The questions were annoying her, for some reason. Vanja was sure of it.

'I don't know what they were called. We weren't watching that closely. We were chatting and reading and listening to music and so on. Flicking through the channels.'

'I don't see how the content of a television program can be of any importance when it comes to finding whoever killed Roger,' Ann-Charlotte broke in. She put the cup down in front of her with a slightly irritated bang. Vanja turned to face her with a smile.

'It isn't. I was just making conversation.' She turned back to Lisa, still smiling. Lisa didn't smile back. She met Vanja's eyes with a stubborn expression on her face.

'Did Roger mention anything that might be worrying him during the course of the evening?'

'No.'

'No phone calls? No texts he didn't want to talk about, or that he got upset about?'

'No.'

'He wasn't behaving differently, didn't seem to find it difficult to concentrate, nothing like that?'

'No.'

'And he didn't say he was going to see anyone else when he left you at ... about ten o'clock, was that what you said?'

Lisa gazed at Vanja. Who was she trying to trip up? She knew perfectly well that Lisa had said Roger left at ten. She was testing her. To see if she would contradict herself. But there was no chance of that. Lisa was well rehearsed.

'Yes, he left at ten and, no, he said he was going home to see who had been knocked out.' Lisa reached for the bread basket and took a slice of wholemeal. Ann-Charlotte chipped in again.

'But she's already told you all this. I don't understand why she has to answer the same questions over and over again. Don't you believe her?' Ann-Charlotte sounded almost hurt. As if the very idea that her little girl might tell a lie was deeply shocking. Vanja looked at Lisa. It might be shocking to her mother, but she knew Lisa was hiding something. Something had happened that evening. Something Lisa had no intention of telling her. Not with her mother there, at any rate. Lisa cut herself some cheese and placed the slices on the piece of bread with slow, almost exaggerated movements, glancing at Vanja from time to time. She would have to be careful. This one was considerably sharper than the police officer she had spoken to in the school cafeteria. She had to stick to the story she'd practised. Keep repeating the times. She wouldn't remember the details of the evening, if they asked her. Nothing special had happened.

Roger arrived.

Homework.

Tea.

TV.

Roger left.

After all, they wouldn't expect her to remember every single detail of any other ordinary, boring Friday evening either. Besides which, she was in shock. Her boyfriend was dead. If she'd only been better at crying, she would have squeezed out a few tears right now. Made her mother put a stop to the conversation.

'Of course I believe her,' Vanja said calmly. 'But Lisa was the last person we know of who saw Roger that evening. We need to get all the details right.' Vanja pushed her chair back. 'But that's enough for now. You need to get to school and to work.'

'I don't work. Apart from a few hours a week in the community. But that's voluntary.'

A housewife. That explained the impeccable home. At least as far as the cleaning was concerned.

Vanja took out her card and pushed it across to Lisa. She kept her finger on it for long enough to force Lisa to look up and meet her gaze.

'Give me a ring if you think of anything you haven't mentioned about that Friday.' Vanja shifted her focus to Ann-Charlotte. 'I'll see myself out. Leave you to your breakfast.'

Vanja left the house and drove back to the station. On the way she thought about the dead boy, and was struck by a realisation that made her feel slightly sad and uncomfortable at the same time.

So far she hadn't met anyone who seemed particularly upset or sorry that Roger was dead.

Fredrik thought it would take ten minutes. Maximum. In, tell the police, out. He had known Roger was missing, of course. Everybody had been talking about it at school. In fact, people had never talked about Roger at Runebergs School as much as they had done last week. Never paid him that much attention. And yesterday, after they found him: an emergency counselling service had immediately been put in place, and people who hadn't given a shit about Roger during the short time he had been a pupil there had excused themselves from lessons, weeping copiously, and had sat in groups holding hands and sharing happy memories in subdued voices.

Fredrik hadn't known Roger and wasn't exactly grieving for him. They had passed one another in the corridors – familiar faces, no more. Fredrik could honestly say he hadn't given Roger a thought since he'd left Runebergs in the autumn. But now the local TV station had turned up, and some of the girls who wouldn't even have spoken to Roger if he'd been the last boy on earth had lit candles and laid flowers by one of the goalposts on the football pitch outside the school.

Perhaps that was a nice thing to do? Perhaps it was a sign that empathy and human kindness still existed? Perhaps Fredrik was just being cynical when he saw only falseness and people exploiting a tragic incident to draw attention to themselves. Taking the chance to fill some indefinable vacuum.

To experience a sense of solidarity.

To experience *something*.

He remembered the images they had seen in Social Studies from the NK department store in Stockholm when Anna Lindh was murdered. Mountains of flowers. Fredrik recalled that he had wondered even then. Where did it come from, this need to mourn people we don't know? People we haven't even met? It obviously existed. Perhaps there was something wrong with Fredrik because he was unable to feel and share this collective grief?

But he read the papers. After all it was a contemporary of his, an acquaintance, whose heart had been cut out. The police wanted to hear from anyone who had seen Roger after he disappeared on Friday evening. While Roger was simply missing, Fredrik hadn't seen the point in going to the police, because, after all, he had actually seen Roger *before* he went missing, but now they had said that any sightings on the Friday, both before and after his disappearance, were of interest. Fredrik cycled down to the police station before school, pushed open the doors and thought it probably wouldn't take very long.

He told the uniformed woman behind the desk that he wanted to speak to someone about Roger Eriksson, but before she had time to pick up the phone a plainclothes officer carrying a cup of coffee limped up to him and told him to come through.

That was – Fredrik glanced at the clock on the wall – twenty minutes ago. He had told the limping detective what he had come to say, certain things he had gone over twice, the place itself three times, and the third time he had to mark it on a map. But now the detective seemed satisfied. He closed his notebook and looked at Fredrik.

'Thank you very much for coming in. Could you wait here for a little while?' Fredrik nodded and the man limped away.

Fredrik settled down and looked at the open-plan office where a dozen or so officers were sitting at desks, separated from one another by movable screens decorated here and there with children's drawings, family photos, takeaway menus and more work-related documents. The sound was a muted blend of the tapping of keyboards, conversations, ringing telephones and the hum of the photocopier. Fredrik wondered how anyone could get anything done in an environment like this, in spite of the fact that he always did his homework with his iPod earphones firmly in place. How could you sit opposite someone who was speaking on the telephone without listening in?

The detective was limping towards a door, but before he got there a woman came over to him. A blonde woman in a suit. It seemed to Fredrik that the limping detective slumped wearily as the woman approached.

'Who's that?' Hanser said, nodding towards the boy who was sitting watching them. Haraldsson followed her gaze, even though he knew perfectly well whom she meant.

'His name is Fredrik Hammar, and he has some information about Roger Eriksson.' Haraldsson held up his notebook as if to emphasise that it was all in there. Hanser did her best to remain calm.

'If it's about Roger Eriksson, why aren't Riksmord interviewing him?'

'I was passing the desk when he came in and thought it a good idea if to speak to him first. To see if what he had to say was of any relevance. There's no point in Torkel wasting his time on things that don't contribute to the investigation.'

Hanser took a deep breath. She could imagine it must be difficult to give up the responsibility for a case. However you wrapped up the circumstances, at the end of the day it indicated a lack of confidence in him. The fact that she was the person who had taken the decision didn't make things any less sensitive. Haraldsson had applied for her job, she knew that. You didn't need any great psychological insight to work out what he thought of her. Everything he did, all the time, radiated aversion and hostility. Perhaps she should be glad Haraldsson was sticking to this case with lunatic stubbornness. Praise his obvious dedication. His genuine commitment. Or maybe he just hadn't grasped that he was no longer an active part of the investigation. Hanser tended towards the latter view.

'Deciding what is relevant or otherwise in this investigation is no longer your job.' Haraldsson nodded in a way that indicated that he was simply waiting for her to finish the sentence so that he could correct her. And, indeed, she had barely started to make her next point before he interrupted.

'I know they're responsible, but they did say very clearly that they wanted to work in association with me.'

Hanser cursed Torkel's diplomacy. Now she would have to play the bad guy. Not that it would change anything in their relationship, but even so.

'Thomas, Riksmord have taken over the investigation, which means that you are no longer a part of it, not in any way. Unless they expressly ask you to do something.'

There, it had been said. Again.

Haraldsson stared at her coldly. He knew what she was up to. Since she had found it necessary to call in Riksmord straightaway, with her non-existent routine and her lack of leadership, naturally she didn't want any of her staff working with them. They had to solve the case on their own. Prove to her superiors that she had made the right decision. That the Västerås police just didn't have the ability.

'We can take that up with Torkel. He expressly said that I was to work in association with them. What's more, the boy has some extremely interesting information that I was just about to pass on to them. I mean, I'd prefer it if we could get on with trying to solve the case, but of course if you'd rather stand here discussing the chain of command, perhaps we should do that instead. It's entirely up to you.'

So this was how he intended to play it. Making her out to be a desk jockey while he was the good police officer, interested only in the case and in solving it unselfishly. Hanser now realised that Haraldsson might be a more dangerous opponent that she had previously suspected.

She stepped aside. Haraldsson gave a triumphant smile and limped off, shouting in as familiar a tone as he could muster, 'Billy, have you got a minute?'

Vanja opened her notebook. She had just apologised for asking Fredrik to repeat everything he had already said. She was annoyed. Vanja wanted to be the first to interview witnesses and anyone else who was involved. There was a risk that they might unconsciously become careless the second time. That they would leave out information because they thought they'd already said it. That they might have assessed the information and decided it wasn't interesting. It struck her that this was the second time the person she was talking to in this investigation had lost a bit of their edge because they had already told Haraldsson everything. Two out of two. There wouldn't be a third, she promised herself. She rested her pen on the paper.

'So you saw Roger Eriksson?'

'Yes, last Friday.'

'And you're sure it was him?'

'Yes, we were at Vikinga School at the same time. And then he went to Runebergs at the beginning of last term.'

'Were you in the same class?'

'No, I'm a year older.'

'And where did you see Roger?'

'It's called Gustavsborgsgatan, by the car park at the high school. I don't know if you know where that is?'

'We'll find out.'

Billy made a note. When Vanja said 'we' in these situations she meant him. It would be added to the map.

'Which direction was he going in?'

64

'He was heading into town. I mean, I don't know what direction that is or anything.'

'We'll find that out too.'

Billy made another note.

'What time on Friday did you see him?'

'Just after nine.'

Vanja stopped dead for the first time during the interview. She looked at Fredrik with a hint of scepticism. Had she misunderstood something? She looked down at her notes again.

'Nine o'clock in the evening? Twenty-one hundred hours?'

'Just after.'

'And this was last Friday?'

'Yes.'

'You're sure of that? And the time?'

'Yes, I finished training at half past eight and I was on my way into town. We were going to the cinema, and I remember looking at my watch and seeing that I had twenty-five minutes. The film started at nine-thirty.'

Vanja didn't speak. Billy knew why. He had just finished the time line for Roger's disappearance on the whiteboard in their office. Roger had left his girlfriend at ten o'clock. According to that same girlfriend he hadn't left her room – let alone her house – all evening. So what was he doing on this Gustavsborgsgatan an hour earlier? Vanja was thinking exactly the same thing. So Lisa had been lying, just as she had thought. The young man sitting in front of Vanja seemed very reliable. Mature, in spite of the fact that he was comparatively young. Nothing in his behaviour suggested that he was here for the attention, for the thrill, or because he was a compulsive liar.

'Okay, so you saw Roger. Why did you notice him? There must have been plenty of people out and about at nine o'clock on a Friday evening?'

'I noticed him because he was walking along on his own, and there was this moped circling round and round him, kind of having a go at him, if you know what I mean.'

Vanja and Billy both leaned forward. The time issue was important, but so far the information they had received had concerned only the victim's movements the evening before he went missing. Now all of a sudden there was someone else in the frame. Someone who was messing Roger about. This was getting good. Vanja swore to herself once again, cursing the fact that she was getting the second bite at this.

'A moped?' Billy took over from Vanja. She didn't just let him do it, she actively welcomed it.

'Yes.'

'Can you remember anything about it? The colour, for example?'

'Well, yes, but I know—'

'What colour was it?' Billy interrupted him. This was his field.

'Red, but I know—'

'Do you know what make it might have been?' Billy broke in again, eager to piece the puzzle together. 'Do you know what type of moped it was? Can you remember if it had number plates?'

'Yes – I mean, no, I don't remember.' Fredrik turned to Vanja. 'But I know whose it is – I mean, I know who was riding it. Leo Lundin.' Vanja and Billy looked at one another. Vanja got up eagerly.

'Wait here, I need to go and fetch my boss.'

The man who was not a murderer was proud of himself. Even though he shouldn't have been. The emotional reports, the school in mourning, the frequent press conferences with grim-faced police officers told a different story. Tragic, dark and sorrowful. But he couldn't help it. However hard he tried, he couldn't avoid ending up in the company of that self-affirming feeling. He alone felt like this. No one would ever understand.

However close they were.

Whatever they said.

His pride was uplifting and liberating, almost joyous. He had acted powerfully. Like a real man. Protected what had to be protected. He had not given way, had not failed when it really mattered. The strong, sweet smell of blood and internal organs had penetrated deep into his senses, and his whole body had fought against the rising nausea. But he had carried on. The knife in his hand had not trembled. His legs had not let him down when he moved the body. He had performed at the very peak of his ability in a situation in which most people would not be able to cope. Or would never encounter. This was what he was proud of.

Yesterday he had been so tense that he had found it difficult to sit still. He had gone for a long walk lasting several hours. Through the town that was talking about just one thing: his secret. After a while he passed the police station. His instinct was to turn back when he saw the familiar building. He had been so lost in thought that he hadn't considered where he was going, but since he was there he realised he might as well walk past. He was just someone out for a stroll, someone who happened to be passing. The men and women inside would suspect nothing. Wouldn't know that the person they were looking for was so close. He kept on going. Eyes front. In spite of everything he dared not glance in through the big windows. A patrol car emerged from the garage and braked. He

67

nodded to the uniformed officers in the car as if he knew them. Which he did, of course. They were his opponents. He was the man they were looking for, even though they didn't know it. There was something incredibly exciting and satisfying about being in possession of that knowledge, holding the truth in his hand. The truth they were so frantically seeking. He stopped and allowed the patrol car to pass in front of him. He could permit his opponents that courtesy.

He knew where this strength came from. Not from God. God gave guidance and consolation. His father gave him the strength. His father, who had challenged him, tempered him and made him understand what was required. It had been anything but easy. Somehow the secret he now held as an adult reminded him of the secret he had carried as a child. No one had been able to understand that either.

However close they were.

Whatever they said.

Once, when he had been feeling sad and weak, he had told a blonde school nurse who smelled of flowers. There was uproar. Chaos. The school and social services intervened. Talked, telephoned, visited. Educational psychologists and social workers. His mother wept and he, the young boy, suddenly knew what he was about to lose. Everything. Because he had been weak. Because he hadn't had the strength to keep quiet. He knew his father loved him. It was just that he was the kind of man who showed his love through discipline and order. A man who would rather put across his message with his fists, his belt and the carpet beater than with words. A man who was preparing his boy with obedience. Getting him ready for reality. Where it was necessary to be strong.

He had solved the problem by taking back what he had said. Denying the whole thing. Saying that he had been misunderstood. He restored order. He did not want to lose his father. His family. He could bear the blows. But not the thought of losing him. They had moved to a different place. His father had appreciated his denial. His lies. They had grown closer to one another, he could feel it. The blows did not diminish – rather, the reverse – but to the boy it felt easier. And he kept quiet. Grew stronger. Nobody understood what a gift his father had given him. He himself had barely understood it at the time. But now he could see it: the ability to rise above chaos and act. The man who was not a murderer smiled. He felt closer to his father than ever.

Sebastian had woken just before four o'clock in one of the hard, narrow single beds upstairs. His mother's, he assumed, judging by the rest of the room. His parents had not been sleeping in separate bedrooms when Sebastian had left home, but he wasn't surprised at the new arrangement. Voluntarily climbing into bed next to his father night after night couldn't reasonably be described as sane behaviour. Clearly his mother had reached the same conclusion.

Sebastian usually got up when he was woken by the dream, regardless of the time. Usually, but not always. Sometimes he stayed where he was. Closed his eyes. Felt the cramp in his right hand slowly ease as he invited the dream back into his consciousness.

Sometimes he longed for these mornings. Longed for and feared them. When he allowed the dream to gain a foothold again, when he milked the pure, unadulterated feeling of love from it, then his return to reality afterwards was significantly more difficult and suffused with fear than when he simply let go, got up and moved on. Generally it wasn't worth it. Because after the love came the pain.

The loss.

Unerring, every time.

It was like a form of addiction. He knew the consequences. He knew that afterwards he would feel so bad he could hardly function.

Hardly manage to breathe.

Hardly manage to live.

But he needed it from time to time. The pure core. The stronger, truer feeling that his memories could no longer give him. His memories were, after all, only memories. Compared to the emotions he felt in the dreams they were pale, almost lifeless. Nor were they all real – he was certain of that. He had taken away here, added there. Consciously and unconsciously. Improved and strengthened certain parts, toned down and pared away others. The memories were subjective. His dream was objective. Pitiless.

Unsentimental.

Unbearably painful.

But alive.

This morning in his parents' home he stayed in bed and allowed himself to embrace the dream again. He wanted it. Needed it. It was easy; it was still there within him like an invisible entity, and all he needed to do was give it a little renewed strength.

And when he did, he could feel her. Not remember her. Actually feel her. He could feel her small hand in his. He could hear her voice. He could hear other voices, other sounds. But, most of all, her. He could even smell her. Baby soap and sunscreen. She was there with him in his half sleep. Properly. Again. His big thumb moved unconsciously over the cheap little ring on her index finger. A butterfly. He had found it among a load of cheap rubbish at a sweaty market. She had loved it at once. Never wanted to take it off.

The day had begun in slow motion. It was late by the time they got outside. The plan was to stay at the hotel and relax by the pool all day. Lily had gone for a run. A belated, truncated run. Once they got outside Sabine didn't want to spend all day lying around by the pool. No – her legs were full of energy, so he decided they would go down to the beach for a while. Sabine loved the beach. She loved it when he held her in his arms and played in the waves. She screamed with joy when he swung her little body between sea and air, wet and dry. On the way down they passed several other children. It was Boxing Day and the children were trying out their new toys. He carried her on his shoulders. A little girl was playing with an inflatable dolphin, pale blue and beautiful, and Sabine reached out towards it.

'Daddy, I want one of those.'

That was to be the last thing she ever said to him. The beach

70

was a little way off beyond a large sand dune, and he headed there quickly so that she would have something other than pale blue dolphins to think about. It worked, and Sabine laughed as he trudged through the warm sand. Her soft hands on his stubbly cheek. Her laughter when he stumbled and almost fell.

It had been Lily's idea to go away for Christmas. He hadn't put up much of a fight. Big occasions weren't Sebastian's specialty, besides which he found her family quite difficult, so when she suggested a trip he had agreed immediately. Not because he actually liked sun, sea and sand, but because he realised that Lily, as always, was trying to make life a little easier for him. Besides, Sabine loved the sun and the sea, and everything Sabine loved, he loved. It was a relatively new sensation for Sebastian. Doing things for other people. It had arrived with Sabine. A good feeling, he had thought as he stood there on the beach, gazing out over the Indian Ocean. He put Sabine down and she immediately ran towards the water on her little legs. It was considerably shallower than it had been on previous days, and the shoreline was further out than usual. He assumed it was the tide that had pulled the water so far back. He ran to the water with her. It was slightly overcast, but the temperature of the air and water was perfect. Without a care in the world he kissed her one last time before lowering her up to her tummy in the warm water. She screamed out loud and then laughed, because to her the water was both frightening and wonderful, and for a second Sebastian thought about the psychological term for their game. *Trust exercises.* Daddy doesn't let go. The child becomes more and more daring. A simple term whose true meaning he had never really put into practice before. Trust. Sabine screamed with a mixture of fear and joy, and at first Sebastian didn't hear the roar. He was completely absorbed by the trust between the two of them. When he did hear the noise, it was too late.

That day he learned a new word.

A word that he, who had read so much, had never heard before. *Tsunami.*

On those mornings when he invited the dream in, he lost her

71

again. And the grief tore at him so that he thought he would never be able to get out of bed.

But he did.

Eventually.

And the thing that was his life went on.

Leonard! Clara Lundin knew it was about her son as soon as she saw the young couple on the steps. She knew before they introduced themselves and showed her their ID that they were neither Jehovah's Witnesses nor people trying to sell something. She had known this day would come. She had known, and a ball of anxiety formed in her stomach. Or perhaps it merely intensified. Clara had felt that pressure in her midriff for so long that she hardly noticed it any more. When the phone rang during the evening. When she heard sirens at the weekends. When Leonard woke her up coming home with his mates. When she checked her inbox and saw there was an email from the school.

'Is Leo in?' asked Vanja, putting away her ID card.

'Leonard,' Clara corrected her automatically. 'Yes, he is . . . What do you want with him?'

'Is he ill?' Vanja asked, ducking the question about the reason for their visit.

'No, I don't think so . . . What do you mean?'

'I'm just wondering why he's not in school.'

It struck Clara that she hadn't even given it a thought. She worked irregular hours at the hospital, and she wondered less and less often about her son's school career. He came and went more or less as he wished. Did most things more or less as he wished.

Everything, in fact.

She had lost control. That was how things were. All she could do was admit it. Lost control completely. In less than a year. The books she had borrowed and the advice columns she had read said it was only natural. This was the age at which boys started to free themselves from their parents and tentatively began to investigate the adult world. It was a question of loosening the reins a little,

72

while still holding onto them firmly, and above all you had to provide them with security in the knowledge that you were always there for them. But Leonard never did anything tentatively. He jumped. From one day to the next. As if he was leaping into a black hole. Suddenly she had lost him, and no reins in the world were long enough to hold him. She was there but he no longer needed her. Not at all.

'He's having a bit of a lie-in. What do you want?'

'We'd like to see him, if you don't mind,' Billy insisted as they stepped into the hallway.

Once inside, the bass beat they had heard as soon as they approached the L-shaped one-storey detached house was even louder. Hip hop. Billy recognised it.

DMX. 'X Gon' Give it to Ya'.

2002.

Old school.

'I'm his mother and I want to know what he's done.' Vanja noticed that she didn't want to know what they *thought* or *suspected* her son had done. She simply assumed he was guilty.

'We'd like a word with him about Roger Eriksson.'

The dead boy. Why did the police want to talk to Leonard about the dead boy? Her stomach was definitely contracting in a series of cramps. Clara merely nodded silently, stepped aside to let Billy and Vanja in, then disappeared to the left, walked through the living room and went up to a closed door. The door she was not allowed to open without knocking. Which was what she did now.

'Leonard. The police are here and they'd like to talk to you.'

Billy and Vanja waited in the hallway. Small and tidy. Hooks on the wall to the right with three jackets on coat hangers, two of which seemed to belong to Leonard. A solitary handbag dangled on the fourth hook. Down below, a little shoe rack with four pairs of shoes, two of them trainers. Reebok and Eck , Billy noticed. On the opposite side a small chest of drawers with a mirror above it. The top of the chest was empty apart from a small mat and a bowl of everlasting flowers. Beyond the chest of drawers the wall

73

soon ended and the living room took over. Clara was knocking on the closed door once again.

'Leonard. They want to have a word with you about Roger. Could you come out, please?'

She knocked again. In the hallway Billy and Vanja looked at one another and reached a silent decision. They wiped their shoes on the doormat and walked through the living room. Just by the kitchen door there was a simple dining table on a yellow rug with a pattern of brown squares, and one of two sofas with its back to the table. The other sofa stood opposite, with a low coffee table made of some kind of pale wood between them. Birch, Vanja guessed, although she had no idea. There was a TV on the wall. No films, even though there was a DVD player on a low shelf beneath it. No games consoles or games. The room was clean and tidy. It didn't look as if anyone had sat on the sofas for a long time. The scatter cushions were perfectly arranged, a blanket folded up, the two remotes lying neatly side by side. Behind the second sofa the entire wall was covered in bookshelves, with hardbacks and paperbacks in perfect rows, interspersed here and there with well-dusted ornaments. Vanja and Billy went over to Clara, who was starting to get worried.

'Leonard, open this door!' No reaction. The music continued at the same volume. Perhaps it was even louder, Vanja thought. Or perhaps it was just because they were closer. Billy knocked. Hard.

'Leonard, could we have a word, please?' No reaction. Billy knocked again.

'That's odd. It sounded as if he was turning the key.'

Vanja and Billy looked at Clara. Billy pushed the handle down. Exactly.

Locked.

Vanja glanced quickly through the living room window. Suddenly she saw a well-built red-haired boy land softly on the grass outside and set off running across the lawn in his stockinged feet, out of her field of vision. The whole thing happened at lightning speed.

74

Vanja ran towards the closed patio door, shouting, 'Leo! Stop!'

Which Leo had absolutely no intention of doing. In fact, he increased his speed. Vanja turned back to a somewhat surprised Billy.

'Take the front!' she yelled from the patio door as she struggled to open it. A short distance away she could just see the fleeing boy. She wrenched the door open and stepped quickly over the flowerbeds. Then she sped up. And shouted to the boy again.

By eight o'clock Sebastian had got up, showered and taken himself off to the Statoil petrol station a few hundred metres away. He bought breakfast and a latte and ate there as he watched the morning commuters buying cigarettes, coffee and unleaded. When he got back to his temporary accommodation he gathered up the newspapers, letters, bills and junk mail from the overflowing mailbox. He dropped everything except for today's paper in a recycling sack he had found neatly folded in the cleaning cupboard. He hoped that estate agent would ring soon, so that he didn't have to make a habit of eating Statoil food. Feeling bored, he went and sat outside at the back of the house, where the sun had already begun to warm up the recently laid wooden decking. When Sebastian was little there had been paving stones here. The ones with pebbles forming a relief pattern; everybody had had them in those days, he remembered. Now everybody seemed to have decking instead.

He picked up the paper and was about to start on the culture section when he heard a woman's voice shouting 'Leo! Stop!' and a few seconds later a tall, red-haired teenager emerged through next door's evergreen hedge, ran across the narrow cycle-and-pedestrian track separating the two properties, and with a quick leap cleared the metre-high white fence and landed in Sebastian's garden. After him came a woman in her thirties. Fast. Agile. She wasn't far behind as she broke through the hedge, steadily catching up the young man. Sebastian watched the chase and silently placed a bet with himself that the lad wouldn't reach the fence on the other side of the garden. He was right. Just a few metres before the fence the woman put on a spurt and brought him down with a well-aimed tackle. To be honest she had the advantage on the soft surface because she was wearing shoes, Sebastian thought as he watched them both roll over a couple of times thanks to the speed they had been running.

The woman quickly seized the young man's arm and twisted it up his back. Police. Sebastian stood up and took a few steps across the lawn. Not that he had any intention of intervening in any way; he just wanted to get a better view. The woman appeared to have the situation under control, and if she hadn't then a man of about the same age was coming running from the opposite direction to help her. Evidently he was a police officer as well, because he took out a pair of handcuffs and started to secure the young man's arms behind his back.

'Let me go, for fuck's sake! I haven't fucking done anything!' The red-haired boy twisted and turned on the grass as best he could in the woman's firm grip.

'So why run?' asked the woman, pulling the teenager to his feet with her colleague's help. They set off towards the front of the house and a waiting car, Sebastian presumed. During the short walk the woman noticed they were not alone in the garden. She looked over at Sebastian, whipped an ID card out of her pocket and flipped it open. From that distance it might just as well have been a library card. Sebastian had no chance of reading a single word.

'Vanja Lithner, Riksmord. Everything is under control. You can go back inside.'

'I wasn't inside. Is it okay if I stay out here?'

But the woman had obviously finished with him. She put away her ID card and grabbed the boy's arm once more. He looked like one of those boys whom life had sent off on a downward path at an early stage. So this was doubtless neither the first nor the last time he would be led to a waiting police car. Another woman was coming along the pavement. She stopped, her hands flew to her mouth to suppress a scream as she saw what was happening on Sebastian's lawn. Sebastian gazed at her. The mother, of course. Red hair in soft, pretty curls. Around forty-five. Not very tall – one metre sixty-five maybe. Looked pretty fit. Probably a regular at the gym. She must be the neighbour from the other side of the hedge. When Sebastian used to live here a German couple with two schnauzers had occupied the house. They were old even then. Bound to be dead by now.

'Leonard, what have you done? Where are you taking him? What's he done?' The woman appeared to be ignoring the fact that no answers were forthcoming; the questions just kept bubbling out. Rapid and strained, in a voice that was approaching a falsetto. Like the safety valve on a pressure cooker. If she had kept the questions inside, she would have exploded with anxiety. The woman advanced across the grass. 'What's he done? Tell me, please! Why do you always end up in trouble, Leonard? What's he done? Where are you taking him?'

The female police officer let go of the boy's arm and took a few steps towards the worried mother. The male officer kept on walking.

'We just want to talk to him. His name came up in the course of our enquiries,' she said, and Sebastian noted the calming hand on the agitated woman's upper arm. Physical contact. Good. Professional.

'"Came up"? What do you mean, "came up"? In what way?'

'We're taking him to the station now. If you come down in a little while we can go through everything quietly and calmly.' Vanja broke off, ensuring that she made eye contact with the woman before continuing. 'Clara, we don't know anything at the moment. Don't get upset for no reason. Come down to the station, ask for me or Billy Rosén. My name is Vanja Lithner.' Vanja had, of course, introduced herself when they arrived at the Lundin house, but it was by no means certain that Clara had remembered or even picked up her name. Vanja therefore produced one of her cards and handed it over. Clara took it with a nod, too shocked to protest.

Vanja turned and left the garden. Clara watched her disappear around the corner by the flowering currant. For a moment she simply stood there. Utterly lost. Then she turned to the nearest port of call, which happened to be Sebastian.

'Can they do that? Can they just drive off with him, without me? I mean, he's still a minor.'

'How old is he?'

'Sixteen.'

'Then yes, they can do that.'

Sebastian went back to the decking and the morning sunshine and the culture section. Clara stayed where she was, gazing at the corner around which Vanja had disappeared, as if she was expecting all three of them to leap out, smiling and laughing and telling her the whole thing was just a joke. A well-planned practical joke. It didn't happen. Clara turned to Sebastian, who had just settled down in his white cane armchair once more.

'Can't you do something?' she said pleadingly. Sebastian looked at her with a quizzical expression.

'Me? Like what?'

'You're the Bergmans' son, aren't you? Sebastian? You work on this kind of thing.'

'Worked. Past tense. I don't do anything these days. And even when I was working, I didn't have anything to do with querying arrests. I was a criminal psychologist, not a lawyer.'

Out in the street, the car taking her only son away started up and drove off. Sebastian looked at the woman who was still standing on his lawn. Totally at a loss. Deserted. 'What's he done, your son? Why are Riksmord interested in him?'

Clara took a few steps towards him. 'It's something to do with that boy who was murdered. I don't know. Leonard would never do something like that. Never.'

'So what does Leonard do, then?' Clara looked at Sebastian, her expression one of complete incomprehension as he nodded at the fence. 'When you came over the fence you were telling him off for ending up in trouble all the time.' Clara took stock. Had she done

78

that? She didn't know. So many questions. So much confusion in her head, but perhaps she had. Leonard had got into quite a lot of trouble, particularly of late, but this was something else entirely.

'But he's not a murderer!'

'Nobody is until they kill someone.' Clara looked at Sebastian, who now seemed completely uninterested in and unmoved by the events that had played out in his garden. He was drumming his fingertips on the newspaper as if nothing unusual or important had happened.

'So you're not going to help me?'

'I've got a copy of the Yellow Pages in the house. I can look up L for lawyer.'

The lump of anxiety and fear in Clara's stomach was joined by rage. She had heard a few things about the Bergmans' son over the years when Esther and Ture had been her neighbours. And none of it had been good. Ever.

'And to think I used to be convinced Esther was exaggerating when she talked about you.'

'That would surprise me – my mother was never one for grand gestures.'

Clara glanced briefly at Sebastian, then turned and left without a word. Sebastian picked up a section of the paper from the decking. He had noticed the article, but hadn't been particularly interested. Now he turned to it once more: RIKSMORD BROUGHT IN TO INVESTIGATE BOY'S MURDER.

'Why did you run?'

Vanja and Billy were sitting opposite Leonard Lundin in the impersonally furnished room. A table, three fairly comfortable chairs. Wallpaper in muted colours, the odd framed poster, a floor lamp in one corner behind a small armchair. Daylight through the window – which admittedly was made of frosted glass, but it was daylight nonetheless. It looked more like a room in a simple ramblers' hostel than an interview room, minus a bed but with the addition of two surveillance cameras that recorded everything from an adjoining room.

Leonard was slumped on the chair with his bottom perched on the very edge, his arms folded across his chest, his shoeless feet sticking out at the side of the table. He wouldn't look at the police officers and kept his gaze fixed on a point somewhere down on the left. His entire body exuded a lack of interest and perhaps a certain amount of contempt.

'Dunno. Reflex.'

'Your reflex when the police want to speak to you is to run? Why is that?' Leonard shrugged his shoulders. 'Have you done anything illegal?'

'You seem to think so.'

The irony was that they hadn't thought any such thing when they went to the Lundins to speak to him, but doing a runner in your socks through the window definitely increased both their interest and the degree of suspicion. Vanja had already decided Leonard's room would have to be searched. Leaving via the window was pretty extreme. Perhaps there were items in the room he really didn't want them to see. Items that linked him to the murder. All they had so far was that he had been circling around the victim on his moped on Friday evening. Vanja steered the conversation in that direction.

'You saw Roger Eriksson last Friday.'

'Did I?'

'A witness saw you together. On Gustavsborgsgatan.'

'In that case I expect I was there. So what?'

'"In that case I expect I was there" – is that an admission?' Billy looked up from his notepad and stared at the boy. 'Did you see Roger Eriksson last Friday?' Leonard met his gaze briefly, then nodded. Billy translated the nod into words for the tape recorder on the table. 'Leonard's answer to the question is "yes".'

Vanja continued. 'You and Roger used to attend the same school, but then he moved to another school. Do you know why?'

'You'll have to ask him that.'

So bloody stupid. So ... disrespectful. Billy just wanted to grab hold of him and give him a good shake. Vanja could feel it, and discreetly placed her hand on her colleague's forearm. Without a trace of irritation or the least sign that she had allowed herself to be provoked, she opened the folder in front of her on the table.

'I would like to do just that. But he's dead, as you might know. Someone cut out his heart and threw him in a bog. I have some pictures here.'

Vanja started to lay out shiny A4-sized high-resolution pictures from the scene where the body was found and from the mortuary. Both Vanja and Billy knew that it didn't matter one iota how much death a person had experienced in films and computer games. No medium could do death justice. Not even the most skilful expert in special effects could recreate the feeling of seeing a real dead body. Particularly if, like Leonard, you had seen the person alive just a week ago.

Leonard glanced at the photos. Tried to appear unmoved, but both Vanja and Billy could see that it was difficult, if not down-right impossible, for him to look at the pictures. But that meant nothing; it could be shock just as easily as guilt. Pictures like these had the same impact on perpetrators and on those who were innocent. Almost without exception. So the reaction was not the important thing. The important thing was to make him take this interview seriously. Get past that truculent, evasive attitude. Vanja carried on laying out the pictures one by one, slowly and calmly, and Billy was struck by the fact that he never ceased to be impressed by her. Even though she was a year or so younger than him, she was like his big sister. A big sister who had top marks in everything, but still managed to be cool rather than a geek. And who stuck up for her younger siblings. She leaned forward.

'We are here to catch the person who did this. And we will. Right now we have only one suspect, and that's you. So if you want to get out of here and boast to your mates about how you ran away from the cops, you'd better drop the attitude and start answering my questions.'

'I told you I saw him last Friday, didn't I?'

'But that wasn't what I asked you. I asked you why he moved to another school.'

Leonard sighed.

'I suppose we might have been a bit unpleasant to him. I dunno if that was why. But it wasn't just me. Nobody at school liked him.'

'Now you're disappointing me, Leonard. The real tough guys don't blame other people. You were one of the main culprits, weren't you? That's what we've heard, anyway.' Leonard looked at her and was presumably just about to answer when Billy chipped in.

'Nice watch. Is it a Tonino Lamborghini Pilot?'

The room fell silent. Vanja looked at Billy with some surprise. Not because he had identified the watch on Leonard's arm, but because he had suddenly jumped in. Leonard shifted the position of his folded arms so that the watch was concealed by his right arm. But he didn't speak. There was no need. Vanja leaned forward again.

'If you don't have a receipt for that, you're in serious trouble here.'

Leonard looked up at them.

Registered their grave expressions.

Swallowed.

And started to tell them. Everything.

'He admits he stole the watch. He was out on his moped and saw Roger here.' Vanja made a cross on the map on the wall. The whole team was there. Ursula and Torkel were listening attentively to Billy and Vanja, who were going over the key points from their interview with Leonard.

'He says he was just messing about, and started riding around Roger on his moped. Then, according to Leonard, Roger knocked him over. They started quarrelling properly, fighting. Roger's nose started bleeding. After a few blows Leonard got Roger down on the ground, and he took the watch as some kind of punishment.'

No one spoke. The only thing they had on Leonard at the moment was the watch. There was nothing in the witness statement or forensic evidence to suggest that what he was saying couldn't be true. Vanja went on.

'But, of course, this is only what Leonard is saying. The fight could just as easily have got out of hand, and he pulled a knife and stabbed Roger.'

'More than twenty times? On a fairly central street? Without anyone seeing anything?' Ursula sounded justifiably sceptical.

'We don't know what the area looks like. He might have panicked. One blow with the knife, Roger's lying there screaming. Leonard realises he's in deep shit, drags him behind some bushes and carries on stabbing. Just to shut him up.'

'And the heart?' Ursula still sounded far from convinced.

Vanja understood her doubts.

'I don't know. But whatever happened, it happened just after nine. Leonard confirmed the time. He looked at the watch when he took it off Roger's wrist. Which means that Roger wasn't with Lisa until ten, as she insists.'

Torkel nodded.

'Okay, good work. Anything from where the body was found?' He turned to Ursula.

'Not much. The tyre tracks we found are from a Pirelli P7. Not exactly a standard tyre, but fairly common. And obviously we don't know for sure that the tracks come from the car that brought the body.'

Ursula took a sheet of paper and a picture of the tyre tracks out of her folder and handed them to Billy, who went over to put the new information in the right place on the board.

'Does Leonard Lundin have access to a car?' asked Torkel as Billy pinned up the picture and fact sheet about the Pirelli tyre.

'Not as far as we know. There wasn't one parked on the drive this morning.'

'So how did he move a dead body to Listakärr, then? On his moped?'

Everyone fell silent. Of course not. An already weak theory about how the murder might have been committed suddenly became even weaker. But it had to be investigated before it was written off completely.

'Ursula and I will take a couple of uniformed officers and search the Lundin house. Billy, can you go over to Gustavsborgsgatan and see if there's any possibility that the murder could have taken place there. Vanja, I'd like you to—'

'Go and talk to Lisa Hansson again,' Vanja finished for him with ill-concealed glee.

Clara was standing outside the house smoking. Some other officers from Riksmord had turned up about half an hour ago, along with a couple of uniformed colleagues. When Clara had asked if she could go to the station to speak to that Vanja Lithner whose card she had, she was told tersely that they were still holding Leonard while they checked the information he had given them. And while they searched her house. So if she wouldn't mind ... Clara was standing in the garden, driven out of her own house, smoking and shivering in spite of the spring warmth as she tried to gather her thoughts. Or, rather, to push aside the thought that kept on coming back, the one that frightened her more than anything: that Leonard might actually have had something to do with Roger's death. Clara knew they weren't the best of friends. Oh, come on, who was she trying to kid? Leonard had bullied Roger. Hassled him. Resorted to violence, on occasion.

When the boys were at junior school Clara had been summoned to see the headmaster on a number of occasions. The last time there had been some talk of excluding Leonard from school, but of course school attendance was compulsory. Was there any possibility that Clara might be able to talk to Leonard, solve the problem on home ground, so to speak? It was of the utmost importance that this issue was resolved, Clara was informed. Compensation claims against schools that failed to tackle bullying were becoming more and more frequent and increasingly expensive. And Vikinga School had no interest in becoming part of the growing statistics.

Somehow they had survived. After the spring term − when Clara had felt as if she was doing nothing but threatening and bribing Leonard − the boys finished school, and during the summer holiday she managed to convince herself that things would be better at the high school. It would be a new start. It wasn't. Because they both ended up at the same high school, Leonard and Roger.

Runebergs School. Leonard was still there; Roger had left after only a month or so. Clara knew that Leonard was probably a major part of the reason for Roger's move to another school. But was there more to it? Clara was angry with herself for even allowing the thought to enter her head. What kind of a mother was she? But she couldn't push it away completely. Was her son a murderer?

Clara heard footsteps approaching from the drive and turned around. Sebastian Bergman was lumbering towards her, carrying two plastic bags from Statoil. The lines around Clara's mouth hardened.

'I see they're back,' he said, nodding towards the house as he came up to her. 'You're welcome to wait in my house if you like. They'll be a while.'

'So now you're interested all of a sudden?'

'Not particularly, but I'm well brought up. And we are neighbours, after all.'

Clara snorted and looked at him coldly.

'I'll be fine, thank you.'

'I'm sure you will, but you're shivering and the whole neighbourhood knows the police are here. Which means it's only a matter of time before the press turn up as well. And they won't stop at the garden fence. If you think I'm hard work, that's nothing compared to them.'

Clara looked at Sebastian again. Two journalists had, in fact, already rung. One of them four times. Clara had absolutely no desire to meet them in person. She nodded and took a few steps towards him. Together they headed for the gate.

'Sebastian?'

Sebastian immediately recognised the voice, and turned to face the man he hadn't seen for a very long time. On the steps outside Clara's house stood Torkel, wearing an expression that was puzzled, to say the least. Sebastian quickly turned back to Clara.

'You go on, the door's open. Can you take these?' He handed her the bags. 'And if you feel like making a start on lunch, be my guest.'

Clara took the bags, slightly surprised. For a second it looked as if she was thinking of asking a question, but then she changed her mind and set off towards Sebastian's house. Sebastian looked at Torkel, who had almost reached him. The expression on the latter's face suggested that he could hardly believe his eyes.

'What the hell are you doing here?'

Torkel held out his hand and Sebastian took it. Torkel squeezed it hard. 'Great to see you. It's been a long time. What are you doing in Västerås?'

'I live over there.' Sebastian waved at the house next door. 'It's my mother's house. She died. I'm going to sell it, that's why I'm here.'

'Sorry to hear that. About your mother, I mean.'

Sebastian shrugged his shoulders. It wasn't really anything to be sorry about, and Torkel ought to know that. In spite of everything, they had been very close for a number of years. A long time ago, admittedly – twelve years, to be precise – but they had discussed Sebastian's parents and his relationship with them on countless occasions. No doubt Torkel was just being polite. What else would he be? Too much time had passed for them to simply pick up where they left off. Too much time even to be able to say they knew each other any more. Too much time for the conversation to flow like a stream in spring. Consequently there was a brief silence.

'I'm still with Riksmord,' said Torkel, breaking the silence after a few seconds.

'I realised that. I heard about the boy.'

'Yes . . .'

Another silence. Torkel cleared his throat and jerked his head back at the Lundin house. 'I'd better get on . . . ' Sebastian nodded understandingly. Torkel smiled at him.

'Might be best if you keep out of the way, so Ursula doesn't see you.'

'So you're still working together?'

'She's the best.'

'I'm the best.'

Torkel looked at the man whom he would have described as a friend, many years ago. Not his closest friend or even a good friend, but definitely a friend. He could allow Sebastian's comment to pass unremarked, nod in agreement, smile, give him a pat on the shoulder and go back into the house, but that wouldn't really be fair. To either of them. And so he said, 'You *were* the best. At lots of things. Completely useless at others.'

Sebastian hadn't really meant anything by his little retort. It was more of a reflex. Gut instinct. Over the four years during which he and Ursula had worked together, they had competed constantly. Different areas. Different tasks. Different methods. Different everything. But on one thing they had been touchingly united: only one of them could be the best in the team. That was how those two were made. But Torkel was right. Sebastian had been unbeatable in many – or, at least, some – areas. In others he had been completely useless. Sebastian smiled weakly at Torkel.

'Unfortunately it's the useless side I've been cultivating. Take care of yourself.'

'You too.'

Sebastian turned and set off towards the gate. To his great relief there was no 'we must meet up one evening' or 'let's have a beer some time' from Torkel. He obviously felt as little need to resume their relationship as Sebastian.

Once Sebastian had turned to go home, Torkel noticed that Ursula had emerged from Clara's house and was standing on the steps. She watched the man disappearing behind the place next door. If Torkel's expression had been one of utter surprise when he saw Sebastian, Ursula's was radiating something entirely different.

'Was that Sebastian?'

Torkel nodded.

'What the hell is he doing here?'

'Evidently his mother lived next door.'

'I see. So what's he doing these days?'

'Cultivating his useless side, apparently.'

'No change there, then,' Ursula snapped.

Torkel smiled to himself as he recalled how Ursula and Sebastian had battled over every detail, every analysis, every single step in an investigation. They were actually very much alike, which was probably why they couldn't work together.

They turned to go back into the house. Ursula handed Torkel a sealed plastic bag. He took it and looked at her questioningly.

'What's this?'

'A T-shirt. We found it in the laundry basket in the bathroom. It's covered in blood.'

Torkel looked with renewed interest at the item of clothing in the bag. Things weren't looking good for Leonard Lundin.

*

It had taken rather longer than Vanja had hoped to speak to Lisa Hansson. She had gone to Palmlövska High, just outside Västerås. It was obviously a school with aspirations. Trees neatly planted in rows, stone walls painted yellow with not a trace of graffiti, always in the top ten when it came to national tests. A school that wasn't even on the radar for kids like Leonard Lundin.

This was Roger's school. This was where he had moved from Runebergs, right in the middle of town. Vanja had a feeling there might be something in this change of school that she ought to check out. Roger had moved from one environment to another. Had anything happened in connection with the move? Big changes can lead to conflict. Vanja decided to find out more about who Roger really was. That would be the next step. First of all she needed to sort out those missing hours that Lisa Hansson so stubbornly refused to acknowledge.

By the time Vanja had finally discovered what class Lisa was in, found the right room and interrupted the English lesson, half an hour had passed.

The other pupils started whispering curiously to each other when Lisa stood up and, in Vanja's opinion, made her way with almost provocative slowness towards her. A girl in the front row put up her hand but didn't bother waiting for any kind of response from either her teacher or Vanja before she spoke.

'Do you know who did it yet?'

Vanja shook her head.

'No, not yet.'

'I heard it was a boy from his old school.'

'Yes. Leo Lundin.' That came from a boy with a buzz cut and two huge fake jewelled earrings. 'From his old school,' he clarified when Vanja didn't react to the name.

She wasn't really surprised. It was a relatively small town, and the kids were constantly connected. Of course they had been texting, tweeting and posting on MSN that one of their contemporaries had been taken in for questioning. And under fairly spectacular circumstances. However, Vanja had no intention of doing anything to spread the rumours. On the contrary.

'We are speaking to as many people as possible and we are still investigating every possible avenue,' she said, before allowing Lisa to pass and closing the classroom door behind her.

In the corridor Lisa had folded her arms across her chest, boldly stared at Vanja and asked what she wanted. Vanja explained that she needed to double-check on a couple of things Lisa had told her.

'Are you allowed to question me without my parents being present?'

Vanja felt a stab of irritation but did her best not to show it. Instead, she smiled at Lisa and said as steadily as she could, 'I am not questioning you. You are not accused of anything. I'd just like a chat.'

'I'd still prefer it if my mother or father were here.'

'But why? It'll only take a few minutes.'

Lisa shrugged her shoulders.

'I'd still prefer it.'

Vanja had been unable to suppress a sigh of annoyance, but she knew better than to continue the conversation against Lisa's will. The girl had called her father, who evidently worked nearby, and after Lisa had refused Vanja's offer of a cup of coffee or a cold drink in the cafeteria, they had gone down to the ground floor to wait for him.

Vanja had taken the opportunity to call Billy and Ursula. Billy had told her that it was virtually impossible for such a brutal murder to have taken place on Gustavsborgsgatan. The proximity of Mälardalen College, a swimming pool and a sports ground meant that there was a fairly high volume of traffic and passers-by. The areas that were not built up were occupied by car parks and open spaces. It was certainly too early to dismiss Leonard Lundin from the investigation, but they had to come up with a different, more realistic scenario. The good news was that Billy had spotted CCTV cameras on the street. If they were lucky, the events of that Friday night would still be accessible somewhere. He was about to go and check it out.

Ursula didn't have much to report, except that the bloodstained T-shirt had been sent for analysis. She had gone over the garage and the moped – no traces of blood on that – and was about to make a start on the house. Vanja reminded her to be particularly meticulous in Leonard's room, only to be informed that it was not possible for Ursula to be any more meticulous than she already was, on every occasion.

Lisa had been sitting on the floor with her back to the wall, watching Vanja wandering around with her mobile clamped to her ear. Lisa gave the impression of being pretty bored, but her brain was busy trying to work out what that policewoman wanted to ask her this time. And how she was going to answer. Eventually she decided simply to stick to her strategy. If she was asked about details, she wouldn't remember.

Roger arrived.

Homework.

Tea.

TV.

Roger left.

An ordinary, slightly boring Friday evening. The question was whether or not it would be enough.

Lisa's father arrived after twenty minutes. Vanja didn't know if it was because the gigantic beaded Jesus was still fresh in her mind, or if it was the cheap pale blue suit and the neatly combed Ken-inspired haircut, that made her think 'God-botherers' as the extremely agitated man came rushing down the corridor. He introduced himself as Ulf, then spent the next three minutes informing Vanja that he had every intention of reporting the fact that a police officer had tried to interview a minor without the presence of a parent or guardian, and in his daughter's school! They might as well hang a sign saying 'suspect' around her neck! Did she have any idea how teenagers gossip? Could she not have been a little more discreet?

Vanja explained as calmly as she could that Lisa was not actually

91

a minor in the eyes of the law, and that she was still the last person to see Roger alive – apart from the murderer, she added just to be on the safe side – and all Vanja wanted to do now was to check on certain pieces of information. Moreover, as soon as Lisa had expressed a wish for her father to be present, Vanja had agreed, and so far she had not asked Lisa one single question. Ulf looked at Lisa for confirmation, and Lisa nodded. Vanja also offered to accompany Lisa back to class and to explain that she was in no way suspected of any involvement in the murder of Roger Eriksson.

Ulf seemed satisfied with this. He calmed down somewhat, and they moved to a clean and tidy common room and sat down on the soft sofas.

Vanja explained that, during the course of the investigation, they had learned from two independent sources that Roger was in town just after nine o'clock on Friday evening, and not at home with Lisa as she had stated. To Vanja's surprise Ulf didn't even turn to Lisa before commenting on her assertion.

'In that case they're wrong. Your sources.'

'Both of them?' Vanja couldn't conceal her surprise.

'Yes. If Lisa says Roger was with her until ten, then that's where he was. My daughter does not lie.' Ulf placed a protective arm around his daughter as if to reinforce his statement.

'But she might have made a mistake about the time – that kind of thing happens,' Vanja ventured, turning her attention to Lisa, who was sitting by her father's side in silence.

'She says Roger left when the news started on Channel 4. It starts at ten o'clock every evening, unless I've been misinformed.'

Vanja gave up and spoke directly to Lisa instead.

'Is there a chance you might have made a mistake about the time Roger left? It's important that we get everything as accurate as possible so that we can find the person who killed him.'

Lisa pressed a little closer to Daddy's arm and shook her head.

'Right, that's all clear then. If there's nothing else, I need to get back to work,' said Ulf.

Vanja didn't mention that she'd waited half an hour for the

opportunity to ask her question, and that she also had a job to do. Probably one more important than his. She made one last attempt.

'Both of the people we've spoken to are sure about the time, completely independently of one another.'

Ulf stared at her, and when he spoke his voice took on a harsher tone. Vanja sensed that he was a man who wasn't used to being contradicted.

'And so is my daughter. Which means it's just one person's word against another, wouldn't you agree?'

Vanja could get no further. Lisa didn't say a word, and Ulf made it clear to Vanja that he intended to be present at any future interview. Vanja didn't bother telling him that his presence or otherwise would be up to her and her colleagues, and not him. Instead she waited in silence as Ulf got to his feet, hugged his daughter then kissed her cheek, shook Vanja's hand, and gave a brief nod before leaving the common room and the building.

Vanja stood gazing after him. It would be great to have a parent who was 100 per cent on the side of his child. All too often in her job Vanja encountered the polar opposite. Or, rather, families in which the teenagers seemed to be more or less strangers, and the parents hadn't a clue what their kids were doing, or with whom. So a father who came rushing over from work, put his arm around his daughter, trusted her and defended her, ought to be a welcome change in Vanja's world. *Ought to be.* Because she couldn't quite shake off the feeling that Ulf was defending the image of the perfect family with the well-brought-up daughter who never lied, rather than sticking up for Lisa herself. That avoiding gossip and speculation at any price was more important than getting to the truth about what had happened that Friday night. Vanja turned to Lisa, who was chewing on the nail of her ring finger.

'I'll walk back to class with you.'

'You don't need to do that.'

'I know, but I'll come anyway.'

Lisa shrugged her shoulders. They walked in silence past rows of lockers, and by the door of the cafeteria they turned right and went up the broad stone staircase to the first floor. Lisa kept her head down, and her fringe prevented Vanja from seeing the expression on her face.

'What have you got now?'

'Spanish.'

'¿Que hay en el bolso?' Lisa looked up at Vanja with total incomprehension. 'It means, "What have you got in your bag?"'

'I know.'

'I did Spanish at school, and that's virtually the only thing I can remember.'

'Right.' Vanja fell silent. With that brief 'right' Lisa had made it very clear how uninterested she was in Vanja's pathetic knowledge of Spanish. They had obviously arrived at Lisa's classroom, because she slowed down and reached for the door. Vanja placed a hand on her arm. Lisa stiffened and looked up at Vanja once more.

'I know you're lying,' Vanja said very quietly as she looked the girl in the eye. Lisa stared back, her face completely blank. 'I don't know why, but I'm going to find out. Somehow.'

Vanja stopped and waited for some kind of response from Lisa. Nothing.

'So now you know that I know, is there anything you'd like to say?'

Lisa shook her head.

'Such as?'

'The truth, for example.'

'I'm supposed to be in Spanish now.' Lisa looked down at Vanja's hand, still resting on her arm. Vanja removed it.

'In that case, no doubt I'll be seeing you again.'

Vanja set off down the corridor, and Lisa watched her until she disappeared through the glass doors at the end. Slowly Lisa let go of the doorhandle and moved a few steps away while getting out her mobile phone. She quickly keyed in a number. She kept neither the name nor the number of the person she was calling in her address book, and deleted her list of calls every time. She never knew if someone might check her mobile. After a few rings the person answered.

'It's me.' Lisa glanced down the corridor again. Completely empty. 'The police were just here.' Lisa rolled her eyes in response to a question from the person at the other end. 'No, of course I didn't say anything, but they're going to find out. One of them has spoken to me twice already. And she'll be back, I'm sure of it.'

Lisa, who had managed to appear uninterested throughout the entire conversation with Vanja, now looked anxious. She had been hiding this for such a long time; she had put the truth in a little corner deep inside and buried it. Now she was beginning to realise that there were many powers determined to wrest it from her, and her strength was beginning to fail. The person on the other end of the phone tried to give her courage. Pep her up. Provide her with things to say. She nodded. Felt a bit better. Everything would probably be fine. She quickly ended the call when she heard footsteps in the corridor behind her, pushed back a strand of hair from her fringe that had got caught in her eyelashes, suppressed the anxiety and went into her Spanish lesson. Looking as unconcerned as she could manage.

Lena Eriksson had spent the morning in the same armchair as yesterday. Now she had started wandering around the apartment. Chain-smoking. A thin blue mist of nicotine and tar filled the small three-roomed flat on the first floor. It was as if she couldn't stay in one place for very long. For a while she had sat on Roger's still unmade bed, but she couldn't bear to see his jeans, the piles of school books, his old video games, the lingering evidence that a sixteen-year-old boy had lived in this room. She tried to find peace in the bathroom, the kitchen, her own bedroom. But everywhere reminded her too strongly of him, so she moved on to the next, and the next. Around and around, like the grieving mother she was.

But then there was the other thing too, the other thing that made her wander around so restlessly.

The voice.

The little voice deep inside her soul.

Was it her fault? *Was it her fault?* She wished she'd never made those bloody phone calls. But she had been angry. She had wanted to hit back. And so it had begun. The money. The calls, the money, the calls. Round and around, just like her wanderings around the apartment. But could it have led to this? She didn't know; she really didn't know. And she had no idea how to find out. But she needed to know. She needed to know for sure that she was just a mother who had lost her son, an innocent person who had suffered the most terrible thing of all. Lena lit another cigarette. Today they would have gone shopping. As usual they would have argued about money, clothes, attitude, respect – all those words she knew Roger was so tired of. Lena started to cry. She missed him so much. She dropped to her knees and let the grief and the pain take over. It was cleansing, in a way, but behind the tears she could hear the voice again.

What if it was you?

'You feel like such a bad parent. You think you're doing everything you can, but they just slip away from you.'

Clara emptied her coffee cup and put it down on the table. She looked at Sebastian, who was sitting opposite her. He nodded in agreement, although he wasn't really listening. Clara had talked about nothing but her poor relationship with her son Leonard since they walked in. Perfectly understandable in view of the morning's events, but not particularly interesting for anyone other than the person directly involved.

Sebastian was considering whether to point out that her use of the word 'you' instead of 'I' when she talked about herself was a verbal defence mechanism, a way of making her failure more universal, less personal, thus keeping some of the pain at bay. But he realised that such a comment would be perceived as spiteful, and would merely reinforce her negative view of him. He didn't want that.

Not yet, anyway.

Not when he still hadn't decided if he should try to get her into bed. He stuck to the soft approach instead. Calm and collected. Understanding, not judging. He glanced at her breasts. They looked enormously inviting in that yellowish-brown pullover.

'That's the way it is with children. Sometimes it works, sometimes it doesn't. Blood ties are no guarantee of a functioning relationship.'

Sebastian was cringing inside. Bloody hell, that was incisive! Seven years of studying psychology, twenty years of working in the profession, and that was his conclusion, his words of comfort for the woman whose entire life had been turned upside down in just a few hours: 'Sometimes it works, sometimes it doesn't.'

Incredibly, Clara was nodding in agreement, apparently satisfied with his shallow analysis. She even gave him a grateful smile. There was definitely the possibility of a shag if he played his cards right. He got up and started to clear the plates and glasses from the table.

Clara had already made a start on lunch when he had returned to the house. Bubble and squeak and fried eggs. She had even found a jar of pickled beetroot in the fridge that was still edible. And two low-alcohol beers. Sebastian had eaten with a good appetite, although Clara had mostly picked at her food. The lump in her stomach seemed to be growing by the minute, and she felt slightly nauseated all the time. But it still felt good to sit at a properly laid table. To have someone to talk to.

To go over things with.

Someone who listened. Who was so wise.

It felt calming. He was quite nice after all, even if he was a bit stand-offish.

She addressed Sebastian's back as he loaded the dishwasher.

'You didn't come to visit very often, did you? We moved here in '99, and I don't think I've seen you here once.' Sebastian didn't answer immediately. If Clara had discussed him with Esther – as she had indicated in the garden earlier – then she was presumably

97

already familiar with the frequency of his visits to his parents' house. He straightened up.

'I never came.'

'Why not?'

Sebastian caught himself wondering what explanation his mother had given for his total absence. The question was whether or not she had admitted the real reason for their minimal contact, even to herself.

'We didn't like each other.'

'Why not?'

'They were idiots. Unfortunately.'

Clara looked at him and decided to drop the subject. True, his parents hadn't come across as the most entertaining couple in the world, but she thought his mother had started to liven up a bit after his father's death a few years earlier. She'd become easier to talk to. They'd even had coffee together a few times, and Clara had been really upset the day she realised Esther didn't have long left.

The doorbell rang, and the next second they heard the sound of the front door opening. Torkel shouted a greeting and appeared. He turned to Clara.

'We're done now, so you can go home. I apologise if we've caused you any inconvenience.'

It was impossible to detect any real regret in Torkel's voice. Correct as always. Sebastian shook his head almost imperceptibly. *Inconvenience*. That particular phrase must have been included in some set of regulations, or a handbook on how a police officer should behave towards members of the public, in around 1950. Obviously he had caused Clara inconvenience. He had taken her son in for questioning and turned her home upside down. Clara, however, didn't appear to react. She got up and turned to Sebastian, almost as if she was making a point.

'Thank you for lunch. And for the company.' Then she left the kitchen without so much as a glance at Torkel.

When the front door had closed behind Clara, Torkel took a

step into the kitchen. Sebastian stayed where he was, leaning against the draining board.

'I see you haven't changed a bit. Still the ladies' knight in shining armour.'

'She was standing outside, shivering.'

'If it had been Leonard Lundin's father, he would still have been standing there. May I?' Torkel gestured towards the coffee machine, which still had coffee left in the pot.

'Sure.'

'Cups?'

Sebastian pointed to one of the kitchen cupboards and Torkel took out a red-striped Iittala mug.

'It's good to see you again. It's been too long.'

Sebastian feared this could be an introduction that would end up with Torkel suggesting a get-together or a beer after all. He played it cool.

'Well, it's certainly been a long time.'

'What are you up to these days?'

Torkel poured the last of the coffee into his mug and switched off the machine.

'I'm living on royalties and my wife's life insurance. And now my mother's died, so I'll sell this place and live off her for a while. But to answer your question: nothing. I'm not up to anything these days.'

Torkel had stopped dead. A lot of information all at once, and not the standard 'oh, just the usual, you know' that he'd probably been expecting, Sebastian thought. But total disengagement combined with deaths in the family might put Torkel off seizing the opportunity to 'catch up'. Sebastian glanced at his former colleague and saw a look of genuine sorrow in his eyes. Empathy had always been one of Torkel's finest qualities. Formal but sympathetic. In spite of everything he had seen in the course of his work.

'Your wife's life insurance . . .' Torkel took a sip of his coffee. 'I didn't even know you'd got married.'

'Yes, indeed, married and widowed. A lot can happen in twelve years.'

'I'm very sorry.'

'Thanks.' They fell silent. Torkel sipped at his coffee, pretending it was hotter than it really was so that he could avoid trying to kick-start their awkward conversation. Sebastian jumped in and saved him. Torkel was obviously seeking contact and his company. For some reason. Sebastian could afford another five minutes of feigned interest after twelve years.

'So, what about you? How's it going?'

'I got divorced again. Just over three years ago.'

'Shame.'

'Yes. Otherwise, everything's fine, I suppose. I'm still there. With Riksmord.'

'Yes, you said.'

'Yes . . . '

Another silence.

Another sip of coffee.

Another rescue. Lowest common denominator. The job.

'So did you find anything in the Lundins' place?'

'Even if we did I couldn't tell you.'

'No, of course not. I'm not really interested. Just making conversation.'

Was that a hint of disappointment on Torkel's face? Whatever it was, it was there for only a brief second before Torkel glanced at the clock and stood up straight.

'Time I made a move.' He put the half-full cup on the draining board. 'Thanks for the coffee.'

Sebastian followed him into the hallway. He leaned against the wall with his arms folded as he watched Torkel pick up a shoehorn that was hanging on the hat stand and slip on his loafers, which he had taken off just inside the door. Suddenly Sebastian saw a somewhat greying, ageing man, an old friend who had only meant well, and towards whom Sebastian had behaved with a rather dismissive brusqueness.

100

'I could have sent a postcard or something.'

Torkel stopped in the middle of putting on his shoes and looked at Sebastian with an almost quizzical expression, as if he hadn't heard properly.

'What?'

'If you're thinking it's your fault that it's been such a long time, that we lost contact. I'm saying I could have got in touch if I'd thought it was important.'

It took Torkel a few seconds to take in Sebastian's words as he replaced the shoehorn.

'I don't think it was my fault.'

'Good.'

'Not only my fault, anyway.'

'That's all right, then.'

Torkel hesitated for a moment with his hand resting on the doorhandle. Should he say something? Should he explain to Sebastian that if you tell a person you think your relationship with them was unimportant, not worth maintaining, it doesn't come across as some kind of consolation, even if that's how it was meant? Quite the reverse, in fact. Should he say it? He dismissed the idea. He shouldn't have been surprised. They had joked about it many times, the fact that, for a psychologist, Sebastian didn't really understand other people's feelings. Sebastian had always countered with the assertion that understanding feelings was overrated. It's the motives that are interesting, not the emotions – those are just waste products, he used to say. Torkel smiled to himself as he realised he was probably just a waste product in Sebastian's memory right now.

'See you,' said Torkel, opening the door.

'Maybe.'

The door closed behind Torkel, and he heard the key being turned. He set off, hoping that Ursula had waited for him with the car.

Torkel got out at the station while Ursula went to park the car. They hadn't talked about Sebastian. Torkel had made an attempt, but Ursula had made her feelings very clear, and for the rest of the journey they had discussed the case. A preliminary analysis of the bloodstained T-shirt had been completed, and Ursula found out via her mobile that the blood came from only one person. Roger Eriksson. Unfortunately the amount of blood was more in keeping with Leonard's explanation of how it had got there during their fight, than with the theory that it might be the result of a violent and frenzied stabbing.

In addition, the boy's truculence had given way to weeping and sobbing in the latest round of interviews, and Torkel found it more and more difficult to imagine that the pathetic figure in front of him could be capable of something so considered and well planned as placing the body in a pool. Using a car he didn't have. No, it was too weak. In spite of the fact that they had found the T-shirt in Leonard's house, it just wasn't realistic.

They weren't, however, ready to write off Leonard completely. Enough mistakes had been made in this investigation. They would keep Leonard in custody overnight, but if they didn't find anything else it would be difficult to get the prosecutor to agree to his arrest. Torkel and Ursula decided to gather the whole team to see if between them they could come up with a way forward.

It was with this thought in mind that Torkel pushed open the main door of the police station, but the woman on reception waved him over.

'You've got a visitor,' she said, pointing to the green seating area by the window. An overweight, badly dressed woman was sitting there. She stood up when she saw the receptionist pointing to her.

'Who is she?' asked Torkel quietly, keen not to be taken completely unawares.

'Lena Eriksson. Roger Eriksson's mother.'

The mother, not good, Torkel just had time to think before she tapped him on the shoulder.

'Are you the one who's in charge of finding out who murdered my son?' Torkel turned around.

'Yes. Torkel Höglund. My condolences on your loss.'

Lena Eriksson merely nodded.

'So it was Leo Lundin who did it?' Torkel met the woman's eyes as she stared at him, her expression challenging. She wanted to know. Of course she wanted to know. Knowing that the murderer had been identified, caught and convicted meant a lot in the process of working through grief. Unfortunately, Torkel couldn't give her the answer she wanted to hear.

'I'm sorry, I can't discuss the details of the investigation.'

'But you've arrested him?'

'As I said, I can't discuss that.'

Lena didn't even appear to be listening. She took a step closer to Torkel. Too close. He resisted the impulse to back away.

'He was always having a go at Roger. Always. It was his fault Roger moved to that stuck-up bloody school.'

It had definitely been his fault. Leo Lundin. Or Leonard, whatever fucking kind of a name that was. Lena didn't know how long it had been going on. The bullying. It had started in junior school, she knew that, but Roger hadn't said anything at first. Hadn't said anything about the name-calling and the shoves in the corridor, the torn books and the fact that his locker was broken into. He'd made excuses when he'd come home without his T-shirt or with soaking wet shoes after school; he hadn't told her that his T-shirt was ripped or that he'd found his shoes down the toilet after gym. He'd come up with explanations when his money and his things disappeared. But Lena had had her suspicions, and eventually Roger had admitted a certain amount.

It was okay, though.

Under control.

He could take care of it himself. If she got involved things would only get worse. But then the violence started. The blows. The bruises. The split lip and the black eye. The kicks to the head. At that point Lena had contacted the school. She had a meeting with Leo and his mother in the head's office, and realised immediately after the meeting that lasted almost an hour that no help would come from there. There was no mistaking who was in charge in the Lundin household.

Lena knew she wasn't the sharpest knife in the drawer from an academic point of view, but she understood power. She was good at identifying power relationships, seeing structures. The boss wasn't necessarily the person who made the decisions. The parent wasn't always the one who had the authority. The school principal may not be the leader of his staff. Lena found it easy to tell who really held the power, how it was used and how she should behave in order to gain as many advantages as possible. Or to avoid disadvantages, at least. Some people probably regarded her as scheming. Some might say that she changed according to which way the wind was blowing, and some almost certainly thought she was just an arse-licker. However, that was how you survived when you spent your whole life surrounded by power but never had any yourself.

That's not true, though, said the little voice inside her head that had been with her all day. *You did have power.*

Lena pushed the little voice away; she didn't want to listen. She wanted to hear that Leo had done it. It was him! She knew it. It had to be true. She just needed to get the well-dressed man in front of her to understand that.

'I'm sure it was him. He's hit Roger before. Beaten him up. We never reported it to the police, but you can check with the school. It was him. I know it was him.'

Torkel understood her stubbornness, her conviction. He was seeing what he had seen so many times before. The desire not only for a solution but also for an understanding of what had happened. The person who had been bullying and tormenting her son overstepped the mark. That was understandable. It made sense. It would make reality a little more real again. He also knew they wouldn't get much further in this conversation. He placed a hand on Lena's arm and steered her gently and almost imperceptibly towards the door.

'We'll have to see where the investigation leads. I'll keep you informed every step of the way.'

Lena nodded and started to head for the glass doors under her own steam. But then she stopped.

'One more thing.'

Torkel walked over to her.

'Yes?'

'The newspapers keep ringing.'

Torkel sighed. Of course they did. In her darkest hour. When she was at her most vulnerable. It didn't matter how many times the press promised to put its house in order after publishing interviews with people who were obviously off balance, obviously not really aware of what they were getting into. People in shock and the deepest sorrow.

It was like a law of nature.

A child is murdered.

The newspapers ring.

'In my experience, most people who talk to the press in a situation like yours regret it afterwards,' Torkel said honestly. 'Just don't answer the phone, or refer them to us.'

'But they want an exclusive interview and they're prepared to pay for it. I just wondered if you knew how much I should ask for?'

Torkel looked at her with an expression that Lena took to mean he didn't understand. Which he didn't, in fact, but not in the way she imagined.

'I mean, you've been involved in this sort of thing before. How much can I ask for?'

'I don't know.'

'I've never had anything to do with them, so what are we talking about here? A thousand? Five thousand? Fifteen thousand?'

'I really don't know. My advice is not to speak to them at all.'

The look on Lena's face told him this definitely wasn't an option.

'I haven't so far. But now they want to pay.'

Torkel gazed at her. She probably needed the money. She didn't want to hear about his moral scruples or his considerations based on experience. She wanted a price ticket. Did he really have the right to comment? How long was it since he had really needed money? Had he ever been in that position?

'Do whatever you like. Just be careful, that's all.' Lena nodded, and to his great surprise Torkel heard himself say, 'Put a high price on yourself.'

Lena nodded with a smile, then turned and left. Torkel stood watching her for a few seconds as she headed off down the street in the late spring sunshine. Then he shook off the visit and turned, ready to get back to the job and his colleagues.

But his trials were far from over.

Haraldsson was limping towards him. From the serious expression on his face, Torkel concluded that Haraldsson wanted to talk. About the matter Torkel had put off for as long as possible. The matter that Vanja had asked him to sort out three times so far.

'When someone says you'll be working in association with one another, what would you say that means?'

Haraldsson was lying on his back on his side of the double bed with his hands linked behind his head, gazing into space. Next to him lay Jenny with two pillows under her bottom and the soles of her feet planted firmly on the mattress. From time to time she pushed her lower abdomen up towards the ceiling at which her husband was staring blankly. It was 22:30.

They had made love.

Or screwed.

Or not even that, if Haraldsson was completely honest. He had dutifully emptied his seed into his wife while his thoughts had been somewhere else altogether.

At work.

At the meeting with Torkel, when Haraldsson told him that Hanser – against Torkel's specifically expressed wish – had tried to remove him from the investigation.

'I suppose it means you'll be working together,' Jenny replied, raising her hips off the mattress once more in order to make the downward slope to her waiting womb a little steeper.

'Well, yes, that's what you'd think, isn't it? In my opinion, if you said to a colleague that you'd be working in association with one another, that would mean you'd be working together. On the same thing. Towards the same goal. Wouldn't it?'

'Mmm.'

To be honest, Jenny was only half listening. The situation wasn't exactly unfamiliar. Ever since Haraldsson got his new boss, his main topic of conversation had been the job, and when he talked about the job, he just wanted to air his complaints. The fact that the target for his irritation was now Riksmord rather than Kerstin Hanser didn't really make much difference.

New words, same old song.

'Do you know what that Torkel Höglund means by working in association with one another? Do you?'

'Yes, you told me.'

'He means not working together at all! When I push him on how he sees our collaboration, it eventually emerges that we won't be working together at all! That's a bit bloody peculiar, don't you think?'

'Doesn't make any sense at all.'

Jenny recycled his words from dinner. She had realised this was a good way of appearing to be up to speed even when she wasn't. Not that she was uninterested in her husband's job. Not at all. She loved to hear about everything from incompetent forgers to the details of the security van heist last summer. But then Hanser had arrived, and Haraldsson's tales of police work were pushed aside in favour of lengthy diatribes on the injustice of it all.

Bitterness.

Moaning.

He needed to be thinking about something else.

'But do you know who you can get really, really close to?' Jenny turned to him and slid her hand under the covers, down towards his limp penis. Haraldsson turned to her with the expression of someone who has had three teeth filled and has just found out that there's a hole in a fourth.

'Again?'

'I'm ovulating.' The hand found its goal and clutched. Squeezed. Gentle but demanding.

'Again?'

'I think so. My temperature was up by half a degree this morning. Best to be on the safe side.'

To his surprise Haraldsson could feel himself beginning to harden once more. Jenny moved over to his side of the bed and lay with her back to him.

'Do it from behind, you can push deeper that way.'

Haraldsson shuffled into the right position and slid in easily. Jenny half turned towards him.

'I need to be up early in the morning, so don't take all night.' She patted Haraldsson on the cheek and turned back.

And as Thomas Haraldsson took hold of his wife's hips, he allowed his thoughts to wander.

He would show them.

Show the lot of them.

Once and for all.

He promised himself that he would solve the murder of Roger Eriksson.

While Haraldsson attempted to impregnate his wife without encroaching on her night's sleep, the man who was not a murderer was sitting in his dressing gown just a kilometre or so away in a residential area that was by now only sporadically lit, keeping up to date with the investigation. Via the internet. He was sitting in the dark, illuminated only by the cold light of the screen, in what he proudly referred to as his study.

The local paper was making a big splash with the death – he couldn't bring himself to call it 'the murder' – although they weren't updating the story quite as often by this stage. Today the focus of their report had been 'a school in shock', with four pages on the situation at Palmlövska High. Everybody seemed to have been given the opportunity to express their views, from catering staff to pupils and teachers. Most of them might as well have kept their mouths shut, the man who was not a murderer concluded as he read every banal line, every cliché-filled quote. It was as if everyone had an opinion but nobody had anything to say. The local paper was also able to inform its readers that the prosecutor had decided that a boy who was the same age as the victim was to be arrested, but only on the lowest level of suspicion.

The evening papers had more. Knew more. Made a bigger thing of it. Aftonbladet.se knew that the boy had terrorised and beaten up the victim in the past, and had evidently been the direct cause of Roger Eriksson's move to a new school. A man who had a full-length picture next to his by-line made the already tragic story even more heartrending by writing about the bullied boy who had escaped his tormentors, picked himself up and moved on, made new friends at a new school and was beginning to regard his future with optimism when he was struck down by meaningless violence. Not a dry eye in the house.

The man who was not a murderer read the emotive article and thought back. Did he wish it hadn't happened? Absolutely. But there was no point in thinking that way. It had happened. It couldn't be undone. Did he feel any regret? Not really. To him, regret meant that a person would act differently if faced with the same situation again.

And he wouldn't.

He couldn't.

There was too much at stake.

He switched to expressen.se. Under 'latest' they had a short piece with the headline: CASE AGAINST VÄSTERÅS MURDER SUSPECT WEAKENED. Not good. If the police let the young man go, they would start looking again. He leaned back in his desk chair. He always did that when he needed to think.

He thought about the jacket.

The green Diesel jacket that was hidden in a drawer behind him. Roger's bloodstained jacket. What if it was found at the home of the young man the police were holding?

At first glance this might seem like an egotistical thought and act. Laying a false trail in order to make a fellow human being appear guilty. An immoral, selfish attempt to avoid the consequences of his actions.

But was that really the case?

The man who was not a murderer could help Roger's relatives and friends. They would be able to stop wondering who had taken the teenager's life, and devote their full attention to the process of working through their grief. He could erase the question mark. Help everyone to move on. That was worth a great deal. And as a bonus he would also improve the resolution rate of the Västerås police. The more he thought about it, the more it seemed like an entirely unselfish act. A good deed, in fact.

It didn't take many clicks on the keyboard before he found out whom the police were holding. Leonard Lundin. His name was all over various chat rooms, forums, blogs and logs. The internet really was fantastic.

Soon he had the address too.

Now he really could help.

Sebastian looked at the clock – how many times was that? He didn't know. 23:11. The last time it had been 23:08. Was it possible for time to move so slowly? The restlessness was in his blood. He didn't want to be in this town, in this house. What was he supposed to do? Sit down in one of the armchairs, read a book and feel at home? Impossible. The house hadn't felt like a home even when he was living here. He had flicked through the TV channels without finding anything of interest. Since he didn't drink, the booze cupboard was of no interest. Nor was he the type to browse through his mother's scented bath oils and exclusive bath pearls before sliding down into a relaxing/refreshing/harmonious/energising bath in the decent-sized, almost luxurious bathroom which had been his mother's refuge; it was the only room she had told her husband she wanted to plan and decorate herself, if Sebastian remembered rightly. Her room in His house.

Sebastian had spent a while wandering around and opening cupboards and drawers at random. To a certain extent he was driven by sheer curiosity, just as he always opened the bathroom cabinet whenever he was visiting other people. But he was also driven – he admitted to himself somewhat reluctantly – by a desire to see what had happened in this house since he left it. The abiding impression was: nothing, really. The best Rörstrand china was still in its place in the white corner display cabinet. Wall hangings and tablecloths for every occasion and every season lay laundered and meticulously rolled in the wardrobes. Sure, there were lots of pointless new ornaments made of glass and china, along with souvenirs from various trips and holidays, all sharing the shelf space behind the closed cupboard doors with presents from a whole lifetime: candlesticks, vases, and – from another era – ashtrays. Objects that were rarely or never used, kept simply because someone else had brought them into the house and it was therefore regarded as impossible to get rid of them without appearing ungrateful or – God forbid – giving the impression that you had better taste than the donor. Things he hadn't seen before, but the feeling in the house was the same. In spite of new furniture, knocked-down walls and modern lighting, in Sebastian's eyes, the house was a sea of pointless items that did nothing to contradict the feeling that life in the Bergman home had been lived in exactly the same calm, quiet, conventionally middle-class, timid way he remembered. The very sight of all these objects his mother had left behind bored him even more, and the only genuine feeling he could conjure up was an enormous weariness at the prospect of sorting out all this shit. Getting rid of it.

The agent had called at around three. He had seemed a little surprised at Sebastian's attitude. After all, these days everyone regarded their house as an investment, and people usually guarded their investment with the capitalist approach of modern times. But Sebastian had made no attempt to negotiate. He wanted to sell, essentially at any price. Preferably today. The agent had promised to come round as soon as he could. Sebastian hoped that would be tomorrow.

He thought about the woman on the train. The piece of paper with her phone number on it was by his bed. Why hadn't he had a little more foresight? Called her earlier, suggested dinner at some pleasant restaurant of her choice. Taken time over a good meal, with good wine for her. Talked, laughed, listened. Got to know her for the evening. They could have been relaxing in comfortable armchairs in some hotel lobby now, a drink in hand, discreet lounge music in their ears, and he could tentatively, almost accidentally, allow his fingers to brush against her bare knees just below the hem of her dress.

112

The seduction.

The game.

Which he would win.

The victory.

The pleasure.

All out of reach, because he wasn't functioning as he normally did. He blamed the house. His mother. The fact that Torkel had suddenly popped up from the past. There were reasons, but he still found it immensely annoying. External circumstances didn't usually affect him and impinge on his actions.

Life fitted in with Sebastian Bergman, not the other way round.

Or that was how it used to be.

Before Lily and Sabine.

No, he wasn't going to give in. Not tonight. It didn't matter what had happened, who fitted in with whom, or that certain people would probably class the days he got through as more of an existence than a life. It didn't matter that he had ostensibly lost control. He still had the ability to make the best of the situation.

He was a survivor.

In every sense of the word.

He went into the kitchen and took down a bottle of wine from the plain wine rack above the cupboard. He didn't even look at the label. It didn't make any difference. It was wine, it was red and it would do its job. As he pushed open the patio door he wondered what his approach should be.

Sympathetic. *I thought you might not want to be alone . . .*

Concerned. *I saw the light was still on. Are you okay?*

Or firm but considerate. *You definitely shouldn't be alone on a night like this . . .*

It was irrelevant. The result would be the same.

He was going to have sex with Clara Lundin.

The paint on the ceiling above the bed had started to flake slightly, Torkel noticed as he lay on his back in bed in yet another anonymous hotel room. There had been so many hotel nights over the years that the impersonal had become the norm. Simplicity was preferable to originality. Functionality was more important than cosiness. To be honest, there wasn't much difference between the two-room apartment south of Stockholm he had moved into after the divorce from Yvonne, and a basic Scandic hotel room. Torkel stretched and tucked his hands under the pillow and his head. The shower was still running. She was taking her time in the bathroom.

The investigation. What had they actually achieved so far?

They had the spot where the body had been dumped, but not the scene of the murder. They had a tyre track that might have come from the murderer's car, but then again it might not. They had a young man in custody, but it was looking more and more likely that they would let him go the following day. On the plus side, after being passed from pillar to post and back again, Billy had managed to get hold of a woman in the relevant security company who knew who he needed to speak to in order to get hold of the tape from the CCTV cameras on Gustavsborgsgatan. The man was at a fiftieth birthday party in Linköping, but would start working on it as soon as he got back the following morning. He wasn't sure, however, if the recordings from the Friday in question would still be there. Some tapes were kept for only forty-eight hours. The local council had views on that kind of thing. He would check when he got back. Tomorrow morning. Billy had given him until eleven.

Vanja was convinced that Roger's girlfriend was lying about the times on the evening Roger disappeared, but as Lisa's father had quite rightly pointed out, it was one person's word against another's. The CCTV tapes would help them out there, too. Torkel sighed. It was slightly depressing to think that the progress of the investigation in the immediate future appeared to depend on how long G4S in Västerås kept their recordings from public places. What happened to good old-fashioned police work? Torkel immediately pushed the thought aside. That was the kind of thing those opera-loving, whisky-swigging old detectives in crime films used to think. Using technology *was* the new honest police work.

114

DNA, surveillance cameras, advanced data technology, information sharing and mapping, bugging, tracing mobile phones, retrieving deleted text messages. That was how crimes were solved these days. Trying to fight against it or refusing to embrace it was not only pointless, it was like standing up and extolling the magnifying glass as the most important investigative tool for any officer. Stupid and sentimental. And this was not the time to be either of those things.

A young boy had been murdered. They were under scrutiny. Torkel had just watched the news on Channel 4 followed by a discussion program on the increase in violence among young people: cause – effect – solution. This was in spite of the fact that there were more and more indications that Leonard Lundin could well be innocent, and that Torkel and his team had made a point of emphasising this precisely so that Leonard would not be condemned by the public and the press. But perhaps the program makers thought that as soon as a young person was the victim of violence, it counted as youth violence regardless of how old the perpetrator might be? Torkel didn't know. He only knew that the discussion had not brought anything new to the table. Absent fathers in particular were blamed, absent parents in general, violence in films and above all in games, and finally a woman in her thirties with piercings came out with what Torkel had just been waiting to tick off the list.

'But we mustn't forget that society is much more aggressive these days.'

So those were the causes. Parents, video games and society.

The solutions were conspicuous by their absence, as usual, unless you counted a legal obligation to take equal maternity/paternity leave, increased censorship and more hugs as solutions. Evidently it wasn't possible to do anything about society. Torkel had switched off before the program ended and started to talk about Sebastian. He hadn't given his old colleague much thought in recent years, but he had still thought an encounter would turn out differently.

With more warmth.

He was disappointed.

That was when she had gone for a shower. She emerged from the bathroom now, naked except for a towel wound around her hair. Torkel carried on as if there hadn't been a fifteen-minute break in the conversation.

'You should have seen him. I mean, he was pretty odd when we worked together all those years ago, but now ... It seemed as if he was deliberately trying to annoy me.'

Ursula didn't answer. Torkel watched her as she went over to the dressing table, picked up a bottle of body lotion and started to rub it in. Lait de Beauté Aloe Vera, he knew. He'd seen her do that quite a few times now.

Over quite a few years.

When had it started? He wasn't sure. Before the divorce, but after things started to go wrong. Quite a lengthy period. Anyway, he'd got divorced. Ursula had stayed married. She had no plans to leave Mikael, as far as Torkel knew. But, then, he knew very little about Ursula and Mikael's relationship. Mikael had gone through some difficult times with too much alcohol. An intermittent alcoholic. He knew that, but if Torkel understood correctly these periods were more infrequent these days, and lasted for a much shorter time. Perhaps they had an open marriage and could sleep with anyone they liked, whenever they liked, as often as they liked? Perhaps Ursula was deceiving Mikael with Torkel? Torkel felt as if he was close to Ursula, but when it came to life with her husband outside work, he knew virtually nothing. He had asked questions in the beginning, but it was obvious Ursula thought it had nothing to do with him. They sought each other's company when they were working together, and they could carry on doing so. It didn't have to be any more than that. He didn't need to know any more than that. Torkel had chosen to drop the subject, to refrain from digging any more for fear of losing her completely. He didn't want that. He wasn't really sure what he did want from their relationship, except that it was more than Ursula was prepared to give. Therefore he made

116

the best of it. They spent the nights together when it suited her. Like now, as she turned back the covers and slipped into bed beside him.

'I'm warning you. If you say one more word about Sebastian, I'm leaving.'

'It's just that I thought I knew him, and . . .' Ursula placed a finger on his lips and propped herself up on one elbow. She looked at him, her expression serious.

'I mean it. I've got my own room. I shall go back to my room, and you don't want that.'

She was right.

He didn't want that.

He kept quiet and turned off the light.

Sebastian woke from the dream. As he straightened out the fingers of his right hand, he quickly orientated himself.

The house next door.

Clara Lundin.

Unexpectedly good sex.

In spite of this, he awoke with a feeling of disappointment. It had been so easy. Far too easy for him to wake up with the sense of temporary satisfaction.

Sebastian Bergman was good at seducing women. Always had been. Over the years other men had sometimes been surprised at his success with the opposite sex. He wasn't good looking in a classic way. He had always veered between being overweight and almost overweight, and in recent years he had come to a halt somewhere in the middle. His features were neither distinct nor sharp, more bulldog than doberman, if you wanted to go for a dog comparison. His hair had started to retreat, and his choice of clothes always tended more towards the professor of psychology than the fashion magazine. Admittedly there were women who went for money, appearance and power. But that was only certain women. If you wanted to have a chance with *all* women, you had to have something else. Which was what Sebastian had:

117

charm, intuition and a range. A realisation that all women are different, and an ability to develop a selection of different tactics to choose between. Try one, change halfway through, check how it's going, change again if necessary.

Sensitivity.

The ability to listen.

When it worked best, the woman believed *she* was seducing *him*. That was a feeling the rich men who flashed their Platinum Amex in the bar would never understand.

Sebastian got a kick from steering the course of events, parrying, adjusting, and eventually, if he had played his cards right, complementing it all with the physical pleasure. But with Clara Lundin it had just been too easy. Like a master chef in a five-star restaurant being asked to fry an egg. He had no opportunity to show what he could do. It was boring. It was just sex.

On the way over he had decided to go for the sympathetic option, and when she opened the door he held out the bottle of wine.

'I thought you might not want to be alone . . .'

She had let him in and they had sat on the sofa, opened the bottle of wine, and he had listened to the same thing he had heard at lunchtime, only in a longer and more refined version in which her shortcomings as a parent received more attention. He had made the right noises and nodded in the right places, topped up her wine glass, carried on listening, and occasionally answered questions on police procedure, about the routine when a person was taken into custody, what might be expected to happen next, what the different degrees of suspicion meant and so on. When at last she was unable to hold back the tears any longer, he had placed a consoling hand on her knee and sympathetically leaned closer. He almost felt a jolt run through her body. The silent sobbing stopped, and her breathing altered, grew heavier. She turned to Sebastian and looked into his eyes. Before he really had time to react, they were kissing.

In the bedroom she had welcomed him with total abandonment.

Afterwards she wept, kissed him and wanted him all over again. She fell asleep with as much skin contact as possible.

She still had one arm resting on Sebastian's chest and her head nestled in the hollow between his chin and shoulder when he woke up. Gently he extricated himself from her embrace and got out of bed. She didn't wake up. He looked at her as he dressed quietly. As much as Sebastian was interested in the seduction phase, he was equally uninterested in prolonging the association beyond sex. What would that give him? Nothing but repetition. More of the same, but without the excitement. Utterly meaningless. He had left enough women after these one-night stands to know that this was a mutually shared view only on very rare occasions, and as far as Clara Lundin was concerned he was sure she expected some kind of continuation. Not just breakfast and small talk, but something more.

Something real.

So he left.

A guilty conscience wasn't normally part of Sebastian's repertoire, but even he understood that things would be difficult for Clara Lundin when she woke up. He had realised how lonely she was earlier in the day when they were in the garden, and their encounter on the sofa had confirmed it. The way she pushed her lips against his, the way her hands clutched his head, the way she pressed her body against him. She was almost desperate for closeness. On every level, not only physically. After years of being rebuffed or, at best, having her feelings and thoughts ignored, or, at worst, being shouted at and threatened, she was starved of tenderness and consideration. She was like sand in the desert, simply sucking up anything resembling normal human kindness. His hand on her knee. Contact. A clear sign that she was desirable. It was like opening a floodgate of need.

For skin.

For closeness.

For someone.

That was the problem, Sebastian thought as he walked the short

119

distance back to his parents' house. It had been too easy, and she had been grateful. He could deal with most emotions when it came to his conquests, but gratitude always revolted him slightly. Hatred, contempt, sorrow – they were all better. Gratitude made it so obvious that everything happened on his terms. He knew that already, of course, but it was nicer if he could convince himself that the situation was somehow equal. *Maintain the illusion.* Gratitude broke it. Showed him up as the complete bastard he was.

It was only a quarter to four in the morning when he got home, and he had absolutely no desire to go back to bed. So what should he do? Even though he didn't really want to do it, and kept hoping that it would all sort itself out somehow, he realised that sooner or later he would have to tackle all the cupboards and drawers. Putting it off wasn't going to make it any easier.

He went into the garage and found some flattened removal boxes leaning against the wall in front of the old Opel. He took three of them, and stopped when he was back in the house. Where to start? He decided on the former guest room and study. He dismissed the desk and the old office equipment, opened up one of the boxes and started piling in books from the shelves covering one wall. They were a mixture of fiction, non-fiction, reference works and textbooks. Everything went in. No doubt the same applied to the books as to the Opel in the garage: the second-hand value was zero. Once the first box was full he tried to close it. He couldn't do it, but that would be some removal firm's problem, thought Sebastian, dragging it over to the door with some difficulty. Then he opened up another box and carried on. By five o'clock he had fetched another four boxes from the garage and emptied virtually the entire shelving unit. There were only two shelves to go, over on the right-hand side. Full of photograph albums. Neatly labelled with the year and a note of the contents. Sebastian hesitated. After all, it was his parents' so-called life sitting on those shelves. Should he just shove the whole lot into a cardboard box and send it off to the dump? Could he do that? He put off the decision; they had to come off the shelves anyway, but where they ended up could be determined at a later stage.

Sebastian had cleared more than half, starting with the top shelf and getting as far as WINTER/SPRING 1992 – INNSBRUCK, when his hand touched something concealed behind the thick albums. A box. He grasped for it, got hold of it and took it down. It was a shoebox: small, pale blue with a sun in the middle of the lid. For children's shoes, presumably. But it was an odd place to keep shoes. Sebastian sat down on the bed and opened the box with a certain amount of expectant curiosity. It wasn't even half full. A sex toy from the infancy of sex toys, neatly sealed up in its original box, which was covered in pencil drawings from something that might have been the Kama Sutra. A safety deposit box key and some letters. Sebastian picked up the letters. Three of them. Two were addressed to his mother. A woman's handwriting. The third was from his mother to someone called Anna Eriksson in Hägersten. 'Returned to sender, address unknown' was stamped on the envelope. More than thirty years ago, judging by the postmarks. From Hägersten and Västerås. The box seemed to contain things his mother didn't want the rest of the world to know about. Obviously important enough to keep, but in secret. What had she done? Who were they from? A lover? A brief, amorous adventure away from home and his father? Sebastian opened the first letter.

Dear Fru Bergman,

I don't know if I am sending this letter to the right person. My name is Anna Eriksson, and I need to get in touch with your son, Sebastian Bergman. He taught Psychology at the University of Stockholm, and I met him there. I have tried to get in touch with him via the university, but he doesn't teach there any more and they don't have his new address. I spoke to some of his colleagues, who told me he had moved to the USA, but I can't find anyone who knows where he's living over there. Eventually someone told me he came from Västerås, and that his mother's name was Esther. I found you in the phone book and hope I am writing to the correct

121

person, and that you can help me get in touch with Sebastian. If
you are not Sebastian Bergman's mother, my apologies for bothering
you. But whether you are or not, could you please let me know? I
really do need to get in touch with Sebastian, and to know whether
I have sent this letter to the right place.

With best wishes,
Anna Eriksson

Then there was an address. Sebastian gave the matter some thought. *Anna Eriksson.* The autumn after he moved to the USA. The name didn't ring a bell, but perhaps that was hardly surprising. It was thirty years ago, and the number of women who had passed through his life while he was at the university was considerable. He had been given a one-year post in the Psychology department the year after he had graduated with top grades. He had been at least twenty years younger than his colleagues, and had felt like a puppy in a room full of dinosaur skeletons. If he really made an effort he might be able to remember at least the name of someone he'd slept with, but probably not. No Anna sprang to mind, anyway. Perhaps the next letter would make things clearer.

Dear Fru Bergman,
Thank you for your speedy and kind reply, and I apologise for
writing and bothering you again. I understand that it must feel
strange to give out your son's address to a total stranger writing to
you out of the blue, but I really MUST get in touch with Sebastian
very soon. It doesn't really feel right to be telling you this, but I
think I have to so that you will understand how vital it is. I am
carrying Sebastian's child, and I have to get in touch with him. So
if you know where he is, please, please tell me. As you will
understand, this is extremely important to me.

There was more, something about moving house and writing again, but Sebastian didn't get any further. He just kept reading the same sentence over and over again. He had a child. Or, at least, he might have. A son or daughter. He might be a father again. Maybe. *Maybe*. A brief realisation that his life could suddenly have been completely different almost made him faint. He leaned forward with his head between his knees and breathed deeply. His thoughts were in turmoil. A child. Did she get rid of it? Or was it still alive?

He tried desperately to remember who Anna was. Put a face to the name. But no memories surfaced. He was finding it difficult to concentrate. He took a deep breath in order to focus his visual memory. Still nothing. The conflicting emotions of happiness and shock were overshadowed for a moment by a sudden surge of anger. He might have a child, and his mother had never said a word. The familiar feeling that she had let him down washed over him. Twisted and turned in his stomach. To think he had begun to want to forgive her. Or, at least, had hoped to find some peace in the internal battle he constantly waged with her. That feeling was gone. The battle would always be there now. For the rest of his life, he realised.

He had to find out more. He had to remember who Anna Eriksson was. He got up. Walked around the room. Recalled the last letter – there had been three letters in the box. Perhaps it contained more pieces of the puzzle. He picked it up. His mother's rounded handwriting on the envelope. For a second he wanted to throw it away. Disappear and never look back. Leave this secret and bury it where it had already been preserved for so long. But his hesitation was soon replaced by action – anything else was unthinkable – and with trembling hands Sebastian carefully took the letter out of the envelope. It was his mother's handwriting, her sentence construction, her words. At first he didn't understand what he was reading, his brain was too overloaded.

Dear Anna,

The reason why I didn't give you Sebastian's address in the USA is not because you are a stranger but because, as I wrote in my last letter, we do not know where Sebastian is living. We have no contact whatsoever with our son. This has been the situation for

*many years. You must believe me. I feel a little sad to hear that you
are pregnant. It goes against my beliefs completely, but yet I feel I
must give you a piece of advice: if it is still possible, I think you
should terminate the pregnancy. Try to forget Sebastian. He will
never take any responsibility, either for you or the child. It pains me
to write this, and you will probably wonder what kind of mother I
am, but most people are better off without Sebastian in their lives. I
really do hope that things work out for you in spite of the
circumstances.*

Sebastian read the letter one more time. His mother had followed the script for their relationship to the letter. Even after her death she still managed to hurt him. He tried to calm his thoughts, concentrate on facts, not feelings. Stand outside. Act professionally. What did he know? Thirty years ago when he was working at the University of Stockholm, he got someone called Anna Eriksson pregnant. Perhaps she had an abortion, perhaps she didn't. At any rate she had moved from – he looked at Anna's address – Vasaloppsgatan 17, at some point thirty years ago. He had gone to bed with her. Was she one of his former students? Probably. He had had sex with several of them.

It was possible to trace his former head of department, Arthur Lindgren, via directory enquiries. Arthur, who was now retired, answered after three separate calls; the last time Sebastian had let the phone ring out more than twenty-five times. Arthur was still living on Surbrunnsgatan, and when he had woken up a little and grasped who was calling him at half-past five in the morning, he had been surprisingly helpful. He promised to look through the documents and files he had at home in search of an Anna Eriksson. Sebastian thanked him. Arthur had always been one of the few people Sebastian respected, and that respect was mutual; he knew that Arthur had actually defended him when the university first tried to kick him out. In the end, however, the situation had become untenable even for Arthur. Sebastian's womanising was no longer restricted to discreet little affairs; there were so many rumours about him that the board managed to have him suspended at the third attempt. That was when he went to the USA, to the University of Carolina. He had begun to realise that his days were numbered and applied for a Fulbright scholarship.

Sebastian started to draw up a time line, noting down the date of the first letter: 9 December 1979. The second letter was dated 18 December. He counted back nine months from December, which took him to March 1979.

He had arrived in Chapel Hill in North Carolina at the very beginning of November 1979. So March to October was the relevant period, eight possible months. She had probably discovered she was pregnant around the time of the first letter, so September–October would seem to be the most likely months. Sebastian tried to recall as many memories as he could of sexual encounters during the autumn of 1979. It wasn't easy: that particular period at the university had been one of the most intensive in his catalogue of sexual misdemeanours. This was partly because the stress of the department's constant investigations into his behaviour simply exacerbated his need for affirmation, and partly because after a number of years spent experimenting, he had perfected the role of seducer. The clumsiness was gone, along with the fear, the ineptitude. He simply enjoyed what he was good at, and he had crossed every boundary during the course of several hectic years.

When he looked back on those days later on, he had been amazed at his behaviour. When the AIDS panic had begun to rage at the beginning of the '80s, he had realised with horror just how bad his abuse had actually been. He had started trying to find ways to resist, and gained a great deal of strength from his more detailed research into serial killers in the USA. He remembered the moment when, sitting in Quantico, the FBI training centre, and working on a joint project with the University of Carolina, he had realised that the way he acted had much in common with the motivation behind a serial killer's actions. Admittedly, these actions had completely different consequences. It was as if he were playing poker for matchsticks and the serial killers for gold chips. But the basis was the same: difficult upbringing with a lack of empathy and love, poor self-esteem and a need to show the individual's strength. And then that constant cycle of fantasy – execution – angst, spinning around all the time. The individual needs affirmation and fantasises about control. In his case it was sexual, in the serial killer's it was a matter of another person's life and death. The fantasy becomes so strong that in the end it is impossible to resist acting it out. This is followed by angst over what he has done. The affirmation was, in fact, worthless. He is bad. A bad person. With the despair the fantasies return, assuaging the angst. These fantasies soon grow so strong that the need to find an outlet for them is reawakened. Around and around it goes.

This realisation had frightened Sebastian, but had also better equipped him for his work in helping the police track down serial killers. He made progress in his analysis. His profiling became sharper. It was as if he had that little something extra that made him unusually well suited to understanding the psychology of a perpetrator. And it was true, of course. Deep inside, behind the academic veneer, the wide knowledge and the intelligent comments, he was actually very similar to those he was hunting.

Arthur called back an hour later. By that time Sebastian had already rung directory enquiries and discovered that there were so many Anna Erikssons in Sweden that their computers simply said 'too many matches'. He then tried restricting the query to Stockholm and was told there were 463 matches. Of course, he didn't even know if she still lived in Stockholm. Or if she had married and changed her name.

Arthur had good news and bad news. The bad news was that, according to the notes Arthur still had, no Anna Eriksson had registered in the Department of Psychology in 1979. Someone of that name had started in 1980, but obviously it couldn't be the same woman.

The good news was that he had managed to gain access to Ladok.

Of course – why hadn't Sebastian thought of that? The system for the storage and management of higher education results had only been a few years old when he left the university. Addresses, name changes and similar information were updated automatically from the electoral roll. And the best part of all: this information was public property. It wasn't usually given out over the telephone, but one of the administrators at the university had made an exception for the former head of department on this early morning. He had the addresses and numbers of the three Anna Erikssons who had been registered at the university during the period in question.

Sebastian couldn't thank Arthur enough. With the promise of an excellent dinner at one of Stockholm's best restaurants when he was back in town, he hung up. His heart was pounding. Three Anna Erikssons.

Was one of them the right person?

The first Anna on the shortlist had been forty-one at the time, and Sebastian quickly dismissed her. Not that she couldn't have been pregnant, but he'd never been much of a one for that whole MILF thing. Not at the time, anyway. These days age was less important.

Which left two. Two possible Anna Erikssons. It was a long time since Sebastian had felt such a mixture of energy, fear and anticipation as when he picked up the phone to call the first one. She lived in Hässleholm and had been studying film. He got hold of her on her way to work. Sebastian decided to be brutally honest, and told her the whole story of the letter he had found earlier that morning. She was somewhat surprised by the unexpected call and the private details so early in the morning, but still explained quite pleasantly that she had absolutely no idea who he was, and that she definitely hadn't had a child by him. She did have children, but they were born in 1984 and 1987. Sebastian thanked her and crossed her off the list.

One left.

He called her. Woke her up. Perhaps that was why she was significantly more wary. She said she didn't know who he was. She admitted that she had studied Social Sciences and graduated in 1980, but she certainly hadn't slept with any of the tutors in the Psychology department. She would have remembered. And if she had got pregnant, she would definitely have remembered that. No, she didn't have any children. If he had managed to find her and get hold of her telephone number after all these years, no doubt he could check on that as well. Then she hung up.

Sebastian crossed the last Anna Eriksson off his list.

He exhaled as if he had been holding his breath for the last few hours. The energy that had carried him along drained away. He sank down onto a chair in the kitchen. His thoughts were all over the place. He needed to get them in some kind of order.

So the Anna Eriksson he was looking for had not been a student. That made things more difficult. But she had some link to the university; she had written that they had met there. So what was it? Had she been a tutor, a temporary lecturer, or just a friend of someone who was studying there? Perhaps they had met at a party?

Lots of possibilities.

No answers.

A name, an address, a year and a link to his time at the University of Stockholm – that was all. He didn't even know her age – that might have helped a bit. But he needed to know. More. Everything. For the first time in ages Sebastian felt something other than the endless weariness that had been his companion for so long. It wasn't hope, but it was something. A small connection with life. He recognised the feeling. Lily had given it to him, the sense of a context. Of belonging to something. In the past Sebastian had always felt alone, as if he was living alongside life and other people. Lily had changed that. She had found her way inside him, got past his wall of attitude and intelligence and touched him as no one else had done. She saw through him. Forgave his stumbles but made demands. That was something new for Sebastian.

Love.

He had stopped screwing around. It had been a struggle, but

somehow, in some magical way, Lily had always managed to find the words to console him in his moments of doubt or despair. Suddenly he realised that she hadn't been the only one who was fighting for them. He had been part of it too. Before her, he had always searched for a way out, and then he wanted to find the way forward. It had been a wonderful feeling. He had no longer been the lone soldier; they were together. When Sabine was born that August day, he was enveloped by life. He had felt complete. He was a part of something. He was not alone.

The tsunami had changed all that. Ripped away every connection, every finely woven thread linking him to everything else. Once again he had stood alone.

Lonelier than ever.

Because now he knew how life could feel.

How it ought to feel.

Sebastian went out onto the decking. He felt strangely uplifted. As if a lifebuoy had suddenly been sent in his direction. Should he grab it? No doubt it would end badly. No doubt at all. But that morning he felt something bubbling up inside him that he hadn't felt for a very long time – an energy, a desire. Not for sex, not for conquest, but for life. He would go along with it. After all, he was already doomed. So he had nothing to lose. Only something to gain. He had to know. *Did he have another child?* He had to find this Anna Eriksson. But how? Suddenly he was struck by an idea. There were those who could help him. But it wouldn't be easy.

Torkel and Ursula arrived in the hotel dining room for breakfast at the same time, but they didn't come down together. When Ursula spent the night in Torkel's hotel room she set the alarm for 04:30, got up as soon as it went off, dressed and went back to her own room. Torkel also got up and said goodbye to her in the doorway, fully dressed and perfectly correct. If anyone should be passing in the corridor at such an ungodly hour, it would look as if two colleagues had been working all night and one of them was now heading back to her room for a few hours' well-earned sleep. The fact that they had met on the stairs this morning and arrived in the dining room at the same time was, therefore, pure chance. They also heard the shrill whistle at the same time, and looked over at one of the tables by the window. Sebastian was sitting there. He raised a hand in greeting. Torkel heard Ursula sigh as she left his side, pointedly turned her back on Sebastian and busied herself with the breakfast buffet.

'Over here, Torkel! I've got you a coffee!' Sebastian's voice filled the dining room. The guests who had shown no interest when he whistled were now paying attention. Torkel marched over to the table.

'What do you want?'

'I want to get back to work. With you. With that boy.' Torkel looked at Sebastian for some sign that he was joking. When he couldn't see any such thing, he shook his head.

'It's impossible.'

'Why? Because Ursula doesn't want me around? Come on, give me two minutes.'

Torkel looked over at Ursula, who still had her back to them. He pulled out a chair and sat down. Sebastian pushed a cup of coffee across to him. Torkel glanced at his watch and put his head in his hands.

130

'Two minutes.'

There was a brief silence as Sebastian waited for Torkel to go on. Ask a question. He didn't.

'I want to get back to work. With you. With that boy. What was it you didn't understand about that?'

'But *why* do you want to get back to work? With us. With that boy.' Sebastian shrugged his shoulders and took a swig of coffee from the cup on the table in front of him.

'Personal reasons. My life is . . . a little fluid at the moment. My therapist says routine would be good for me. I need discipline. Focus. Besides which, you need me.'

'Really?'

'Yes. You've completely lost the plot at the moment.'

Torkel should be used to this. How many times had he or his colleagues put forward a theory or sketched out a scenario, only to be shot down in flames by Sebastian? In spite of this, Torkel still caught himself feeling annoyed at his former colleague's casual dismissal of all their work so far. Work he knew nothing about.

'Have we?'

'The neighbour's kid didn't do it. The body was moved to a remote and pretty clever dump site. The attack on the heart seems almost ritualistic.' Sebastian leaned in close and lowered his voice. 'The murderer is more sophisticated and considerably more mature than a bully who can hardly get himself to school.'

He leaned back with his coffee cup and met Torkel's gaze over the rim. Torkel pushed back his chair.

'We know, that's why we'll be releasing him today. And the answer to your question is still "no". Thanks for the coffee.'

Torkel stood up and pushed his chair in. He could see that Ursula had sat down at a window table further down the room, and was about to go and join her when Sebastian put down his cup and raised his voice.

'Do you remember when Monica was unfaithful? All that business of your divorce.' Torkel stopped and turned back to Sebastian, who met his gaze with a relaxed expression. 'Your first divorce, that is.'

Torkel stood in silence, waiting for the follow-up he knew was inevitable.

'You really were in a bad way then, weren't you?'

Torkel didn't answer, but gave Sebastian a look that made it clear he didn't want to talk about that. A look that Sebastian ignored completely.

'I'd put money on the fact that you wouldn't be the boss today if someone hadn't covered up for you in the dark days of that autumn. The whole fucking year, in fact.'

'Sebastian . . .'

'What do you think would have happened if someone hadn't got the reports in on time? Fixed your mistakes? Carried out damage limitation?'

Torkel put both hands on the table, palms down.

'I don't know what you're up to, but this has to be some kind of personal low. Even for you.'

'You don't understand.'

'Threats? Blackmail? What is it I don't understand?'

Sebastian didn't say anything for a moment. Had he gone too far? He really did need to get into this investigation. And he did actually like Torkel – or he used to, once upon a time long ago, in a different life. The memory of that life made Sebastian try, at least. A more friendly tone this time.

'I'm not threatening you. I'm asking you. For a favour.' Sebastian looked up and met Torkel's gaze, his face open. In his eyes there was an honest plea that Torkel couldn't remember ever seeing from Sebastian before. But he was still trying to shake his head when Sebastian got in first.

'A favour for a friend. If you know me half as well as you think you do, then you know I would never ask you like this unless I really needed it.'

They had gathered in the conference room at the station. Ursula had given Torkel a particularly nasty look when she had walked in and seen Sebastian ensconced in one of the chairs. Vanja appeared mostly puzzled by the presence of this unknown person when she arrived. She introduced herself, but Sebastian thought he noticed her enquiring expression change to open dislike when he told her his name. Had Ursula been holding forth about him?

Of course she had.

Talk about an uphill struggle.

The only person who had shown no obvious reaction to his presence was Billy, who was sitting at the table with his 7-Eleven breakfast. Torkel knew there wasn't actually a good way of saying what he was about to say. The simplest approach was often the best. So he said it as simply as he could.

'Sebastian is going to be working with us for a while.'

Brief silence. An exchange of glances. Surprise. Anger.

'Is he?' Torkel could see Ursula's jaw hardening as she clenched her teeth. She was professional enough not to call Torkel an idiot and have a go at him in front of the team, even though he was convinced that was what she really wanted to do. He had let her down. Twice. For a start, he had brought Sebastian back into her professional life, but, worse than that, he had said nothing about his plans during breakfast or while they were walking to the station together. Yes, she was angry. With good reason. He would be sleeping alone during the rest of this investigation. Perhaps longer.

'Yes.'

'Why? What's so special about this case that we need the great Sebastian Bergman?'

'We haven't solved it, and Sebastian is available.' Torkel could hear for himself how hollow that sounded. It was less than two days since the body had been found, and they could expect a breakthrough on several fronts today if the films from the CCTV cameras delivered what they promised. And available? Was that enough of a reason to bring him into the investigation? Of course not. Any number of psychologists were available. Several of them better than Sebastian in his current state, Torkel was convinced. So why was Sebastian sitting here? Torkel owed him nothing. Quite the reverse. His life would be simpler without his former colleague on the scene. But there had been something nakedly honest about Sebastian's request. Something desperate. Sebastian might try to appear detached and unmoved, but Torkel sensed an emptiness there. A sorrow. It sounded exaggerated, but Torkel had the feeling that Sebastian's life – or, at the very least, his mental health – depended on his being allowed into this investigation. To put it simply, Torkel's only reason was that it had felt right.

At the time. In the hotel dining room.

He could feel a seed of doubt beginning to grow inside him.

'Plus I've actually lost a bit.'

All four of them turned as one to Sebastian, who was straightening up in his chair.

'Sorry?'

'Ursula called me "the *great* Sebastian Bergman". But I've lost a bit of weight. Unless, of course, you were referring to the size of something else.' Sebastian smiled meaningfully at Ursula.

'That's enough, for fuck's sake! Thirty seconds and you've already started!' Ursula turned to Torkel. 'Are you seriously telling me we're supposed to try to work together?'

Sebastian threw his hands wide in a gesture of apology.

'I'm sorry. I apologise. I didn't realise a reference to a great intellect would cause such offence within this particular team.'

Ursula snorted, shook her head and folded her arms across her chest. The way she looked at Torkel clearly indicated that she expected him to come up with a solution, and that this would involve Sebastian's disappearance. Vanja, who had no previous experience of Sebastian, was gazing at him with a mixture of disbelief and fascination. As if he were a great big insect under a microscope.

'Are you for real?'

Sebastian spread his arms wide once more.

'The whole of this fantastic body is for real.'

Torkel could feel the seed of doubt growing. Usually things worked out extremely well when he went with his gut feeling. But now? How long had it been? Three minutes? And the atmosphere in the room was worse than it had been for many years. If ever. Torkel raised his voice.

'Okay, that's enough. Sebastian, I'd like you to leave us now. Go and find a seat somewhere else and read up on the case.'

He held a folder out to Sebastian. Sebastian grabbed it but Torkel didn't let go, forcing Sebastian to meet his gaze.

Sebastian looked up at him with a searching expression.

'And you will treat me and my staff with respect in future. I brought you in. I can kick you out. Clear?'

'Oh, absolutely, it must be terribly difficult to cope with my lack of respect when everyone has done their very best to make me feel welcome.'

The irony was wasted on Torkel.

'I'm not joking. If you don't get your act together, you're out. Clear?'

Sebastian realised that this was not the right moment to take on Torkel. He nodded obediently.

'I apologise unreservedly to every single one of you. For every-thing. From now on you'll hardly even notice I'm here.'

Torkel let go of the folder. Sebastian tucked it under his arm and gave a little wave to the four people in the room.

'See you later.'

Sebastian pushed open the door and left. Ursula turned to Torkel, but before she had time to launch into her harangue, Haraldsson tapped on the doorframe and came into the room.

'We've had an email.'

He handed a printout to Torkel. Vanja moved closer so that she could read over his shoulder, which proved unnecessary as Haraldsson was about to tell them what it said.

'It's from someone who says Roger's jacket is in Leonard Lundin's garage.'

Torkel didn't even need to say anything. Ursula and Billy pushed past Haraldsson in the doorway and disappeared.

*

Sebastian walked through the office with the folder he had no intention of opening under his arm. So far, so good. He was part of the investigation; now all he had to do was get what he had come for. If you really wanted to find someone, the police computer system was the place to look. There was the criminal records database for a start; not everybody was on there, and hopefully Anna Eriksson wasn't there either, but the amount of information – apart from a possible criminal record – that the right person could get hold of via the police was impressive. That was the power he needed.

It was just a matter of finding the person who was going to help him.

The right person for the job.

He allowed his gaze to roam over the workstations. He decided on a woman of about forty over by the window. Short, practical hairstyle. Subtle make-up. Small, neat earrings. Brown eyes. Wedding ring. Sebastian walked over to her and switched on his smile.

'Hi. My name is Sebastian Bergman, and I'm working with Riksmord from today.' Sebastian jerked his head in the direction of the conference room when the woman looked up from her work.

'I see. Hi. Martina.'

'Hi, Martina. Listen, I need help with something.'

'No problem. What is it?'

'I need to find an Anna Eriksson. She was living at this address in Stockholm in 1979.'

He placed the envelope that had been returned to his mother on the desk in front of Martina. She glanced at it then looked up at Sebastian with a hint of suspicion in her eyes.

'Does she have some connection to the investigation?'

'Yes, indeed. Absolutely. Definitely.'

'So why don't you look her up yourself?'

Yes, why didn't he? Fortunately the truth worked, for once.

'I only started today, and I haven't been given my username and password and so on.' Sebastian gave her his most captivating smile, but could see from Martina's expression that it wasn't working. She fingered the envelope on the desk and shook her head.

'So why don't you ask somebody on your team to do it, then? They've got access to the entire system.'

And why aren't you just happy to be able to help out in a high-profile murder investigation? Why don't you find what I'm asking for and stop asking so many bloody questions, Sebastian thought as he leaned a little closer. Confided in her.

'To be perfectly honest, it's a bit of a long shot on my part, and you know, it's my first day, I don't want to make a fool of myself.'

'I'd be happy to help you, but I just need to check it out with your boss first. We can't just look people up when we feel like it.'

'It's not a matter of . . .'

Sebastian broke off as he saw Torkel emerge from the conference room and gaze around the office. Evidently he found what he was looking for: Sebastian. Torkel was heading straight for him. Sebastian grabbed the envelope and straightened up quickly.

'Never mind. Forget it. I'll get someone on the team to help instead. That's probably the easiest thing to do. Thanks, anyway.'

Sebastian started walking before he had finished speaking. He wanted to put enough distance between himself, Torkel and Martina so that she wouldn't decide to ask Torkel in passing if it was okay to look up Anna Eriksson from 1979. That would make Torkel wonder why, call into question Sebastian's motives for wanting to join the investigation, put Torkel on his guard for no reason. So Sebastian kept on walking away from Martina. Step by step. Until . . . 'Sebastian.'

Sebastian conducted a quick debate with himself. Did he need to give a reason for his conversation with the female officer? Perhaps it would be best. He decided to go for the explanation Torkel probably had in mind anyway.

'I was just on my way to read this, but I was distracted by a tight, well-filled top.'

Torkel wondered if this was the time to explain to Sebastian that from today he was part of Riksmord. That everything he did reflected on the whole team. And that it was therefore not a good idea to try to get married colleagues from the local force into bed. But Torkel knew that Sebastian already knew that. Knew and didn't care.

'We've had an anonymous tip directing our attention back to Leonard Lundin. Ursula and Billy have gone to check it out, but I wondered if you wanted to go over there and have a chat with the mother.'

'Clara?'

'Yes, you seemed to be getting on well.'

Well, yes, you could say that. Extremely well. Clara was another woman who would not only put Torkel on his guard but get Sebastian kicked out before he knew what had hit him. You didn't go to bed with the mother of a boy suspected of murder. Sebastian was pretty sure Torkel would be firm on that particular point.

'I don't think so. It's probably better if I read up on the case, see if I can come up with something new.'

For a moment it looked as if Torkel might object, but then he nodded.

'Okay, you do that.'

'Just one more thing – could you arrange for me to have access to the computers here, please? Criminal records, the whole lot.'

Torkel looked genuinely puzzled.

'Why?'

'Why not?'

'Because you're well known for running your own race.' Torkel moved closer. Sebastian knew why. There was no reason to let curious ears know there were potential rifts within the team. To the outside world they were united. That was important. It also meant that whatever Torkel was about to say, it was unlikely to be entirely positive. And it wasn't.

'You are not a full member of the team. You are a consultant. Any investigations you wish to carry out, any leads you want to follow up, everything goes through one of us. Billy, preferably.'

Sebastian tried not to show his disappointment. He didn't quite manage it.

'Do you have a problem with that?'

'No. Not at all. Your decision.'

Bloody Torkel. Now it was going to take longer than he'd thought. He had no intention of being part of this investigation for too long. And definitely not an active part. He was not about to speak to, interview or analyse anything or anyone. Nor was he going to come up with possible scenarios or perpetrator profiles. He would get hold of what he had come here for – an updated, current address for Anna Eriksson, or whatever her name might be these days – and then he would quickly and efficiently disentangle himself from the team, leave town and never come back.

Sebastian held up the folder.

'In that case I'll start reading.'

'One more thing, Sebastian.'

Sebastian sighed to himself. Couldn't he just go and sit down somewhere with a cup of coffee and pretend to read?

'You're here as a favour to a friend. Because I believed you when you said you really needed this. I don't expect gratitude, but now it's up to you to make sure I don't end up regretting my decision.'

Before Sebastian had time to respond, Torkel turned and left. Sebastian gazed after him.

He felt no gratitude.

Of course Torkel would end up regretting his decision.

That's what happened to everyone who let Sebastian into their lives.

Billy opened the garage door. No car at the moment, although there was plenty of room for one. Which was unusual. Over the years Billy and Ursula had been inside a number of garages. Most of them were full of just about everything, apart from a vehicle. But in the Lundins' garage they were faced with an empty expanse of floor, dirty and stained with oil, and with a drain in the centre. Billy pushed the door all the way up as Ursula reached for the light switch.

They stepped inside. The two bare fluorescent tubes on the

ceiling flickered into life but they both took out their torches anyway. Without needing to say a word they each began to examine one side of the garage. Ursula took the right, Billy the left. The floor on Ursula's side was virtually bare. There was an old croquet game and, in the corner, a plastic boules set with one ball missing. And an electric lawnmower. Ursula picked it up. Empty. Just like last time. The shelves lining the walls were crowded, but there was nothing to indicate that there had ever been a car in the garage. No oil, spark plugs, lock de-icer or light bulbs. There was, however, plenty of gardening equipment: edging tools, half-empty seed packets, gloves and weed-killer sprays. Nowhere to hide a jacket. Ursula would be very surprised if the information in the email proved to be correct. If the jacket was in here, she would have found it the first time.

'Did you check the drain?'

'What do you think?'

Billy didn't reply. He started shifting the three sacks of compost piled up along one wall, next to the white plastic garden furniture. Stupid of him to ask. Ursula didn't like being called into question. Without knowing much about their previous relationship, Billy thought that was why she disliked Sebastian Bergman so much. The little Billy had heard about Sebastian suggested that he constantly questioned everything and everyone. Questioned and knew better, if not best. It didn't matter to Billy, as long as Sebastian knew what he was doing. Every single day Billy worked with officers who were better than him. No problem. Billy hadn't really formed an impression of Sebastian yet. A slightly off-colour joke could be down to nerves as much as anything. But Ursula didn't like him. Neither did Vanja, so the odds were pretty good that Billy would end up in the same camp.

He reached the corner on his side. There were a number of garden tools in a rack on the floor, and various other tools hanging neatly from hooks on the wall.

'Ursula ...'

Billy had stopped by the garden tools. There was a large white

140

plastic bucket containing Leca aggregate next to the wooden rack that held a rake, a hoe and something resembling a pickaxe that Billy didn't know the name of. Ursula came over and Billy shone his torch down into the bucket. Something green was clearly visible among the balls of burnt clay.

Immediately Ursula started taking photographs. After a while she lowered the camera and turned to Billy. She had no trouble interpreting the look on his face as sceptical, even though he thought it was neutral.

'I wouldn't miss a jacket half hidden in a bucket in a suspect's garage. Just so you know.'

'I didn't say a word.'

'I can see the look in your eyes. That's enough.'

Ursula took out a large evidence bag and carefully fished the jacket out of the bucket with a pair of tongs. Both of them stared at it, their expressions serious. Most of the jacket was covered in congealed blood. At the back the material was barely holding together. It became very clear to both of them how it must have looked with a living body wearing the jacket. Without another word Ursula slid it into the bag and sealed it.

At the station on Västgötegatan Haraldsson was sitting at his computer waiting for messages. He was still in the game.

No doubt about it.

They were all doing everything they could to get rid of him, but he was hanging on. Thanks to his foresight, his ability to realise who was privy to the most information in this building. The people most of his colleagues simply greeted in passing every day: the staff on reception. Haraldsson had realised at an early stage in his career that the people who worked in the foyer found out the most. From both inside and outside. For that reason he had made a point of having coffee with them from time to time over the years, asking about their families, taking an interest and occasionally covering up for them if necessary. So now they automatically got in touch with him if something connected to Roger Eriksson turned up. Whether it came via the telephone or the form on the local police authority website which members of the public with information could fill in, it came to Haraldsson too. When the anonymous tip about the jacket in the Lundins' garage came in they had phoned him from reception and, a second later, the forwarded message landed in his inbox. All he had to do was print it out and deliver it.

Good, but not enough. Anybody could turn up with a printout.

That was a job for a work experience student.

Somebody with no qualifications.

Tracing the sender, though – now, that was police work. There was nothing in the message to suggest that the person who had supplied the information was guilty of anything. But if it turned out to be accurate, then this person had some knowledge of the crime. The murder squad was bound to be interested, and Haraldsson would be able to point them in the right direction.

The station's IT department was a joke. It consisted of Kurre Dahlin, a man in his fifties, whose main skill lay in pressing Ctrl/Alt/Delete, shaking his head, then sending the offending machine away to be fixed. It would probably have taken Kurre Dahlin less time to learn to fly than to trace an incoming email.

The computer from which the message had been sent had an IP address, and Haraldsson had a seventeen-year-old nephew. As soon as Haraldsson received the message he forwarded it to his nephew, then texted him and offered him 500 kronor if he could come up with an actual address for the sender. Yes, he knew that his nephew was in school, but as soon as possible, please.

His nephew read the text, put his hand up, excused himself and left the classroom. Two minutes later he had picked up the message from his inbox on one of the school computers. As soon as he saw the sender's address on the original email he leaned back in his chair, his expression troubled. Haraldsson thought his nephew was some kind of whiz-kid when it came to computers, and usually the things he asked about were ridiculously simple, but this time he was going to have to disappoint his uncle. There was no problem tracking down an IP address, but it could have been sent via one of the big internet operators, in which case it would be impossible to find anything really usable. Oh well, he might as well give it a try anyway.

After two minutes he leaned back in his chair again, this time with a broad grin on his face. He'd been lucky. The message had been sent from a freestanding server. He would get his 500. He clicked on *Send*.

At the station Haraldsson's computer pinged. He quickly opened the new message and nodded to himself with satisfaction. The server from which the original message had been sent was just outside town.

At Palmlövska High, to be exact.

'Next left.'

Sebastian was sitting in the passenger seat of an unmarked police car. A Toyota. Vanja was driving. She glanced quickly at the small screen above the dashboard.

'The GPS says straight on.'

'But it'll be quicker if you go left.'

'Are you sure?'

'Yes.'

Vanja decided to go straight on. Sebastian sank down in his seat and looked out of the grubby side window at the town, feeling nothing but a great emptiness towards it.

He had been sitting in the conference room with Torkel, Vanja and Billy, having failed to come up with a good reason why he couldn't be there, when Torkel came to tell him they had new information on the case. He learned that they had found the victim's jacket. True, the blood had yet to be analysed, but none of them really believed it could be anyone else's jacket or anyone else's blood. Which meant that Leonard Lundin was once again a person of interest in the investigation. Vanja was to question him again after the meeting.

'Feel free, but it's a waste of time.'

They had all turned to face Sebastian, who was sitting at the end of the table tipping his chair back and forth. He could have sat there in silence, letting the others make whatever mistakes they liked while he worked out a way to gain access to the computers and the information he needed. Or, to put it more accurately, while he found another woman in the department who was more susceptible to his charms than Martina had been. It couldn't be that difficult, surely. On the other hand, nobody liked him anyway. He might as well be true to his inner know-it-all.

'It doesn't fit.' Sebastian allowed the front legs of his chair to make contact with the carpet again. Ursula came in and sat down on one of the chairs nearest the door without saying a word.

Sebastian went on.

'Leonard would never hide the victim's jacket in his garage.'

'Why not?' Billy seemed genuinely interested. Not at all defensive. He might be someone worth cultivating.

'Because he wouldn't even remove it from the body.'

'He took the watch.' Vanja's tone wasn't defensive either. It was more a question of being on the offensive. Keen to put him right. Break down his argument. She was like Ursula. Or, indeed, like him, the way he had been when he'd actually cared.

Competitive.

Focused on winning.

Unfortunately, she wasn't going to win this particular match. Sebastian met her gaze calmly.

'There's a difference. The watch was valuable. We have a boy of sixteen, single mother who works in the care industry. He's constantly trying to keep up in the materialistic race that's going on around him all the time. Why would he struggle to remove a ripped, bloodstained jacket and take it with him when he left Roger's wallet and mobile? It doesn't make any sense.'

'Sebastian is right.' They all turned to Ursula, Sebastian with an expression that suggested that he was finding it difficult to believe his ears. Those were three words Ursula had rarely uttered in her life. In fact, Sebastian couldn't ever remember her saying them.

'It pains me to say so, but it's true.' Ursula quickly got to her feet and took two photographs out of a C4 envelope.

'I know you think I might have missed the jacket the first time. But look at these.' She placed the first picture on the table, and they all leaned forward.

'When I went through the garage yesterday, I was particularly interested in three things: the moped, for obvious reasons; the drain, in case there were traces of blood, or in case someone had rinsed the moped or a weapon in the garage; and then the garden tools, since we don't have a murder weapon. I took this photograph yesterday.'

She placed her finger on the picture, which showed the garden tools stacked in their wooden rack. The picture was taken at an angle from above, and the white bucket containing the Leca aggregate was clearly visible in one corner.

'I took this one today. Spot the difference.' Ursula put down the second picture. Almost identical to the first one. This time, though, the green fabric was clearly visible in several places through the thin layer of aggregate. The room fell silent for a moment.

'Someone put the jacket there overnight.' Billy was the first to articulate what they were all thinking. 'Someone wants to frame Leonard Lundin.'

'That's not the main reason.' Sebastian caught himself looking at the pictures with a degree of interest. There was something energising about what had just happened. The murderer had taken items belonging to the victim and was now using them to plant evidence. And not at random, but in the house of the main suspect. This indicated that the murderer was closely following the progress of the investigation, and was acting accordingly, with deliberate planning. He was determined to get away with it. He probably didn't even regret what he'd done. A man entirely after Sebastian's own heart.

145

'The main reason for placing the jacket in the garage is to divert suspicion from himself. He has nothing personal against Leonard, it's just that Leonard fitted the bill because we're already focused on him.'

Torkel looked at Sebastian with a certain amount of satisfaction. His earlier doubts faded slightly. Torkel knew Sebastian better than Sebastian liked to think. He knew that his colleague was incapable of getting involved in something that didn't interest him, but he also knew how absorbed Sebastian could become if he encountered a challenge. When that happened, he was a real asset to an investigation. Torkel had a feeling they were on the way to something good. He gave silent thanks for the email and the discovery of the jacket.

'So the person who sent the email is probably the murderer.'

It was Vanja who quickly came to the correct conclusion.

'We need to try to trace it. Find out where it came from.'

It was almost like a theatrical performance. There was a discreet knock on the door, as if Haraldsson had been standing outside just waiting for his cue in order to make his entrance.

Sebastian undid his seatbelt and got out of the car. He looked up at the building in front of him and was filled with an immense weariness.

'So this was where he went?'

'Yes.'

'Poor bastard. Have we completely ruled out suicide?'

Above the double doors leading into Palmlövska High was a large painting of a man who could only be Jesus. His arms were outstretched in a gesture that the artist undoubtedly meant to be welcoming, but which looked distinctly threatening to Sebastian. Keen to take away the freedom of anyone who walked through those doors.

Beneath the picture it read: *John 12:46.*

'"I have come into the world as light, so that whoever believes in me shall not remain in darkness",' Sebastian reeled off.

'You know your Bible?'

'I know that thing.'

Sebastian went up the last couple of steps and pushed open one door. With a final glance at the enormous painting, Vanja followed him.

Ragnar Groth, the Principal of Palmlövska High, waved expansively towards a small sofa and an armchair in one corner of his office. Vanja and Sebastian sat down. Ragnar Groth, on the other hand, unbuttoned his jacket and sat down behind the old-fashioned rustic desk. Without even realising what he was doing, he straightened a pen until it was perfectly parallel with the edge of the desk. Sebastian noticed, and allowed his gaze to sweep over the desk, then to the rest of the room. The principal's workplace was almost empty. To his left was a pile of plastic folders. Edge to edge. No part of any folder was sticking out. They were in the bottom left-hand corner of the desk, with a gap of two centimetres below and at the side. To his right lay two pens and one pencil in parallel lines, all pointing in the same direction. At a right angle above them were a ruler and an eraser, which looked unused. The telephone, computer and lamp were arranged with precision in relation to the edges of the desk and to each other.

The rest of the room was ordered along the same lines. No crooked pictures. Not a Post-it note in sight. Everything on the noticeboard neatly pinned up and evenly spaced. Every file precisely in line with the edge of the bookshelf. No hint of a mark left by a coffee cup or a glass of water. The furniture arranged with absolute precision in relation to the walls and the rug. Sebastian quickly reached a diagnosis on Ragnar Groth: a pedant with elements of obsessive behaviour.

Wearing an expression of the utmost seriousness, the principal had met Vanja and Sebastian outside his office, his outstretched hand so rigidly straight it looked ridiculous, and had immediately embarked upon a lengthy narrative on how terrible it was that one of the school's pupils had been found murdered. Everyone would, of course, do their best to help solve this dreadful crime. No obstacles would be placed in the way of the police. Total cooperation. Vanja couldn't help feeling that every single word sounded as if it came from some PR firm's crisis management handbook. The principal offered them coffee. Vanja and Sebastian declined.

'How much do you know about the school?'

'Enough,' said Sebastian.

'Not much,' said Vanja.

'We started as a boarding school in the 1950s, and now we're an independent grammar school. We have a social studies and natural sciences program, with options in languages, economics and leadership. We have 218 students from the whole Mälardalen area, and from as far away as Stockholm. That is why we have retained the boarding-school element.'

'So that the rich kids won't have to mix with the plebs.'

Groth turned to Sebastian, and even though his voice remained low and well modulated, he was unable to hide a hint of irritation.

'Our reputation as an upper-class school is disappearing. These days the parents who come to us are those who actually want their children to learn something in school. Our results are among the best in the country.'

'Of course they are. That makes you competitive and justifies your ridiculously high fees.'

'We no longer charge fees.'

'Of course you do, you just have to call it "a reasonable donation" these days.'

Groth glared at Sebastian and leaned back in his ergonomically perfect desk chair. Vanja could feel the whole thing slipping through their fingers. In spite of the principal's exaggerated formal tone, he had at least seemed keen to help with the investigation. Sebastian's inappropriate remarks could change that situation after just three minutes, which would leave them fighting for every scrap of information about students and staff. If Ragnar Groth didn't give his blessing, they wouldn't even be able to look at a school photograph without applying for permission. Vanja wasn't sure if Groth was aware of how difficult he could make their job, but at this stage she wasn't prepared to take the risk. She shifted forward on the sofa and gave him a winning smile.

'Tell me more about Roger. How come he ended up here?'

'There were problems with bullying at his junior school and at the high school he first attended. A member of my staff knew him well – he was a friend of her son's, so she put in a good word for him and we found him a place here.'

'And he was happy here? He didn't get into any kind of trouble with other students?'

'We're very proactive in our efforts to prevent bullying.'

'You've got another word for it, haven't you? "Hazing", isn't that what it's called?'

Groth ignored Sebastian's comment. Vanja gave Sebastian a look that she hoped would make him keep his mouth shut. Then she turned back to the principal.

'Do you know if Roger was behaving differently over the last few days or weeks? Whether he was worried about anything, playing up, that kind of thing?'

Groth shook his head slowly as he thought about it.

'No, I wouldn't have said so. But you should speak to Beatrice Strand, his class teacher – she saw him far more often than I did.'

He was now addressing only Vanja.

'It was through Beatrice that Roger came here.'

'How did he manage the reasonable donation?' Sebastian piped up. He had no intention of being ignored. That would make things rather too easy for Herr Groth. The principal looked a little surprised, almost as if he had managed to forget for a little while that this slightly overweight and rather scruffy man was sitting in his office.

'Roger was exempt from making the donation.'

'So he was your little social project? Filled your quota of charitable deeds? That must have felt good.'

Groth pushed back his chair very deliberately and got to his feet. He remained standing behind the desk, straight backed and with his fingertips resting on the dust-free surface. Like Caligula in the old film *Torment*, Sebastian thought as he noticed the way the principal buttoned his jacket with a reflex action as he got up.

'I have to say that I find your attitude towards our school rather annoying.'

'Oh dear. The thing is, I spent three of the worst years of my life here, so it'll take a bit more than your sales patter before I join in the chorus of approval.'

Groth looked at Sebastian with a certain amount of scepticism.

'You're a former student?'

'Yes. Unfortunately it was my father's idea to found this temple of knowledge.'

Groth processed this information, and when he realised what he had heard, he sat down again. Jacket button undone. The irritated expression replaced by one of sheer disbelief.

'You're Ture Bergman's son?'

'Yes.'

'There's not much of a resemblance.'

'Thank you, that's the nicest thing anyone's said to me since I got here.'

Sebastian stood up and waved his hand in a gesture that encompassed both Vanja and Groth.

'You two carry on. Where will I find Beatrice Strand?'

'She's teaching at the moment.'

'But presumably she's doing that somewhere on the premises?'

'I'd prefer you to wait until break before you speak to her.'

'Okay, I'll find her myself.'

Sebastian left the room. Before he closed the door behind him he heard Vanja apologising for him. He'd heard it before. Not from Vanja, but from other colleagues to other people in different contexts. Sebastian was beginning to feel more and more at home in this investigation. He headed quickly towards the stairs. Most of the classrooms used to be one floor down. That was hardly likely to have changed. In general most things looked the same as they had forty years ago. The walls might have been a different colour, but otherwise Palmlövska High hadn't changed much.

After all, hell doesn't usually change.

That was probably the very definition of hell.

The endless torment.

It took Sebastian longer than he had expected to find his way. He spent some time wandering around the familiar corridors, knocking on various doors before finding the classroom in which Beatrice Strand was teaching. On the way he had decided to feel nothing. The school was just a building. A building in which he had spent three years under protest. His father had forced him to attend Palmlövska when he started the place, and from the first day Sebastian was determined not to like it. Not to fit in. He broke every imaginable rule, and in his capacity as the founder's son he challenged every teacher and every authority figure. His behaviour might possibly have given him a certain status among the other students, but Sebastian had decided that there would be *nothing* positive about his years at this school, and he therefore had no hesitation in telling tales or playing his fellow students off against one another or against the staff. This made him extremely unpopular with everyone, and cast him in the role of outsider, which he welcomed. In some way he thought he was punishing his father by systematically alienating himself from everyone and everything, and there was no denying the fact that his status as a complete outsider gave him a new kind of freedom. The only thing that was expected of him was that he would do whatever he felt like doing in any given situation. He became very good at that. For the rest of his life he had carried on along the route he had embarked upon in his teens.

My way or the highway.

All his life. No, not all his life. Not with Lily. He hadn't been like that with her. Not at all. How could it be that one person – eventually, two – could have had such an influence on his life? Changed him so completely?

He didn't know.

151

He only knew that it had happened.

It had happened, and then it had been taken away from him.

He knocked on the pale brown door and walked in with one single movement. A woman of about forty was sitting at the teacher's desk. Thick red hair tied back in a ponytail. The freckled, open face free of make-up. A dark green blouse with a bow resting on the not inconsiderable bust. Long brown skirt. She looked at Sebastian, who introduced himself and gave the students the rest of the lesson off. Beatrice Strand didn't object.

When they were alone in the classroom, Sebastian pulled out a chair in the front row and sat down. He asked her to tell him about Roger, and waited for the emotional outburst he suspected would follow. Absolutely right. Beatrice had had to be strong in front of her students, the person with all the answers, the person who represented security and ordinary, everyday life when something incomprehensible forced its way in. But now she was alone with another adult. Someone who was part of the investigation, and who therefore took over the role of security and control. She didn't have to be the strong one any more. The dam burst. Sebastian waited.

'I just don't understand it . . . ' The words came shuddering out between sobs. 'We said goodbye as usual last Friday, and now . . . now he's never coming back. We kept on hoping, but then when they found him . . . '

Sebastian said nothing. There was a knock on the door and Vanja stuck her head in. Beatrice blew her nose and dried her eyes as Sebastian introduced the two women. Beatrice gestured towards her tear-stained face with her handkerchief, then excused herself and left the classroom. Vanja perched on one of the desks.

'The school doesn't monitor computer usage in any way, and there are no cameras anywhere. It's a question of mutual respect, according to the principal.'

'So anybody could have sent the message?'

'It doesn't even have to be a student. You can just walk in straight off the street.'

'But it does need to be someone with a certain knowledge of the school.'

'Yes, but that still means two hundred and eighteen students plus parents, plus friends, plus all the staff.'

'He knew that.'

'Who?'

'The person who sent the message. He knew it would be impossible to trace it beyond the school. But he's been here before. He has some kind of link to this school. We can take that as read.'

'Probably. If it is a he.'

Sebastian looked at Vanja, his expression sceptical.

'I'd be very surprised if it wasn't a he. The way the murder was carried out, and in particular that business with the heart, indicates a male perpetrator.' Sebastian was about to begin a monologue on the male perpetrator's need for trophies, a desire to retain his power over the victim by keeping something belonging to him or her, something that almost never occurs in the case of a female perpetrator. But Beatrice came back, interrupting him before he could get going. She sat down at her desk with another apology and turned to face them, looking much more composed.

'You were responsible for Roger moving to this school?' Vanja began.

Beatrice nodded.

'Yes, he and my son Johan are friends.' She realised which tense she had used and corrected herself. '*Were* friends. He often used to come round to our house and I knew he hadn't been happy at junior school, but eventually it emerged that things were just as bad, if not worse, at Runebergs.'

'But he was happy here?'

'He was settling in well. It was difficult at first, of course.'

'Why?'

'It was a big adjustment for him. The students here are highly motivated when it comes to their work. He wasn't used to either the tempo or the level at which we work. But it was getting better.

He was staying behind after school, getting some extra tuition. He really was getting to grips with it all.'

Sebastian didn't say anything. Beatrice's attention was focused on Vanja. Sebastian sat there gazing at her profile and caught himself wondering what it would feel like to run his fingers through that thick red hair. Kiss that freckled face. Watch those big blue eyes close with pleasure. There was something about her that was giving off a signal suggesting ... loneliness, perhaps? Sebastian wasn't sure. But she wasn't like Clara Lundin. She wasn't as vulnerable. Beatrice was more ... secure. More mature. Sebastian had a feeling she would be more difficult to get into bed, but probably worth the effort. He dropped the idea. One woman connected to the investigation was enough. He went back to concentrating on the conversation.

'Did Roger have friends here?'

'Not many. He used to hang out with Johan and sometimes with Erik Heverin, but Erik is in the USA this term. And then there was Lisa, of course, his girlfriend. He wasn't an outsider, or unpopular. He was just a bit of a lone wolf.'

'No real problems, though?'

'Not here. But sometimes he bumped into people from his old school.'

'Did he seem worried about anything?'

'No. He was just the same as always when he left here. Glad it was Friday, like everybody else. They'd had a Swedish exam and he called by to say he thought it had gone well.'

Beatrice fell silent and shook her head, as if she'd just realised how absurd the situation was. The tears sprang to her eyes once more.

'He was a really lovely boy. Sensitive. Mature. This just doesn't make any sense.'

'Is your son here?'

'No, Johan is at home. This has hit him very hard.'

'We'd really like to speak to him.'

Beatrice nodded with a resigned expression.

'I realise that. I'll be home around four.'

'There's no need for you to be there.'

Beatrice nodded again, looking even more resigned. That sounded familiar. No one needed her. Sebastian and Vanja stood up.

'We might be back if we need to speak to you again in the future.'

'Fine. I really hope you find out who did this. It's so ... it's so difficult. For everyone.'

Sebastian nodded, giving every impression of sincere sympathy. Beatrice stopped them.

'There's something else – I don't know if it's important, but Roger rang our house. That Friday evening.'

'What time?'

This was completely new information, and the effect on Vanja was clear. She moved closer to Beatrice.

'About a quarter past eight. He wanted to speak to Johan, but he was out with Ulf, his dad. I said he could ring Johan's mobile, but according to Johan he never called.'

'What did he want? Did he tell you?'

Beatrice shook her head.

'He wanted to speak to Johan.'

'At a quarter past eight on Friday?'

'Round about then.'

Vanja thanked her and they left. Quarter past eight.

When Roger was with his girlfriend, Lisa.

Vanja was becoming more and more certain he'd never even been at Lisa's house.

The material was on two LaCie hard drives. They had arrived by courier from the security company an hour ago. Billy quickly linked the first of the steel grey boxes to his computer and started work. The disk was marked FRI 23 APRIL 06:00–00:00, CAMERAS 1.02–1.16. According to the notes Billy had received with them, cameras 1.14–1.15 covered Gustavsborgsgatan, or at least parts of it. The last place they knew Roger had been on that fateful evening.

Billy found camera 1.14 in the various subfolders and started the film with a double click. The quality of the image was better than usual: the CCTV system was less than six months old, and the company hadn't cut corners when it had come to the cost. This cheered Billy up no end. Most of the time the material from surveillance cameras was so poor and blurred that it was of very little help in their investigations. But this was a different matter. *Practically Zeiss optics*, thought Billy as he scrolled through to 21:00. After only half an hour he rang Torkel, who came straightaway.

Torkel sat down next to Billy. On the ceiling the projector linked to Billy's computer was whirring away. On the wall the images from camera 1.15 were running. From the angle of the picture it was easy to work out that the camera was located some ten metres off the ground. It was staring down at an open square, and in the centre a road disappeared between two tall buildings. The building on the left was the college, the other a school. The empty open square directly in front of the camera looked cold and windy. A digital clock marked the time in one corner of the screen. The silence was suddenly broken as a moped appeared. Billy froze the image.

'There. Leonard Lundin passes by at 21:02. Shortly afterwards Roger appears, walking from the west.'

Billy pressed a key and the recording continued. A minute or so later another figure appeared. He was wearing a green jacket and walking quickly and purposefully. Billy froze the image again and they gazed at the figure. Even though he was wearing a baseball cap with the peak hiding his face, it was definitely Roger Eriksson, without a shadow of doubt. The height, the medium-length hair and that jacket, the one that was now hanging in the police evidence lock-up, brown with dried blood, was undamaged and unmarked.

'He appears at precisely 21:02:48,' said Billy, restarting the film. Roger gave a little jump and carried on walking. There was something about moving pictures of a person who had only hours to live. It was as if the knowledge of the impending catastrophe meant that every step was scrutinised more closely, every movement acquired a greater significance. Death was lurking just around the corner, but in fact this ordinary walk carried nothing of it. The knowledge of what was to come lay with the person watching, not with the sixteen-year-old boy quietly moving past camera 1.15. He knew nothing of what was waiting for him.

Torkel saw Roger stop and look up. A second later the moped re-entered the picture. From Roger's body language Torkel and Billy could see that he knew the rider and was aware that the appearance of the moped would cause him problems. Roger stiffened and looked around, as if seeking a way out. He seemed to decide quickly to ignore the moped, which was now circling around him like an irritating wasp. Roger tried to move on but the circling moped prevented him, coming closer and closer, around and around. Roger stopped, and after a few more circuits so did the moped. Leonard got off. Roger looked at the other boy as he removed his helmet and straightened up, as if to make himself look bigger. He looked as if he knew there was going to be trouble and was preparing himself. Steeling himself for what he knew was bound to happen.

This was Torkel's first real encounter with the dead boy, and it gave him some idea of who he had been. He hadn't run away. Perhaps he hadn't been just a victim. It looked as if he too was trying to make himself look a little taller. Leonard said something. Roger replied, and then came the first shove. Roger stumbled backwards and Leonard followed. As Roger regained his balance Leonard grabbed hold of his left arm and tugged at the jacket, exposing his watch. Presumably Leonard said something, because Roger made an attempt to pull his arm away. Leonard responded by punching him in the face.

Hard and fast.

With no warning.

Torkel could see the blood trickling down Roger's right hand when he raised it to his face. Leonard hit him again. Roger wobbled, grabbing Leonard's T-shirt as he fell to his knees.

'That's how Leonard got blood on his T-shirt,' Billy commented briefly. Torkel nodded to himself; that explained it. Seeing the blood on his T-shirt seemed to be the trigger, the impetus Leonard needed to justify an increased level of violence. He hurled himself at Roger in a fury. It wasn't long before Roger was lying on the ground, suffering a barrage of kicks. The clock on the screen mechanically registered the time as Roger lay there curled up in the foetal position, taking what Leonard thought he deserved. Eventually, at 21:05, Leonard stopped kicking, bent over Roger and ripped the watch off his arm. With one last look at the boy lying on the ground, he put on his helmet with exaggerated slowness, as if to emphasise his superiority, got back on his moped and rode out of the picture. Roger stayed where he was for a while. Billy looked at Torkel.

'He wasn't watching *Let's Dance* with his girlfriend.'

Torkel nodded. Lisa was lying. But the information Leonard had given during questioning was also incorrect. Roger hadn't started something by knocking Leonard off his moped.

They hadn't had a quarrel.

As far as Torkel knew, a quarrel required two active participants.

He reached back and put his hands behind his head. They could certainly do Leonard Lundin for robbery with violence.

But not murder. At least not there and then. And not later either, Torkel was sure of it. Leonard was a thug. But cutting out someone's heart ... No, he didn't have it in him. In a few years maybe, if his life really went down the pan, but not right now.

'Where does Roger go next?'

'I don't know. Look.' Billy got up and went over to the map on the wall.

'He carries straight on and reaches Vasagatan, where he can go right or left. If he goes left he eventually comes to Norra Ringvägen. There's a camera at the junction there, but he never appears on it.'

'So he must have gone right?'

'In that case he would have turned up on this camera here.' Billy pointed to a spot outside the sports ground, a fraction to the north on the map. A couple of hundred metres, in reality. 'But he doesn't.'

'So he turned off somewhere before he got there.'

Billy nodded and pointed to a smaller road leading off Vasagatan at an angle.

'Probably here. Apalbyvägen. Straight into a residential area. No cameras. We don't even know which direction he went in.'

'So check them all. He might reappear on one of the bigger roads. Get a team knocking on doors in the area. Someone must have seen him. I want to know where he went.'

Billy nodded, and both men picked up their phones.

Billy called the slightly hung-over birthday boy at the security company to request more CCTV footage.

Torkel called Vanja. She answered immediately, as always.

Vanja and Sebastian were just leaving Palmlövska High when Torkel rang. The bell had gone for the lunch break and many of the students were outside. Torkel briefed her quickly. He liked to be efficient when he was speaking on the telephone, and the conversation lasted less than a minute. Vanja ended the call and turned to Sebastian.

'They've seen the film from Gustavsborgsgatan. Roger was there just after nine.'

Sebastian considered this new information. Vanja had stubbornly maintained that Lisa Hansson, Roger's sixteen-year-old girlfriend, had lied repeatedly about where Roger was on the night of the murder. Now they had proof that this was indeed the case. It seemed more important to Lisa to hide the truth than to solve the murder of her boyfriend. That kind of secret interested Sebastian. In fact, the whole bloody case was starting to interest him more and more. He had to admit that a little break from his own brooding had been welcome. He might as well stick with it for as long as he needed to, make the best of the situation. Make new decisions about his collaboration and the future when the opportunity arose.

'Shall we go and have a little chat with Lisa?'

'I thought you'd never ask.'

They headed back into the school. Lisa had gone home after English; this was her shortest day. Hopefully she would be home by now. Vanja didn't feel like ringing to check; that would just mean her parents would be ready with their line of defence. They got in the car and Vanja put her foot down, ignoring the speed limit.

They drove in silence, which suited Vanja very well. She felt no compulsion whatsoever to get to know the partner who had been forced upon her, and hoped this would be a very temporary arrangement. She already knew Sebastian wouldn't make small talk to pass the time. Ursula had called him a 'social meltdown'. She had also said it was much better when he kept quiet. As soon as he opened his mouth he was crass, sexist, critical, or just plain nasty. As long as he kept his mouth shut, he couldn't infuriate you.

Just like Ursula, Vanja had been very annoyed when Torkel had introduced Sebastian and said that he would be working with them on this investigation. Not so much because it was Sebastian. True, she had heard more crap about him than the rest of the police service put together, but what bothered her most was that Torkel had made his decision without asking her. She knew he had no obligation to consult her on such matters, but even so ... She felt as if they worked together so closely, and meant so much to each other in a professional capacity, that her views ought to be considered before a decision that would affect the entire team was made. Torkel was the best boss she had ever had, which was why she was so surprised when he made such major changes over her head. Over all their heads. Surprised and, to be honest, disappointed.

'What are the names of her parents?'

Vanja's train of thought was interrupted. She turned to Sebastian, who hadn't moved. He was still staring out of the side window.

'Ulf and Ann-Charlotte. Why?'

'No reason.'

'It was in the case folder you were given.'

'I didn't read it.'

Vanja couldn't possibly have heard him correctly.

'You didn't read it?'

161

'No.'

'Why are you actually part of this investigation?'

Vanja had been asking herself that question ever since she heard Torkel's explanation of Sebastian's presence, which had been vague, to say the least. Did he have some kind of hold over Torkel? No, that was impossible. Torkel would never jeopardise an investigation for personal reasons, whatever they might be. Sebastian's answer came more quickly than she had expected.

'You need me. You'll never solve this without me.'

Ursula was right. It was very easy to get annoyed with Sebastian Bergman.

Vanja parked the car and switched off the engine. She turned to Sebastian before they got out.

'One thing.'

'What?'

'We know she's lying. We have proof. But I want her to talk. So we're not going to go marching in and shove the evidence down her throat so that she doesn't say a word. Okay?'

'Sure.'

'I know her. I'm leading. You keep quiet.'

'Like I said, you'll hardly even notice I'm there.' Vanja gave him a look that made it clear she was serious, then she got out of the car and headed for the house. Sebastian followed.

Just as Vanja had hoped, Lisa was at home alone. She looked shocked when she saw Vanja and a strange man standing on the doorstep. She tried a few feeble excuses, but Vanja walked straight in uninvited. She had made her decision, particularly when she learned Lisa was alone.

'It'll only take a minute. We can talk in here.' Vanja led the way into the neat and tidy kitchen. Sebastian stayed in the background. He had greeted the girl pleasantly enough, then shut up. So far he was sticking to their agreement, Vanja was pleased to note. The truth was that he was incapable of speech at the moment. He had just spotted the bead picture of Jesus and was utterly dumbstruck. He had never seen anything like it.

162

'Sit down.' Vanja thought she detected a slight change in the girl's expression. She seemed more tired. She didn't have the same defiant fire in her eyes: it was as if her defences had begun to crack. Vanja tried to sound as amenable as possible. She didn't want her words to seem aggressive.

'Let me explain, Lisa. We have a problem. A big problem. We *know* Roger wasn't here at nine o'clock that Friday evening. We know where he was, and we can prove it.' Was she imagining it, or had Lisa's shoulders relaxed and dropped a fraction?

But she didn't say anything.

Not yet.

Vanja leaned forward and touched her hand, her tone softer now.

'Lisa, you have to tell us the truth. I don't know why you're lying. But you can't do it any more. Not for our sake, but for your own.'

'I want my parents here,' Lisa managed to say. Vanja kept her hand on the girl.

'Is that what you really want? Do you really want them to know you're lying?' For the first time Vanja saw that fleeting flicker of weakness that usually precedes the truth.

'Roger was on Gustavsborgsgatan at five past nine. He was caught on CCTV. Gustavsborgsgatan is quite a way from here,' Vanja went on. 'I should imagine your boyfriend left here at about quarter past eight. Half past at the latest. If he was here at all.'

She didn't go on. She looked at Lisa, whose expression was weary and resigned. All trace of defiance and teenage cockiness gone. She just looked worried. A worried child.

'They'll be so angry,' she said eventually. 'Mum and Dad.'

'If they find out.' Vanja squeezed the girl's hand, which seemed to be getting warmer and warmer as their conversation went on.

'Fuck, fuck, fuck,' Lisa said suddenly, and the forbidden words were the beginning of the end. Her defences were down. She pulled away from Vanja and buried her face in her hands. She released a long, almost relieved sigh. Secrets are a heavy burden, and carrying them is a lonely business.

163

'He wasn't my boyfriend.'

'Sorry?'

Lisa raised her head and her voice slightly.

'He wasn't my boyfriend.'

'No?'

Lisa shook her head and turned away from Vanja. She gazed unseeingly into the distance. Out of the window. As if she wished she could go there. Get away.

'So what was he then? What were you up to?'

Lisa shrugged her shoulders.

'We weren't up to anything. He was approved.'

'What do you mean, "approved"?'

Lisa turned her head and gazed wearily at Vanja. Didn't she get it?

'Approved by your parents, you mean?'

Lisa dropped her hands and nodded.

'I was allowed to go out with him. Or spend time alone with him at home. Although we always went out.'

'But not together.'

Lisa shook her head.

'So you've got another boyfriend?' Lisa nodded again, and for the first time the look she gave Vanja was pure pleading. A girl whose life presumably consisted of being the perfect daughter, a mask that was about to slip off.

'A boyfriend your parents don't like?'

'They'd kill me if they knew.'

Vanja looked at the bead picture again. It meant something different now. *I am the Way*. Not if you're sixteen years old and in love with the wrong boy.

'You know we're going to have to speak to this boy? But your parents don't need to know, I promise.'

Lisa nodded. She could no longer fight. The truth shall set you free, the youth leader at church always said whenever he got the chance. For a long time Lisa had included these words in the growing tissue of lies she had been forced to live by for so many years.

But right now, at this particular moment, she realised they had to be recatalogued. The truth shall set you free, and it shall make your parents fucking furious. No question. But at least it was the truth, and it did actually feel liberating.

'What's wrong with him? Too old? Criminal record? Drugs? Muslim?'

The questions came from Sebastian. Vanja looked at him and his expression was apologetic. She nodded, it was okay.

'There's nothing wrong with him,' said Lisa, shrugging her shoulders. 'It's just that he's not ... all this.' Lisa's small gesture encompassed not only the house but the entire area, the tidy gardens in front of the houses that were exactly the right size on the quiet street. Sebastian understood completely. He had been unable to analyse his own situation and express it in the same way when he was Lisa's age, but he recognised the feeling. The security that became a prison. The care and consideration that became suffocating. The conventions that turned into chains.

Vanja took her hand again. Lisa let her do it, or, to be more accurate, she seemed to want it.

'Was Roger here at all?'

Lisa nodded.

'But only until a quarter past eight. Until we were absolutely sure Mum and Dad had gone.'

'And where did he go then?'

Lisa shook her head.

'I don't know.'

'Was he meeting someone?'

'I think so. He usually did.'

'Who?'

'I don't know. Roger never told me. He liked having secrets.'

Sebastian looked at Lisa and Vanja, sitting close together at the spotless table and talking about an evening that had contained everything but Roger. The tidy kitchen reminded him of his own childhood home and those of all their neighbours, the people who had been so happy to associate with his successful parents. To be honest, he felt as if he'd walked into a copy of his own bloody upbringing. He had always fought against it. Seen the superficial maintenance of order and convention, never love or courage. Sebastian's opinion of the girl sitting at the table was going up all the time. She could turn into something quite special. A secret lover at the age of sixteen. Her parents were going to have a lot of trouble with her when she was older. This cheered him up no end.

They heard the front door open, and a voice shouted brightly from the hallway, 'Lisa, we're home!'

Lisa pulled back her hand in a reflex action and stiffened on her chair. Vanja quickly pushed her card across.

'Send me a text to let me know how I can get hold of your boyfriend, and we won't talk about it now.' Lisa nodded, grabbed the card and just managed to slip it into her pocket. Her father came in first.

'What are you doing here?' The pleasant tone of voice from the hallway was gone.

Vanja stood up and faced him with a smile that was rather too cheerful. A smile that made him realise he was too late. Vanja was satisfied. Ulf did his best to re-establish his authority.

'I thought we had agreed that you were not to speak to my daughter unless I was present. This is completely unacceptable!'

'It's not up to you to make that decision, and in any case we just wanted to check a couple of details with Lisa. We're leaving now.' Vanja turned and smiled at Lisa, who didn't notice because her gaze was fixed on the table. Sebastian got up. Vanja headed for the door, passing Lisa's parents on the way.

'I don't think we'll need to disturb you again.'

Ulf looked from Vanja to his daughter, and back to Vanja again. For a few seconds he didn't know what to say, but then he trotted out the only viable threat he could come up with.

'I shall be speaking to your superior officer, make no mistake. You won't get away with this.' Vanja couldn't even bring herself to respond. She just carried on towards the door. She had what she came for. Then suddenly she heard Sebastian's voice behind her.

It sounded particularly powerful, as if he had been waiting a long time for this moment.

'There is one thing you ought to know,' he said as he pushed his chair towards the table with an almost exaggerated movement. 'Your daughter has been lying to you.'

What the fuck is he doing! Vanja turned around in shock, and flashed Sebastian a filthy look. For Sebastian to be a pig in his dealings with colleagues and other adults was one thing, but to betray a child! For no reason. Lisa looked as if she wanted to slide under the table and disappear. Her father said nothing. Everyone was staring at the man who had become the kitchen's focus.

It was moments like this that Sebastian Bergman had missed the most during his self-imposed absence. He took his time, it was important to make the most of the magic. It didn't come that often these days.

'Roger left much earlier on that Friday than Lisa was prepared to admit initially.'

Lisa's parents looked at one another, and her mother broke the silence.

'Our daughter does not lie.'

Sebastian took a couple of steps towards them.

'Yes, she does.' He had no intention of letting the real liars get away. Not now he had them on the hook. 'But the question you should be asking is why she lies. Perhaps there's a reason why she daren't tell you the truth.'

Sebastian fell silent and stared at the parents. The spotless kitchen was heavy with anxiety about what was to come. What he was going to say next. Vanja's brain was working overtime. How could she get a foothold in the quicksand in which she suddenly found herself? The only thing she could come up with was a faint plea.

'Sebastian . . .'

Sebastian didn't even register her presence. He dominated the room, holding the life of a sixteen-year-old girl in his hands. Why should he listen to anyone else?

'Lisa and Roger had a quarrel that evening. He left at eight. They quarrelled and he died. How do you think that makes her feel? If they hadn't quarrelled, he would still be alive today. It was her fault that he left early. That's a huge burden of guilt for a young girl to carry.'

'Is this true, Lisa?' Her mother's voice was pleading, and her eyes had begun to fill with tears. Lisa looked at her parents as if she had just woken from a dream and didn't really know what was true or false any more. Sebastian winked at her discreetly. He was enjoying himself.

'What Lisa did wasn't really lying. It's more of a defence mechanism, something that enabled her to carry on, to cope with the guilt. That's why I'm telling you,' said Sebastian, adopting a serious expression as he looked at Lisa's parents. Then he lowered his voice in order to further stress the gravity of the situation. 'It's important now for Lisa to realise she's done nothing wrong.'

'Of course you haven't, sweetheart.' Daddy Ulf this time. He moved over to his daughter and put his arm around her. Lisa looked surprised more than anything. The transition from being exposed as a liar to being enveloped in love and concern had been somewhat rapid.

'Oh, poppet, why didn't you say anything?' her mother began, but she didn't get far before Sebastian interrupted.

'Because she didn't want to disappoint you. Don't you understand? She feels an enormous burden of guilt. Guilt and grief. And all you've talked about is whether she was lying or not. Don't you realise how lonely that made her feel?'

'But we didn't know ... We believed her.'

'You chose to believe what suited you. No more and no less. But that's understandable. It's human. However, your daughter needs love and consideration now. She must feel that you trust her.'

'But of course we do.'

'Not enough. Give her love, but give her freedom too. That's what she needs now. Lots of trust and freedom.'

'Of course. Thank you. We didn't know. I'm sorry if we over-reacted, but I hope you understand,' said Lisa's mother.

'Of course. We all want to protect our children. From everything. Otherwise we wouldn't be parents.'

Sebastian's face broke into a warm smile directed at Lisa's mother. She reciprocated gratefully, with a little nod. How true that was.

Sebastian turned to Vanja, who had gone from fury to confusion. 'Shall we make a move?'

Vanja tried to nod as if it were the most obvious thing in the world.

'Absolutely. We won't disturb you any longer.' She and Sebastian threw a final smile at the parents.

'Now, just remember, you have a wonderful daughter. Give her plenty of love and freedom. She needs to know that you trust her.'

With those words, they left. Sebastian was bubbling over with joy at having planted a little time bomb in the middle of the Hanssons' family life. Freedom was exactly what Lisa needed in order to blow the whole shit-heap sky high even more quickly. The sooner the better.

'Was that really necessary?' Vanja asked as they opened the gate.

'It was fun, isn't that enough?' Sebastian turned to Vanja, whose expression made it clear that the entertainment value didn't justify his actions. He sighed. Did he have to explain everything?

'Yes, it was necessary. Sooner or later it would come out in the press that Roger wasn't where Lisa said he was. We were able to be there and explain why. Help her.'

Sebastian kept on walking. He almost felt like whistling as he strode towards the car. It was a long time since he had whistled.

A very long time.

Vanja was a few steps behind, trying to keep up. Of course. Just leaving Lisa to sort things out by herself would have been stupid. She should have thought of that. It was a long time since she felt someone had got the better of her.

A very long time.

*

Torkel and Hanser were sitting in her office on the third floor. Torkel had requested the meeting to discuss where they were up to regarding evidence. The information from the CCTV cameras was certainly a breakthrough, since they could now definitively place Roger on Gustavsborgsgatan shortly after nine on that fateful Friday. At the same time though, this information meant that their suspicions about Leonard were further weakened. There was sufficient correlation between his earlier account and the reality, and in consultation with the prosecutor Torkel had decided to let Leonard go in order to avoid wasting time and losing focus in a difficult investigation. Naturally, all hell would break loose in the press. After all, they had already tried and convicted Leonard Lundin, the bully who went too far. They would highlight the fact that certain discoveries pointed to Leonard. The victim's blood on his T-shirt was already a matter of common knowledge. The green jacket wasn't all over the papers yet, but several reports had stated that the police had made a further discovery in the Lundins' garage. The fact that this 'further discovery' had actually been planted there was not mentioned in the press, and nor would it be. This information was known only to Torkel's team, and that was the way it would stay.

Torkel wanted to inform Hanser of his decision in person before he rang the prosecutor. She was still formally responsible for the investigation, and under pressure to produce results. Torkel knew it was never easy to release a suspect without being able to introduce a new one. Hanser understood the situation and shared his view. However, she insisted that Torkel should conduct the imminent press conference. Torkel understood why. It was all the better for her career if Riksmord were fumbling in the dark. Torkel promised to take care of the press, and went off to ring the prosecutor.

Their car pulled up on another street, in front of another house in another residential area. *How many places like this were there in Västerås? In the county? In the country*, Sebastian wondered as he and Vanja walked up the stone path to the yellow two-storey house. He assumed it was possible to be happy in an area like this. He had no personal experience of this, but that didn't mean it was out of the question. Well, it was for him. There was a sense of 'quiet dignity' about the whole place that he despised.

'Right, that's enough – clear off, the pair of you!'

Sebastian and Vanja turned and saw a man of about forty-five heading towards them from the open garage door. He had a blue cylinder made of some kind of fabric under one arm. A tent. He was marching towards them with speed and determination.

'My name is Vanja Lithner and this is Sebastian Bergman.' Vanja held up her ID. Sebastian raised his hand in greeting. 'We're from Riksmord, and we're investigating the murder of Roger Eriksson. We spoke to Beatrice at school.'

'My apologies. I thought you were journalists. I've already chased away a couple today. Ulf Strand, Johan's father.'

Ulf held out his hand. Sebastian was struck by the fact that this was the second of Johan's parents to introduce himself like this. As a parent. Ulf – Johan's father, not Beatrice's husband. Beatrice had spoken about Ulf in the same way. As her son's father, not as her husband: 'his dad' not 'my husband'.

'Aren't you married? You and Beatrice?'

Ulf seemed surprised at the question.

'Yes, why?'

'Just curious, I had the feeling that … doesn't matter. Is Johan home?'

Ulf glanced at the house, his brow furrowed with concern.

'Yes, but do you have to do this today? Everything that's happened has hit him really hard. That's why we're going camping. Just to get away for a little while.'

'I'm sorry, but for various reasons we're behind with most aspects of this investigation, and we really do need to speak to Johan as soon as possible.'

Ulf realised there wasn't much he could say to that, so he shrugged his shoulders, put down the camping equipment and showed them into the house.

They took off their shoes in the hallway, where a number of shoes, trainers and slippers lay in a jumbled heap. Dust bunnies on the floor. At least three different combinations of coats, scarves and gloves lay tossed on the black wooden bench along one wall. As they moved into the house Vanja got the impression that this was the absolute opposite of Ann-Charlotte and Ulf Hansson's well ordered home. An ironing board stood in one corner of the living room with a pile of clean laundry on top of it, alongside an assortment of letters, bills, a daily newspaper and a coffee mug. There were another two mugs among the crumbs on the sticky surface of the table in front of the TV. Yet more clothes lay strewn across armchairs and the back of the sofa: it was impossible to tell whether they were dirty or clean. They carried on upstairs. A skinny, bespectacled boy who looked younger than his sixteen years was in his room playing on a computer.

'Johan, these are police officers, and they'd like to have a little chat with you about Roger.'

'In a minute.'

Johan kept his attention fixed on the screen. It appeared to be some kind of action game. A man with an extremely overgrown and distorted arm was running around fighting figures that looked like soldiers. He was using his arm as a weapon. Billy would probably have known what the game was called. The character in the game got into a tank standing on a street corner and the screen froze, showing the word *Loading*. When the picture returned you were inside the tank, and apparently you could steer it. Johan pressed a key. The picture froze. He turned to Vanja, a tired look in his eyes.

'I'm sorry for your loss. As I understand it, you and Roger were close friends.'

Johan nodded.

'So I would assume Roger told you things he didn't tell anyone else.'

'Like what?'

Nothing new, as it turned out. Johan didn't think Roger had

been worried about anything, or afraid of anyone in particular, although he did bump into some of the boys from Vikinga School from time to time. He was happy at Palmlövska High, didn't owe anyone any money, hadn't shown an interest in anyone else's girl-friend. He had a girlfriend of his own, after all. Johan thought that was where Roger had been that Friday evening. Roger had spent a lot of time at Lisa's. *Too much*, Sebastian and Vanja suspected Johan really meant. And no, he didn't know who Roger would have been meeting if he wasn't with Lisa. Nor did he know why Roger had phoned him at home that evening. And he hadn't rung Johan on his mobile later. Johan's favourite word appeared to be 'no'.

Vanja was beginning to despair. They were getting nowhere. Everybody kept saying the same thing. Roger was a quiet, well-behaved boy who kept himself to himself and didn't fall out with anyone. What if this was one of those rare cases where the perpe-trator didn't know his victim? What if someone had just decided to go out and commit a murder one Friday evening, and chose Roger?

By chance.

Just because he could.

Admittedly this was extremely unusual, at least given the cir-cumstances in this case. Removing the heart. Moving and hiding the body. Planting evidence.

Unusual, but not impossible.

At the same time there was something not quite right about all these near identical descriptions of Roger. Vanja was starting to feel this more and more strongly. Lisa's comment that Roger liked to have secrets had stuck in her mind. She felt as if those few words were closer to the truth than all the rest. It was as if there had been two Roger Erikssons: one who was barely notice-able and never stuck out from the crowd, and another with lots of secrets.

'So you can't think of anyone who might have had a reason to be angry with Roger?'

173

Vanja was already on her way out of the room, certain that she would get another shake of the head in response.

'Well, yes, Axel was furious with him of course. But not *that* furious.'

Vanja stopped dead. She could almost feel the adrenaline level rising. A name. Someone who had a grudge against Roger. A straw to clutch at. Perhaps the beginning of yet another secret.

'Who's Axel?'

'He was the caretaker at school.'

An adult male. Access to a car. The straw was getting bigger.

'And why was this Axel angry with Roger?'

'Roger got him sacked a few weeks ago.'

'Ah yes, that unfortunate incident.'

Ragnar Groth unbuttoned his jacket and sat down behind his desk looking as if he might have eaten something unpleasant. Vanja was standing just inside the door, arms folded. She was finding it difficult to keep the fury out of her voice.

'When we were here earlier, I said that someone at this school could have been involved in Roger Eriksson's murder. But you didn't think about an employee sacked because of Roger?'

The principal threw his arms wide in a gesture that managed to be both apologetic and belittling.

'No, I'm afraid not. I do apologise. I didn't make the connection.'

'Could you tell us a little about "that unfortunate incident"?'

Groth was staring with open dislike at Sebastian, who had settled down in one of the armchairs with a brochure about the school that he had found in a rack outside the principal's office while they were waiting.

Palmlövska High. Where your opportunities begin.

'There isn't much to tell. It became apparent that our caretaker, Axel Johansson, was selling alcohol to the students. Bootlegging, you might say. Of course he was dismissed with immediate effect, and that was the end of the matter.'

174

'And how did you find out what he was up to?' Vanja said. Ragnar Groth gave her a weary look as he leaned forward and brushed a few specks of dust from the surface of his desk.

'That's why you're here, I suppose? Roger Eriksson came to me as the responsible student he was and told me what was happening. I asked a girl in one of the lower years to ring Axel and place an order. When he turned up to meet her with the goods, we caught him red-handed.'

'Did Axel know it was Roger who had given the game away?'

'I don't know. Probably. I think several of the students knew.'

'But you didn't report this to the police?'

'I couldn't really see that there was anything to be gained by doing so.'

'Could it be that your reputation as "an outstanding educational environment, encompassing security, inspiration and extensive developmental opportunities for each individual from a Christian point of view with underlying Christian values" might have been slightly sullied?' Sebastian looked up from the brochure and couldn't suppress a malicious smile.

Ragnar Groth fought to keep the distaste out of his voice when he replied. 'It's no secret that our excellent reputation is our principle resource.'

Vanja simply shook her head, unable to understand.

'So you don't report crimes committed on school premises?'

'It was just bootlegging. Small amounts. Admittedly those involved were under age, but even so. Axel would have been fined, wouldn't he? If that?'

'Probably, but that's not the point.'

'No!' Groth interrupted her sharply. 'The point is that the loss of the parents' confidence would have cost me a great deal more. It's a question of priorities.' He stood up, buttoned his jacket and headed for the door. 'If that's all, I have other things to do. But the receptionist will provide you with Axel Johansson's address if you wish to speak to him.'

*

175

Sebastian was in the corridor waiting for Vanja. The walls were covered in portrait photographs of former principals and other members of staff who had earned the right to be remembered by future generations. In the middle of the display hung the only oil painting. Of Sebastian's father. A full-length portrait. He was standing by a desk that was full of items and symbols relating to a classical education. The painting was done slightly from a worm's eye view, so that Ture Bergman was constantly looking down on the person gazing at him.

Which probably suited him perfectly, Sebastian thought.

Looking down on everyone and everything.

Judging.

From the very centre of things.

Sebastian allowed his thoughts to wander. What kind of father had he been during the four years he had been permitted with Sabine? The answer was probably 'so-so'. Or, rather, he had been as good a father as he could, but that was still only 'so-so'. In his darker moments, when Sebastian doubted his ability as a parent, he had thought it was just like when Sabine was watching TV: the quality of the program was irrelevant. As long as it was fairly colourful and moved around on the screen, she was happy. Was it the same with him? Was Sabine happy with him just because he happened to be there? She made no demands as far as the quality went. He had spent a lot of time with his daughter, there was no doubt about that. More than Lily. It wasn't a conscious decision based on a desire to share things equally, but more a result of their everyday lives. Sebastian had often worked from home, followed by short, intensive periods of working away, then a fair amount of time off before starting to work from home again. So yes, he had been there. And yet Sabine had still turned to Lily whenever something happened. Always Lily first. That had to mean something, surely? Sebastian refused to believe it was merely genetic. Some women he knew maintained that it was impossible to replace a mother, but that was nonsense. So he had constantly picked over his own abilities.

What had he actually given his daughter, apart from the security of always having someone there? Sebastian hadn't found the first couple of years with Sabine all that special or – to be honest – all that much fun. No, that wasn't true – they had been special. Dizzying. He had heard of many people who convinced themselves that nothing would change when they had children. They would carry on living their lives just as they had always done, with the minor difference that they were now parents. Sebastian hadn't been quite that naive. He knew he would have to change his whole life. Everything he was. And he had been willing to do that. So those first years *had* been special, but he hadn't got a great deal out of them. To put it crudely: Sabine gave him too little in those first years.

That's what he had thought at the time.

Now he would give anything to get them back.

Things had improved, he had to admit. The older she got, the better things were, and he felt as if their relationship was growing and becoming closer as she developed an ability to give something back to him. But what did that show, apart from the fact that he was an egotist? He had hardly dared to think about what things would be like when she grew up.

When she started making demands.

When she became more of a person than a child. When he no longer knew best. When she could see through him. He loved her more than anything in the world. But had she known that? Had he been able to show her that? He wasn't sure.

He had loved Lily, too. He had told her.

Sometimes.

Not nearly often enough.

He didn't feel comfortable saying those words. Not when he was supposed to mean them, anyway. He assumed she knew that he loved her. That he showed it in other ways. He had never been unfaithful during the time he was with her. Could you show love through the things you didn't do? Was he capable of showing it at all?

177

And now he was standing here, perhaps with a grown-up son or daughter somewhere. Anna Eriksson's letter had knocked him sideways, and since then he had been operating on autopilot. He had immediately decided that he had to find her. He had to find his child. But did he, if he really thought about it? Was he really going to track down a person who was almost thirty years old, and who had lived their whole life without him? What would he say if he did? Anna might have lied, told the child someone else was the father. She might have said he was dead. He might just end up causing problems.

For everyone.

But mainly for himself.

Sebastian didn't really give a damn whether it was right or wrong to go trampling into the life of an adult and turn it upside down, but what would he get out of it? Did he think there was a new Sabine waiting for him somewhere? There wasn't, of course. No one was going to slip a hand wearing a butterfly ring into his; no one was going to fall asleep on his shoulder, drowsy and warm with sunshine. Nobody was going to cuddle up to him in bed in the mornings, snuffling almost inaudibly down his ear. The overwhelming risk was that he would be sent packing. Or, at best, clumsily embraced by a complete stranger who could never be anything more than an acquaintance. Possibly a friend, in the very best-case scenario. He certainly didn't have too many of those. What if he wasn't allowed into his child's life at all? Would he be able to cope with that? If he was going to embark on yet another selfish course of action, then at least he ought to be sure that he would be the one who was going to benefit the most. And he was no longer sure of that at all. Perhaps he should just forget the whole thing. Sell the house, leave the investigation and Västerås, go back to Stockholm.

His thoughts were interrupted by Vanja closing the door of the office down the corridor a little too loudly. She marched towards him with rapid, angry steps.

'I've got an address,' she said as she passed Sebastian without slowing down.

He followed her.

'What does it take before they actually report something to the police in this place?' Vanja asked as she pushed open the doors and strode outside. Sebastian assumed this was a rhetorical question and didn't answer. There was no need for him to do so, Vanja carried straight on.

'Seriously, how far are they prepared to go to protect the school's reputation? Ten days before he dies Roger gets an employee sacked, and Groth doesn't even mention it. If some girl is gang raped in the toilets, would he try to keep that quiet as well?'

Once again Sebastian assumed that Vanja wasn't really expecting a reply, but at least he could show he was listening. Besides which, he found the question quite interesting.

'If he thought he had more to gain than to lose, then yes, absolutely. He's not difficult to understand. His priorities are always the school and the reputation of the school. On some level it's understandable: it's their main selling point.'

'So when we're told there's no bullying here, that's bullshit as well, is it?'

'Of course it is. Establishing hierarchies is part of human nature. As soon as we become part of a group, we have to know where we stand, and we do whatever is necessary to maintain our place or to climb higher. Sometimes it's obvious, sometimes not. Sometimes it's deliberate, sometimes not.'

They had reached the car. Vanja stopped by the driver's door and turned to face Sebastian, her expression sceptical.

'I've worked as part of this team for several years. We don't do anything like that.'

'That's because your hierarchy is static, and because Billy, who is down at the bottom, has no ambition to climb higher.'

Vanja looked amused and quizzical.

'Billy's down at the bottom?'

Sebastian nodded. It had taken him less than three seconds to work out that Billy was at the bottom of the pile.

'And where am I, according to your analysis?'

'Immediately below Torkel. Ursula allows you to occupy that position because you don't work on the same things. She knows she's the best in her field, so you're not really competing with each other. If that had been the case, she would have bumped you down the ranking order.'

'Or I might have done it to her.'

Sebastian smiled at her as if she were a little girl who had unwittingly said something highly amusing.

'I think everybody should believe what they want to believe.'

He opened the passenger door and got in. Vanja stood there for a moment, trying to shake off a growing feeling of irritation. She wasn't going to give him the satisfaction of annoying her. She cursed herself. *Don't start a conversation.* As long as he kept his mouth shut, he couldn't infuriate her. Two deep breaths, then she opened the door and got in. She glanced briefly at Sebastian. Against her better judgement, she spoke to him again. She wasn't going to give him the pleasure of having the last word, anyway.

'You don't know us. You're just talking rubbish.'

'Am I? Torkel brought me in. Billy wasn't bothered. You and Ursula don't really know where you are with me, you just know I'm bloody good, and you've both very clearly distanced yourselves from me.'

'And that's because we feel threatened, is it?'

'Why else would it be?'

'Because you're a bastard.'

Vanja started the car. *Ha! Victory!* She had the last word. And now they were going to drive to Axel Johansson's house in complete silence, if it was up to her.

It wasn't.

'It's important to you, isn't it?'

For fuck's sake, couldn't he just keep quiet? Vanja sighed.

'What is?'

'Having the last word.'

Vanja gritted her teeth and kept her eyes fixed on the road

ahead. At least she wouldn't have to see that smug smile on his lips as he leaned back in his seat and closed his eyes.

Vanja kept her finger on the doorbell. The monotonous ringing penetrated out through the door and into the echoing stairwell where she and Sebastian were standing. But that was the only sound from inside the apartment. Vanja had pushed open the letter box and listened before she rang the bell the first time.

Not a movement.

Not a sound.

So now Vanja had parked her finger on the button. Sebastian wondered whether he ought to point out that if Axel Johansson was in the apartment, he would probably have opened the door at some point during her first eight onslaughts on the bell. Even if he'd been fast asleep he would have come to the door by now. For fuck's sake, even if he'd been lying in state in there he would have been on his feet by now.

'What do you think you're doing?'

Vanja took her finger off the bell and turned around. A little grey old lady was peering out from behind a half-open door. That really was Sebastian's first impression: she was grey. It wasn't just the thin, straight hair. The woman was wearing a grey knitted cardigan, grey velour trousers and thick socks. Thick grey socks. In the middle of the wrinkled face perched a pair of glasses with colourless frames, which added to the impression of greyness and transparency. She was peering at the intruders with a challenging look in her eyes. Which were grey, of course, thought Sebastian.

Vanja introduced herself and Sebastian and explained that they were looking for Axel Johansson: did she have any idea where he might be? Instead of a 'yes' or a 'no', the response was an unexpected question.

'What's he done?'

The little grey neighbour received the standard reply.

'We'd like a chat with him.'

'Just routine,' Sebastian chipped in. Mostly for fun. Nobody said

181

'just routine' in real life, but somehow it fitted the situation. It was as if the little grey lady was expecting it. Vanja gave him a look that made it clear she was not amused. Not that he thought she would be. Vanja turned back to the neighbour, glancing quickly at the name above the letter box.

'Fru Holmin, do you have any idea where he is?' No, Fru Holmin did not have any idea where he was. She knew he wasn't at home. He hadn't been there for more than two days now. She knew that. Not that she kept an eye on what was happening in the apartment block, on all the comings and goings, but you couldn't help noticing some things, after all. Like the fact that Axel Johansson had got the sack a while ago. Or that his girlfriend, who was far too young, had moved out a few days before that. It had been high time. Fru Holmin couldn't understand what she had ever seen in Axel. Not that he was unpleasant or anything, but he was very odd. Kept himself to himself. Unsociable. Hardly even bothered to say 'hello' if you met him on the stairs. The girl, on the other hand, was very chatty. Very pleasant. Everybody in the block thought so. Not that she had been spying on people, but it was easy to hear things in this building, and she was a light sleeper, which was why she knew so much. No other reason.

'Was there a lot of coming and going at Axel's apartment?'

'A fair amount, yes. Lots of young people – the phone and the doorbell were always going. What's he done?'

Vanja shook her head and repeated her earlier answer.

'We'd just like a chat with him.'

Vanja smiled, passed over her card and asked the neighbour to call if she heard Johansson come back. The little grey lady peered at the card bearing the Riksmord logo, and it seemed to help her put two and two together.

'Has this got something to do with that boy who was killed?' There was a spark in the grey eyes as she looked from Vanja to Sebastian for confirmation. 'He used to work at the school the boy went to, but perhaps you knew that already?' Vanja was digging for something in her inside pocket.

182

'Do you know if he's been here?' Vanja took out a picture of Roger. It was from the last batch of school photos, and was the one all the police officers involved were using. She handed it over to the grey lady, who glanced quickly at the picture then shook her head.

'I don't know – they all look the same to me, with their baseball caps and hoods and their great big jackets. So I don't know.'

They thanked her for her help and reminded her to get in touch if Axel turned up.

On the way downstairs Vanja took out her mobile and rang Torkel. She briefly explained the situation and suggested they put out a call for Axel Johansson. Torkel promised to arrange it immediately. As they reached the door leading to the street they almost crashed into a man on his way in. A familiar face: Haraldsson. Vanja's expression darkened noticeably.

'What are you doing here?'

Haraldsson explained that they were carrying out door-to-door enquiries in the area. Roger Eriksson had been picked up by a CCTV camera on Gustavsborgsgatan, but not on any of the others, which he should have been if he had carried on up the main road. Therefore, he must have turned off somewhere, and this block was in the possible search area. They were trying to find someone who had seen him on that Friday evening.

Knocking on doors. Vanja had the feeling that Haraldsson had finally ended up in the right place. Axel Johansson's apartment was in the search area. The straw at which they were clutching had become a fraction thicker.

The group sitting around the pale birch-wood table in the conference room looked exhausted. As they reviewed their progress, it was painfully clear that they hadn't got very far. The fact that the email had been sent from Palmlövska High didn't exactly reduce the number of suspects. Being able to prove that Lisa was lying had simply confirmed suspicions Vanja had harboured, but it got them nowhere. The most important thing that had emerged from the interview with Lisa was that Roger probably hid things from those around him. They were all convinced there was more to discover about his life outside school. And the suggestion that he might have been having a relationship with someone who nobody knew about was particularly interesting. Someone he used to see when everybody thought he was with Lisa. They decided some of the team would focus on getting to know Roger better. Who was he really?

'Have we looked at his computer?' Billy wondered.

'He didn't have one.'

Billy looked at Vanja as if he had misheard.

'He didn't have a computer?'

'Not according to the list the local cops made when they went to his house.'

'But he was sixteen. Could it have been stolen? Like his watch?'

'He didn't have a laptop with him on the CCTV footage,' Torkel interjected. Billy shook his head as he tried to imagine the suffering the poor boy must have endured. Imagine not being online. Isolated. Alone.

'He could still have been active on the internet, of course,' Torkel went on. 'On Lisa's computer, or at a youth centre or internet café. See if you can find him anywhere.' Billy nodded.

'And then there's Axel Johansson.' Torkel looked around the table, and Billy picked up the ball.

'We got nothing from today's door-to-door enquiries. Nobody could remember seeing Roger in the area on Friday evening.'

'That doesn't mean he wasn't there,' Vanja said quickly.

'It doesn't mean he *was* there, either,' Billy countered.

'What have we got on him, apart from the fact that he lives in an area where Roger may or may not have been on the Friday when he disappeared?' said Sebastian.

'Roger got him sacked from his job at the school,' said Vanja, 'and that's the closest thing we've got to a motive so far.'

'He's been gone for two days,' said Billy. Sebastian felt a stab of impatience. He had been with Vanja all day. Heard exactly the same things as her. He was well aware that there was something which could be interpreted as a motive, and that Axel Johansson hadn't been home for a couple of days.

'Apart from that, I meant.'

There was a brief silence around the table. Billy leafed through his papers, found what he was looking for.

'Axel Malte Johansson. Aged forty-two. Single. Born in Örebro. Has moved around a lot within Sweden. During the past twelve years he's lived in Umeå, Sollefteå, Gävle, Helsingborg and Västerås. Came here two years ago. Got the job at Palmlövska. Several payment default notices. No court judgments against him, but he has featured in several investigations into cheque fraud and forgery. All dropped due to lack of evidence.'

Vanja still felt slightly better. At least he was mentioned in criminal records. That definitely made Axel Johansson more interesting to the investigation. One of the incontrovertible truths about murder enquiries was that it was rarely those who had never committed any kind of offence who committed murder or manslaughter. Usually such extreme crimes were merely the pinnacle of an escalating scale of criminality or violence. The road to perdition was generally paved with other offences, and there was almost always some kind of relationship between the murderer and the victim.

Almost always.

Vanja wondered whether she should mention the thought that had occurred to her earlier: that perhaps the murderer hadn't known Roger at all. That they were just wasting their time putting all this effort into building up a detailed picture of the boy. Perhaps they should be tackling this from a completely different angle. But she kept quiet. She had been involved in solving fourteen murders so far. In every case the perpetrator and the victim had known each other, even if it had been no more than a fleeting acquaintance. It was highly unlikely that a complete stranger had murdered Roger. If this was the case, then the four of them sitting around the table were well aware that this particular murder would almost certainly remain unsolved. The chances of the police tracking down an unknown murderer with no link to his victim were very small, particularly in view of the minimal forensic evidence in this case. The breakthrough in DNA technology in the 1990s was the main reason such cases could be cleared up, but when a body had been lying in water, there were usually no traces of DNA from the perpetrator. The task they faced was not an easy one.

'Are we sure that Axel Johansson is keeping out of the way? I mean, could he have gone away for a few days, visiting an elderly parent or something?' Sebastian's reasonable contribution didn't exactly help.

Billy glanced at his papers to check.

'Both his parents are dead.'

'Okay, but perhaps he's gone to visit somebody who's still alive?'

'Possibly,' Torkel agreed. 'We don't know where he is.'

'Can't Ursula go and poke around a bit in his apartment?' Sebastian suppressed a yawn. The air quality in the room had deteriorated quickly. Obviously the air-conditioning system wasn't as new as everything else.

'We haven't got enough for a search warrant. Maybe if we'd been able to link Roger to the area, but not as things stand.'

A resigned silence pervaded the room.

Billy lifted the gloomy atmosphere. One of his great strengths was his constant ability to look forward, even when the doubts began to pile up.

'I've been in touch with SKL. They'll let us have the existing texts on Roger's phone, and they're retrieving those that have been deleted. Plus the lists of calls are on the way from the operator. I'm expecting those this evening.' Billy broke off as Vanja's phone rang. She looked at the display, apologised and left the room. Torkel and Billy watched her go. They couldn't remember Vanja ever prioritising a private call over the job. It must have been important.

The call from her father had stirred up a lot of feelings, and Vanja left the station to get her head straight. She generally managed to keep her work and her private life far apart, two parallel lines that seldom crossed. But things had become much more difficult over the past six months. Her colleagues hadn't noticed anything – she was too disciplined for that – but it had taken its toll.

The speculation.

The anxiety.

In the centre of her whirling thoughts was the man she loved more than anything in the world: her father, Valdemar. If you push anxiety aside, it always comes back. The more firmly you drive it away, the stronger it is on its return. Lately it had been getting worse. Vanja had started to wake earlier and earlier each morning, and found it impossible to get back to sleep.

She headed off to the left towards the little park by the castle. There was a gentle breeze blowing off Lake Mälaren, making the fresh green shoots and the newly unfurled leaves rustle and sway. The smell of spring was in the air. Vanja cut across the soft ground without any real idea of where she was going.

The picture came back to her. The hospital. Eight months ago, when they got the news. Her mother had wept. The doctor standing beside her father, looking professional. It had made Vanja think of all the times she had adopted that role: calm and focused in the face of the victims and the grieving. This time the roles were reversed. She had stood there and simply allowed the emotions to wash over her. It was a simple enough diagnosis to understand.

Cell changes in the lungs.

Lung cancer.

Vanja had sunk down on the chair next to her father, her lips trembling, her voice finding it hard to strike its normal balanced tone. From his hospital bed her father tried to appear calm, as always. He was the only member of the family who was still capable of playing his normal role.

Vanja had gone back to work that day eight months ago with the doctor's assurances about the possibilities offered by modern science ringing in her ears. *Chemotherapy and radiotherapy. There was a strong chance that her father would make a full recovery. Beat the cancer.* She had sat down opposite Billy and listened to his review of the previous day's gig by some band she'd never even heard of; she would probably switch the radio off if they came on. For a second he had looked at her and stopped. As if he could see that something had happened. His kind eyes met hers steadily, just for a second. Then she had heard herself saying something sarcastic about his taste in music, pointing out that he would be thirty-two next month and not twenty-two, in case he'd forgotten. They had exchanged banter for a little while, just as they always did. Vanja decided there and then that things would stay that way. It wasn't that she didn't trust him. Billy wasn't just her colleague: he was her best friend. But at that moment she needed him to be as normal as he could possibly be. It made everything slightly less painful. One part of her life might end, but another part would carry on. As usual. She needed to feel that.

That day her banter with Billy had had an extra energy.

She followed the river down to the shore. The afternoon sun sparkled on the water. A few daring boats were battling in the cold wind. She took out her phone, pushed away the idea that she ought to get back to her colleagues, and pressed her parents' number on speed dial. Her mother had taken Valdemar's illness very badly. Vanja had wanted to sob, scream and feel like a little girl at the thought that she might lose Valdemar. But that role was already taken. Normally that was the way she wanted things. The dynamic had been worked out over the years: the mother was sensitive, the daughter more controlled, like her father. This last year was the first time Vanja had realised there were times when she actually wished they could swap roles, if only for a second. She had suddenly felt as if she was teetering on the edge of an abyss, with no idea how deep it might be. And the person who had always been there making sure she didn't fall was suddenly leaving her.

For ever.

But maybe not.

Medical science had tossed hope into the equation. He was probably going to be all right. Vanja smiled to herself. Gazed out across the sparkling water and allowed the feeling of happiness to sweep over her.

'Hi, Mum.'

'Have you heard?' Too eager even to say hello.

'Yes, he just rang me. It's fantastic.'

'I can't believe it's true. He's coming home!' Vanja could hear in her mother's voice that she was only just holding back the tears. Tears of joy. It had been a long time.

'Give him a hug from me. A great big hug, and tell him I'll come over as soon as I can.'

'When?'

'This weekend at the latest, I hope.'

They decided to have dinner the following week, all three of them. It was difficult to get her mother to hang up. Vanja, who usually hated protracted goodbyes, loved it. Both she and her mother babbled on, the anxiety they had carried spilling out in a plethora of words. As if they both needed to confirm that everything was back to normal again.

Her mobile beeped. A text message.

'I love you, Vanja.'

'And I love you. But I have to go.'

'Do you?'

'You know I do, Mum, but I'll see you soon.'

Vanja ended the call and opened the incoming message. From Torkel. Her other world was demanding her attention.

where have you gone? ursula on her way in.

A quick reply.

on my way.

She wondered about a smiley, but decided against it.

189

Beatrice Strand had caught the bus home as usual. She got off one stop earlier. She needed some air. At school it was impossible. And at home. Roger's death had got into everything. It was as if a dam had burst, taking everyone with it. Her student, in whom she had invested so much. Johan's friend. The person he had spent so much time with. That kind of thing just didn't happen.

Friends didn't die.

Students weren't found murdered in the forest.

It usually took her eight minutes from leaving the bus stop to stepping onto the gravel path leading up to the pale yellow two-storey house. Today it took her thirty-five. Not that Ulf would notice. It was a long time since he cared what time she got home.

The house was silent when she walked in.

'Hello?'

No response.

'Johan?'

'We're up here,' came the reply.

But that was all. No 'I'll come down' or 'How are you?' Just silence.

We're up here.

We.

Ulf and Johan.

Always. More and more infrequently all three of them.

Who was she trying to fool?

Never all three of them.

'I'm making some tea,' she shouted, but once again there was no response.

Beatrice put the kettle on, then stood there gazing at the little red light, lost in thought. For the first few days she had tried so hard to get them to spend time together as a family, to talk, support each other. After all, that was what families did at difficult

190

times. Supported each other. But Johan didn't want that. He with-drew from her. In this family he did everything with his father, and that included grieving. Leaving her on the outside. But she had no intention of giving up. She took out the big teacups with the French fruit pattern and placed them on a tray with honey and sugar cubes. Looked out of the window at the quiet residential street. Soon the shades of pale pink that she loved would greet her. Their cherry tree had just come into bud. It was early this year. The family had planted it together a long time ago. It felt like an eternity. Johan, only five years old, had insisted on helping to dig the hole, and they had giggled together and let him. She remem-bered what she had said.

A proper family has fruit trees.

A proper family. The kettle switched itself off and she poured the steaming water into the cups. Three teabags. Then she went upstairs. To what was left of her proper family.

Johan was sitting at the computer playing some violent game which involved shooting as many people as possible. She had learned the name: 'First Person Shooter'. Ulf was sitting com-fortably on the edge of his son's bed, watching the game. When she opened the door and walked in, at least Ulf looked up at her. Which was something.

'Are you two hungry?'

'No, we've just eaten.'

Beatrice put down the tray on the cupboard that housed her son's manga books.

'Have the police been here today?'

'Yes.'

Silence once more.

Beatrice moved over to her son and gently placed her hand on his shoulder. Let it lie there, feeling the warm skin beneath his T-shirt. For a second she hoped he wouldn't mind.

'Mum . . .' A shrug which clearly indicated *get off!*

Beatrice reluctantly removed her hand, but she wasn't about to give up. Not yet. She sat on the bed a short distance from Ulf.

'We have to talk about this. There's nothing to be gained by just shutting everything in,' she began.

'I talk to Dad,' came from the direction of the desk. Johan didn't even turn around.

'Well, I need to talk as well,' she said, her voice breaking slightly. It wasn't just that she needed to talk. She needed her family. Above all, her son. She had hoped that Johan would come back to her when Ulf had come back.

Erase and rewind.

Forgive, forget, move on.

She had hoped that everything would get back to normal. Like before. Before it all happened. When she was someone Johan would come to with his problems in the evenings, when they had shared the trials and joys of life in long, close conversations and she was the person she needed to be: a mother, a woman, a part of something. But now those times seemed as distant as that day long ago when a family proudly planted its cherry tree. Ulf turned to her.

'Later. Everything went well with the police. Johan told them what he knew.'

'Good.'

'Listen, we're going off soon, Johan and I. Camping somewhere. Get away from it all.'

Away from her, Beatrice couldn't help thinking, but she merely nodded.

'Good idea.'

Silence again. What else was there to say?

Johan's computer game carried on.

Ursula walked into the room. She was smiling.

'Oh, please tell me that means you've got good news,' Torkel begged.

'I've got the autopsy report. It's full of surprises. Just like a Kinder egg!'

Vanja, Sebastian and Torkel sat up in their seats. Ursula opened the folder she was carrying and started pinning up a handful of photographs that showed Roger's torso and arms from every possible angle and from various distances.

'Twenty-two knife wounds to the back, torso, arms and legs. Those are the ones we can count. In addition there are the wounds sustained when the heart was removed.' She pointed to one picture, which showed a deep, asymmetrical opening in the back between the shoulderblades.

Sebastian looked away. He had always found stab wounds difficult. There was something about the grotesque combination of pale, smooth skin and the deep lacerations exposing what the skin was meant to conceal.

'No defensive wounds on the palms of the hands or the forearms,' Ursula went on. 'And do you know why?' She didn't wait for a reply. 'Because all the stab wounds were inflicted post mortem.'

Torkel looked up from his notepad and took off his glasses.

Ursula looked at them all with a grave expression, as if to emphasise her discovery.

'So what did he die of, then?'

Once again Ursula pointed at the close-up of the open wound in Roger's back. Approximately eight centimetres at the widest point. Pieces of broken ribs were visible here and there. It had taken a considerable amount of strength to inflict these injuries. Strength and determination.

'Most of the heart is missing, but it has nothing to do with any kind of ritual or weird sacrifice. Someone has dug out a bullet. That's all.'

Ursula put up another picture. No one around the table said a word.

'He was shot in the back. The bullet is missing, but we found traces of it on one of the ribs.' Ursula pointed to the extreme enlargement of Roger's wound that she had just pinned up. On one of the ribs it was just possible to see a small half-moon-shaped mark left by a bullet.

'We're talking about a relatively fine-calibre weapon. A twenty-two, judging by the mark.'

The information galvanised everyone. They immediately started talking about the guns they knew that were the same calibre. Torkel started to extract a list from the database. Sebastian had nothing to contribute, so he got up and went over to the wall. He forced himself to take a closer look at the photographs. Behind him the discussion died out. The printer whirred into life and started to spit out Torkel's list. Torkel looked over at his former colleague.

'Found anything?'

Sebastian continued to stare at the gaping wound in Roger's back.

'I don't think Roger was meant to die.'

'If you shoot someone then stab him twenty-two times, I think you probably have to bear in mind that it's a possibility,' Vanja said drily.

'Okay, bad choice of words. I don't think someone had planned to kill Roger Eriksson.'

'Because?'

'Digging out that bullet wasn't an easy task. It would have been gory. It took time. It increased the risk of being caught in the act. But the murderer had to do it. Because he knew it would identify him.'

Vanja immediately understood what he meant. For a moment she cursed herself – why hadn't she thought of that? She should have. She spoke up, keen not to let Sebastian take all the credit.

'And if he had planned the murder, he would have used a different gun. One that couldn't be traced.'

Sebastian nodded approvingly. She was quick.

'So what happened?' Torkel wondered out loud. 'Roger was ambling along in a fairly central area in Västerås, met someone with a twenty-two, walked past, got shot in the back. The person who shot him realised that, "Oh dear, the bullet could give me away", and decided to get it back, put the body in his car and dumped it in Listakärr.' Torkel looked at the others. 'Does that sound likely to you?'

'We don't know what happened.' Sebastian looked at his boss with a hint of weary irritation. He had merely delivered a small piece of the puzzle, not completed the whole thing.

'We don't even know where he died. I'm only saying it probably wasn't planned.'

'So there's the possibility that we're talking about manslaughter rather than murder, but it doesn't get us any closer to who killed the boy, does it?'

Silence. Sebastian knew there was no point in responding when Torkel got grumpy like this. Evidently the others felt the same. Torkel turned to Ursula.

'Those marks on the rib – will it be possible to match them with a bullet if we do find the gun?'

'No. Unfortunately.'

Torkel slumped in his chair and spread his arms wide.

'So we have a new cause of death, but fuck-all else.'

'Not quite.' Sebastian pointed to another of the photographs on the wall. 'We have the watch.'

'What about the watch?'

'It's expensive.'

He gently touched the shiny pictures showing Roger's clothes.

'Acne jeans. Quiksilver jacket. Nike trainers. All designer labels.'

'He was a teenager.'

'Yes, but where did he get the money from? His mother doesn't seem to be very well off. And after all, he was Palmlövska High's little charity experiment.'

Lena Eriksson was sitting in her armchair in the living room, tapping the ash from her cigarette into an ashtray by her side. She had opened a fresh packet that morning, and another just an hour ago. This was the third cigarette from the second packet. Which meant it was the twenty-third of the day. Too many. Particularly as she had eaten next to nothing all day. She was feeling slightly dizzy as she cleared her throat and looked over at the police officers sitting on the sofa on the other side of the coffee table. New ones. Both of them. All three of them, if you counted the woman who was in Roger's room. The one Lena had met at the mortuary wasn't there. Nor were any of those who had come to see her earlier on. These officers were in plain clothes and came from something called Riksmord. They had asked where Roger got his money from.

'He had a grant to support his studies.'

She took another drag of her cigarette. The movement was so familiar, so much a part of her everyday life, almost a reflex action. What else had she done today, apart from sitting in the armchair smoking? Nothing. She couldn't summon up the energy. This morning she had woken up after about an hour's sleep and thought she might go out for a while. Get some fresh air. Do a bit of shopping. Perhaps tidy the apartment. Take the first small step towards getting back to some kind of normal life. Without Roger.

She had to go out to buy *Aftonbladet*, the evening paper, in any case. They were the ones who had offered the most money in the end. Fifteen thousand kronor for talking to a young woman for a couple of hours. Cash in hand. A photographer had been there for the first half-hour then he had left. The young woman whose name Lena had forgotten had placed a tape recorder on the table and asked about Roger – what he was like, his childhood, what he enjoyed doing, how she felt now he was gone. To her surprise, Lena hadn't cried during the interview. She had thought she would. It was the first time she had talked to anyone other than the police about Roger since he disappeared. Really talked, that is. Maarit, a work colleague, had phoned and awkwardly offered her condolences, sounding most uncomfortable, and Lena had quickly ended the call. Lena's boss had been in touch, but that was mainly to say that he understood if Lena couldn't come into work according to the roster, and that they would divide her shifts between the rest of the staff, but that it would be helpful if she could ring a day or so before she was coming back. The police who had been to see her had only wanted to know more about Roger's disappearance – had he run away from home before, did he have problems, had anyone threatened him? They didn't want to know anything about him as a person. As a son.

Anything about who he had been.

How much he had meant to her.

That was exactly what the journalist *had* wanted to know. They had looked at photo albums, and she had let Lena tell her about Roger at her own pace, just asking the odd question for clarification here and there. When Lena had finished telling her everything she thought she could say and wanted to say about her son, the woman started to ask more specific questions. Was Roger the kind of person his friends turned to for help? Was he involved in any voluntary work? Did he help train a youth team, did he mentor a younger child? Anything along those lines? Lena had told the truth and answered no to every question. The only friends he had brought home were Johan Strand and a boy from the new school. Once. Erik something. Lena had thought she detected a hint of disappointment on the journalist's face. Could Lena tell her a little more about the bullying, in that case? How she felt when she heard that her son's former tormentor was being held on suspicion of murder? Even if that was old news by now, the journalist – whose name was Katarina – thought they could give it another whirl. With a picture of two cuddly toys sitting on Roger's bed, it might just work.

So Lena had talked. About the bullying. The violence. The move to a new school. But mostly she had talked about how convinced she was that Leo Lundin had murdered her son, and that she would never forgive him. Katarina had switched off the tape recorder, asked if she could borrow a few pictures from the family albums, handed over the money and left. That had been yesterday. Lena had put the cash in her pocket. So much money. She had wondered whether to go out for a meal. She could really do with getting out of the apartment. And she would need to eat. But she stayed where she was. In the armchair. With her cigarettes, and the money in her pocket. She could feel it against her leg every time she changed position. Every time that little voice woke up.

197

This money didn't kill him, anyway.

In the end she had got up and put the bundle of notes in a drawer. She didn't go out. She didn't eat. She sat in the armchair and smoked. Just as she had done all day today as well. And now there were two different police officers here, wanting to talk about money.

'The child benefit and the study allowance were enough before he moved to that bloody posh school. Once he got there he had to have new stuff all the time.' Vanja gave a start of surprise. She had assumed Lena would have nothing but good things to say about Palmlövska High, which took her son away from his tormentors and offered him a place at what Vanja was convinced was a good and attractive school, regardless of her opinion of the principal.

'Weren't you pleased when he changed schools?'

Lena wouldn't meet her gaze. She looked over at the big window. On the window sill stood a lamp with a blue shade, and two shrivelled dieffenbachia plants. When had she last watered them? A long time ago. The peace lilies had fared better, but they too were wilting. In the fading sunlight from the window she could see that the apartment could, in fact, be classed as smoke filled.

'She took him away from me,' she said as she stubbed out her cigarette, got up from the armchair, walked over to the balcony door and opened it.

'Who took him away from you?'

'Beatrice. Everyone in that stuck-up place.'

'In what way did they take Roger away from you?'

Lena didn't answer straightaway. She closed her eyes and breathed in the oxygen-rich air. Sebastian and Vanja felt a welcome gust of cold, fresh air swirl around their feet. In the silence they could all hear Ursula going through the boy's room. She had insisted on coming with them, partly to avoid being left alone with a grumpy Torkel – with whom she was still furious – and partly because the room had been searched only by the local police. Ursula's faith in the local police was almost non-existent. They'd missed the report of the boy's disappearance for two days, for God's sake. If she wanted to be sure it had been done properly, she would do it herself. And that was what she was doing now.

Lena could hear the wardrobe being opened, drawers being pulled out, pictures and posters taken down from the walls, as she stood there gazing blankly at a tree by the car park. It was the only bit of greenery visible from the window. The rest of the view was taken up by the grey exterior of the block next door.

In what way did they take Roger away from her? Could she even explain it?

'It had to be the Maldives in the Christmas holidays and the Alps in February and the Riviera in summer. He didn't want to be at home. The apartment wasn't good enough any more. Nothing we did or had was good enough any more. I didn't have a chance.'

'But Roger was happier at Palmlövksa, wasn't he?'

Oh yes, of course he was. He wasn't being bullied any longer. Or beaten up. But in her darkest hours Lena had thought that might almost have been preferable. At least he had been at home back then. When he wasn't training or at Johan's, he had been at home. With her. He had needed her just as much as she had needed him. Now the unpalatable truth was that no one needed her.

This last year she hadn't been alone.

She had been abandoned.

That was worse.

Lena became aware of the silence in the room. They were waiting for an answer.

'I suppose so.' Lena nodded to herself. 'I suppose he was happier there.'

'Do you have a job?' Vanja asked when she realised she wasn't going to get a more comprehensive answer about Roger's new school.

'Part time. At Lidl. Why?'

'I just wondered if he perhaps stole money. Without your knowing about it.'

'He might have done, if there had been any money to steal.'

'Did he ever talk about it? Did he ever say it was important for him to have money? Did he seem desperate? Could he have borrowed money from someone?'

Lena pushed the balcony door to, without shutting it. She returned to the armchair. Resisted the urge to light yet another cigarette. She felt so tired now. Her head was spinning. Couldn't they just leave her in peace?

'I don't know. Why is it so important to know where he got money from?'

'If he borrowed or stole it from the wrong person, it could provide a motive.'

Lena shrugged her shoulders. She didn't know where Roger had got his money from. Was she supposed to have known that?

'Did he ever mention Axel Johansson?' Vanja said, trying a new tack. Nobody could accuse Roger's mother of being unduly cooperative. They had to drag every bloody answer out of her.

'No, who's he?'

'The caretaker at Palmlövska. Former caretaker.'

Lena shook her head.

'When you spoke to my colleagues, you said . . .' Vanja flicked back a couple of pages in her notebook and read, '. . . that Roger didn't feel threatened, and hadn't quarrelled with anyone. Is that still the case?'

Lena nodded.

'If he had been threatened or got into a scrap with anyone, would you have known about it?'

It was the man who asked the question. He hadn't said anything up to now. He had introduced himself when they arrived, then sat in silence – no, that was wrong, he hadn't even done that. The woman had introduced both of them when she showed her ID. The man hadn't shown his. *Sebastian*, Lena remembered. Sebastian and Vanja. Lena looked into Sebastian's calm blue eyes and realised that he already knew the answer. He could see right through her.

He knew this wasn't just about the rented three-room apartment in a dull neighbourhood, that the DVD should have been a Blu-ray and that you had to get a new mobile every six months. He knew she hadn't been good enough – the way she looked, her weight problem, her badly paid job. He knew Roger had been ashamed of her. That he had no longer wanted her to be a part of his life, that he had thrown her out. What this man didn't know was that she had found an opening. A way back to Roger. Back to one another.

But then he died, said the little voice. *So much for your way back*.

With trembling hands Lena lit up number twenty-four before she gave the answer Sebastian already knew.

'Probably not.'

Lena fell silent and shook her head, as if she had just realised what a terrible relationship she had had with her son. Her gaze was lost somewhere in the distance.

The conversation was interrupted as Ursula emerged from Roger's room with her two bags, the camera around her neck.

'I'm done. See you back at the station.' She turned to Lena. 'Once again, my condolences on your loss.'

Lena nodded absently. Ursula looked meaningfully at Vanja, ignored Sebastian and left the apartment. Vanja waited until they heard the outside door close.

'Would it be possible for us to speak to Roger's father?' Vanja again. Fresh attempt. New tack. See if it was possible to get more than three words in a row out of Roger's mother at any point about anything.

'There is no father.'

'Wow, it's two thousand years since that last occurred!'

Lena gazed steadily at Vanja through the smoke.

'Are you judging me? You'd fit in perfectly at Roger's new school.'

'Nobody's judging you, but there has to be a father somewhere,' Sebastian said bluntly. Was it Vanja's imagination, or was there a different tone in his voice?

Interest?

Involvement?

Lena tapped the ash off her cigarette and shrugged.

'I have no idea where he is. We were never together. It was a one-night stand. He doesn't even know Roger exists.'

Sebastian leaned forward. Definitely more interested now. He met Lena's eyes with an open expression on his face.

'So how did you deal with that? I mean, surely Roger must have asked about his father at some point?'

'When he was little.'

'And what did you say?'

'I said he was dead.'

Sebastian nodded to himself. Was that what Anna Eriksson had said to her son or daughter? That Daddy was dead? In which case, what would happen if Daddy suddenly turned up? After thirty years? Disbelief, of course. It might require some proof that he really was the person he claimed to be. Presumably the man or woman would be angry with the mother, or possibly disappointed in her. She had lied. Robbed her child of its father. Perhaps Sebastian's appearance would wreck their relationship. Cause more harm than good. However he looked at things, he came to the conclusion that it would be best simply to carry on living as if he had never come across those letters. Never found out.

'Why did you say he was dead? If Roger had known the truth he could have gone looking for him.'

'I thought of that, but it felt better saying that he was dead than that he didn't want Roger. For the boy's self-esteem, I mean.'

'But you can't know that! You don't know what he wanted! He never got the chance!' Vanja stole a sideways glance at Sebastian. He was getting caught up in this. His voice had grown both louder and higher. He had shifted to the edge of the sofa and looked as if he was about to get to his feet at any second.

'What if he'd have wanted Roger! If he'd only known!'

Lena seemed fairly unmoved by Sebastian's outburst. She stubbed out her cigarette and expelled the last of the smoke from her lungs.

'He was already married. He had other kids. Kids of his own.'

'What was his name?'

'Roger's father?'

'Yes.'

'Jerry.'

'If Jerry had come looking for Roger when he was older, how do you think Roger would have reacted?'

Vanja leaned forward. What on earth was Sebastian doing? This was getting them nowhere.

'How could he have done that? He didn't even know the boy existed.'

'But if he had?'

Vanja gently laid her hand on Sebastian's arm to attract his attention.

'This is a hypothetical discussion that doesn't really belong here, wouldn't you say?'

Sebastian pulled himself up short. He could feel Vanja looking at him quizzically from the side.

'True ... I ... ' For the first time since he couldn't remember when, Sebastian didn't know what to say, so he simply repeated, 'That's true.'

Silence. They stood up, decided they'd finished. Sebastian headed for the hallway and Vanja followed him. Lena showed no sign of either getting up or accompanying them out. Just as they reached the door leading into the hallway, she spoke.

'Roger's watch.'

Sebastian and Vanja both turned back to face Lena. Vanja couldn't help feeling that there was something not quite right about the woman in the shabby armchair. Something she couldn't quite put her finger on.

'What about it?'

'The journalist I spoke to said Lundin stole a watch from Roger before he murdered him. A valuable watch. I presume it belongs to me now?'

Vanja took a step back into the room. She was surprised that

Lena didn't know; Torkel was usually very scrupulous about informing the relatives.

'All the indications at the moment are that Leonard Lundin had nothing to do with the murder of your son.' Lena received this information with the same level of reaction as if Vanja had just told her what she'd had for lunch.

'Okay, but the watch still belongs to me, doesn't it?'

'I presume so.'

'I'd like to have it.'

Sebastian and Vanja were on their way back to the station to finish off the day. Vanja was driving fast. Too fast. She had a clump of irritation somewhere around her midriff. Lena had provoked her. Vanja rarely allowed herself to be provoked. It was one of her strengths. The ability to remain cool, keep her distance. But Lena had got under her skin.

Sebastian had his mobile clamped to his ear. Vanja listened to his side of the conversation. He was talking to Lisa. After a final question about how things were at home and what was evidently a very short answer, Sebastian ended the call and slipped the phone into his pocket.

'Lisa was paying Roger to pretend to be her boyfriend.'

'So I gathered.'

'Not a huge amount of money, not enough to cover the things he bought, but there could be something there. He was enterprising.'

'Or greedy. Thinking about money and nothing else seems to run in the family. I mean, her son has been murdered, and all she can think about is cashing in.'

'Making the best of the situation you've ended up in is a way of dealing with the pain.'

'It's a sick way.'

'Maybe it's all she has.'

Typical psychologist. So understanding. All reactions are natural. Everything can be explained. But Vanja had no intention of letting

204

Sebastian get off so easily. She was furious, and had no qualms about taking it out on him.

'Come on, seriously. Her eyes were red from all that bloody smoke. I'd put money on the fact that she hasn't even cried, not once. I've seen people in shock, but that's not what this is. She's just at rock bottom.'

'I got the impression she has no contact with the feelings we're expecting. Grief. Despair. Maybe not even empathy.'

'So why not?'

'How the fuck should I know? I've only spent forty-five minutes with the woman. I suppose she's shut them down.'

'You can't just "shut down" your feelings.'

'No?'

'No.'

'You've never heard of people who have been hurt so badly by someone that they choose never to grow attached to anyone again?'

'There's a difference. Her child has died. Why would you choose not to react to that?'

'So that you can manage to go on living.'

Vanja drove on in silence. There was something.

Something about Sebastian.

Something different.

First of all he had seized on the issue of Roger's father like a terrier, even though that particular topic had turned out to be of no interest to the investigation after just two questions, and now Vanja thought she could hear a new tone in his voice. More subdued. Less confrontational. Not so keen to be quick, witty or condescending. No, there was something else. Grief, perhaps.

'I don't buy it. It's just sick, not grieving for her son.'

'She is grieving, as best she can.'

'Like hell she is.'

'How the fuck do you know?' Vanja jumped at the sudden sharpness in Sebastian's voice. 'What the hell do you know about grief? Have you lost someone who means everything to you?'

'No.'

'So how do you know what a normal reaction is?'

'Well, I don't, but—'

'No, exactly,' Sebastian broke in. 'You have no bloody idea what you're talking about, so maybe it's best if you keep your mouth shut from now on.'

Vanja glanced sideways at Sebastian, surprised by his outburst, but he kept his eyes fixed on the road ahead. Vanja drove on in silence. *We know so little about each other*, she thought. *You're hiding something. I know how that feels. Better than you think.*

The open-plan office at the station was more or less in darkness. Here and there a computer screen or a forgotten desk lamp illuminated a small area of the room, otherwise it was dark, empty and silent. Torkel slowly made his way between the desks towards the staffroom. He hadn't expected Västerås police station to be humming with activity around the clock, but it still came as something of a surprise that large parts of the building were completely dead after five o'clock.

He reached the staffroom, which was fairly impersonal. Three round tables, eight chairs at each. A fridge freezer, three microwaves, a coffee machine, a sink, draining board and dishwasher along one wall. A plastic flower on a round purple mat in the middle of each table. Scratched lino on the floor, easy to clean. No curtains at the three windows. A single telephone on the window sill. Sebastian was sitting at the table furthest away from the door with a cardboard cup of coffee in front of him. He was reading *Aftonbladet*. Torkel had also flicked through it; they'd given Lena Eriksson four pages.

Well written.

Exposing her vulnerability.

According to the article, Lena still believed it was Leonard Lundin who had murdered her son. Torkel wondered how she had taken the news that they had released him today. He had tried calling her several times, but she had never picked up. Perhaps she didn't know yet.

Sebastian didn't look up from the paper, even though he must have heard Torkel's approach. Only when Torkel pulled out the chair opposite him and sat down did he glance up before resuming his reading. Torkel linked his hands on the table and leaned towards Sebastian.

'How did it go today?'

Sebastian turned a page.

'How did what go?'

'Everything. The job. You were out with Vanja for some time.'

'Yes.'

Torkel sighed. Obviously he wasn't going to get anything for nothing. He probably wasn't going to get anything at all.

'So how did it go?'

'Fine.'

Torkel watched Sebastian turn another page and reach the pink supplement. Sport. Torkel knew that Sebastian had no interest in any kind of sport, whether it involved active participation, being a spectator or reading about it. And yet he seemed to be examining the pages with great interest. As clear a sign as any. Torkel leaned back and watched Sebastian in silence for a few seconds before moving over to the coffee machine for a cappuccino.

'Do you fancy having dinner somewhere?'

Sebastian stiffened slightly. There it was. As expected. Not 'We must meet up one evening' or 'Let's have a beer some time'. Dinner.

Same shit. Different name.

'No, thanks.'

'Why not?'

'I have other plans.'

A lie. Just like his sudden interest in the sports supplement. Torkel knew it, but decided not to push things. He would only get more lies in response. He took his cup out of the machine, but instead of leaving the room, as Sebastian had expected, he came back to the table and sat down again. Sebastian gave him a brief, quizzical glance then turned his undivided attention to the newspaper once more.

'Tell me about your wife.'

He hadn't expected that. Sebastian looked at Torkel with genuine surprise as his former colleague raised the cup to his lips, completely relaxed, as if he had merely asked what time it was.

'Why?'

'Why not?'

Torkel put down the cup and wiped the corners of his mouth with the thumb and forefinger of his right hand before he met Sebastian's gaze across the table and held it. Sebastian quickly ran through his options.

Get up and leave.

Carry on pretending to read.

Tell Torkel to go to hell.

Or.

Tell him about Lily.

His instinct was to go for one of the first three, but what harm would it do if Torkel knew a little more? No doubt he was asking out of some genuine concern, rather than curiosity. Another outstretched hand. An attempt to revive a friendship that, if not actually dead, was certainly in a deep sleep. You had to admire his persistence. Time for Sebastian to give something back? After all, he could set the boundaries, decide how much. Better that than have Torkel decide to search on the internet and find out more than Sebastian wanted him to know.

Sebastian pushed the newspaper away.

'Her name was Lily. She was German; we met in Germany when I was working there and got married in '98. Unfortunately I'm not the type who carries a photo around in his wallet.'

'What did she do?'

'She was a sociologist. At the university in Cologne. That's where we lived.'

'Older than you? Younger? Same age?'

'Five years younger.'

Torkel nodded. Three quick questions, three apparently straight answers. Now things were going to get a bit more tricky.

'When did she die?'

Sebastian stiffened. Okay, enough. Question time was officially over. There was the line, and Torkel had crossed it.

'Several years ago. I don't want to talk about it.'

'Why not?'

'Because it's private and you're not my therapist.'

Torkel nodded. True, but there had been a time when they had known most things about each other. Perhaps it would be overstating the case to say that Torkel had missed those days. He hadn't given Sebastian more than a passing thought for several years. However, now he was back, now Torkel saw him at work, he realised that his job, and perhaps his life, had been more boring for those years when Sebastian hadn't been around. There were other factors as well as Sebastian's absence, but still Torkel couldn't shake off the feeling that he had missed his former colleague. His old friend. More than he had thought he would. Torkel had no expectations that the feeling was mutual, but at least he could give it a try.

'We used to be friends. All those times you had to hear about my problems, about Monica and the kids and all that crap.' Torkel looked directly at his colleague across the table. 'I'm happy to listen.'

'To what?'

'To anything you like. If there's anything you want to tell me.'

'There isn't.'

Torkel nodded. He hadn't expected it to be easy. After all, he was talking to Sebastian Bergman.

'Is that why you invited me to dinner? So you could hear my confession?'

Torkel picked up his coffee cup, buying himself a little time before he answered.

'I just get the impression you're not feeling too good.' Sebastian didn't answer. No doubt there was more to come. 'I asked Vanja how things went today. Apart from the fact that she thinks you're an awkward bastard, she said it seemed as if ... I don't know ... She got the feeling that perhaps you were carrying some kind of burden.'

'Vanja ought to concentrate on her work.' Sebastian stood up, left the newspaper but took his cup and screwed it up. 'And you shouldn't take any notice of all the crap you hear.'

He left the room, throwing the cup in the bin by the door on his way out. Torkel was left alone. He took a deep breath and let the air out very slowly. What had he expected? He should have known better. Sebastian Bergman didn't allow himself to be analysed. And he'd lost his dinner companion for the evening. Billy and Vanja were working, and there was no point in thinking about Ursula. But he really didn't want to sit through another dinner all on his own. He took out his mobile.

Sebastian strode through the deserted office. He was furious. With Torkel, with Vanja, but mostly with himself. Never before had Sebastian given a colleague the feeling that he was 'carrying some kind of burden'. Nobody had even been able to hazard a guess at what he was thinking before. The only things they knew about Sebastian were the things he allowed them to know. That was how he had reached the position he used to occupy.

At the top.

Admired.

Feared.

But he had given himself away in the car. Lost control. And in Lena Eriksson's apartment, too, when he thought back. Unacceptable. It was his mother's fault. Hers and those letters. He had to make some kind of decision on what to do about that. Right now it was affecting him more than he could permit.

There was a light on in the conference room. Through the glass Sebastian could see Billy sitting with his laptop open. Sebastian slowed down. Stopped. Every time he had thought about Anna

Eriksson during the day he had come to the conclusion that he ought to forget it. There was too little to gain, too much to lose. But could he do that? Could he just forget what he knew and carry on as if nothing had happened? Probably not. Besides which, it wouldn't do any harm to have that address if someone could find it. Then he could decide later what he was going to do. Use it or throw it away. Go round there or stay away. He could even go and suss out the lie of the land. See what kind of people lived there. Get an idea of how he might be received if he introduced himself. He made a decision. It was just stupid not to keep all his options open.

He pushed open the door. Billy looked up from his computer.

'Hi.'

Sebastian nodded, pulled out a chair and sat down on the edge of the seat, legs outstretched. He pulled over the fruit bowl on the table and took a pear. Billy had turned back to the computer.

'What are you doing?'

'Just checking out Facebook and a few other social networking sites.'

'Does Torkel let you do that during working hours?'

Billy looked up at him over the top of the screen, smiled and shook his head.

'No chance. I'm checking up on Roger.'

'Found anything?'

Billy shrugged his shoulders. It depended on how you looked at it. He had found Roger, but nothing of interest.

'He wasn't particularly active. I know he didn't have a computer of his own, but it's still more than three weeks since he wrote anything on Facebook. Actually, it's not so strange that he wasn't on there more often. He only had twenty-six friends registered.'

'Is that a small number?' Sebastian knew what Facebook was, of course – he hadn't spent the last few years living under a rock – but he had never felt the urge to find out exactly how it worked or to become a member, or whatever it was called. He had no desire to keep in touch with old school friends or former work colleagues.

The very thought that they might 'add' him as a friend and terrorise him with artificially imposed intimacy and stupid trivialities made him feel quite exhausted. In fact, he made a real effort not to associate with anyone, either in real life or in the digital world.

'Twenty-six friends is nothing,' said Billy. 'You get more than that just by registering, virtually. Same thing on MSN. He hasn't been on there for over four months, and his only contact was with Lisa, Erik Heverin and Johan Strand.'

'So he had hardly any cyber friends.'

'Looks that way. No enemies either, though – I haven't found any bad stuff about him on the net.'

Sebastian decided he had pretended to be interested long enough to broach what he had really come for. Why not smooth the way with a little flattery?

'You're pretty good with computers, from what I've heard.'

Billy couldn't suppress the smile that said that it was true.

'Above average. It's cool, I enjoy it,' he said, rather more modestly.

'Do you think you might be able to help me with something?'

Sebastian took the letter out of his inside pocket and tossed it over to Billy.

'I need to find someone called Anna Eriksson. She was living at this address in 1979.'

Billy picked up the letter and examined it.

'Is she connected to the investigation?'

'Could be, yes.'

'In what way?'

Bloody hell, why were they all so keen on sticking to the rulebook in this place? Sebastian was too tired and too slow to come up with a good lie, so he decided to go with something vague, hoping it would suffice.

'It's just something I'm following up on my own, a bit of a long shot. I haven't said anything to the others, but with a bit of luck it may work out.'

Billy nodded and Sebastian relaxed slightly. He was just about to get up when Billy stopped him.

'But in what way is it related to Roger Eriksson?'

Okay, so that didn't work. What happened to people just doing as they were told? If it all went pear-shaped Billy could always blame Sebastian, who in turn would claim that Billy had misunderstood him. Torkel would get a bit upset. There would be talk of revising procedures. Everything would carry on as normal. Sebastian gave Billy the chance to take the hook without adding any further bait.

'It's a long story, but it would be a good thing for you too if you could help me out. I really think this could lead somewhere.'

Billy turned the envelope over, studied it. Just in case Billy wasn't going to bite, Sebastian started working out a story in his head. He thought he might say there was a chance that Anna Eriksson could be Roger's biological mother. No, it wasn't listed in any adoption register – this was inside information. No, he couldn't say whom from. That might work. If it was biologically possible. Sebastian started calculating. How old would Anna Eriksson have been when she had Roger, in that case? About forty? It worked.

'Okay.'

Sebastian came back to reality, unsure of what he had heard, whether he might have missed something.

'Okay?'

'Sure, but it'll have to wait a while. I've got a load of files from the CCTV cameras to look at by tomorrow.'

'Of course, there's no rush. Thank you.' Sebastian headed for the door. 'Just one more thing.'

Billy looked up from his computer.

'I'd appreciate it if we could keep this between ourselves. It's a long shot, as I said, and people like nothing more than to gloat if someone gets it wrong.'

'Sure. No problem.'

Sebastian smiled gratefully and left the room.

Limone Ristorante Italiano. She had made the booking, but Torkel got there first and was shown to a corner table next to two windows, with metal spheres the size of bowling balls hanging from the ceiling. A table for four. Two sofas instead of chairs. Hard, straight backed. Upholstered in a dark purple fabric. Torkel sipped a beer straight from the bottle. Had this been a bad idea? Inviting Hanser to dinner? Although he hadn't really asked her out as such. He just wanted to have a more in-depth discussion about the case with her. Their brief meetings during the day had only scratched the surface, and he might as well do that over a meal as in her office. Admittedly Hanser had voluntarily taken a step back and allowed them to run the investigation as they wished, but it was important to remember that she was ultimately responsible, and Torkel had the feeling he had been a little grumpy with her of late.

Hanser arrived, apologised for being late, sat down and ordered a glass of white wine. The local chief superintendent had sought her out to check on the current state of play. He was concerned at the news that they had released Leonard Lundin, and keen to hear that another arrest was imminent. Of course she had to disappoint him. He was also under pressure: the interest from the press, particularly the tabloids, had not diminished at all. At least four pages, every single day. The interview with Lena Eriksson was repackaged and presented as something new. They focused on Roger's loneliness, speculated that the perpetrator may not have been known to Roger. In which case it could happen again. An 'expert' explained that when a person killed for the first time – which could be the case in this instance – they crossed a line from which there was no way back. It was likely that this person would kill again. Probably quite soon. Good old-fashioned scaremongering journalism, in the same category as the latest pandemic hysteria, or the 'Could your headache be a brain tumour?' headlines. *Expressen* had managed to sniff out the cock-up from the first weekend when the boy's disappearance wasn't followed up, and they were questioning the efficiency of the police. In connection with the article they had already produced information panels on other unsolved murder cases, with the murder of Olof Palme at the top. Hanser explained that she was meeting Torkel, and hoped to have more information for the chief superintendent the following day. He had settled for that, but before he left he made it clear that, (a) he hoped it had not been a mistake to call in Riksmord, and (b) if it had been a mistake, then she and no one else would bear the responsibility.

When the waiter brought her glass of wine and asked whether they were ready to order, they spent a short while studying the menus. Torkel already knew what he wanted. *Salmone alla calabrese*: fried fillet of salmon with cherry tomatoes, leeks, capers, olives and a potato cake. He wasn't one for starters. Hanser quickly decided on *agnello alla griglia*: grilled rack of lamb with parmigiana potatoes and a red-wine sauce. More expensive than his choice. Not that it mattered. He was the one who had asked for her company. He regarded it as a working dinner, in which case of course he was paying. Riksmord was paying.

While they were waiting for their food they went over the case. Yes, Torkel had read the papers. Vanja had followed the same line of thought, but only briefly. Unknown perpetrator. But the discovery that Roger had been shot disproved that theory, according to Sebastian. A person who had decided to kill, regardless of who his victim might be, didn't use a gun that would mean he'd have to carve out the bullet afterwards in order to avoid being identified. Unfortunately this was not something Hanser could release to the media. They didn't want the public – and, thus, the murderer – to find out that they knew Roger had been shot. Apart from that, Torkel didn't have much to tell. They hadn't made any impressive progress except for the Axel Johansson angle, and a great deal would depend on the following day and the forensic reports from SKL. Torkel's mobile vibrated in his inside pocket. He took it out and looked at the display. *Vilma*.

'Sorry, I have to take this.'

Hanser nodded and took a sip of her wine.

'Hi, sweetheart.' Before he even heard her voice his face broke into a smile. She had that effect on him, his youngest daughter.

'Hi, Dad, what are you doing?'

'I'm having dinner with a colleague. What about you?'

'I'm going to a party at school. Are you here in town?'

'No, I'm still in Västerås. Did you want something?'

'I just wondered if you could pick me up tonight. After the party. We didn't know if you were back, so Mum said I should ring and check.'

'If I'd been at home I'd have been happy to pick you up.'

'It's cool. Mum will do it. I just thought if you were home …'

'What kind of party is it?'

'Fancy dress.'

'And what are you going as?'

'A teenage chav.'

Torkel had a vague idea what that meant. He wasn't entirely happy with his twelve-year-old daughter's choice, but on the other hand he wasn't there to talk her out of it or to come up with creative alternatives. Besides which, he was confident Yvonne would make sure everything was kept in check. Unlike the split with Monica, his divorce from Yvonne had been good. As good as a divorce could be, that is. Their relationship had been terrible. Both of them had thought so. He had been unfaithful. So had she, he was sure of it. Both of them had wanted out, but with Vilma's and Elin's best interests at heart. The fact was that things were better between them now than when they were married.

'Okay. Say hello to Mum and have a good time.'

'Will do. She says hello too. See you when you get back.'

'Definitely. Miss you.'

'Miss you too. Bye, Dad.'

Torkel ended the call and turned to Hanser.

'That was my daughter.'

'So I gathered.'

Torkel slipped his mobile back in his inside pocket.

'You have a son, don't you? How old is he now?'

Hesitation. Although Hanser had gone through this many times over the past six years, whenever her son came up in conversation

216

she always hesitated. At first she had answered honestly, told the truth, but it made people extremely uncomfortable, and after a painful silence or desperate attempt to keep the conversation going, they would find a reason to get away from her. So these days when people asked her if she had children, she usually said no. It was the easiest thing to do, and it was true.

She had no children.

Not any more.

But Torkel knew that she had been a mother.

'He's dead. Niklas died six years ago. When he was fourteen.'

'Oh, I'm sorry. I didn't know. I'm so very sorry.'

'No, how could you know?'

Hanser knew what Torkel was thinking. It was what everyone who found out that Niklas had died wanted to know. Fourteen-year-olds don't just collapse in most cases. Something must have happened. What? What happened, that's what everyone wanted to know. Torkel was no exception, Hanser was sure of it. But the difference was that he asked.

'How did he die?'

'He was taking a short cut. Across a train. He got too close to the high-voltage cable.'

'I can't imagine how you and your husband must have felt. How did you get through it?'

'We didn't. They say that eighty per cent of those who lose a child end up getting a divorce. I wish I could say that I belonged to the other twenty per cent, but unfortunately . . . ' Hanser took another gulp of her wine. It was easy to tell Torkel about it. Easier than she had thought.

'I was so angry with him. With Niklas. He was fourteen years old. I don't know how many times we'd read about kids who had burned to death on top of trains. Every single time we said they ought to know better. They were teenagers. Some of them almost adults. And Niklas always agreed with me. He knew it was dangerous. Lethal. And he still . . . I was so angry with him.'

'That's understandable.'

217

'I felt like the worst mother in the world. In every way.'

'That's understandable as well.'

The waiter came over with a plate in each hand. That could have given them an excuse to stop, to concentrate on the food in silence. But they carried on talking as they started to eat, and after a few minutes Torkel realised they would know considerably more about each other when dinner was over than they had done before. He smiled to himself. It was nice when that kind of thing happened.

Haraldsson was shivering in his green Toyota outside Axel Johansson's address, even though he was wearing long johns and a fleece sweater under his padded jacket. He clutched his coffee mug. The first real warmth of spring had begun to filter through during the day, but the evenings and nights were still cold.

Haraldsson felt he had played a large part in the fact that the day had resulted in a call being put out for Johansson. A very large part. His contribution had been absolutely crucial. It was his work in tracing the sender of the email that had led Riksmord to Palmlövska High, and thus to the sacked caretaker. Torkel Höglund had nodded to him and given him a little smile when he walked past in the afternoon, but that was all. Apart from that, no one had given him the credit he deserved for providing the information that led to a breakthrough in the investigation. He wasn't surprised. Disappointed, but not surprised. Haraldsson knew he would never get any appreciation for his work. Not from Torkel and his colleagues, at any rate. How would it look if one of the locals solved the case under the very noses of Riksmord?

Before he'd limped home Haraldsson had checked with Hanser to find out if the search for Johansson included twenty-four-hour surveillance on the suspect's place of residence. It didn't. The first phase had merely involved a message to all personnel asking them to be extra vigilant during their normal patrols and call-outs. They had contacted friends, neighbours and relatives and said that they would like to speak to Axel, but they had been careful to emphasise that he was not suspected of anything at the moment. Whether his home was placed under surveillance was a matter for Riksmord to decide.

Haraldsson made his own decision immediately. It was obvious the man was deliberately staying away. Innocent people didn't do that, and what Haraldsson did in his free time and where he spent the night was his own affair.

So now he was sitting here.

In his Toyota.

Shivering.

He toyed with the idea of starting the car and driving around for a while just to get some heat going, but then there was always the risk that he would miss Axel Johansson if he came home. Simply sitting there and running the engine for a few minutes was out of the question, partly because the suspect might react to the fact that there was a car chugging away outside his apartment block so late at night, and partly because it was only permitted to run the engine for one minute in town. That would be a minor offence, of course, but even so. Rules and laws were there to be obeyed. Besides which, it was completely unjustifiable from an environmental point of view. To warm himself up Haraldsson poured a little more coffee into his cup. Wrapped his hands around it. He should have worn gloves.

He breathed warm air onto his hands and looked at the dressing. Jenny had crept up behind him while he was pouring the coffee from the pot into his Thermos flask, and he had jumped when she slipped her arms around his stomach and quickly slid her hands downwards. He had gone into the bathroom to put some Xylocaine ointment and a dressing on the small burn on the back of his hand. Jenny had accompanied him, and as he threw the empty packaging into the stainless steel bin she had come up behind him again and wondered if he was in a terrible hurry.

They'd done it in the shower. Afterwards he'd had to change the sodden dressing and put on fresh ointment. In spite of the quickie in the shower Jenny had looked disappointed when he'd left. Wondered when he'd be back. Perhaps he'd be home half an hour or so before she had to leave for work in the morning? Hopeful. Haraldsson was doubtful. The plan was to go straight to the station. He would see her tomorrow evening. Kiss-kiss bye-bye.

Haraldsson thought about it as he took a sip of his rapidly cooling coffee. Jenny had been annoyed when he'd left. He knew it. Now he was sitting here feeling annoyed because she was annoyed. He really wanted to ... Wrong. He was *going* to solve the murder of Roger Eriksson, but it was as if she had no concept of how important this was to him. Her desire to get pregnant overshadowed everything else in their lives. To a certain extent Haraldsson could understand her. He wanted children too. He longed to be a father, and it grieved him that the process was so difficult. But for Jenny it was an obsession. These days their relationship consisted of nothing but sex. He tried to persuade her that they should go out, to the cinema or a restaurant, but she just said they could watch a DVD and eat at home, then they could 'do it' as well. On the few occasions they visited friends they always left early, and neither of them drank any more. Inviting anyone around was out of the question. The guests might overstay their welcome, preventing Haraldsson and Jenny from getting down to business. He tried to talk about his work, about the problems, first with Hanser and now with Riksmord, but more and more frequently he got the feeling she wasn't listening. She nodded, made the right noises, answered him – increasingly feeding his own words back to him – and then she wanted to have sex again. It was quite the reverse for the few male colleagues who occasionally spoke about their relationship or marriage: too little sex was the problem there.

Too infrequent.

Too boring.

Haraldsson hadn't dared mention the situation at home. But he thought about it more and more often. What if this carried on? When Jenny did get pregnant? Would he turn into one of those people who read every beat-up story about every kind of food, and hunted for twenty-four-hour petrol stations kilometres away from home, trying to get hold of pickled gherkins and liquorice ice-cream? He shook off his thoughts. He had a job to do. That was why he was here. He certainly wasn't avoiding his wife – was he?

Haraldsson decided to go for a walk to warm up, making sure he could see Axel Johansson's door the whole time.

Vanja was leaning over her desk and gazing out of the window. Most of the view was obscured by the building opposite – a modern glass monstrosity – but at least she could see the night sky and a strip of trees leading down to Lake Mälaren. In front of her were several notepads, a few loose sheets of paper and a number of black pocket diaries. They had come from Roger's desk and were just some of the items Ursula had removed from his room.

An hour earlier Vanja and Billy had eaten a salad down at the Greek restaurant recommended by the girl on reception. The food more than met their expectations, and they both knew they would be back. It was always stupid to take a chance in a small Swedish town. If they found a good place they quickly became regular customers. On the way back she had called in at the hotel to ring her father. Valdemar had sounded happy but tired. The whole day had been something of an emotional roller coaster for him, and the treatment made him drowsy. But for Vanja it was a wonderful conversation. For the first time in ages she didn't hang up thinking she might lose him. She was bubbling with joy and thought she might as well put her energy to good use. She went back to the station. The truth was that she always worked as hard as she could when they were on a case away from home, but this time the thought of an extra evening shift felt better than it had for a long time. Ursula had finished at six, which both Vanja and Billy had thought was a little odd. Ursula usually worked late, just like the others, and while they were eating they had speculated that perhaps the real reason was Torkel. However discreet Ursula and Torkel might be, Billy and Vanja had long suspected that they were more than just colleagues.

Vanja started with the loose sheets of paper. Mostly old exams and class tests, a few notes from school. Vanja started to catalogue them: exams in one pile, notes in another, various bits and pieces in a third. She ended up with three basic piles, which she then went through again, sorting the contents according to date and subject. Eventually she had twelve piles in front of her and began to go through these with a little more focus on the content. She had learned this method of cataloguing material from Ursula. The great advantage was that you quickly gained an overview of the material, and that you looked at the same document several times with an increasing degree of focus. This made it easier to spot patterns or events that didn't seem to fit, and it improved accuracy. Ursula was good at that kind of thing. Building up systems. Vanja suddenly remembered Sebastian's comments on the hierarchy within the team. He was right. She and Ursula had an unspoken agreement not to encroach on each other's areas of expertise. It wasn't just about respect, but also about a mutual awareness that otherwise it would be easy for them to end up competing, thus challenging each other's position. Because they did actually compete on where they stood in the chain of command.

And results.

And being the best.

Vanja turned to the rest of the material. The loose papers hadn't turned up anything, except that Roger was worse at Maths than Swedish, and that he really needed to work on his English. She picked up the black pocket diaries. They looked as if they were little used, and dated from 2007 onwards. She picked up the most recent and started from the beginning. Roger hadn't written very much. It looked as if he had been given a diary for Christmas and had gradually stopped using it. A few birthdays had been entered, some homework, the odd test, and the further she got from January, the fewer entries there were.

The abbreviation PW first appeared at the beginning of February, then again at the end of February and the first week in March, then every other Wednesday at ten o'clock. Vanja picked up on what seemed to be the only recurring entry, and turned the pages until she reached that fateful Friday in April. Every other Wednesday, PW. Always at ten o'clock. Who or what was PW? Since it was during the school day, it ought to have something to do with school. She carried on turning the pages and realised that Roger had missed a meeting with PW since he died. She quickly checked the previous year's diary to see if PW was in there, too. Indeed it was. The first time was at the end of October, then every other Tuesday at three o'clock until the end of term in November.

Roger's circle of friends was very limited, and so far had provided the investigation with little information. But here at least was a person he saw on a regular basis – if it was a person and not an activity. She looked at the clock: only a quarter to nine. Not too late to make some calls. She tried Roger's mother first. No answer. She wasn't surprised: the phone had rung several times when she and Sebastian were there and Lena had made no attempt to pick it up. She decided to call Beatrice Strand. As his class teacher she ought to know what Roger was doing at ten o'clock every other Wednesday.

'He had a free period then.' Beatrice sounded a little tired, but she would do her best to help.

'Do you know what he used to do at that time?'

'I don't, I'm afraid. The next lesson started at eleven-fifteen and he was always on time.' Vanja nodded and picked up the previous year's diary.

'What about last autumn? Tuesday afternoons at three?'

There was a brief silence.

'I think school was over then. Yes, that's right, we finished at quarter to three on Tuesdays.'

'Do you have any idea what the abbreviation PW might stand for?'

'PW? No, not off the top of my head.'

Vanja nodded. This was getting better and better. It seemed that Roger had hidden his meetings with PW from Beatrice. She felt as if that was important. After all, she wasn't just his teacher – they knew each other outside school.

'Was he meeting this PW on Wednesdays?' Beatrice asked after a while. She had obviously been giving the abbreviation some thought.

'Exactly.'

'It could be Peter Westin.'

'Who's that?'

'He's a psychologist who does some counselling with the students. I know Roger went to see him a few times just after he started at the school. It was actually me who mentioned Peter to Roger. But I didn't realise he was still seeing him.'

Vanja thanked Beatrice for her help and took down Peter Westin's contact details. She rang him, but got his answering machine, which informed her that his office would be open at nine in the morning. A quick look at the map showed her that the office was only ten minutes from the school. Roger could easily have got there and back in his free period without anyone knowing where he'd been, and if there was one thing you talked to a psychologist about, it was secrets. The kind of thing you didn't want to discuss with anyone else.

Her mobile beeped. A text message.

found axel j's ex-girlfriend. want 2 come & talk 2 her? billy

Quick reply.

yes

This time she did add a smiley.

Axel Johansson's ex-girlfriend, Linda Beckman, had been at work when Billy got hold of her. She had pointed out several times that she and Axel were no longer together, and that she had no idea where he was or what he was up to. It had taken a great deal of persuasion on Billy's part to get her to agree to a meeting. When she finally gave in she insisted there was no way she could come to the police station. If they wanted to talk to her tonight they would have to come to the restaurant where she worked, and she would take a short break. So now Vanja and Billy were sitting at a table in a pizzeria on Stortorget. Neither of them ordered anything to eat but settled for a cup of coffee.

Linda came and sat down opposite them. She was a blonde, fairly ordinary-looking woman aged about thirty. Her hair was shoulder length, and her full fringe ended just above her blue–green eyes. She was wearing a black-and-white-striped sweater and a short black skirt. The sweater didn't particularly flatter her figure. She had a gold heart on a thin chain around her neck.

'I've got fifteen minutes.'

'In that case we'll try to get through this in fifteen minutes,' said Billy, reaching for the sugar. He always took sugar in his coffee. And not a small amount either.

'As I said on the phone, we'd like to know a bit about Axel Johansson.'

'You didn't say why.'

Vanja took over. It would be stupid to reveal that they knew about Axel's little sideline, at least until they had an idea of Linda's attitude towards her ex. Instead Vanja started a little more circumspectly.

'Do you know why he got the sack?'

Linda smiled at the two police officers. She knew what this was all about.

'Yes. The booze.'

'The booze?'

'He was selling it to the kids. Idiot!'

Vanja looked at Linda and nodded. She didn't seem to be a member of Axel's fan club.

'Exactly.'

Linda shook her head wearily, as if to reinforce her negative view of Axel's activities.

'I told him it was a stupid thing to do. But did he listen? No. And then he got the sack, just like I said. Idiot.'

'Did he ever mention a Roger Eriksson?' Vanja ventured optimistically.

226

'Roger Eriksson?' Linda seemed to be thinking about it, but her face showed no spark of recognition.

'A sixteen-year-old boy,' Billy went on, handing over a picture of Roger.

Linda took the picture and studied it. She recognised him.

'The boy who died?'

Vanja nodded. Linda looked at her.

'Yes, I think he came by once.'

'Do you know why? Was he buying alcohol from Axel?'

'No, I don't think so. They had a chat. He didn't have anything with him when he left, as far as I remember.'

'When was this?'

'Maybe two months ago. I moved out shortly afterwards.'

'Did you see Roger again? Please think carefully – this is important.'

Linda sat in silence for a while, then shook her head. Vanja changed tack.

'What was Axel's reaction when you moved out?'

Linda shook her head again. It seemed to be her default response whenever she thought of Axel.

'I don't think he cared one way or the other. He didn't seem angry or upset or anything. He didn't make any attempt to get me to stay. He just ... carried on. As if it didn't matter whether I was there or not. He was completely fucking unbelievable.'

When Vanja and Billy thanked Linda Beckman twenty minutes later and set off back to the station, their picture of Axel Johansson had not only acquired contours, every little detail was clearly visible. In the beginning Axel had been the perfect gentleman. Attentive, generous, amusing. After only a few weeks she had moved in. At first everything had continued to go well. Then things had started to crop up. Not too serious to start with. Hardly noticeable, really. There was slightly less money in her purse than she'd thought, that kind of thing. Then a piece of gold jewellery she had inherited from her grandmother disappeared, and Linda began to realise that to Axel their relationship was mainly a way of reducing his costs. She had confronted him, and he had been full of regrets. He had gambling debts and had been afraid she would leave him if he told her, so he'd done what he had to do to get straight. Just so that he could start afresh with Linda. No baggage. She had believed him. But before long money was going missing again. The last straw was when she found a hidden rent agreement and realised that she was, in fact, paying the whole of the rent, not half as she had supposed. Linda coloured in the rest of the picture. Their sex life was hopeless. He was hardly ever interested, and on the few occasions when it did happen he was dominant almost to the point of violence, and always wanted to take her from behind with her face buried in the pillow. *Too much information*, Vanja thought, but she nodded encouragingly to Linda. Axel was always out at odd times, sometimes all night. He would come home first thing, or late in the morning. The rest of his time, when he wasn't working at the school, was spent coming up with different ways to make money. Axel's entire world revolved around screwing the system.

Only idiots do as they're told was his motto. The only reason he applied for the job at Palmlövska High was because the students had richer parents and a stricter upbringing, which in Axel's world led to fewer problems. The families tended to solve any problems on the quiet. Just as the principal had in the end.

Sell to those who can pay the most, and who have the most to lose if they get caught, he had said. But Linda never saw any money. That was the thing she found most difficult to understand. In spite of all the 'business' he did, Axel was always broke. Where the money went was just one big mystery to Linda. He didn't seem to have many friends, and he was always cursing those he did have because they wouldn't lend him any money. Or if they did lend him some, he cursed them because they wanted it back.

He was always dissatisfied.

With everything and everybody.

The most important question for Vanja and Billy was what Roger had to do with Axel. Roger had been to his apartment, they knew that now. Was there a link to the fact that Roger had got Axel sacked a few weeks later? That was one possible scenario, at any rate. By the time Vanja and Billy said good night, they were quite happy with the last hour's work. Axel Johansson had become even more interesting. And they were going to see a psychologist with the initials PW the following morning.

Torkel nodded to the woman on reception and walked over to the lift. Once inside he hesitated as he slid his key card into the reader, then pressed 4. His room was 302. Ursula was on the fourth floor. The sound of the Rolling Stones was coming through the hidden speakers. Torkel thought back to when he was young and the Stones had produced the hardest rock he'd ever heard. Now they were lift music. The doors slid open and Torkel didn't move. Should he forget it? He didn't even know if she was still angry with him. He just assumed she was. He would still have been angry with her if she'd done that to him. But it was probably best to know. Torkel walked down the corridor to room 410 and knocked on the door. A few seconds passed before Ursula opened it. The neutral expression on her face gave Torkel a pretty good clue what she thought of the visit.

'Sorry if I'm disturbing you.' Torkel did his best to prevent the nervousness from showing in his voice. Standing here in front of her, he realised he really didn't want them to fall out.

'I just wanted to check how things stand between us.'

'How do you think they stand?'

As he had feared. Still angry. Understandably. But Torkel had never found it difficult to apologise when he had done something wrong.

'I'm sorry, I should have told you I was intending to bring Sebastian in.'

'No, you shouldn't have brought him it at all.' For a brief moment Torkel felt a stab of irritation. Now she was being unreasonable. He was apologising. He admitted that he had handled the situation badly, but he was the boss. He had to make the decisions and bring in the people he thought were best for the investigation, whether everybody else was happy with that or not. It was a case of maintaining a professional approach. Torkel quickly decided not to say any of this, partly because he didn't want to upset Ursula even more, but also because he still wasn't completely convinced that Sebastian's presence really was the best thing for the investigation. He had the feeling he didn't just need to explain his actions to Ursula, he also needed to sort it out for himself. Why hadn't he simply said 'thanks but no thanks' to Sebastian in the hotel dining room that morning? His expression was almost pleading as he spoke to Ursula.

'Listen, I really need to talk to you. Can I come in?'

'No.' Ursula made no attempt to open the door. Quite the reverse. She pushed it slightly further shut, as if she was expecting him to kick it down. From inside the room came the sound of three short, three long, three short beeps. SOS. Ursula's ringtone.

'That's Mikael. He said he'd call.'

'Okay.' Torkel realised the conversation was over. 'Say hello from me.'

'You can do it yourself, he'll be here tomorrow.' Ursula closed the door.

Torkel remained where he was for a second, letting it sink in. Mikael hadn't come to visit Ursula during an investigation since ... well, never, as far as Torkel could recall. He couldn't even begin to start contemplating what that meant. With a heavy tread he headed back towards the staircase that would take him to his own room. His life was considerably more complicated now than it had been twenty-four hours earlier.

But what did he expect?

He had let Sebastian in again.

Sebastian woke up lying on his back on the sofa. He must have nodded off. The television was on. Low volume. The news. His right hand was so tightly clenched that the pain was shooting right up his forearm. He closed his eyes and began to straighten his fingers slowly from their cramped position. The wind had got up. It was blowing hard, roaring down the chimney of the open fire, but in his half-awake state the sound blended with the dream that had just left him.

The roar.

The power.

The superhuman power in that wall of water.

He held onto her. Held on tight. Through all the screams, all those people screaming. The water. The swirling sand. The power. That was the only thing he knew in the midst of all the madness. That he was holding onto her. He could even see their hands. Of course it was impossible but, no, he really could see their hands. He could still see them. Her little hand. With the ring on it. Clutched in his right hand. He was holding on to her tighter than he had ever held on to anything before. There was no time to think about anything, but yet he knew that he was thinking. Just one thought. More important than any other. *He must never, ever let go.*

That was what he thought.

The only thing he thought.

He must never, ever let go.

But he did.

Her hand slipped out of his.

Suddenly she wasn't there. Something in the huge volume of water must have hit her. Hit him? Or had her small body got stuck on something? Had his? He didn't know. He only knew that when he came to several hundred metres from what had been the beach – bruised, battered and in shock – she wasn't there.

She wasn't nearby.

She wasn't anywhere.

His right hand was empty.

Sabine was gone.

He never found her.

Lily had left them that morning to go for a run along the beach. She did the same thing every morning. She used to bore him with

231

her preaching about all the beneficial effects of exercise. Digging her fingers into the softness that had once been his waistline. He had promised to go for a run. At some point during their holiday. But he hadn't said when. Not today, Boxing Day. He was going to spend today with his daughter. Lily was late going out. She usually ran before it got too hot, but this morning they had had breakfast together in the big double bed, then just stayed there giggling and having fun. The whole family. Eventually Lily had got up, kissed him, given Sabine one last kiss and left the hotel room with a cheerful wave. She wasn't going to run very far today.

Too hot already.

Back in half an hour.

He never found her either.

Sebastian got up off the sofa. Shuddered. It was chilly in the silent room. What time was it? Just after ten. He picked up his plate from the coffee table and went into the kitchen. When he'd arrived home last night he had microwaved something from the freezer that purported to be a pub meal, and sat down in front of the TV with his plate and a bottle of low-alcohol beer. It had struck him that the pub which served the kind of food he had just shovelled down had probably closed its doors for good fairly quickly. 'Depressing' didn't even begin to describe it. But the meal matched the offerings on TV: watery, lacking in imagination and without any texture. Whichever channel he turned to, there seemed to be some young presenter staring straight into the camera and trying to persuade him to ring in and cast his vote. Sebastian had eaten half his meal, leaned back and evidently fallen asleep.

Fallen asleep and dreamed.

Now he was back in the kitchen, with no idea what to do. He put the plate and the bottle on the draining board. Stood there. He had been unprepared. He didn't usually allow himself to fall asleep. He never took a nap after dinner, or slept through a flight or a train journey. It usually destroyed whatever was left of the day. For some reason he had relaxed. It had been a different kind of day.

He had worked.

Been a part of a wider context, which hadn't happened since 2004. He wouldn't go so far as to say it had been a good day, but it had been different. He had obviously thought that would continue, that the dream wouldn't creep up on him. How wrong could he have been. So now he was standing here. In his parents' kitchen.

Restless.

Irritable.

He was unconsciously opening and closing his right hand. If he wasn't going to have a sleepless night, there was only one possible course of action.

First of all he would have a quick shower.

Then he would go and fuck someone.

The house really did look appalling. Everywhere. Piles of ironing. Dirty laundry. Dust. Dirty dishes. The beds needed changing, the wardrobes needed airing and during the day the spring sunshine made it painfully clear that the windows needed cleaning. Beatrice didn't even know where to start, so instead she did nothing, just as she had done every evening, every weekend lately. She didn't even dare to think how much time was encompassed by the word 'lately'. A year? Two? She didn't know. She just knew she didn't have the strength. To do anything. All her energy went into keeping up the appearance of the popular, conscientious teacher and colleague at school. Keeping the facade intact so that no one would notice how tired she was.

How lonely.

How unhappy.

She pushed aside a pile of clean underwear that had failed to get any further and sat down on the sofa with her second glass of wine. If anyone looked in through the window – and ignored the mess in the room – they could easily get the impression that she was a professional woman, wife and mother relaxing on the sofa after a hard day. Feet tucked underneath her, a glass of wine on the coffee table, a good book waiting, relaxing music in the background from the hidden speakers. The only thing missing was a crackling open fire. A middle-aged woman enjoying some time alone. Time to herself.

Nothing could be further from the truth. Beatrice was alone. That was the problem. She was alone even when Ulf and Johan were at home. Johan, aged sixteen, right in the middle of the process of breaking free, and Daddy's boy. Always had been. It had intensified ever since Johan had started at Palmlövska High. To a certain extent Beatrice could understand him: it couldn't be much fun to have your mother as your class teacher. But she felt more shut out than she thought she deserved to be. She had spoken – or tried to speak – to Ulf about it. Without getting anywhere, of course.

Ulf.

Her husband, who left the house in the morning, came back in the evening. Her husband, with whom she ate, watched TV and went to bed. The man with whom she was alone. He was in the house, but he was never at home with her. Not since he came back. Not before that either.

The doorbell rang. Beatrice glanced at the clock. Who could that be? At this time of night? She went into the hallway, pushed a pair of trainers to one side in a reflex action and opened the door. It took a few seconds before she was able to place the face with which she had only a fleeting acquaintance. The police officer who had been to the school. Sebastian something-or-other.

'Hi, sorry to disturb you so late but I just happened to be passing.' Beatrice nodded and glanced over her visitor's shoulder. No car parked on the drive or out on the street. Sebastian realised immediately what she was looking for.

'The thing is, I was out for a walk and I just thought you might need someone to talk to.'

'Why would I need someone to talk to?'

This was the critical point. On his way over, Sebastian had worked out a strategy based on what he thought he knew about Beatrice Strand and her husband. The fact that they had both introduced themselves as the parent of their son and not as each other's husband or wife told him that the relationship probably wasn't all that good. He had seen and heard it before. It was an unconscious way of punishing the other person within a couple: 'I do not principally think of myself as your partner.' The father and son had gone away to work through the events of the last few days instead of the three of them doing so as a family. This gave Sebastian a clear signal that things weren't going too well between mum and dad right now. He had, therefore, decided on the role of the good listener. It didn't matter what he had to listen to. It could be about Roger's death, Beatrice's crap marriage or a lecture on quantum physics. He was convinced that a listener was exactly what Beatrice needed at the moment. Apart from a cleaner.

'When we met in school today I got the feeling that you had to be strong, to be there for your students while all this is going on. And at home too, I presume, since your son was Roger's best friend. You have to hold back your own feelings.' Beatrice nodded without even being aware that she was doing so, confirming his diagnosis. Sebastian went on:

'But Roger was your student. A young boy. You need to be able to go over it all. You need someone who will listen.' Sebastian ended by tilting his head slightly to one side and firing off his most sympathetic smile, a combination that made him look like someone who had only the other person's interests at heart, with no ulterior motive whatsoever. He could see that Beatrice was taking in what he had said, but that she still couldn't quite make sense of it.

'But I don't understand – I mean, you're a police officer. Part of the investigation.'

'I'm a psychologist. I work with the police occasionally as a profiler, but that's not why I'm here. I knew you were on your own tonight, and I thought perhaps that was when the thoughts would come crowding in.'

Sebastian considered whether to underline his words with a light touch. A hand on her upper arm. But he stopped himself. Beatrice nodded again. Wasn't that a hint of a tear in her eyes? He had struck exactly the right note. Bloody hell, he was good! He had to fight to suppress a smile as Beatrice stepped to one side and let him in.

The man who was not a murderer plumped up the pillow. He was tired. It had been a long and, in many ways, wearing day. He caught himself thinking constantly that he must behave in a natural way, which in turn meant he was afraid that he was making too much effort, and therefore behaving oddly. Then he tried to stop thinking about behaving in a natural way, but after a while that led to a feeling that he was behaving oddly, and so he started thinking about it again. It was tiring. Besides which, the police had let Leonard Lundin go. That meant they were searching more actively again.

For someone else.

For him.

The man who was not a murderer settled down on his back and joined his hands together. A short evening prayer. Then sleep. A thank you for enabling him to find the strength to get through another day. A wish that life would get back to normal as soon as possible. Back to the everyday routine. He had read somewhere that the first twenty-four hours after a murder were the most important when it came to catching the perpetrator. In this case, nobody had even started looking for the boy until three days had passed. The delay could only mean that his actions were justified. Finally a request that he might sleep all night, without dreams. Not like last night.

It had been such a strange dream.

He had been standing behind the embankment at the football ground. Illuminated by the car headlights. The boy was lying on the ground in front of him. Blood everywhere. The man who was not a murderer was holding the damaged heart in his hand. Still warm. Had it been beating? Yes, in the dream it had. Slow beats. Fading.

Dying.

At any rate, in the dream he had turned to the right, aware that someone was standing there, a few metres away. Completely motionless. He was fairly certain who it was. Who it ought to be. But he was wrong. To his surprise he saw his father, silently watching him. A sense of unreality came over him, even though this was a dream. His father had been dead for many years. The man who was not a murderer made a sweeping gesture with his hands, taking in the gory scene.

'Don't just stand there. Aren't you going to help me?'

His voice was high, and when he spoke it broke like the voice of a small child who was upset. His father didn't move, he carried on gazing at the scene, his eyes clouded by cataracts.

'Sometimes the best thing you can do if you have problems is to talk about them.'

'Talk about what? What is there to talk about?' shouted the man who was not a murderer in his childish voice. 'The boy is dead! I'm holding his heart in my hand! Help me!'

'But sometimes when we talk, we say too much.'

Then his father had disappeared. The man who was not a murderer looked around. Confused.

Afraid.

Let down.

His father couldn't just disappear. Not now. Daddy had to help him. Just as he'd always done. He had to. It was his fucking responsibility. But his father did not reappear, and the man who was not a murderer became aware that the heart he was still holding had grown cold. Cold and still.

Then he had woken up. He couldn't get back to sleep. He had thought about the dream from time to time during the day, wondering what it could mean, whether it meant anything at all, but as the hours passed and everyday life took over, the memory of it began to fade.

But now ... now he was going to sleep. He needed it. He needed to remain one step ahead. The lead he had sent from the

237

school hadn't produced the result he had hoped for. Somehow the police must have worked out that Leonard hadn't hidden the jacket in his garage. That it had been planted. What should he do now?

He read everything he could find about the dead boy, but there wasn't much new information. He wondered whether he knew anyone who worked in the police station, someone who could give him some inside gossip, but he couldn't come up with anyone. Evidently the team that was investigating the murder had been expanded. *Expressen* wrote that the police had brought in a specialist: Sebastian Bergman. Well known within his field, apparently. Played a crucial and decisive role in catching the serial killer Edward Hinde in 1996. The man who was not a murderer was aware that his thoughts were becoming more and more unfocused. He was just about to fall asleep when he suddenly woke up. Sat bolt upright. He understood now.

'If you have problems, talk about them.'

His father *had* tried to help him.

As usual.

As always.

He had just been too stupid to understand. Who did you talk to if you had problems? A psychologist. A therapist.

'But sometimes we say too much.'

He knew. He had known all the time, it was just that he had never made the connection. Never thought he would need it. There was one man in Västerås who could destroy everything he had accomplished so far. Everything he had fought for. A man who could threaten him.

A professional listener.

Peter Westin.

238

It was twenty past two and bitterly cold. Not below freezing, perhaps, but it must have been very close. At any rate, Haraldsson's breath was coming out of his mouth as white vapour as he sat there, his gaze fixed on the apartment block across the street. He had heard somewhere that freezing to death was a painless, almost pleasant way to die. Apparently your entire body felt warm and relaxed just before you passed away. Which meant that at the moment Haraldsson's life was in no danger whatsoever. He was shivering in the driver's seat, his arms tightly folded across his chest. Every time he moved – even the smallest amount – he twitched uncontrollably and felt as if his body temperature dropped another tenth of a degree. There were still lights showing here and there in the building he was watching, but most of the apartments were in darkness. People were fast asleep under their duvets. In the warmth. Haraldsson had to admit that he envied them. Once or twice during the evening he had been on the point of giving up and going home, but each time he had felt tempted to turn the key in the ignition he had pictured himself arriving at work tomorrow as the person who had solved the murder of Roger Eriksson. The person who had caught the murderer. The person who had cracked the case. He had seen the reactions.

The praise.

The envy.

He could hear the chief superintendent thanking him and praising his initiative, the dedication to his work which had made him go a step further than duty demanded, a step further than even Riksmord thought necessary. The step that only a real police officer could take. This last comment would be delivered by the chief superintendent with a meaningful look at Hanser, who would stare down at the floor with a mixture of shame and embarrassment.

Perhaps Haraldsson's outstanding contribution had even prevented the loss of further lives.

Haraldsson felt warm inside just thinking about it, sitting there in his deep-frozen Toyota. Imagine how he would feel when it actually happened! Everything would turn around for him. The downward spiral in which his life was caught would be halted, and he would be back. In every way.

Haraldsson woke up from his drowsy deep-frozen daydream. Someone was approaching the main door of the apartment block. A tall, gangling figure. A man. He was walking quickly, hands thrust deep in his jacket pockets, shoulders hunched. Obviously Haraldsson wasn't the only one who was shivering inside. The man passed beneath a light fixed to the outside of the building, and for a brief moment Haraldsson had a clear view of his face. He glanced at the photograph attached to the dashboard with a paperclip. Not a shred of doubt. The man heading for the door was Axel Johansson.

Welcome home, thought Haraldsson, feeling every scrap of frozen weariness melt away. Axel Johansson reached the entrance and keyed in the four-digit code. The lock clicked and he pulled open the door. He was about to step into the warmth and darkness when he heard another click and a metallic sound that could only be a car door opening. Axel stopped dead and looked around. Haraldsson sat motionless for a moment. He had been too eager. He should have let the suspect enter the building before he opened the car door. What was Johansson doing now? The main door was still open, and he was staring straight at the Toyota. Sitting there with the car door ajar looked even more suspicious, if that were possible, so Haraldsson got out. Twenty metres away he saw Axel Johansson let go of the doorhandle and take a step backwards. Haraldsson set off across the street with determination.

'Axel Johansson!' Haraldsson did his best to make it sound as if he had unexpectedly caught sight of an old friend. Pleasantly surprised, not in any way threatening. Not like a police officer at all. Evidently he failed.

Axel Johansson turned and ran.

Haraldsson set off after him, cursing the fact that he had sat in the car for so long and got so cold. Slow. When he rounded the corner of the building he could see that the distance between him and Axel Johansson had grown. Haraldsson increased his speed, ignoring the fact that his thighs and legs were stiff and not at all inclined to cooperate. He was operating on sheer willpower. Johansson was running quickly and easily between the buildings. He jumped over the low wooden RESIDENTIAL PARKING ONLY sign, raced across the car park, up onto the grass and away. But Haraldsson was after him. He could feel his strides getting longer and longer as his whole body responded to his efforts. His speed was steadily increasing. The distance between Haraldsson and Johansson was no longer growing. It wasn't even staying the same. Haraldsson was catching up. It was a gradual process, but he was fit and unlikely to tire. As long as he didn't lose the suspect or slip on the wet grass, he would catch up with him eventually, he was sure of it.

Not bad for a man with a badly sprained right foot. Now where had that thought come from?

Haraldsson slowed down instinctively, swore to himself and speeded up again. Ran. Heard his pulse throbbing at his temples. Got his second wind, his legs pounding rhythmically. Strong. Axel Johansson showed no sign of slowing down. He crossed Skultunavägen, heading for the bridge over the river Svartån. Haraldsson was still behind him, but he couldn't shake off that thought. Officially he was injured. A badly sprained foot. He had been particularly careful to maintain the illusion. He could still barely get to the coffee machine and back to his desk without grimacing in pain. Sometimes he had to stop halfway to have a chat with one of his colleagues, simply because his foot was aching so much. Throbbing, kind of. If he caught the suspect after a night chase of several kilometres, then everybody would know he'd been faking. Lying. They would have proof that he had left his place in the search party. Deserted his post. But would it matter? If he

241

caught a child murderer, surely nobody would make an issue of the fact that he had been economical with the truth in relation to certain circumstances several days earlier?

Wrong. Hanser would. He was sure of that. He would never hear the speeches and the praise. Would he become the subject of an internal inquiry? Perhaps not, but what would his colleagues say? It would hardly be the step up he so desperately needed. His head was spinning. Haraldsson saw Axel Johansson cross the river and turn left, heading down the cycle track along Vallbyleden. Soon he would reach the park at Djäkneberget and it would be impossible to find him in the darkness. Haraldsson slowed down. Stopped. Johansson disappeared from view. Haraldsson stood there panting, swearing out loud to himself. Why had he come up with the sprained foot? Why hadn't he said that Jenny had been taken ill, or that he'd got food poisoning or any fucking thing that didn't last long? He turned around and set off back towards the car.

He would go home to Jenny.

Wake her up and have sex with her.

So that he wouldn't feel completely worthless.

One of the bedroom windows was ajar and the fresh night air had cooled the untidy bedroom. Sebastian stretched and cautiously straightened his clenched right hand. The feeling of Sabine remained on his skin, and he stroked his palm just to stay close to her for a little while longer. It was warm beneath the covers, and a part of Sebastian thought it would be nice to stay there for a while, postponing the moment when he had to face the cold. He turned to Beatrice. She was lying quietly beside him, watching his face.

'Bad dream?'

He hated it when they were awake. It always made the departure so much messier.

'No.'

She edged closer to him, and the warmth of her naked body

242

wrapped itself around him. He let it happen, even though he knew he should have chosen the cold. She stroked his neck and back.

'Does that feel silly?'

'No, but I have to go.'

'I know.' She kissed him. Not too hard. Not too desperate. She provoked a response from him. Her red hair tumbled over his cheeks. Then she turned away, adjusted her pillow and settled down comfortably.

'I love early mornings. It feels as if you're the only person in the world.' Sebastian sat up. His feet met the cold wooden floor. He looked at her. He had to admit that she surprised him. He hadn't really been aware of it before. She was a potential grower. This was the term Sebastian used for women who were really dangerous. The ones who grew on you. Who gave you something. More than sex. The ones you could grow fond of, feel you had to come back to. Particularly if you were a bit out of sorts. He got up to put a little distance between them. It already felt better. To Sebastian, most women were more beautiful when you went to bed than when you woke up with them. But with some it was quite the reverse, and a grower was at her most beautiful just before you left her. A grower left a promise at the end, rather than promising something from the start. She smiled at him.

'Would you like a lift home?'

'No, thanks, I'll walk.'

'I'll give you a lift.'

He nodded. After all, she was a grower, in spite of everything.

They drove through the quiet morning. The sun was resting below the horizon, just waiting for the night to disappear. David Bowie's 'Heroes' was on the radio. They didn't say much. Bowie took the place of conversation. Sebastian felt stronger. It was always easier with clothes on. Many of the things that had happened over the past few days were tumbling around in his head. A lot of emotions, and then this: an emotional connection, albeit a faint one. No doubt the situation was to blame. He was in a weakened state, that was all, not his normal self.

243

Beatrice pulled up outside his parents' house and switched off the engine. She looked at him with a certain amount of surprise.

'Is this where you live?'

'At the moment, yes.'

'It doesn't look like your style, I have to say.'

'You don't know how right you are.' He smiled at her and opened the door. The interior light came on, making her freckles look prettier. He leaned towards her. She smelled good. What was he doing? No kiss good night or good morning. He was supposed to be keeping his distance, for fuck's sake, that's what he'd decided. She grabbed hold of him and kissed him on the lips, as if to make it even more difficult for him. The car was cramped, but there was a warmth between them. Her hands stroked his hair and the back of his neck. He freed himself. Gently, but even so. He'd achieved something at least.

'I have to go.'

He closed the door quickly, thus extinguishing the treacherous light that made her far too tempting. Beatrice started the car and put it into reverse. The halogen lights dazzled him, but he was able to see her final wave before she turned the wheel and the headlights swept across his parents' house, then Clara Lundin's. A pair of eyes and a pale blue padded jacket glimmered in the beam over at the house next door. Clara Lundin was sitting on the steps with a cigarette in her hand, watching him with an expression full of anger and pain. Sebastian nodded in her direction and thought he would test the water.

'Morning!'

No reply. Not that he'd expected one. Clara stubbed out her cigarette and, with a last long stare at Sebastian, went back inside. *Not good*, he thought. But he was too tired to care. He walked up the path to his parents' house. In less than forty-eight hours he had acquired a house, a possible child, and a job. He had also met a grower and someone who would probably want their revenge. He had been wrong. Things did happen in Västerås after all.

The practice was 600 metres from Palmlövska High in a three-storey building, with offices on the ground floor and families living above. Vanja had waited at the station for Sebastian until 08:25 before she got fed up and decided to go and see Peter Westin on her own. She was relieved. Under normal circumstances she thought it was better to have two officers present at an interview, however trivial it might be. Partly because it was always helpful to have several points of view on any story, and partly because the information could then be shared informally with more members of the team. This meant a reduction in the time spent sitting in lengthy briefings, which Vanja found increasingly tedious. But when it came to Sebastian, things were different. Definitely not boring, but he had the ability to turn most things into a battle. So she hadn't waited too long for him.

The sign on the glass door said WESTIN & LEMMEL, with ACCREDITED PSYCHOLOGISTS in smaller letters underneath. Vanja went in. A reassuringly pleasant atmosphere, pale furniture, and better lighting than most traditional doctors' surgeries, with small white designer lamps on the coffee table. A lovely sofa to sit on while you were waiting. A glass door led from the waiting room to what Vanja assumed were the consulting rooms. She tried it. Locked. She knocked firmly, and after a little while a man in his forties emerged and introduced himself as Rolf Lemmel. Vanja showed her ID and explained why she was there.

'Peter hasn't arrived yet, but he shouldn't be long,' said Rolf, inviting her to sit. Vanja settled down on the sofa and started to glance through the previous day's *Dagens Nyheter*, which was lying on the table. The waiting room was quiet and peaceful. After a while a girl of about fifteen came in. She was slightly built and had freshly washed hair. Vanja gave her a friendly smile.

'Are you here to see Peter Westin?'

245

The girl nodded in response.

Good, that meant he should be here soon.

'I need a few minutes of your time.' Sebastian realised at once that something had happened. He knew Torkel and his tone of voice very well. Admittedly Sebastian had gone back to sleep for once when the alarm went off and hadn't arrived at the station until after nine, but this wasn't about turning up late. This was something more serious.

'Of course,' Sebastian replied, ambling after Torkel, who marched into one of the three interview rooms on the first floor, waving his hand to hurry Sebastian along. This was serious. Hurrying him along. A private conversation. In a soundproof room. This didn't bode well. Sebastian slowed down a fraction. As usual he was preparing himself for the worst by pretending to be even more nonchalant. This didn't impress Torkel.

'Get a move on, I haven't got all day.'

Torkel closed the door and looked Sebastian straight in the eye.

'The day before you turned up and said you wanted to work with us, you had sex with Leonard Lundin's mother. Is that true?'

Sebastian shook his head. 'No, it was the night before.'

'Enough! Are you out of your mind? She was the mother of our chief suspect at the time!'

'What does that matter? I mean, Leonard was innocent.'

'You didn't know that at the time!'

Sebastian smiled at Torkel. Self-assured. Self-important, some might say.

'I did, actually. I was absolutely certain, as you well know.'

Torkel shook his head, pacing angrily around the cramped room.

'It was wrong on every level, and you know it. She's phoned to tell me about it. Threatened to ring the press if I didn't take appropriate action. You have to be able to keep your cock in your pants, for fuck's sake!'

Sebastian suddenly felt sorry for Torkel. He had brought an

unknown troublemaker into the investigation against the will of most of the others. No doubt he had had to defend his decision in many ways – not least to himself. One of his rationales was no doubt the old classic, 'Don't worry, he's different now, he's changed.' But the truth is that no one changes. Sebastian knew that. We merely revolve around the same axis, so that the sides of ourselves that we show vary, but the basic foundation is always the same.

'Absolutely. But when Clara and I ended up in an intimate situation, I wasn't working with you, was I?'

Torkel looked at him. Couldn't bring himself to respond.

'Nothing like that will happen again,' Sebastian said as honestly as he could, and added, 'I promise.' As if that extra promise could chase away the memory of a naked Beatrice last night. Beatrice Strand, the murder victim's class teacher. And her son was Roger's best friend. However you looked at it, it was wrong in every possible way. God, he really was a complete idiot – even he had to admit that.

Why do I always, always have to test everything to destruction?

Torkel looked at him, and for a second Sebastian thought he was going to be asked to leave right there and then. That would have been the right decision. But it was a fraction too long before Torkel spoke; he hesitated, for some reason Sebastian was unable to fathom.

'Are you sure?' he said eventually.

Sebastian nodded, still wearing his most honest expression.

'Absolutely.'

'You don't have to have sex with every woman you meet,' Torkel went on, his tone slightly softer. Sebastian suddenly worked it out. It was actually quite simple. Torkel liked him. Sebastian decided to make an attempt. He felt as if Torkel deserved it, somehow.

'I find it difficult to be alone. The nights are the worst.'

Torkel met his gaze.

'Let me make one thing clear: there will be no more chances. Now get out of here. I don't want to set eyes on you for a while.'

Sebastian nodded and left. Normally he would have felt superior, cocky and smug. He had tricked his way out of yet another sticky situation. Got away with it.

'You put me in the shit,' he heard Torkel's voice behind him, 'and I don't like it.' If Sebastian possessed any capacity for regret or a bad conscience, he would experience those feelings now. But perhaps there was a hint of those emotions as he headed for the door. Beatrice was a one-off. He promised himself that.

The girl with the freshly washed hair had given up after twenty minutes, when Peter Westin still hadn't turned up. After a while Vanja had taken a stroll around the outside of the building. It wasn't in her nature to sit still, and she took the opportunity to call her parents. They were just on their way out but still had time to chat. It was just like the good old days. First of all she had a long chat with her mother, then a shorter one with her father. Oddly enough, they never needed as many words to say the same amount. A certain level of ordinariness had already returned to their conversations after the last few months, when everything had revolved around life and death. Vanja realised how much she had missed this normality and laughed when her mother embarked on one of her favourite topics: Vanja's love life. Or, rather, the absence of it. As always, Vanja brushed her questions aside, but not as brusquely as before.

Hadn't she met anyone in Örebro?

Västerås, and no, she hadn't time.

But what about that nice Billy she worked with? She liked him, didn't she?

Yes, but it would feel like going to bed with her brother.

And then of course they were back to Jonathan, the inevitable final destination of her mother's argument.

Was she really not going to get in touch with him again? He was so nice!

A few months earlier Vanja had always adopted a furious defensive stance whenever Jonathan was mentioned. The fact that her

248

mother kept on trying to get her to go back to her ex, without any concept of how this diminished Vanja, used to drive her crazy. Now it just felt gloriously normal. She even allowed the nagging and pleading to go on for a while. Her mother seemed surprised when she didn't encounter the usual counterattack. Indeed, she seemed to lose heart after a little while, and concluded with the point Vanja so often used.

'Oh well, you're a big girl now. You can make your own decisions.'

'Thanks, Mum.'

Her father came on the line shortly after that. He had decided to come up and see her that evening. No excuses. Vanja didn't even try. She usually made an effort to keep her two worlds apart, but this time she was happy for them to collide. He was catching the six-twenty train, and Vanja promised to pick him up at the station. She ended the call and went back to the psychology practice. She got Peter Westin's address from his colleague, who was tiring of her by this stage, but Rolf Lemmel did promise that when Peter eventually arrived he'd let him know that the police were looking for him.

Vanja got in the car. Rotevägen 12. She entered it into the GPS. It would take around half an hour to get there. She had promised to be back at the station by ten for a briefing with the rest of the team. Westin would have to wait.

Torkel walked into the conference room. The others were already gathered, and Ursula raised an eyebrow at them, following Torkel inside.

'So what have you done with Sebastian, then?'

Was Torkel just being oversensitive this morning, or was there a difference between 'Where's Sebastian?' and 'What have you done with Sebastian, then?' The latter made it sound as if they were inseparable. Tom and Jerry. Yogi Bear and Boo-Boo. Torkel and Sebastian. 'So what have you done with Sebastian, then?' A passive-aggressive way of making it clear to Torkel that Ursula had the impression Sebastian was more important to him than she was. As if he needed any further reminders. If she only knew. Right now Torkel was prepared to sell Sebastian for painful medical experiments. But this morning had been bad enough without starting a row with Ursula as well.

So he simply answered, 'He's on his way.' Pulled out a chair and sat down. He reached across the table, grabbed the thermos and poured some coffee into a polystyrene cup. 'Has Mikael arrived yet?'

Neutral tone of voice. Everyday small talk.

'He'll be here this afternoon.'

'Lovely.'

'Absolutely.'

Vanja looked up. There was a particular tone between Ursula and Torkel, a tone she couldn't recall hearing before. A bit like when Mum and Dad didn't want to give away the fact that they'd been quarrelling, when she was little. When they made a huge effort to be polite so that she would think everything was fine. It hadn't worked then and it didn't work now. Vanja glanced at Billy. Had he picked up on it too? Obviously not. He was absorbed in his laptop.

Sebastian came in, nodded to the assembled company and sat down. Vanja stole a glance at Ursula, who gave Sebastian a black look, did the same to Torkel then fixed her gaze on the table. What was going on here? Torkel took a sip of his coffee.

'Okay, Billy, would you like to start us off?'

Billy closed his laptop, picked up a small pile of A4 sheets and got to his feet.

'I received the list of calls from the telephone operator last night and the lists from SKL this morning, so I've put them all together in one document.'

He went around handing a sheet of paper to each person. Vanja wondered why he didn't just put them in the middle of the table and let everyone help themselves. She didn't say anything, just looked at the first page of her printout.

'The first page is outgoing calls. Roger's last call was on Friday at 20:17, to his class teacher's home number.' Billy wrote up the call on the time line on the wall. Sebastian looked up from his list.

'Can you tell if he tried to call anyone after that, but didn't get an answer?'

'Yes, that was the last call he made.'

'What were you thinking?' asked Vanja, turning to Sebastian.

'He said he wanted to speak to Johan when he rang the Strands, didn't he? But he never tried Johan's mobile.'

Billy turned to face them and shook his head.

'Yes. I mean no, he didn't.'

'Perhaps something prevented him,' Torkel suggested.

'A murderer, for example,' said Ursula.

'Next page,' Billy went on. 'Incoming calls. The last is from Lisa just before half past six. Well, you can see that for yourselves.'

He added that call to the time line then moved on.

'Next page. Text messages. First of all we have the messages that were left on the water-damaged phone. There aren't many. Most are to and from Johan, Erik and Lisa. We already knew that Roger wasn't all that big on friends, so no surprises there. If you could turn to the last page, you'll see the incoming texts that were deleted, and those are obviously of interest.'

Sebastian skimmed the sheet of paper in front of him. He sat up straight. 'Obviously of interest' wasn't even the half of it.

'Two of them are from a prepaid phone,' Billy went on. 'One on the Thursday and one on the Friday, a few hours before he disappeared.

Sebastian read the first message.

this has to stop now! for everyone's sake!

And the second

please get in touch! it's all my fault! nobody is blaming you!

Sebastian put down the printout and turned to Billy.

251

'The technical stuff has never been my strong point. Does a pre-paid phone mean what I think it means?'

'If you think it means we have a number but not the name of a subscriber, then yes,' Billy replied as he wrote up the number. 'I've requested lists of all calls and messages from that phone, so we'll see where that takes us.'

Sebastian watched as Vanja unconsciously raised her arm and stuck her index finger in the air while studying the pages in front of her, as if she were putting her hand up in class. For a brief second Sebastian pictured her in school uniform then immediately dismissed the thought. He had already overstepped enough boundaries in this investigation, and if there was one thing all the years of fleeting relationships had taught him, it was how to recognise more or less instantly when he had a chance and when he didn't.

'Were the messages written in upper case, in capital letters, on the phone itself, or is it just on the printout?'

Billy looked at Vanja with a certain weariness in his expression.

'I know what upper case means.'

'Sorry.'

'They were written exactly as they are there. In upper case.'

'It's like shouting.'

'Or perhaps it's just that the person who wrote the messages wasn't all that familiar with texting.'

'Most people in that category are older.'

Sebastian read the short messages again and was inclined to agree with Vanja. He didn't know whether capital letters meant you were shouting or not, however, the choice of words suggested that an adult, an older person, was the sender.

'So we've got no chance of finding out who sent these?' Torkel asked, a hint of resignation in his voice. Billy shook his head.

'Has anyone tried ringing the number?'

The room fell silent. Everyone looked at Vanja, who had asked the question, then at one another, and finally at Billy. He leaned over to the phone in the middle of the table, switched it to speakerphone and keyed in the number. A tense air of expectation filled the room. The number did not ring out. Instead they heard, 'The person you are calling is not available. Please try later.'

Billy switched off the speakerphone. Torkel looked at him, his expression serious.

'Make sure somebody keeps trying that number.'

Billy nodded.

'What are the rest of these?' Ursula gestured to the papers in her hand.

Sebastian studied the printout.

One text: 12 BEER + VODKA.

Next: 20 BEER + GIN. Followed by a smiley.

Next: 1 BTL RED & BEER.

And so on.

'These are orders.'

The others looked up.

'For what?'

'For what it says.'

Sebastian turned to Billy.

'When did he get the last of these messages?'

'About a month ago.'

Sebastian met Vanja's eyes across the table. He could see that she knew where he was going with this, but he said it anyway.

'That was when Axel Johansson got the sack for bootlegging.'

Vanja got up and looked at Sebastian, who stared down at his papers. He knew where she wanted to go. To the very place where he didn't want to go.

Vanja set off towards the house, with Sebastian a few steps behind. At first he had intended to stay in the car, but had quickly realised that would look odd. Not that he really cared whether Vanja thought he was odd or not. No, it was more a case of pure survival instinct. He had decided that he needed to stay with this investigation for a while longer, at least until Billy had managed to track down an address for him. Beatrice Strand thanking him for a wonderful night would definitely throw a spanner in the works. Vanja

253

didn't even manage to ring the bell before the door opened. It was Beatrice. She had put her hair up and was wearing a simple blouse and a pair of jeans. She looked surprised.

'Has something happened?'

'We need a word with Johan,' Vanja began.

'He's not here, he and Ulf have gone camping.' Beatrice looked at Sebastian, but didn't give the slightest indication that they had seen each other just a few hours ago.

'We know that,' Vanja went on. 'But have you any idea where they've gone?'

They drove west on the E18. Beatrice's directions took them past the small community of Dingtuna, then south on small roads heading towards Lake Mälaren and the inlet known as Lilla Blacken, which was where Beatrice thought they would be. Neither Vanja nor Sebastian spoke. Vanja tried calling Peter Westin, but there was still no reply. She was becoming annoyed with the psychologist's failure to return her calls. She had left four messages by now. Sebastian closed his eyes and tried to sleep.

'Late night?'

Sebastian shook his head.

'No, I just didn't sleep very well.' He closed his eyes again to make it clear that he wasn't interested in having a conversation, but was soon forced to open them as Vanja braked sharply.

'What's going on?'

'Do we turn left or right here? You're supposed to be navigating.'

'Oh, please.'

'You like making decisions. Now's your chance.'

Sebastian sighed, picked up the map and studied it. He didn't have the strength to fight back. She could have her victory this time.

He hated Västerås.

God, how he hated Västerås.

He felt as if he had seen every single square metre of the town on CCTV footage of varying quality. It had been nice to see something of the place live, so to speak, but the only time he got the opportunity to tear himself away from the tapes was when he was compiling lists of telephone calls or – Billy gave a start. His fingers flew over the keyboard. Stop. Rewind. Play. Yes, at last. Ladies and gentlemen, entering from the right: Roger Eriksson. Stop again. Billy looked at the key that had arrived with the films. Which camera was this? 1.22. Drottninggatan. Where was that? Billy grabbed his map of Västerås, searched, found and marked the place. The time showed in the top corner of the picture: 21:29.

Play.

Billy watched as Roger walked towards the camera with his head bowed, dragging his feet. After about ten metres he looked up, turned off to the right and disappeared behind a parked car, which was in a side street and out of the picture.

Billy sighed. His joy was short-lived. The boy was alive and had carried on walking. Which meant that Billy had to carry on as well. See more of Västerås, whether he wanted to or not. Roger was heading north. Billy looked at the key again, checked on the map. Discounted a number of cameras that were in the wrong direction and started searching again.

He hated Västerås.

Lilla Blacken was a popular leisure area by an inlet in Lake Mälaren. At least, it was in the summer. Today it seemed to be deserted. They had driven around on dirt tracks for a while before finding the right place.

A Renault Mégane was parked in front of a dilapidated noticeboard. Sebastian got out and walked over to the empty car. Thought he recognised it from Beatrice's house the previous day when they had seen Ulf there. A battered sign on the noticeboard proclaimed WELCOME TO LILLA BLACKEN – FRESH AIR AND FUN. Below the sign a number of notices had been pinned up offering items for sale or exchange, information on fishing permits, but the winter dampness had blurred most of the text. He turned to Vanja.

'I think this is the place.'

They looked around. In front of them a few scattered clumps of deciduous trees were growing on an open field leading down to the water. Right down at the bottom on the shoreline stood a blue tent, flapping slightly in the wind.

They made their way down through the damp grass to the tent. The sky was overcast, but the cold of the night had gone. As always, Vanja took the lead. Sebastian smiled. Always first, always the last word. That was Vanja. Just like him when he was young and hungry. These days he usually settled for the last word. As they approached the lake they could see two people sitting on a rickety jetty extending out into the water, not far from the camp. They seemed to be fishing. Side by side. As Sebastian and Vanja got closer they recognised Ulf and Johan. It was a real father-and-son picture, the kind of thing Sebastian had never experienced.

Ulf and Johan were warmly dressed, well equipped with hats and green Wellingtons. Beside them stood several buckets, a knife and a box containing hooks and weights. They were each holding a fishing rod. Johan remained seated, while Ulf got up and came towards them, anxiety etched on his face.

'Has something happened?'

The water in Lake Mälaren was high after the spring thaw, and the underside of the jetty was dangerously close to the surface. Cold water surged up through the gaps in the planks, soaking the wood as Ulf walked towards them. Sebastian moved back a couple of paces to avoid getting wet.

'We need to speak to Johan again. Some new information has come to light.'

'And we thought we might be left in peace for a while. Get away from it all. This has been really tough for him.'

'Yes, you told us that, but we need to speak to him again.'

'It's okay, Dad.'

Ulf gave a resigned nod and allowed them to pass him. Johan put down the rod and slowly got to his feet. Vanja just couldn't wait any longer.

'Johan, was Roger selling alcohol along with Axel Johansson?'

Johan stopped and stared at Vanja. He looked like a little boy dressed in clothes that were far too big. He paled, nodded. Ulf reacted immediately. This was obviously news to him.

'What are you saying?' All three adults were now staring at the sixteen-year-old, who had gone even paler.

'It was Roger's idea from the start. He took the orders. Axel did the buying. Then they sold at a higher price and split the profits.'

Ulf looked at his son, his expression serious.

'Were you in on this?'

The boy shook his head immediately. 'No, I didn't want anything to do with it.' Johan's eyes were pleading, but his father remained stern.

'Listen to me, Johan. I understand that you feel you have to protect Roger, but you need to tell me and these officers everything you know.' Johan had moved along the jetty to stand beside his father. 'Do you understand?'

Johan nodded without speaking. Vanja decided to continue.

'When did it start?'

'Some time last autumn. Roger talked to Axel, and then it was all under way. They made good money.'

'What went wrong? Why did Roger tell on Axel?'

'Axel didn't want to share the money with anyone, so he started selling on his own. He didn't really need Roger, after all. He could take the orders himself.'

'So Roger went to the principal?'

'Yes.'

'Who fired Axel Johansson.'

'Yes, the same day.'

'Didn't Axel tell the principal that Roger had been in on it from the start?'

'I don't know. I think Roger might have told Herr Groth

himself. That he'd got involved but changed his mind. That he didn't want to be a part of it any longer.'

The last questions had come from Sebastian. He could almost see Roger standing in front of the pedantic principal, playing the regretful and conscientious student. Accusing the man who had betrayed him. Roger had been more calculating than Sebastian thought. He kept revealing new sides of his character. It was intriguing.

'Why did Roger start selling in the first place?'

'He needed the money.'

Ulf felt compelled to chip in, presumably because he needed to draw attention to the fact that this was something that affected his family.

'For what?'

'Didn't you see what he looked like, Dad? What he was wearing when he started at the school? He had no intention of being bullied again.'

There was a short silence, then Johan went on.

'Don't you understand? He just wanted to fit in. He did whatever he had to do to fit in.'

Roger, who had been a somewhat anonymous figure at first, was beginning to take shape. The hidden aspects of his character were starting to emerge into the light and, with them, his motives. It was both sad and human. A young person who wanted to be someone else. Something else. At any price. Vanja recognised the situation from her time in uniform. But it surprised her that this struggle could lead to violence, even murder. She took out the printed text messages from Roger's mobile that Billy had given her and passed them over to Johan.

'Do you know who could have sent these?'

Johan shook his head.

'No idea.'

'You don't recognise the number?'

'No.'

'Are you sure? This could be really important.'

Johan nodded to show that he understood, but he still didn't know. Ulf put his arm around his son.

'I think you and Roger had started to lose touch a little bit this term, wouldn't you say?'

Johan nodded.

'Why was that?' said Vanja.

'Oh, you know how it is, boys develop differently at that age.' Ulf shrugged as if to indicate that this was a natural law, and nothing anyone could do about it.

Vanja didn't give up. She made a point of turning to Johan this time.

'Was there a reason why you didn't spend so much time together any more?'

Johan hesitated, thought about it, and then he too shrugged his shoulders.

'He kind of changed.'

'In what way?'

'I don't know . . . In the end he was only interested in money and sex.'

'Sex?'

Johan nodded.

'He talked about it all the time. I didn't like it.'

Ulf hugged his son. *Classic*, Sebastian thought. Most parents feel compelled to protect their children as soon as sex is mentioned, mostly for the benefit of those who might be observing. To show everyone else that in this family the children are protected from the animal side of things, from everything dirty. If only Ulf knew what his wife and Sebastian had been doing last night while he was shivering in a cold tent. Then again, that would probably have ruined any chance of a constructive interview.

They spoke to Johan for a few more minutes, trying to find more clues to Roger's true character, but Johan didn't appear to have any more to give. He was worn out – they could both see that – and they had got more from him than they had hoped for. Eventually they thanked both Ulf and Johan and headed back to the car. Sebastian looked back at the father and son, standing on the shoreline watching them.

A loving and protective father.

His son.

No room for anyone else.

Perhaps it wasn't Sebastian who had seduced Beatrice.

Perhaps it was the other way round.

On the way back from Lilla Blacken Vanja decided to call at Peter Westin's house on Rotevägen. Her irritation at his failure to call her back had been replaced by a sense of unease. After all, an entire morning had elapsed. As they drew closer to the address it became clear that her anxiety was justified, as the acrid smell of smoke filled the car. Through the side window she could see a faint dark-grey column of smoke rising above the trees and houses. She slowed down and turned left into a side street, then left again into Rotevägen. It was a residential street lined with chestnut trees, but the peace and quiet had been destroyed by the large number of fire engines blocking the road up ahead. Blue lights flashing. Firefighters walking to and fro with equipment, with no sense of urgency. Groups of curious onlookers behind a cordon. Even Sebastian woke up.

'Is that where we were going?'

'I think so.'

They got out of the car and walked quickly up to the house. The closer they got, the worse it looked. Large sections of the out-side wall were missing from one side of the upper floor, and inside they could see the charred remains of furniture and possessions. Black, stinking water was running down the street and into the drains. Drawing closer, the smell became more pungent. A small number of firefighters were busy damping down. On the grey fence – which was presumably the same colour as the house had been before the fire – was a metal sign with the number twelve on it. It was Peter Westin's house.

Vanja showed her ID and after a few minutes she was able to speak to Sundstedt, the officer in charge. He was a man in his fifties with a moustache, wearing a high-visibility jacket with the words CHIEF FIREFIGHTER on the back. He was a calm man who spoke with a Norrland accent. He was surprised to see plainclothes police already on the spot. He had just called in to report that they had found a body on the upper floor. Vanja stiffened.

'Could it be the man who lived here? Peter Westin?' she said.

'We don't know, but it's highly likely. The body was found in what was left of the bedroom,' said Sundstedt and went on to explain that one of his team had noticed a charred foot sticking out from underneath the collapsed ceiling. They would try to remove the body as soon as they could, but since they were still damping down and the risk of further structural collapse was high, it could take several hours.

The fire had started early in the morning, and the call to the fire service had come at 04:17 from the next-door neighbour. By the time they had arrived, large parts of the upper floor were already ablaze, and they'd had to focus on preventing the fire from spreading to neighbouring properties.

'Do you suspect arson?'

'It's too early to say, but the concentrated seat of the fire and the rapid spread would suggest that's the case.'

Vanja looked around. Sebastian had gone over to speak to some of the nosy neighbours a short distance away. Vanja took out her phone and called Ursula. She explained the situation and asked her to come as soon as she could. Then she rang Torkel to tell him, but there was no reply. She left a message on his voicemail.

Sebastian was heading towards her. He nodded in the direction of the neighbours he had just been talking to.

'Some of them saw Westin late yesterday evening, and they're sure he was in there last night. He was nearly always at home.'

They looked at one another.

'It seems to me as if this is a bit too much of a coincidence,' said Sebastian. 'How sure are you that Roger was one of his clients?'

'Not sure at all. I know he went there once or twice at the beginning when he first moved to the school – Beatrice told me that – but as to whether he went to see Westin recently, I've no idea. All I have is those initials and the time on Wednesdays.'

Sebastian nodded and touched her arm.

'We have to know.' He set off towards the car. 'That school is too small for anyone to be able to keep a secret like that. Trust me, I used to go there.'

They turned the car around and drove back to Palmlövska High. This case seemed to keep on taking them back there.

The perfect school on the surface.

With bigger and bigger cracks appearing in the facade.

Vanja called Billy and asked him to find out everything he could about one Peter Westin, psychologist, registered address Rotevägen 12. He promised to get onto it as soon as possible. Meanwhile, Sebastian rang Lena Eriksson to see if she knew what her son used to do every other Wednesday at ten o'clock. Just as Vanja had suspected, Lena knew nothing about any educational psychologist. Sebastian thanked her and ended the call. Vanja looked at him. Realised that over the past few hours she had forgotten that she had promised herself she would dislike him. He was actually a pretty good sounding board in critical situations. She couldn't suppress a smile. Naturally Sebastian seized the opportunity to misinterpret it.

'Are you flirting with me?'

'What? No!'

'Well, you're sitting there checking me out like a lovesick teenager.'

'Fuck off.'

'It's nothing to be ashamed of. That's just the effect I have on women.' Sebastian gave her a ridiculously self-confident smile. She looked away and floored the accelerator.

This time he had definitely had the last word.

'Do you have a moment?' From the tone of her voice Haraldsson understood immediately that Hanser actually meant, 'I want to speak to you. Now!' Indeed. When he looked up from his work he saw her standing there with her arms folded, and her expression was grim as she nodded towards the door of her office. But she wasn't having things that easy. Whatever was going on, Haraldsson had no intention of allowing her to play on home ground.

'Couldn't we do it here? I'm trying to stay off my foot as much as possible.'

Hanser looked around the open-plan office as if to establish how many colleagues sitting closest to Haraldsson would be able to hear the conversation, then, with a sigh and a movement indicative of suppressed irritation, she pulled over a chair from a vacant work-station. She sat down opposite Haraldsson, leaned forward and lowered her voice.

'Were you outside Axel Johansson's apartment block last night?'

'No.'

Pure reflex.

Denial.

No logical thought process.

Was she asking because she already knew he'd been there? Probably. In which case a 'yes' would have been better, then he could have tried to come up with a good reason for being there, if there was a problem. Presumably there was, otherwise she wouldn't have come to speak to him, would she? Or did she just suspect he'd been there? In which case a denial would work. Perhaps she merely wanted to praise his initiative? Not very likely. Haraldsson's mind was whirling. He had a feeling this was going to be a damage-limitation exercise, and that it would have been better to answer 'yes' to the first question. Time up.

'Are you sure it wasn't you?'

Too late to change his answer now, but there was no need for him either to confirm or deny what he had already said.

'Why?'

'I had a call from one Desiré Holmin. She lives in the same block as Axel Johansson. She said she saw him last night, and that somebody who was waiting in a car started to chase him when he got home.'

'And you think that was me?'

'Was it?'

Haraldsson thought frantically. Holmin. Holmin . . . Wasn't that the little grey lady on the same floor as Johansson? Yes, it was. She'd been so interested when he'd knocked on the door and spoken to her. He'd thought he was never going to get away. He could easily imagine she was the type who sat up keeping an eye on things. To assist the police. To bring a little excitement into her grey, monotonous pensioner's life. On the other hand, it had been dark and the old lady must have been tired and maybe a little short-sighted. Perhaps slightly senile. He could get away with this.

'No, it wasn't me.'

Hanser sat in silence, studying his face. Not without a certain level of satisfaction. Haraldsson didn't know it but he had just made a solid start on digging his own grave. She didn't say a word, convinced that he would carry on shovelling.

Haraldsson was beginning to feel uncomfortable. He hated the way she was looking at him. He hated the silence, which clearly said that she didn't believe him. And wasn't that a little smile playing around her lips? He decided to play his trump card right away.

'How could I chase anyone, when I can hardly limp to the toilet?'

'Because of your foot?'

'Exactly.'

Hanser nodded. Haraldsson smiled at her. *There you go, sorted.* Hanser would realise how impossible the suggestion was and leave him alone. To his surprise she stayed where she was, still leaning forward.

'What kind of car do you drive?'

'Why?'

'Fru Holmin said that the man who chased Johansson got out of a green Toyota.'

Okay, thought Haraldsson, *time to play the slightly weaker cards in my hand: dark, tired, short-sighted and senile.* How far from the building had he been? Twenty to thirty metres. At least. His face broke into a disarming smile.

'Not that I wish to discredit Fru Holmin, but if we're talking about last night then I presume it was dark, so how could she have seen what colour the car was? And how old is she – getting on for eighty? I have spoken to her, and I must say she didn't seem all that reliable. It would surprise me if she could distinguish between different makes of car.'

'It was parked under a street light and she had a pair of binoculars.'

Hanser leaned back, her eyes fixed on Haraldsson. She could practically see his brain working. Like a cartoon, with the cogs spinning faster and faster. She was a little surprised. Surely he could see where she was going with this?

'Well, I'm hardly the only person who owns a green Toyota. If that's what it was.'

Obviously not, thought Hanser. Not only was Haraldsson still digging, he had jumped down into the grave and started filling it in.

'She wrote down the registration number. You're the only person who has that number.'

Haraldsson was lost for words. He couldn't come up with a thing. His head was empty. Hanser leaned right across the desk.

'Now Axel Johansson knows we're looking for him, and he will probably make even more of an effort to stay away.'

Haraldsson tried to respond, but the words wouldn't come. Nothing. His vocal cords refused to cooperate.

'I will have to inform Torkel Höglund and his team about this. It. Is. Their. Investigation. I'm putting it as clearly as possible, since you don't seem to have grasped the idea yet.'

Hanser stood up and looked down at Haraldsson, whose eyes were darting all over the place. If it hadn't been such a gross error of judgement and, to be honest, if it hadn't been Haraldsson, she would have felt a little sorry for him.

'We also need to discuss exactly where you were when you should have been at Listakärr. Desiré Holmin said the man who chased Axel Johansson wasn't limping. Quite the reverse, in fact. He was really fast.'

Hanser turned and left. Haraldsson watched her go, his face expressionless. How had that happened? He was supposed to have gotten away with it. Damage limitation was the worst-case scenario. This wasn't even on the map. The chief superintendent's speech was a long, long way away. Haraldsson could feel the downward spiral that was his life spinning faster and faster, growing steeper and steeper. And he was falling. Helplessly.

Ursula already knew Sundstedt. He had been an investigator for the Swedish Accident Investigation Board for a while before returning to his profession as a firefighter. They had met when she was working at SKL during a complex investigation involving a private plane that had crashed in Sörmland: it was suspected that the pilot had been poisoned by his wife. They had got on well from the start. Sundstedt was exactly like Ursula: not afraid to get stuck in. Didn't take any crap. He had spotted her as soon as she got out of the car and given her a friendly wave.

'My, we are honoured!'

'Kind of you to say so!'

A warm hug, a quick word about how long it had been since they'd seen each other. Then he gave her a hard hat and led her over to the ruined house.

'So you're still with Riksmord?'

'Yes.'

'Are you here about the murder of that boy?'

Ursula nodded. Sundstedt waved in the direction of the still-smoking house.

'Do you think there's a connection?'

'We don't know. Have you removed the body?'

He shook his head and took her around the house. He opened the door of his car, dug out a big fireproof jacket and held it out to her.

'Put this on. I might as well show you where the body is. You'll only moan if you're not involved from the start.'

'I don't moan. I complain. With good reason. There's a difference.'

They smiled at one another and carried on towards the house. They went in through the opening where the front door had been. It now lay to one side in the hallway. The kitchen furniture was untouched by the flames, and it looked as if it was just waiting for someone to come and sit down for lunch. The floor, however, was covered with filthy, sooty water that was still dripping from the ceiling and trickling down the walls. They went up the stairs, which were slippery with the water. The acrid smell grew stronger, making Ursula's nose prickle and bringing tears to her eyes. In spite of the fact that Ursula had seen more than her fair share of fires, she was always fascinated. Fire transformed everyday objects in a terrifying and almost seductive way. An undamaged armchair stood among the rubbish. Beyond it, where there used to be an outside wall, she could see the garden and the house next door. The transience of life met the remains of normality. Sundstedt slowed down and began to move forward more carefully. He waved to Ursula to stay where she was. The floor creaked ominously beneath his weight. He pointed to a white cover lying beside what remained of the bed. Parts of the roof had fallen in, and they could see the sky above them.

'There's the body. We need to make the floor safe before we can move it.'

Ursula nodded, crouched and took out her camera. Sundstedt knew what she wanted to do, and without a word he reached down, got hold of the end of the cover and pulled it away. Beneath it lay charred wooden rafters, along with broken and unbroken tiles from the collapsed section of the roof. But protruding from under the rubble was something that was clearly a foot. It was blackened by the fire but the flesh had not been burned away. Ursula took a number of pictures, starting with the wider shots. As she cautiously moved in to take close-ups she became aware of a sweeter aroma coming through the pungent smell of the fire, like a combination of the mortuary and a forest fire. It was possible to get used to many things in her job, but the smells were always the most difficult.

She swallowed.

'Judging by the size of the foot it's probably an adult male,' Sundstedt began. 'Shall I help you take a tissue sample? There are some soft parts left around the ankle.'

'I can do that later if necessary. At the moment it would be more helpful if I had something to compare with dental records.'

'It's going to be a few hours before I can move the body.'

Ursula nodded.

'Okay, if I'm not here then, call me right away.' She dug her card out of one of her pockets and handed it to Sundstedt. He tucked it in his pocket, replaced the cover over the body and got to his feet, as did Ursula.

Together they began to investigate the cause of the fire. Ursula was no expert, but even she could see that a number of details in the bedroom indicated that the fire had spread extremely rapidly. Far too rapidly to be natural.

Rolf Lemmel was devastated. A close friend had rung to tell him about the fire at Peter's house. However, he didn't know that a body had been found in the bedroom, and when Vanja told him, he turned even paler. Flopped down onto the sofa in the waiting room with his head in his hands.

'Is it Peter?'

'We don't know yet, but it's a strong possibility.' Lemmel's body twisted, as if it didn't know where to go. His breathing was heavy and laboured. Sebastian fetched him a glass of water. Rolf took

268

a few gulps, which seemed to calm him a little. He looked at the two officers. Realised that one of them had been looking for Peter earlier in the day, when he still believed his colleague had merely been delayed. At the time he had found her quite irritating. Now he felt as if he hadn't understood the seriousness of her visit.

'Why were you here this morning? Could it be to do with this?' he asked, looking deep into Vanja's eyes.

'We don't know. I needed to know if a particular person had been seeing Peter as a patient.'

'Who?'

'His name is Roger Eriksson. He's a sixteen-year-old from Palmlövska High.'

Vanja reached for the photo of Roger, but it wasn't necessary.

'The boy who was murdered?'

'Exactly.'

She handed him the picture anyway, just to be on the safe side. He stared at it and thought long and hard, he wanted to be sure.

'I don't know. I mean, Peter had a counselling arrangement with the school, so lots of the kids came here. It's possible.'

'Every other Wednesday at ten o'clock this term? Was he here then?'

Lemmel shook his head.

'I only work here three days a week. I'm at the hospital on Wednesdays and Thursdays, so I don't know. But we can check Peter's room. His notebook will be in there.'

'Don't you have a receptionist?' Sebastian wondered as they walked through the glass doors and along a small corridor.

'No, we can manage things ourselves. It would be an unnecessary expenditure.' Lemmel stopped at the second door on the right and took out his keys. He looked a little surprised when he tried to turn the key and the door suddenly opened.

'That's odd . . . '

Sebastian pushed the door right back. Their eyes were met by a scene of utter chaos, with files and papers all over the place.

Drawers pulled out. Folders emptied on the floor. Shattered glass. Rolf looked shocked. Vanja quickly pulled on a pair of latex gloves.

'Stay where you are. Sebastian, call Ursula and tell her she's needed here as soon as possible.'

'I think it might be better if you rang her.' Sebastian attempted a smile.

'Tell her what it's about. She might hate you, but she's a professional.'

Vanja turned to Lemmel.

'So you haven't been in here today?'

He shook his head. She started to look around.

'Can you see Peter's notebook anywhere?'

Lemmel was still in shock and his answer was slow to come.

'No, it's a big green book with a leather cover, almost A4.'

Vanja nodded and began hunting carefully among the discarded papers. It was no easy task, because she didn't want to crash about too much and run the risk of destroying any possible forensic evidence. At the same time she felt it was of the utmost importance to find out if there was a link between Peter Westin and Roger Eriksson. Because if there was, it would mean the investigation had taken an unexpected turn.

After ten minutes Vanja gave up. As far as she could see, there was no notebook in the room. But she couldn't turn everything upside down and search the whole place. Ursula had called back to say that she would be tied up at Rotevägen for the next few hours, but she had spoken to Hanser, who had promised that the Västerås police would send their best CSI technician. Ursula didn't like it, but how hard could it be to secure one room? Vanja locked the door with Lemmel's key and went to have another word with him. He was back on the sofa, talking to someone on the phone. His eyes were full of tears, his tone of voice controlled but full of sorrow. He caught sight of Vanja and tried to pull himself together.

'I have to go, darling. The police want to speak to me again.'

'A technician is on the way. No one is allowed into that room. May I keep your keys?'

He nodded. Vanja looked around.

'Where's my colleague?'

'He said he was going to check on something.' Vanja sighed and took out her mobile, then realised she didn't have Sebastian's number. She had never expected to need it.

Sebastian walked into the cafeteria at Palmlövska High. In his days as a pupil there had been no warm and cosy venue resembling a coffee shop on the ground floor. At that time this space had been a study room for those wishing to do extra homework. The walls had not been white with little spotlights. Nor did he recall any black leather armchairs, low tables made of pale wood or small wall-mounted speakers playing lounge music. As far as he remembered, the walls had been lined with bookshelves and on the floor there had been long tables with hard chairs. Nothing else.

Sebastian had grown tired of playing second fiddle at the psychologists' practice. He had battled all day to fit in, not to go too far, to be a team player and all that crap. It hadn't been particularly difficult – all he'd had to do was drift along and keep his mouth shut in most cases. But it was boring, it was so fucking soul-destroyingly mind-numbingly boring. Even though he had managed to score a few points off Vanja in the car, it hadn't gone far enough. It was like existing at subsistence level, and Sebastian just didn't do that.

As he had watched Vanja cautiously moving papers around amid the chaos of Peter Westin's room, to avoid ruining things for Ursula later, he had decided to fly solo for a while. There was information everywhere. Somebody knew something about everything. It was just a matter of knowing who to ask.

Which was why he was standing here gazing around the cafeteria. He spotted Lisa Hansson sitting a short distance away chatting to her girlfriends, empty latte cups on the table in front of them. He went over. She didn't exactly look pleased to see him. But there was acceptance in her eyes. That would have to do.

'Hi, Lisa. Can you spare two seconds?'

The other girls looked at him in surprise, but he didn't wait for a reply.

'I could do with your help.'

When Sebastian walked back into Westin & Lemmel's psychology practice twenty-two minutes later, he had received confirmation from two sources that Roger Eriksson had been seeing Peter Westin every other Wednesday at ten o'clock. As with all clearly defined groups with strong internal control (and there are fewer groups with a more effective system of keeping a check on one another than teenagers), it would have been impossible for Roger to sneak off to see a counsellor without anyone finding out. Lisa had no idea who Roger had been seeing every other Wednesday, but she was familiar with the hierarchies within the school, and had proved very helpful in finding someone who did know. A girl in Year 2 had seen him, and another girl in Roger's parallel class confirmed it. They had met in the waiting room on two occasions.

Vanja was on the phone. She looked at Sebastian with a sour expression as he strolled nonchalantly into the room. He smiled at her. He noticed that a technician was dusting the doorframe to Westin's room for fingerprints. He had timed it perfectly. He waited until Vanja finished her conversation.

'How's it going? Found any forensic evidence?'

'Not yet. Where have you been?'

'Doing a little job. You wanted confirmation that Roger came here every other Wednesday at ten o'clock. He did.'

'Who says?'

Sebastian gave her the names of the two students. He had even written down what they said on a little piece of paper for her. He knew that would annoy her even more.

'Give them a call and check if you like.'

She looked at the piece of paper.

'I will. Later. Right now we're going back to the station. Billy's found something.'

*

Torkel hoped it was something good. He needed progress, something to smile about. In fact, he was ready to settle for something that wasn't heading straight down the pan. He had just been in a meeting with Hanser. After a polite exchange along the lines of 'thank you for dinner' and 'it was very nice', she had told him about Thomas Haraldsson. It didn't matter how well meaning his efforts had been, the incompetent arsehole had probably managed to get their one and only suspect so far to go underground. Which meant that the information they had acquired from the lists of phone calls and the retrieved text messages were now almost worthless. On top of all that, it looked as if Roger's counsellor had been murdered. Well, he was dead, they knew that much. Torkel had been doing this job for too long to think it was just an unfortunate coincidence.

So now they had a double murderer. It was small consolation that Sebastian didn't believe the first murder had been planned. The second one definitely was. Westin had presumably died because of something he knew about Roger Eriksson. Torkel swore to himself: why hadn't they been quicker? Why hadn't they got there first? Nothing was going their way in this bloody investigation. It wouldn't be long before the press made the connection between the deaths. It was just what they needed to keep the story going.

And Ursula was angry with him.

Mikael was on his way.

He pushed open the door of the conference room. Ursula was still at the scene of the crime, but the others were already there. Billy had called them all. Torkel sat down and nodded to Billy to start. The projector on the ceiling hummed into life, so Torkel assumed they would be looking at more CCTV footage. Correct. Roger came ambling in from the right.

'At 21:29 Roger Eriksson was here.' Billy circled a street on the map on the wall. 'Just about a kilometre from Gustavsborgsgatan. As you can see, he crosses the road and disappears. I mean, really disappears.' Billy rewound the film and froze the picture just before Roger disappeared behind a parked car.

'He turns into Spränggränd, a cul-de-sac which ends in foot-paths leading off in three directions.' Billy pointed at the map with his pen. 'I checked every camera to the north and west of Spränggränd. There aren't many. Roger doesn't appear on any of them, so I checked to see whether he had turned around and gone back. Nothing. I've seen more nondescript streets than any person needs to see in an entire lifetime. This is the last image of Roger Eriksson.'

They all looked at the frozen picture on the wall. Torkel was already in a bad mood and he could feel it dropping by several degrees. Or whatever bad moods dropped by. It was definitely dropping, anyway.

'If we play with the idea that he carried straight on, heading north, what's up there?' This came from Vanja. Torkel felt grateful that there was still someone on the team who was trying to get as much as possible out of nothing.

'On the other side of the E18 is Vallby, which mostly consists of large areas of apartment blocks.'

'Does he have any connections to that part of town? A classmate who lives there, anything like that?'

Billy shook his head. Sebastian got up and went over to the map.

'What's this?' He pointed to a large building only twenty metres or so from the end of Spränggränd.

'A motel.'

Sebastian started wandering around the room, speaking in a calm, reasoned tone of voice, as if talking to himself.

'Roger and Lisa had been pretending to have a relationship for some time. Lisa said Roger was also seeing someone else, but she didn't know who. He was extremely secretive about it.' Sebastian went back to the map and placed his finger on the motel.

'According to Johan, Roger talked about sex a lot. A motel is perfect for that kind of encounter.'

His gaze swept over the other three.

'Yes, I am speaking from experience.' He gave Vanja a meaningful look. 'Not of that particular motel, but you and I aren't

274

finished yet.' Vanja glanced at him wearily. The second sexual innu-endo today. One more and she would have him off this investigation before he knew what had hit him. But she said noth-ing. Why warn him? Torkel folded his arms and looked at Sebastian, his expression sceptical.

'Isn't the idea of meeting up at a motel a bit ... advanced when you're only sixteen? Surely you usually hang out at somebody's house at that age?'

'Perhaps that wasn't possible, for various reasons.'

Nobody spoke. The same sceptical looks from Billy and Vanja. Sebastian threw his arms wide.

'Come on! We've got a horny sixteen-year-old and a motel. Surely it's worth checking out, at least?'

Vanja got to her feet.

'Billy.'

Billy nodded, and together they left the room.

Edin's Budget Motel was built in the 1960s, and looked scruffy and neglected. There were only three cars in the oversized car park. The place was completely inspired by the USA and consisted of two long storeys with flights of steps on the outside, so that each room had its own entrance with direct access from the car park. In the middle of the ground floor was a small reception area with a neon sign glowing outside: VACANCIES. Billy and Vanja had a feel-ing it was a long time since it had been switched off. If you wanted to meet someone on the quiet, this was the perfect place.

They walked in through the double glass doors, which bore a handwritten notice: WE DON'T TAKE AMERICAN EXPRESS. It was quite dark in reception, which consisted of a tall, curved desk made of dark wood, a dirty dark-blue fitted carpet and two arm-chairs next to a round coffee table. The room felt oppressive and stank of smoke. The small fan humming away at one end of the desk had no chance of making any impact on the atmosphere. Behind the desk sat a woman of about fifty-five with long blonde hair that was probably bleached. She was reading one of those cheap gossip magazines that are packed with as many pictures as possible and very few words. Beside her lay the current edition of the evening paper, *Aftonbladet*, open at an article about Roger. Vanja had glanced through it earlier. Nothing new, except an interview with the principal of Palmlövska High in which he spoke about how proactive his school was in its efforts to stamp out bullying and isolation, and how Roger had found a home from home there, as he put it. The catalogue of lies he had come out with had almost made Vanja feel ill. The woman looked up at the new arrivals.

'Hello, can I help you?'

Billy smiled at her.

'Were you on duty last Friday?'

'Why?'

'We're from the police.'

Billy and Vanja showed their ID and she nodded, slightly apologetically. Vanja took out a picture of Roger and placed it beneath the lamp in front of the woman so that she could see it properly.

'Do you recognise this boy?'

'Yes, from the paper.' The woman touched the open newspaper. 'There's something about him every day.'

'But you don't recognise him from here?'

'No – should I?'

'We think he might have been here last Friday. Just before ten.'

The woman behind the desk shook her head.

'But of course we don't see all the guests, usually it's just the person who pays. I mean, he could have been in one of the rooms with somebody else.'

'Has he been in one of the rooms?'

'Not as far as I know. I'm just saying he *could* have been.'

'We'd like to know a little more about your guests that evening.'

At first the woman's expression was sceptical, but after a little while she moved over to the computer, which was far too old. At least eight years old, Billy noticed. Probably older. An antique. The woman started tapping away at the yellowing keyboard.

'We had nine rooms occupied, Friday into Saturday.'

'Were all nine occupied at around nine-thirty?'

'In the evening, you mean?'

Billy nodded. The woman carried on checking. After a while she found what she was looking for.

'No, only seven.'

'We need all the information you have about those guests.'

The woman's brow furrowed with anxiety.

'I'm pretty sure you need some kind of authority for that, don't you? Some kind of warrant?'

Vanja leaned forward.

'I don't think so.'

But the woman had decided. Not that she knew much about the laws regarding privacy and that kind of thing, but she'd seen it on TV: the police always needed a warrant for everything. She didn't have to give information about her clients just because they asked. She would stand up for her rights.

'Yes, you do. You need a warrant.'

Vanja gave her a dirty look, then glanced at Billy.

'Okay, we'll come back with a warrant.'

The woman gave a satisfied nod. *There you go.* She had protected the private lives of her guests, and thus the entire issue of freedom of speech.

The policewoman went on, 'And we'll bring an auditor with us when we come back. And perhaps someone from Environmental Health – I presume you're responsible for the restaurant as well?'

The woman's expression was a little uncertain as she looked at Vanja. *They couldn't do that, could they?*

The male officer looked around and nodded before adding in a serious tone of voice, 'And let's not forget a fire safety officer. There are a number of escape routes to check, I notice. And you do seem to be very keen to protect your guests.'

They headed for the door. The woman behind the desk hesitated.

'Hang on. I don't want to make things difficult for you. I'll do you a copy now.'

She smiled foolishly at the two officers. Her gaze fell on the open newspaper. She suddenly recognised him. It was a strange feeling. Excitement and triumph. A chance to pick up some bonus points. Perhaps she could make them forget that stuff about Environmental Health. She turned to the female officer, who was on her way back to the desk.

'He was here last Friday.'

The officer came over, a curious look on her face.

'What?'

'He was here last Friday,' she said, pointing to the newspaper.

Vanja gave a start as she saw the photograph.

There was an air of excitement in the big room that had been missing before. There were many questions, the case had opened out in several different directions, and now they had to start prioritising. The latest news was that the motel receptionist was certain she had seen Ragnar Groth, the principal of Palmlövska High, at the motel that Friday night. And it wasn't the first time either. He was there at regular intervals. Always paid cash and called himself Robert something-or-other. That Friday she had caught a glimpse of him as he walked past outside, heading towards the rooms on the west side, but he hadn't checked in himself. She had always assumed he was there to meet a mistress. After all, there were a number of people who used the motel for that kind of thing. You might not read about it in the adverts, but it was a fact. Sebastian was gloating to himself: this was just getting better and better. To think that the pedantic Ragnar Groth might turn out to have some serious skeletons in the cupboard. Torkel looked at Vanja and Billy with an approving nod.

'Okay, well done. This means that the principal becomes an obvious priority. As I see it, there is a strong possibility that he and Roger were in the same place on the night Roger was murdered.'

Billy took out a picture of Ragnar Groth and passed it to Torkel.

'Could you put this up? I haven't had a chance to check him out yet, but the interesting thing is that both Roger and Peter Westin have links to Groth. Westin had an arrangement with the school and Roger was a student there.'

Torkel pinned up the picture of Groth and drew arrows pointing to Roger and to Westin.

'Perhaps we should pay our principal another visit. With some new questions.' Torkel turned to the others. There was a brief silence.

'I think we need to proceed carefully, gather more information

279

before we confront him,' said Sebastian. 'After all, so far he's proved very adept at keeping quiet about relevant details. So the more we know when we do see him, the more difficult it will be for him to duck and dive.'

Vanja nodded in agreement. That was her analysis too.

'Particularly as we still know too little about Peter Westin. We don't even know for certain if he is the person in the bedroom, or how the fire started,' Vanja went on. 'Ursula is still at Rotevägen and has promised a preliminary report as soon as possible.'

'What about the break-in at Westin's practice? Did we get anything from the scene?' Torkel chipped in.

'No. No forensic evidence, no notebook. So we're at a standstill there. Westin's colleague said he wasn't the type who made extensive notes. Perhaps the odd keyword here and there, but he used to jot those down in the notebook, which of course is missing.'

'We're not having much luck,' Billy said with a sigh.

'Which means we just have to work harder,' Torkel replied, looking at his team with an encouraging expression.

'Luck comes through hard work, we know that. For the moment we assume the break-in is linked to the fire, and that Peter Westin's notebook has been stolen because of what was in it. Until we find out otherwise. I've asked Hanser to organise door-to-door enquiries in the vicinity of Westin's practice, to find out if anyone saw anything suspicious last night.'

'And what about Axel Johansson?' Billy nodded towards the picture of the caretaker that was pinned up in the corner. 'Anything there?'

Torkel laughed and shook his head.

'Ah well, everybody's favourite detective, Thomas Haraldsson, has been undertaking a little private surveillance there.'

'What do you mean?'

'Where do I start . . .'

'You could start by admitting I was right. We should have got rid of him as soon as we met him in the foyer,' said Vanja with a little smile. Torkel nodded.

'I can't argue with that, Vanja.'

A uniformed officer knocked on the door, poked her head in and asked for Billy and Vanja. She gave them each an envelope. Billy peered into his.

'Shall we go through these now?' He looked at Torkel.

'What are they?'

'Preliminary reports on the guests Vanja and I think are worth a closer look.'

Torkel nodded.

'Absolutely. But just to bring you up to date on Axel Johansson: we have no fresh leads there. Thanks to Haraldsson, he now knows we're looking for him, so there's a risk that he's left Västerås. Hanser has promised to put all their resources into finding him, so we'll leave that to her. She's a little bit embarrassed, by the way.'

While Torkel was speaking Billy had gone over to the wall with the new pictures. Once Torkel had finished, he began.

'Okay, at nine o'clock on Friday evening a total of seven rooms had been rented out. We have eliminated three families with children, plus an elderly couple who stayed until Monday. It's hardly likely that Roger or Ragnar Groth were visiting any of the families or this elderly couple. If we put them aside, that leaves us with three names which could be of interest.'

The pictures showed two women and one man.

'Malin Sten, aged twenty-eight; Frank Clevén, fifty-three; and Stina Bokström, forty-six.'

The others moved closer to get a better view of the enlarged passport photographs.

Malin Sten, née Ragnarsson, was the youngest of the guests. She was an attractive woman with long, dark, frizzy hair. According to the information received, she was married to one William Sten. The middle photograph showed Frank Clevén, a father of three who lived in Eskilstuna. He had short dark hair that had begun to recede and turn grey. A lined, weather-beaten face. He looked determined in the photograph. The last picture was of Stina Bokström. She had a narrow face with short blonde hair and

281

quite an angular appearance. Unmarried. Billy pointed to the brunette.

'I managed to get hold of Malin Sten. She's a sales rep who stayed over after a meeting in town. She says she didn't see anybody. She just had an early night. Lives in Stockholm. I haven't spoken to the other two yet, but as you can see neither of them lives in Västerås, not according to the electoral register.'

Torkel nodded and brought in the whole team.

'Okay, good, we need to get hold of the other two guests. Start with the assumption that they have something to hide. That applies to Malin Sten as well.'

They all nodded except for Vanja. She was leafing through the papers she had just received. She looked up.

'Sorry, but I think that will have to wait.'

They all turned and stared at her. Even Sebastian. Vanja enjoyed her moment centre stage, and paused dramatically before she went on.

'It occurred to me that the gun that was used to shoot Roger was a twenty-two calibre. Which is a classic weapon for shooting competitions, isn't it?'

Impatience was written all over Torkel's face.

'And?'

'I've just received the members' list from Västerås Gun Club.'

Vanja paused again, and she was unable to suppress a smug smile as she looked at the others in turn.

'Our esteemed Principal Ragnar Groth has been a member since 1992. An extremely active member, apparently.'

The gun club lay to the north, near the airport. It was a wooden building resembling a barracks, which had doubtless belonged to the military at some point in the past. There seemed to be both indoor and outdoor ranges, and Vanja, Sebastian and Billy could hear the dull reports of gunfire as they approached. Vanja had called in advance and spoken to the club secretary, who lived nearby. He had promised to come down to answer some questions.

A man came out onto the steps to greet them. He was about forty-five and wore a short-sleeved shirt and scruffy jeans. He looked like an ex-soldier and introduced himself as Ubbe Lindström. They went into the barracks together and were invited into the simple office, which acted as both the club's administration centre and storeroom.

'You said this was to do with one of our members,' Ubbe said as he sat down on a threadbare desk chair.

'That's right: Ragnar Groth.'

'Oh, Ragnar. Good shot. He's won bronze at national level twice.' Ubbe went to the overstuffed bookshelves, took out a well-thumbed folder and opened it. Searched through a great pile of papers before he found what he was looking for.

'He's been a member here since 1992. Why do you want to know?'

Billy ignored the question.

'Does he keep his guns here at the club?'

'No, he keeps them at home. Most of our members do. What's he done?'

They ignored the question again. Vanja joined the discussion.

'Could you tell us what guns he owns?'

'He has several – he hunts as well as competing. Is this something to do with that boy from his school? The one who died?'

He was a stubborn man, Ubbe. Sebastian had already grown tired of the discussion and moved out of the office. It didn't take three of them to ignore Lindström's questions. Billy glanced in Sebastian's direction while Vanja pressed on.

'Do you know if he has anything in a twenty-two calibre?'

'He owns a Brno CZ 453 Varmint.'

At least Ubbe had stopped asking questions and started answering instead. Which was something. Vanja made a note on her pad.

'What was it again? A Bruno . . . ?'

'A Brno CZ. A hunting rifle. Terrific weapon. What do you carry? Sig Sauer p225? Glock 17?'

Vanja looked at Ubbe. He really did seem to like following

283

every answer with a question of his own. She was prepared to allow him this one.

'Sig Sauer. Is that the only twenty-two Ragnar has access to?'

'As far as I know. Why? Was the kid shot?'

Sebastian walked down the long corridor and came to a common room containing a coffee machine and a large, battered fridge. Two large glass cabinets full of trophies and medals took pride of place in the room. In front of the cabinets were a number of plain chairs and tables marked with cigarette burns, from the days when men with guns didn't have to go outside for a smoke. Sebastian ambled into the room. A girl of about thirteen was sitting at one of the tables with a can of Coke and a cinnamon Danish in front of her. She gave Sebastian a non-committal teenage look. He nodded to her then went over to the cabinet containing the gold-coloured trophies. He was fascinated by the way in which people insisted on rewarding victory in any sport with ridiculously huge golden trophies. It was as if the participants actually suffered from extremely low self-esteem, and deep down they were aware of the total pointlessness of what they were doing. Their way of denying this truth and showing the world how important their activities really were resulted in total trophy inflation. In terms of both size and lustre.

The walls were adorned with photographs of individual club members and groups. Here and there was a framed news placard or newspaper article. It was a classic club room, in fact. Sebastian glanced idly at the pictures. The majority showed proud men holding their guns, legs apart, beaming at the camera. There was something about those smiles that looked ridiculously false, he thought. Was it really so terrific to be holding those guns, that trophy? He felt the girl's eyes on his back and turned to face her. She still had that same look on her face. Then she spoke.

'What are you doing?'

'Working.'

'At what?'

Sebastian glanced briefly at her.

'I'm a police psychologist. What are you doing?'

'I've got a training session soon.'

'Are you allowed to shoot at your age?'

The girl laughed.

'We don't shoot at each other.'

'Not yet ... Do you enjoy it?'

The girl shrugged her shoulders.

'It's more fun than running around after some stupid ball. Do you enjoy being a police psychologist?'

'It's okay. I'd rather be shooting at things, like you.'

The girl looked at him in silence and went back to her Danish. Obviously the conversation was over. Sebastian returned to his contemplation of the wall. His eyes settled on a picture of six cheerful men standing around one of those enormous trophies. A small gold plaque above the picture described the moment as NATIONAL CHAMPIONSHIPS – BRONZE 1999. Sebastian peered more closely at the photograph. Particularly at one of the six men. He was standing on the left, looking especially cheerful. Big smile. Lots of teeth. Sebastian took down the picture and left the room.

By the time Ursula left Rotevägen, she and Sundstedt had become more and more convinced that the fire at Peter Westin's home had been deliberately lit. The fact that it had started in the bedroom was beyond doubt. The wall behind the bed and the floor beside it showed clear signs of an explosive development of the fire. Once it had taken hold, the flames had spread hungrily to the ceiling and been fed with fresh oxygen when the bedroom windows were blown out by the heat. There was nothing around the bed to explain the rapid spread. When they examined the area more closely, they found clear traces of an accelerant. Definitely arson, then.

Westin's actual cause of death was still unknown, but Sundstedt had managed to get the body out from beneath the rubble. It had taken several hours, because it had been necessary to prop up the damaged floor from below before they could make a start. Ursula made sure the body was carefully packed into a body bag, and decided to go along to the forensic lab herself to attend the autopsy. Sundstedt promised to get his report in as soon as possible.

At the lab they had raised their eyebrows slightly at her presence, but she took no notice. Ursula had promised herself that this time she was going to stay at the centre of things. Otherwise this could turn into a real nightmare for them. A comparison with the dental records she had requested quickly established that the body they had found in the half-burnt-out house was definitely Peter Westin, which meant Ursula was pretty certain that one murder had become two, and that they were now dealing with a double killer. She also knew that someone who is capable of murdering twice could do it over and over again. Each time it would be a little easier.

She called Torkel.

Billy and Vanja didn't get much further with Ubbe Lindström. He became more and more defensive as the conversation went on. They had found out the most important thing: Ragnar Groth had a gun which matched the one that took Roger's life, at least as far as the calibre was concerned. Ubbe kept on trying to get them to reveal the reason for their interest in one of the club's most loyal and successful members. The fewer answers he got, the more terse and reluctant to respond he became. Vanja realised that Ragnar Groth and Ubbe Lindström were probably more than just fellow members, she got the feeling they were friends, and was growing concerned that Ubbe would call his friend and tell him about their visit the minute they left.

'As I'm sure you're aware, your gun licence has to be renewed every five years. If it comes to my attention that this confidential discussion wasn't quite so confidential, then . . . ' Vanja let the rest of the sentence hover unspoken in the air.

'What do you mean?' said the club secretary, fury in his voice. 'Are you threatening me?'

Billy smiled at him.

'All she means is that this conversation is just between us. Okay?' Ubbe's eyes darkened and he nodded crossly. At least they had tried, and he had been warned. Sebastian lumbered into the office.

'Just one more thing.' He placed the framed photograph in front of Ubbe. Pointed at something in the picture. 'Who's that? Top left?'

Ubbe leaned forward and peered at the photograph. Billy and Vanja moved forward and caught a glimpse of the man with the broad smile.

'That's Frank. Frank Clevén.'

Vanja and Billy recognised him at once. His picture was already on the wall back at the station. Minus the broad smile, admittedly, but there was no doubt that this was the man who had booked a room in a run-down motel the previous Friday.

'Is he a member here as well?'

'He was. Moved away the year after they took bronze. He lives in Örebro now, I think. Or Eskilstuna. Is he involved as well?'

'Nobody is involved in anything. Just think about your licence,' Vanja replied curtly, then left with the others. All three of them walked back to the car much more quickly than usual. This was turning out to be a really good day.

Frank Clevén lived on Lärkvägen in Eskilstuna. Billy couldn't get an answer on the landline, however, and they couldn't find a mobile number registered in his name. After a little research Billy found the name of Frank's employer, a building firm known as H & R Bygg. He worked as a construction engineer and had a work mobile. Billy called him. Frank was very surprised to hear that the police were looking for him, but Billy stressed the fact that they just wanted to ask him a few questions.

Which they would like to do at his place of work.

In thirty minutes.

They insisted on it, in fact.

Vanja and Sebastian were already in the car halfway to Eskilstuna when they got the call from Billy, who had stayed back at the station. He read out the brief details available on Frank Clevén. They didn't reveal much. Fifty-three years old, born in Västervik, moved to Västerås at a young age. Four years studying technical options at high school, military service with KA3 Gotland, gun licence for both a pistol and a rifle since the end of 1981, still current. No criminal record, no bad debts. Nothing of note. But they did get an address.

Just outside Eskilstuna they pulled into a building site where a shopping centre was under construction. With girders sticking up where the walls would be, it didn't look much like a future temple of consumerism at the moment, but the huge concrete base was almost finished. Some distance away they could see a group of workers busy with a big yellow machine. Sebastian and Vanja headed over to the builders' huts, where they found someone who appeared to be the foreman. 'We're looking for Frank Clevén.'

The man nodded and pointed to one of the huts in the middle. 'He was over there last time I saw him.'

'Thanks.'

Frank Clevén was one of those people who looked better in real life than in a photograph. His features were finely chiselled, even though his skin was lined from spending so much time outdoors. Sharp eyes, screwed up in the manner of the Marlboro Man as he shook Sebastian and Vanja by the hand. They didn't see that broad smile from the photograph once during their conversation. He suggested they should go into his small office in one of the other huts, where they would be able to talk without being disturbed. Vanja and Sebastian followed him, and it seemed to Vanja that his shoulders grew heavier and heavier with every crunching step across the gravel. They were on the right track, she could feel it.

At last.

Clevén unlocked the door and invited them in. The grey daylight seeped in through two windows white with dust as they stepped into the cramped hut. There was a pungent smell of tannin. A coffee machine occupied the tiny hallway linking two small rooms. Clevén's office was the first. The only furniture was an impersonal desk covered in drawings, and a few chairs. The walls were bare apart from old tape marks and last year's calendar. Clevén looked at the two officers, who remained standing even though he had offered them a seat. He also chose to stand.

'I don't have a great deal of time, so this will have to be quick.' Clevén tried to keep his voice calm, but failed. Sebastian noticed that Clevén's upper lip was beaded with sweat. The room was not warm.

'We've got all the time in the world, so it's up to you how quick this is,' Sebastian replied, making it perfectly clear that this meeting wasn't going to be conducted on Frank's terms.

'I don't even know why you're here. Your colleague just said you wanted to speak to me.'

'If you'd like to sit down, my colleague will explain.' Sebastian looked at Vanja, who nodded but waited for Clevén to sit down. After a short silence he decided to cooperate. He sat down. Right on the edge of the chair. As if he were perching on needles.

'Could you tell us why you stayed in a motel in Västerås last Friday?'

He looked at them.

'I didn't stay in a motel last Friday. Who says I did?'

'We do.'

Vanja didn't say any more. Under normal circumstances the person they were questioning would begin to talk of their own accord at this stage. When they were presented with facts. Surely he ought to realise they wouldn't have come all the way to Eskilstuna if they didn't have solid evidence? Confirm or explain away, those were the usual options. Or there was a third choice. Silence. Clevén went for the third option. He glanced from Vanja to Sebastian but didn't say a word. Vanja sighed.

'Who were you meeting? What were you doing there?'

'I wasn't there, I tell you.' His expression was almost pleading. 'You must have got the wrong person.'

Vanja looked down at her papers. Mumbled to herself. Took her time. Sebastian didn't take his eyes off Clevén. He was licking his lips as if they had suddenly gone dry. A bead of sweat began to emerge just on his hairline above his forehead. The room still wasn't warm.

'Aren't you Frank Clevén, ID number 580518?' Vanja asked, her tone neutral.

'Yes.'

'Didn't you pay 779 kronor for a room using your debit card last Friday?'

Clevén blanched.

'It's been stolen. My card's been stolen.'

'Stolen? Have you reported it to the police, and if so, when?'

He fell silent. His brain seemed to be working overtime. The bead of sweat trickled down his cheek, which had grown significantly paler.

'I haven't reported it.'

'Have you stopped it?'

'I might have forgotten, I don't know . . .'

'Oh come on, you don't seriously expect us to believe your card has been stolen?'

No reply. Vanja decided it was time to let Frank Clevén know just how bad things looked for him at the moment.

'This is a murder investigation. That means we will look into every piece of information you give us in detail. So let me ask you again: did you stay in a motel in Västerås last Friday, yes or no?'

Clevén looked shocked.

'A murder investigation?'

'Yes.'

'But I haven't murdered anyone.'

'So what have you done?'

'Nothing. I've done nothing.'

'You were in Västerås on the night of the murder, and you've lied about it. That sounds rather suspicious to me.'

Clevén jerked, his whole body twisting. He found it difficult to

290

look at the two people sitting in front of him. Sebastian leaped to his feet.

'Bugger this. I'm going to your house to ask your wife if she knows anything. Will you stay here with him?'

Vanja nodded and looked at Clevén, he was staring wanly at Sebastian, who was slowly heading for the door.

'She doesn't know anything,' he sputtered.

'No, perhaps not, but she'll know whether you were at home or not, won't she? Wives usually have a pretty good idea about that sort of thing.' Sebastian's extra broad smile showed how happy he was at the very thought of going to Clevén's house to see his wife and children and ask the question. He managed a few more steps before Clevén stopped him.

'Okay, I was at the motel.'

'I see.'

'But my wife doesn't know anything.'

'So you said. Who did you meet there?'

No reply.

'Who did you meet? We can sit here all day. We can send for a squad car to come and take you away in handcuffs. It's up to you. But let me make one thing very clear: we will find out eventually.'

'I can't say who it was. It's out of the question. Things will be bad enough for me if this comes out, but for him ...'

'Him?'

Frank fell silent and nodded in embarrassment. Suddenly everything became clear to Sebastian.

The gun club.

The embarrassed look on Frank's face.

Palmlövska High, riddled with lies.

'You were meeting Ragnar Groth, weren't you?'

Frank nodded quietly.

He lowered his eyes.

And his world came crashing down.

*

In the car on the way back Sebastian and Vanja were almost elated.

Frank Clevén and Ragnar Groth had been involved in a relationship for quite some time. They had found each other at the gun club. Fourteen years ago. Tentatively at first, then their liaison had become all-consuming. Destructive. Clevén had even moved away from Västerås to try to put an end to the relationship he was so ashamed of. After all, he was married. He had children. He wasn't a homosexual. But he hadn't been able to stay away. It was like a poisonous drug.

The pleasure.

The sex.

The shame.

Around and around it went. They had carried on seeing each other. It was always Groth who rang and suggested they should meet, but Clevén never refused. He longed for their encounters. Never at Groth's home. The motel became their oasis. The cheap room. The soft beds. Clevén always made the booking and paid. He had had to come up with excuses, constantly trying to allay his wife's suspicions. It was easier when he didn't stay over. Coming home late was easier than not coming home at all. Yes, they had met up on that Friday. At about four o'clock. Groth had been almost insatiable. Clevén hadn't left the motel until just before ten. Groth had departed just about half an hour earlier.

Shortly after half past nine.

Just when Roger was probably walking past the building.

292

All five of them could feel the sense of expectation in the air. They recognised it and welcomed it. This was how it felt when they had made a breakthrough, when the investigation gathered fresh pace, when in the best-case scenario they could begin to sense the end. For several days every clue, every idea, had led to a dead end, but Ragnar Groth's tryst at the motel had provided them with completely new pieces of the puzzle to work with. Pieces that seemed to fit together very well.

'So the principal of an independent school with a Christian set of values and ethos is homosexual.' Torkel contemplated his team. In their eyes he could see and feel the fresh energy permeating the room. 'It's not too far-fetched to think that he was ready to go quite a long way to hide that fact.'

'Killing someone isn't going quite a long way, it's going a hell of a long way.' That came from Ursula. Torkel thought she looked tired. True, she had been tied up with the fire and the presumed murder of Westin all day, but he still couldn't help wondering whether she had slept as badly as he had.

'No one was ever meant to die.' Sebastian plucked a pear from the fruit bowl. He took a big, noisy bite.

'Aren't we assuming that the person who murdered Roger Eriksson also killed Peter Westin?' Ursula wondered. 'Surely nobody thinks that was an accident too?'

'No, but I still maintain that Roger's murder wasn't planned.' It was slightly difficult to make out the words as they got caught up in the half-masticated pear. Sebastian took a few seconds, finished chewing and swallowed. Started again. 'I still maintain that Roger's murder wasn't planned. We are, however, dealing with a person who will do whatever it takes to get away with it.'

'So Roger's murder may have been an accident, but he's prepared to kill in cold blood so that nobody will find out he did it?'

'Yes.'

'How does he square that?' Billy wondered. 'With his conscience, I mean.'

'He probably regards himself as being of supreme importance. Not necessarily for selfish reasons. He might believe that one or more people would be harmed if he were caught. Would suffer for his sake. He might have a job he thinks no one else could do, or a task he must complete. At any price.'

'Does the principal of Palmlövska High fit in there?' The question came from Vanja. Sebastian shrugged his shoulders. He could hardly reach a diagnosis on Ragnar Groth from the two short meetings they had had, but nor was he prepared to dismiss him. His commitment to the school had already led to his failure to report a serious matter to the police. Was he prepared to go further? Definitely. As far as necessary? That remained to be seen. Sebastian left it open.

'Possibly.'

'Do we know whether Ragnar Groth knew that Roger used to go and see Peter Westin?' Understandably, Ursula was sticking to the Westin trail.

'He must have done.' Billy looked around, seeking support. 'I mean, Westin had an agreement with the school, so he must have told them who was making use of his services. He must have got paid somehow.'

'We'll find out.' Torkel broke in before their new-found enthusiasm provided answers to questions they hadn't even asked yet. The desire to get everything to fall into place was very strong at this stage of an investigation, and it was important to hold back. To analyse what they actually knew, what was possible and probable, and what they hadn't a clue about.

'Sebastian and Vanja have put together a scenario. The rest of us will listen and concentrate on finding instances where the facts or the forensic evidence don't fit. Okay?'

Everyone nodded. Torkel turned to Sebastian, who indicated with a small gesture that Vanja could begin. She glanced down at her papers and started to speak.

'This is how we see it: Roger is walking towards the motel. He's angry and upset after his encounter with Leonard Lundin. With blood on his face and his self-esteem shattered, he wipes away the tears with the sleeve of his jacket. He turns into the grounds of the motel, on his way to meet the person he has arranged to see. Suddenly he stops. A movement from one of the motel rooms catches his attention. He looks up and sees the school principal. Ragnar Groth turns to the door of the room he has just left, and a hand draws him back. A man Roger doesn't recognise appears in the doorway, leans forward and kisses Ragnar on the lips. He seems to protest momentarily, but as Roger withdraws into the shadows, he sees Ragnar relax and respond to the kiss almost immediately. When the kiss is over and the door closes, Ragnar looks around, his expression alert.

'If Roger was going to meet someone at the motel, he definitely has to change his plans at this point.' Vanja looked at Sebastian, who stood up and started to wander around the room as he took over.

'Roger sneaks off towards the car park, and when Ragnar reaches his car, Roger is standing there waiting for him, a supercilious smile on his face. He confronts Ragnar with what he has just seen. Ragnar denies everything, but Roger sticks to his guns. If nothing has happened, it won't matter if he tells people, will it? Roger can see that Ragnar is frantically trying to come up with a solution. The situation gives Roger great pleasure. After his encounter with Leonard, it feels good to be the one who has the power for a while. He sees Ragnar sweating. Sees someone else suffering for once. He is the strong one now. Roger explains that he can of course keep quiet about the principal's amorous little adventures, but it won't be cheap. He wants money. Lots of money. Ragnar refuses. Roger shrugs his shoulders. In that case it will be on Facebook within fifteen minutes. Ragnar realises he is close to losing everything. Roger turns to leave. The car park is deserted. Poorly lit. Roger misjudges how much Ragnar has to lose as he turns his back on him. Ragnar hits out and Roger slumps to the ground.'

'It hasn't rained for a long time. We ought to go to the motel car park and see if there's any evidence there.' Ursula nodded and made a note on her pad. There may have been no more than the odd shower since they had found Roger, but to imagine that there would be any physical evidence in a relatively busy car park a whole week after a crime might have been committed there was stretching her optimism well beyond its limits. However, she would go and take a look. Perhaps if the boy or the principal had dropped something . . .

Sebastian looked at Vanja, who glanced at her papers once more before taking over again. Torkel didn't say a word. Not just because the emerging hypothesis looked as if it might work. Sebastian was allowing Vanja to share the limelight. Usually there was only room for one person to shine in Sebastian's orbit. He didn't share. Vanja must have done something right.

'With some difficulty, Ragnar bundles Roger into his car. He never meant to harm the boy, but he couldn't just let him leave. Couldn't let him tell everybody. Ruin everything. They had to find a solution that was acceptable to both of them. Talk it over. In a rational, adult manner. Ragnar drives around at random, sweaty and nervous, finding himself in areas of the town that are increasingly deserted, with the unconscious boy beside him. He wonders how he's going to get out of the situation, what he's going to say to his student when he comes round. He is trying to get a grip on the nightmare when Roger suddenly wakes up. Ragnar doesn't even have time to start on his calming, rational speech. Roger hurls himself at him, hitting him over and over again. Ragnar is forced to brake. The car slews over to the side of the road and stops. Ragnar's attempts to calm the boy are unsuccessful. Not only is Roger going to tell everyone that he screws other men, he's also going to report Ragnar for kidnapping and abuse. Ragnar has no time to react as Roger opens the door and tumbles out. Seething with rage, Roger sets off along the badly lit street, trying to work out where he is. Where the hell are they? Where has the sick bastard brought them? The adrenaline is pumping, preventing Roger from realising how frightened he is. The headlights of the car cast long shadows in front of him. Ragnar staggers out of the car, shouts after him, but Roger's only response is to stick his finger up in the air. Ragnar is desperate now. He can see his entire life collapsing. The boy must be stopped. He doesn't think. He just acts instinctively. He runs around the back of the car, flings open the boot and takes out his gun. Raises it quickly and with practised hands into the correct position, gets the fleeing boy in his sights and pulls the trigger. The boy falls to the ground.

'Not even a second passes before Ragnar grasps what he has done. He looks around in shock. No one is coming. No one is there. No one has seen or heard anything. There is still a chance that he might get away with this. That he might survive.

'Ragnar races over to the boy and realises two things as he watches the blood pumping from the bullet hole in his back in the beam of the headlights.

'The boy is dead.

'The bullet is like a fingerprint.

'He grabs hold of Roger and drags him away from the road. Into the bushes. He fetches a knife from the car. Stands over the dead boy and exposes the bullet hole. Acting on autopilot, without really thinking, he cuts out the heart and removes the bullet. His expression is almost one of surprise as he stares at the small, bloody piece of metal that has caused so much damage. Then he looks down at the body. The bullet is gone, but it would be best if he could somehow hide the fact that the boy has been shot. Make it look like a knife attack. His survival instinct has taken over completely by now, and Ragnar begins to stab the body in a frenzied attack.

'Afterwards he puts Roger in the car, drives to Listakärr and dumps the body. We know the rest.'

Sebastian andd Vanja had finished. It had been a vivid description of the course of events, and spiced up with speculation, but it was an account that sounded credible to Torkel. He looked around the room, took off his glasses and folded them up.

'I think it's time we had a chat with Ragnar Groth.'

'No, no, no, it wasn't like that at all.'

Ragnar Groth shook his head, leaned forward on his chair and held up his well-manicured hands in a dismissive gesture. The movement sent a faint whiff of Hugo Boss in Vanja's direction, on the opposite side of the desk. The same aftershave Jonathan used to wear, she thought briefly, although that must be the only thing the two men had in common. Vanja had just gone through the first part of their theory about the night of the murder, suggesting that Groth had met Roger outside the motel and that this might have led to a disagreement. Her assertion resulted in the principal's firm denial.

'So what was it like?'

'It never happened. I didn't see Roger on Friday night, I've already told you that.'

Indeed he had. About an hour ago when they'd picked him up from the school. He had looked tired and cross when Vanja and Billy had turned up in his office. The tiredness had vanished when they explained why they were there, and it had been replaced by hurt incomprehension. They surely couldn't be seriously suggesting that he was in any way involved in this tragic event? They certainly could, he realised that when they asked him to accompany them to the station for questioning. Groth had wanted to know if he was under arrest or being taken into custody, or whatever the correct term might be, but Vanja had assured him that they simply wanted to ask him some questions. The principal had asked if they couldn't talk in his office, as they had done on the two previous occasions, but Vanja had insisted that this interview must take place at the station.

It had taken time to organise the formalities of something as simple as leaving his office and the school. Groth had been very keen to ensure that it didn't look as if he was being arrested.

Vanja had reassured him. There would be no handcuffs, no uniformed officers were waiting, and he would travel in the passenger seat of an unmarked car. She had even provided him with a cover story when one of his colleagues wanted to know where he was going. Ragnar Groth's presence at the station had been requested to see if he could identify a number of young people on some CCTV footage. The principal had thanked her for her help as they walked out beneath the gigantic figure of Christ on the front of the school.

In one of the three interview rooms Groth had then rejected coffee, water, throat lozenges and legal representation. He had met Torkel for the first time and the three of them had sat down, Vanja and Torkel on one side of the desk and Groth on the other. He had dusted off the messy surface with his handkerchief before allowing his arms to come into contact with the desk.

'What's that?' he had asked as Vanja picked up a small piece of moulded plastic.

'This?' Vanja held it up to Groth, who nodded. 'It's an earpiece.'

'And who are you listening to?'

Vanja had chosen not to respond and simply tucked it into her ear. Groth had turned and stared at the slightly oversized mirror on one wall.

'Is Bergman behind there?' He was unable to suppress a tone of pure revulsion. Once again Vanja had chosen not to answer. But Groth had been right: Sebastian was standing in the room next door, studying the interview so that he could make brief comments directly to Vanja if necessary. They had agreed that Sebastian shouldn't be in the interview room. It would be difficult enough to get someone with as much self-control as Ragnar Groth to open up at all, without Sebastian's presence to annoy him.

Vanja had placed the tape recorder on the table, listed those present and stated the time, then she had explained how they had followed Roger via the CCTV cameras, and put forward the theory that Groth met Roger outside the motel. To begin with the principal had simply listened, his face devoid of expression. The

299

first time he showed any kind of reaction was when the motel was mentioned. Then he shook his head silently, folded his arms across his chest and leaned back in his chair, his body language indicating that he was distancing himself.

From Vanja.

From everything she said.

From the entire situation.

It wasn't until Vanja had finished that he leaned forward and spread his hands.

'No, no, no, it wasn't like that at all.'

'So what was it like?'

'It never happened. I didn't see Roger on Friday night, I've already told you that.'

'But you were at the motel at the relevant time?' In the room next door, Sebastian nodded to himself. They could tie him to the time and place, and it was obvious that this bothered him.

A great deal.

So much so that he didn't even answer Vanja's question. Needless to say, she didn't give up.

'That was a rhetorical question. We know you were at the motel at nine-thirty on Friday night.'

'But I didn't see Roger.'

'Ask him about Frank,' Sebastian said into his microphone. He saw Vanja's face brighten up in the interview room, and she glanced at the mirror. Sebastian nodded encouragingly, as if she might be able to see him. Vanja leaned across the table.

'Tell me about Frank Clevén.'

Groth didn't answer immediately. He took the time to tug at his shirt cuffs so that they extended precisely one and a half centimetres below the sleeves of his jacket. Then he leaned back and looked calmly at Vanja and Torkel.

'He's an old friend from the gun club. We meet up from time to time.'

'To do what?' The question came from Torkel, and Groth turned his attention in his direction.

'Chat about old times. We won bronze in the national championships, as you perhaps know. We usually have a glass of wine. Sometimes we play cards.'

'Why don't you meet at your house?'

'We usually meet when Frank is passing through Västerås, on his way home. The motel is in a more convenient location.'

'We know that you and Frank Clevén meet at the motel to have sex.'

Groth turned to Vanja, and for a second it looked as if the very idea made him feel sick. He bent towards her and held her gaze.

'And how, may I ask, do you know that?'

'Frank Clevén told us.'

'Then he's lying.'

'He's married, with three children. Why would he lie about travelling to Västerås to have sex with a man?'

'I don't know; you'd have to ask him.'

'Isn't it true that you're good friends?'

'I thought so, but what I'm hearing is making me doubt that.'

'We can tie you to the motel.'

'I was there. I met Frank. I'm not denying that. What I am most certainly denying is that we indulged in any sexual activities, or that I met Roger during the course of the evening.'

Vanja and Torkel exchanged glances. Ragnar Groth was good. Admit what can be proved, deny everything else. Had they brought him in too soon? All they had in fact was a chain of circumstantial evidence. Secret sexual encounters, membership of a gun club, a position in society that was worth protecting. Did they need more?

In the room next door, the same thought occurred to Sebastian. They knew Groth was a man with an obvious psychological problem that found its expression through pedantic and compulsive behaviour. It wasn't too much of a leap to imagine that over the years he had developed a deep and almost impenetrable defence to protect himself against actions that he found undesirable. Sebastian had the feeling that Ragnar Groth was constantly weighing advantages and disadvantages against one another, and once he had made a decision, he shaped reality according to that decision. It became the truth. He probably didn't even think he was lying when he said that he and Frank Clevén hadn't had sex in that motel room. He believed it. They would probably need photographic evidence to make him confess. Photographic evidence that they didn't have.

'Peter Westin?'

Vanja tried a new tack.

'What about him?'

'You know him.'

'The school has an arrangement with his practice, yes. What's that got to do with anything?'

'Do you know where he lives?'

'No, we don't have any contact except in a professional capacity.' Groth was struck by a thought and leaned forward once more. 'Are you suggesting I'm having a sexual relationship with him as well?'

'Are you?'

'No.'

'Where were you at four o'clock this morning?'

'I was at home, asleep. It's a nasty little habit of mine. I try to have a little nap around that time. Why do you ask?'

Sarcasm. In the room next door, Sebastian sighed. Groth had regained his self-confidence. He had realised they didn't have enough on him. They weren't going to get anywhere. In the interview room Torkel was still trying to salvage what could be saved.

'We need to take a look at your guns.'

'What on earth for?' Genuine surprise. Vanja swore to herself. They had managed to keep it out of the press. No one, apart from the murderer, knew that Roger had been shot. It would have been a great help if Groth had thought the request was eminently reasonable or, even better, refused to let them see his guns.

'Why not?'

'I just don't understand your reasons. I mean, the boy wasn't

302

shot, was he?' He looked from Vanja to Torkel. Neither of them was inclined to confirm or deny.

'Are you refusing to let us examine your guns?'

'Not at all. Help yourselves. Take as long as you like.'

'We'd also like to take a look around your apartment.'

'I live in a detached house.'

'In that case we would like to take a look around your detached house.'

'Don't you need some kind of warrant for that?'

'If we don't have the owner's permission, then all we have to do is speak to the prosecutor.' Vanja knew they couldn't expect the principal to be helpful for much longer, so she decided to go for a threat overlaid with consideration.

'There's a certain amount of administration involved in obtaining a warrant, and of course the more people who see our application, the greater the risk that the details will be leaked.'

Groth gave her a look and she realised that he had seen through the false consideration and completely understood the threat.

'Of course. Search wherever you like. The sooner you realise that I didn't harm Roger, the better.' Vanja had a feeling this was the last time Groth would be so cooperative.

'Do you have a mobile phone?'

'Yes. Would you like to see it?'

'Please.'

'It's in the top drawer of the desk in my study. Are you going to my house now?'

'Soon.'

Groth got to his feet. Vanja and Torkel stiffened, but he simply reached into his trouser pocket and took out a small bunch of keys. Three keys. He put them on the table and firmly pushed them over to Vanja.

'The key to the gun cupboard is hanging up on the right in the cleaning cupboard. I must insist on your discretion. No uniforms, no flashing blue lights. I am a respected person in the neighbourhood.'

'We'll do our best.'

'I hope you will.' He sat down again, leaned back as comfortably as possible, folded his arms once more. Vanja and Torkel exchanged a quick glance. Vanja also looked up briefly at the mirror. Sebastian brought the microphone up to his mouth.

'I don't think we're going to get any further.'

Vanja nodded to herself, read out the time and switched off the tape recorder. She met Torkel's eyes and realised they were both thinking the same thing.

They'd brought him in too soon.

If one wanted to be pedantic, Ragnar Groth actually lived in a link-detached house. His carport was attached to the house next door. It wasn't difficult to spot which house belonged to him. Both Billy and Ursula knew instinctively that they were approaching the right address. The house was . . . cleaner.

Every last bit of gravel from the winter's road gritting had been meticulously swept away from the street and pavements outside the property. Inside the carport everything was hung up, stacked and arranged in impeccable order. As Billy and Ursula walked towards the house they noticed that not one fallen leaf from last year lay on the garden path or on the beautifully kept lawn. When they reached the front door, Ursula ran her finger along the nearest window ledge. She held it up to show Billy. Spotless.

'Keeping things this tidy must take up every waking moment,' said Ursula as Billy inserted the key, opened the door and went inside.

The house was quite small: ninety-two square metres divided into two floors. They walked into a narrow hallway leading to a staircase, with two doors and two archways in between. Billy switched on the hall light and they looked at each other. Without a word they bent down and took off their shoes. They didn't usually bother when they were searching someone's property, but in this house it felt almost like sacrilege to walk in wearing outdoor shoes. They left them on the rug, even though there was room on the shoe rack below the coat stand just inside the door. On the shelf lay a hat, with an outdoor coat on a hanger underneath. At the bottom stood one pair of shoes. Polished. Not a grass stain or a scrap of mud to be seen. It smelled clean. Not of cleaning products, just . . . clean. It made Ursula think of a brand-new house she and Mikael had looked at several years ago. That had smelled like this.

Impersonal.

Uninhabited.

They moved along the hallway and each opened one of the two doors. The one on the right was a cloakroom, the one on the left led to a downstairs bathroom. A quick inspection indicated that both were as irreproachably clean and tidy as everything else in Ragnar Groth's life. The rest of the house provided further confirmation. The archway on the right led to the small, tastefully furnished living room. Opposite a three-piece suite with matching coffee table stood a bookcase, half the shelves taken up by books and the other half by vinyl LPs. Jazz and classical. In the middle of the bookcase was a dust-free record player. Groth didn't have a television. Not in the living room, at any rate.

The opening on the left took them into the spotlessly clean kitchen. Knives hanging neatly from a magnetic strip on the wall. A kettle on the worktop. Salt and pepper mills on the table. Apart from that, every surface was empty. Clean.

Together they headed upstairs, to a small square landing with three doors. A bathroom, a bedroom, a study. Behind the dark, heavy oak desk Ragnar's guns were hanging in a locked, officially approved gun cupboard. Billy turned to Ursula.

'Up or down?'

'Doesn't matter. What would you prefer?'

'If I take downstairs, you can deal with the guns.'

'Okay, and whoever finishes first takes the carport and the car?'

'Deal.' Billy nodded and went back downstairs. Ursula headed into the study.

It wasn't until Vanja was standing with her arms around her father that she felt the immense difference. Before and after. He had lost weight, but it wasn't just that. Over the last few months every hug had held within it a quivering fear engendered by the fragility of life, a desperate tenderness where every touch might be the last. With the positive news from the doctors, this hug suddenly meant something different. Medical science had extended their journey and saved them from the edge of the abyss on which their relationship had been teetering of late. Now their hugs promised a future. Valdemar smiled at her. His blue-green eyes were brighter than they had been for a long time, even though they were shining with tears of joy.

'I've missed you so much.'

'Me too, Dad.'

Valdemar stroked her cheek.

'It's really strange. I feel as if I'm discovering everything afresh. As if it's the first time.'

Vanja looked up at him. 'I can understand that.' She took a couple of steps back. She had no desire to stand in a hotel foyer crying. She made a sweeping gesture towards the window and the gathering dusk outside.

'Let's go for a walk. You can show me around Västerås.'

'Me? I haven't been here for ages.'

'You know the place better than me. You lived here for a while, didn't you?'

Valdemar laughed, took his daughter's arm and walked towards the swing doors.

'That was a thousand years ago. I was twenty-one and I'd just got my first job at Asea.'

'You still know more than me. I've only been to the hotel, the police station, and a few crime scenes.'

They set off. Talked about the days long ago when Valdemar was an enthusiastic young trainee engineer in Västerås. They were both enjoying their time together. The small talk was just that, rather than a way of avoiding the one thing that filled their thoughts every minute of the day.

Darkness was beginning to fall, the weather had changed, and there was a light drizzle in the air. They hardly noticed it as they walked along by the water side by side. It wasn't until it had been raining for half an hour, the drops getting bigger all the time, that Valdemar thought they ought to find some kind of shelter. Vanja suggested going back to the hotel for something to eat.

'Have you got time?'

'I'll make time.'

'I don't want you to get into trouble for my sake.'

'It's fine – the investigation can cope without me for another hour.'

Valdemar gave in. He took his daughter's arm once more and they hurried back to the hotel.

Vanja ordered a glass of white wine and a Diet Coke as her father studied the bar menu. She looked at him. She really did love him. She loved her mother too, but things were always more complicated with her – there was more conflict, more jostling for space. With Valdemar she was calmer. He was more accommodating. He challenged her too, of course, but in areas where she felt more secure.

Not on the subject of relationships.

Or her abilities.

He trusted her. That made her feel secure. She would have liked to have a glass of wine too, but thought she'd better not. She would probably have to work later, or at least catch up on any progress in the case. It was best if she remained alert.

Valdemar looked up from the menu.

'Mum sends her love. She wanted to come with me.'

'So why didn't she, then?'

'Work.'

Vanja nodded. Of course. It wasn't the first time.

'Give her a hug from me.'

The waitress brought their drinks and they ordered. Vanja went for a chilli cheeseburger while Valdemar chose fish soup with aioli and garlic bread. The waitress took their menus and left. They raised their glasses in a silent toast. She was sitting there with her reborn father, as far from the investigation and the hassles of everyday life as she could get, when she heard a voice, a voice that under no circumstances had anything to do with this private moment.

'Vanja?'

She turned towards the voice, hoping that her ears had deceived her. But no. Sebastian Bergman was heading towards them, his coat wet from the rain.

'Hi, have you heard any more about Groth?'

Vanja stared at him with an expression she hoped would make it very clear that he was disturbing them.

'No. What are you doing here? Have you got no home to go to?'

'I've been for something to eat and I was on my way back to the station. I thought I'd check if Billy and Ursula have found anything. Have you heard?'

'No, I'm taking some time off.'

Sebastian glanced at Valdemar, sitting in silence in his armchair. Vanja realised she had to do something before her father decided to introduce himself and, if she was really unlucky, ask Sebastian to join them for a drink.

'We're just going to have something to eat. You go on and I'll be there later. See you at the station.'

No normal person could avoid hearing the dismissal in her voice, but as she watched Sebastian extend his hand to Valdemar with a tentative smile, she realised she'd forgotten. Sebastian was not a normal person.

'Sebastian Bergman. I work with Vanja.'

Valdemar's response was friendly. He half rose from his chair and shook Sebastian's hand.

'Valdemar – I'm Vanja's dad.' Vanja was even more put out. She knew how interested her father was in her work, and she realised this could turn into much more than a brief greeting. Too right. Valdemar settled back down and looked at Sebastian with curiosity.

'Vanja's told me about most of her colleagues, but I don't think she's mentioned you.'

'I'm only attached to the team on a temporary basis. As a consultant. I'm a psychologist, not a police officer.'

Sebastian noticed the change in Valdemar's expression when he said he was a psychologist. As if he were searching through his memory.

'Bergman ... you're not the Sebastian Bergman who wrote that book about Hinde, the serial killer?'

Sebastian nodded swiftly.

'Books. But yes. That's me.'

Valdemar turned to Vanja. He seemed almost exhilarated.

'But that was the book you gave me years and years ago, you remember?'

'Yes.'

Valdemar turned back to Sebastian and gestured towards the empty armchair opposite Vanja.

'Wouldn't you like to sit down?'

'I'm sure Sebastian has other things to do, Dad. We're in the middle of a pretty complex investigation.'

Sebastian met Vanja's eyes. Was that a pleading expression he could see? There was certainly no doubt that she didn't want him there.

'No, no, I've got plenty of time.' Sebastian unbuttoned his wet coat, took it off and draped it over the back of the chair, then sat down. The whole time he was looking at Vanja with a smile and a look on his face that could only be described as teasing. He was enjoying this. She could see that, and it annoyed her even more than the fact that he was staying.

'I didn't know you'd read my book,' Sebastian said to her as he sank down into the chair. 'You didn't mention it.'

'Perhaps I didn't get round to it.'

'She loved it,' Valdemar chipped in, unaware that his daughter's expression darkened with every word he uttered. 'She practically forced me to read it. I think it was one of the reasons why she decided to join the police.'

'Really? How wonderful!' Sebastian sat back in his chair contentedly. 'To think I had such an influence on her!'

Game over. Sebastian smiled at her. She would never, ever have the last word again. Her darling dad had just made sure of that.

Mikael rang Ursula from the train station, wondering whether she was going to meet him or if he should make his own way to the hotel. Ursula swore to herself. She hadn't forgotten that he was coming, but nor had she given it a thought all day. She glanced at the clock. It had been a bloody long day, and it wasn't over yet. She was standing in Groth's bedroom, about to tackle the double wardrobe with the neatly folded shirts, pullovers, underwear, socks and everything else that Ragnar didn't feel should be hanging up, with precisely three centimetres between the coat hangers.

Her initial thought was to ask her husband to wait for an hour or so. She was in a foul mood. The lack of any concrete discoveries annoyed her. She had started with the guns, but had realised immediately that they weren't going to lead anywhere. There were signs that they had been fired recently, but then Groth was a competitive marksman. Without a bullet for comparison, the information was worthless. The rest of the study had been equally disappointing: nothing in the desk, in the bureau by the window or on the bookshelves. Perhaps there might be something on the computer, but Billy would look into that. The bathroom had also been a waste of time. Not so much as a strand of hair in the plughole.

And now she had Mikael in her ear, going on and on. She was the one who had asked him to come, after all. It was getting towards dinnertime. Surely she had to eat at some point? Ursula gave up, went downstairs and stuck her head into the kitchen, where Billy was going through cupboards and drawers.

'I'm going out for a while. I'll be back in an hour or two.' Billy looked at her in surprise.

'Okay.'

'Do you mind if I take the car?'

'Where are you going?'

'I'm just ... going out to dinner.'

It made no sense to Billy at all. He couldn't remember when Ursula had last announced that she was disappearing to get something to eat. In his eyes she was the woman who lived on packaged sandwiches from various petrol stations, which she then ate at various crime scenes.

'Has something happened?'

'Mikael's in town.'

Billy nodded with as much understanding as he could muster, even though the whole situation was just getting odder and odder. Mikael, the husband Billy had seen once for ten minutes when he came to pick up Ursula from the annual Christmas party, had come to Västerås to have dinner with her.

Something had definitely happened.

Ursula left the house and marched crossly to the car. As she opened the door she suddenly realised she had forgotten the whole purpose of Mikael's trip to Västerås for a moment.

It wasn't Mikael she should be angry with.

Absolutely not.

He was completely innocent. It was bad enough that she was using him for her own ends. He presumably thought she had called because she wanted to see him, because she missed him, not so that his presence would teach Torkel a lesson.

She would have to be extra nice to him. She had to keep reminding herself of that. Not to punish the wrong person.

She got in the car and took out her mobile phone. On the way into the town centre she made two quick calls: one to the police station to make sure Torkel was still there, and one to Mikael to arrange where they should meet. Then she slowed down to make sure she would arrive after him. Switched on the radio, listened for a while, let her thoughts drift.

The ball had been set in motion.

The punishment would be meted out.

'Hi, Torkel.'

Torkel turned around and immediately recognised the tall, dark man now rising from one of the sofas in reception. Torkel nodded a greeting. Did his best to smile.

'Mikael, good to see you. Ursula said you were coming up.'

'Is she here?'

'Not as far as I know, but I can check.'

'No problem, she knows I'm here.' Torkel nodded again. Mikael looked fresh. There were a few strands of grey among the dark hair at his temples, but it suited him. They were about the same age, yet Torkel couldn't help feeling both older and more worn out. He certainly hadn't aged as well, and the fact that Mikael had struggled with periods of alcohol abuse didn't show at all in his appearance. Quite the reverse – he looked healthier and fitter than ever.

It has to be genetic, Torkel thought, but he still began to wonder if he shouldn't join a gym after all. The two men stood in silence for a moment. Torkel definitely didn't want to come across as unfriendly, but for the life of him he couldn't come up with a single thing to say. In the absence of genuine interest, he decided to stick to routine. Play a safe card.

'Coffee? Can I get you a coffee?' Mikael nodded and Torkel walked over to the entrance, swiped his card and held open the glass door for Mikael. They went through the open-plan office towards the staffroom.

'I read about the murder. It seems to be a tricky case.'

'It is, yes.'

Torkel led the way in silence. They had met on only a handful of occasions over the years, he and Mikael. Mostly at the beginning, when Ursula was new to the department. Torkel and Monica had invited them to dinner – two or three times, perhaps. At that time he and Ursula had been no more than colleagues, spending time with their respective partners. That was before they had embarked on their hotel-room relationship. How long had it been going on now? Four years? Five, if you counted that late night in Copenhagen. Which he, at least, had thought of – in a cold sweat of remorse – as a one-night stand. Something never to be repeated. But that was then.

Now it had become something else. The remorse and the assurance that it was a one-off were gone, replaced by a set of unwritten rules.

Only at work.

313

Never on home turf.

No plans for the future.

The last point had been the most difficult for Torkel. When they were lying beside one another, naked and satisfied, it had been difficult – almost impossible in the beginning – not to wish for more. More outside those anonymous hotel rooms. But on the few occasions when he had crossed the line and broken their agreement, her expression had hardened and he had been deprived of their encounters for weeks. So Torkel had learned his lesson.

No plans for the future.

They cost too much.

And now he was standing in the impersonal staffroom staring at the brown coffee as it filled his cup. Mikael was sitting at the table next to the coffee machine, sipping his cappuccino.

They had already covered everything Torkel was prepared to say about the case, so small talk took over.

The weather. (*Spring has definitely arrived.*)

How was Mikael's job going? (*Same as usual, really, wall-to-wall problems.*)

And how was Bella? (*Fine, thanks, she's in her final year studying law.*)

Did Mikael play any football these days? (*No, his knee wasn't strong enough. Torn meniscus.*)

Torkel couldn't stop thinking about the fact that he had been in bed with Mikael's wife yesterday morning. He felt false.

Through and through.

Why the hell had Ursula arranged to meet Mikael here? Torkel suspected that he knew exactly why, and his suspicions were confirmed a moment later when Ursula materialised behind them.

'Hi, darling. Sorry I'm late.' Ursula swept past Torkel without so much as a glance and gave Mikael a loving kiss. Then she turned to Torkel with a dismissive expression.

'Have you got time to sit around drinking coffee?'

Torkel was about to respond when Mikael leaped to his defence. 'I was waiting for you in reception – he was just being kind.'

'It's just that we have an enormous amount to do – so much so that we've had to bring in extra staff. Isn't that right, Torkel?'

Spot on. Mikael's presence was Torkel's punishment. Perhaps it wasn't the most refined approach, but it still put him in his place. Torkel didn't reply. There was no point fighting this battle. Not with Mikael there. And not at any other time either. When Ursula was in this mood you just couldn't win.

Torkel made his excuses, and also made a point of shaking Mikael firmly by the hand before he left. He could at least show some pride. He hated the feeling that he was slinking away with his tail between his legs.

Ursula took Mikael's arm and they set off.

'I don't know much about the restaurants around here, but Billy said there's a good Greek place not far away.'

'Sounds great.' They walked a short distance in silence, then Mikael stopped.

'Why am I here?'

Ursula turned to face him, her expression puzzled.

'What do you mean?'

'Exactly what I said. Why am I here? What do you want?'

'I don't want anything. I just thought that since I'm only an hour from Stockholm, we could take the opportunity to . . .'

Mikael looked searchingly at her. Not convinced.

'You've worked closer to Stockholm than this and you haven't called me.'

Ursula sighed to herself, but managed to prevent it from showing.

'And that's exactly why. We don't see enough of each other. I wanted to do something different. Come on, let's eat.'

She took his arm and drew him gently along. As she pressed closer to her husband she cursed the idea that had seemed so clever and so obvious yesterday. What *was* she really trying to do? Make Torkel jealous?

Humiliate him?

Prove her independence?

Whatever the purpose might have been, Mikael's presence already seemed to have fulfilled its function. Torkel was clearly uncomfortable with the situation, and his shoulders had been slumped lower than they had for a long time when he sloped off without a word.

So the question that now occurred to Ursula was this: what was she going to do with her husband?

After just an hour in the Greek restaurant, Ursula felt she had to get back to Ragnar Groth's house. Dinner had been pleasant after all. Better than she had expected. Admittedly Mikael had asked a couple more times why she wanted him there. He seemed to find it difficult to believe that it was just because she wanted to see him. Which wasn't surprising, really.

Her relationship with Mikael had been hard work for many years, and it was a miracle that it had survived, but during the struggle the bonds between them had also grown stronger. There was something about getting to know a partner's innermost weaknesses that either strengthened a relationship or killed it. They both had their faults. Not least as parents. When it came to Bella, it was as if there were a tiny filter, a thin film that prevented Ursula from getting really close to her daughter, and which meant that she often put her work before her family. There were many times when Ursula had been tormented by the realisation that she subconsciously seemed to choose forensic examinations and dead bodies over her vibrant, living daughter. She blamed her upbringing, her parents, her brain that prioritised logic over emotions. But the fact remained: that thin film was there and, with it, the sorrow over her own inability to connect. She always felt that she should have been there more often, been more involved. Particularly during those periods when Mikael had fallen back into alcohol abuse. When that happened over the years both sets of grandparents had come to the rescue.

In spite of his weaknesses, Ursula couldn't help admiring Mikael. He had never allowed his addiction to destroy their financial security, nor made it impossible for her and Bella to stay at home. When things got really bad he withdrew instead. Like a wounded animal. The person he let down the most every time he slipped was himself. His life was one long battle against his own shortcomings.

317

That was what Ursula regarded as the key to her love for him. He never gave up. In spite of all the failures, the lapses, the shattered hopes, he struggled on. More determined than her, stronger than her. He fell, he failed, but he got up and carried on.

For her.

For Bella.

For the family.

And Ursula was loyal to those who fought for her sake. Unswervingly loyal. It wasn't particularly romantic, it wasn't a teenage girl's dream of a perfect relationship, but Ursula had never been very impressed by that kind of thing. She had always valued loyalty above love. You needed people who were there for you, and you stuck with those people. They deserved it. If there was something missing within the relationship, you had to find it elsewhere.

Torkel wasn't her first lover, although he no doubt thought he was. No, there had been others. Early on in her relationship with Mikael she had complemented him with others. In the beginning she had tried to disapprove of herself, but it had been impossible, however hard she had tried. She couldn't accept that she was letting Mikael down. Her extramarital adventures made it possible for her to stay with him. She needed both the emotional complexity she found in Mikael and the undemanding physical closeness of someone like Torkel. She was like a battery that needed both a plus and a minus pole in order to function. Otherwise she felt empty.

There was, however, one thing she demanded from both of them.

Loyalty.

Which was where Torkel had let her down. That was the simple explanation for her decision to bring the two poles together and cause a short circuit. It had been a childish and emotional decision, and she hadn't thought it through. But at least it had worked.

And dinner had been pleasant.

She left Mikael outside the restaurant, promising to be back at the hotel as soon as possible, but explaining that it might take a while. Mikael said he had brought a book with him, so he'd be fine. No need for her to worry.

After the encounter with Mikael, Torkel's evening continued on its downward trajectory. Billy called on his way back from Groth's house, reporting that they hadn't found anything. No blood on any items of clothing, no muddy shoes, no trace that Roger – or anyone else, for that matter – had been in the house. No Pirelli tyres on the car, no traces of blood in the car or the carport. No container of highly flammable liquid, no clothes reeking of smoke. Nothing to link Groth to the murders of either Roger Eriksson or Peter Westin.

Nothing.

Not a thing.

Billy was intending to go through Groth's computer one more time, but advised Torkel not to expect too much.

Torkel ended the call with a sigh. He sat down at the table and stared unseeingly at the wall with all the pictures and information about the case. They could hold Groth for twenty-four hours, but Torkel honestly couldn't see how they could strengthen the case against him at the moment. No prosecutor in the world would agree to his arrest on the basis of what they had now. So it didn't make much difference whether they let him go tonight or tomorrow afternoon.

Torkel was just about to get to his feet when Vanja came hurtling into the room. He hadn't expected to see her again today. She'd said she had some private business to take care of.

'Why the hell did you bring Sebastian Bergman into this investigation?'

Her eyes flashed with anger. Torkel looked at her wearily.

'I think I've explained that enough times.'

'It was a stupid decision.'

'Has something happened?'

'No, nothing's happened. But he has to go. He's ruining everything.'

319

Torkel's phone rang. He looked at the display. The chief superintendent. Torkel gave Vanja a slightly apologetic look and answered. They exchanged information for barely one minute.

Torkel was told that *Expressen* had linked Peter Westin to Palmlövska High, and therefore to Roger Eriksson. It was on the internet.

The chief superintendent was told that Torkel intended to release Ragnar Groth, and why. Torkel was told that the chief superintendent was not happy. The case needed to be solved. And soon.

The chief superintendent was told that they were doing their best.

Torkel was told that the chief superintendent expected Torkel to speak to the journalists who had gathered outside the station before he left for the evening.

The chief superintendent hung up. So did Torkel, but that didn't mean his troubles were over. He realised this as soon as he met Vanja's gaze.

'We're letting Groth go?'

'Yes.'

'Why?'

'You heard what I said on the phone, didn't you?'

'Yes.'

'There you go, then.'

Vanja stood in silence for a moment, as if she was processing the information she had just been given. She quickly came to a conclusion.

'I hate this case. I hate this whole bloody town.' She turned and walked towards the door, opened it, then stopped halfway and looked back at Torkel.

'And I hate Sebastian Bergman.'

Vanja left the room, closing the door behind her. Torkel watched her march through the empty office. He picked up his jacket somewhat wearily from the back of the chair. His snap decision to bring in Sebastian really had cost him.

Half an hour later Torkel had sorted out all the details relating to the release. Ragnar Groth had been polite but said little. He had repeated his hope that they had been discreet, and demanded an unmarked car or a taxi to take him home. From a door at the back of the station. He had no intention of walking out at the front and becoming a target for the press. It wasn't possible to get hold of an unmarked car at this late hour, so Torkel ordered a taxi. They took their leave. Groth expressed the hope that he wouldn't have to see them again. Torkel couldn't help thinking the feeling was mutual. He waited until the rear lights of the cab had disappeared from view. Stood there. Tried to think of something that needed doing. Something he could prioritise with a clear conscience. He failed. He had no option but to go and face the press.

If there was one thing Torkel loathed about his job, it was the way in which the relationship between the police and the press had become increasingly important. He understood the public's need for information, of course, but he had seriously begun to question if that was really what drove journalists these days. It was all about attracting readers, and nothing seemed to sell better than sex, fear and sensationalism. This led to a tendency to frighten rather than inform, and a reluctance to give anyone the benefit of the doubt. The press also decided at an early stage that it was in the best interests of the public to reveal the identity of any possible perpetrator. Names and photographs. Before the trial.

And always, in every single report, Torkel felt there was a terrifying underlying message: *This could happen to you.*

You are never safe.

It could be your child.

That was what Torkel found most difficult. The press simplified complex situations, wallowed in tragedy, and created nothing but fear and suspicion among the public.

Lock yourself in.

Don't go out at night.

Trust no one.

Fear.

That was what they were selling.

When Ursula finally got back to the hotel after a good two hours, she was in a foul mood.

It was only going to get worse.

By the time she had returned to Groth's house, Billy had almost finished. They'd sat down at the kitchen table so that he could tell her what he had found. It hadn't taken long.

Nothing.

Absolutely nothing.

Ursula had sighed. At first she had appreciated Ragnar Groth's love of tidiness, but now that any interesting discoveries were conspicuous by their absence, she felt that his pedantic nature was simply detrimental to the investigation. Groth would never do anything unconsidered or unplanned. He would never carelessly conceal something, never allow key evidence to be discovered by chance. If he hid something, he would make sure it remained hidden.

Nothing.

Absolutely nothing.

They found no porn, no banned substances, no hidden love letters, no suspect links on the computer, nothing to confirm a sexual relationship with Frank Clevén or other men. His mobile phone was not the one that had sent the text messages to Roger Eriksson. For fuck's sake, they didn't even find a reminder to pay a bill. Ragnar Groth was inhumanly perfect.

Billy shared Ursula's frustration, so he had disconnected the computer so that he could take it back to the office and go through it for a third time, with better software.

It wasn't only anything forbidden that was missing, though. There was nothing particularly personal among Groth's belongings at all. No pictures of himself or someone who seemed fond of him, no parents, no relatives, no friends, no letters, no Christmas cards tucked away, no thank you notes, no invitations.

The most personal thing they found was a copy of his qualifications. Perfect, of course. Billy and Ursula became more and more convinced that the principal's inner life – if he had one – must be somewhere else.

They decided that Billy should take the car back to the station and report to Torkel. Ursula stayed on to go through the upstairs one more time. Determined to make sure she hadn't missed anything because Mikael had turned up. She found nothing.

Absolutely nothing.

She took a taxi back to the hotel and went straight up to her room.

Mikael was in front of the TV watching Eurosport. Ursula felt that something was wrong as soon as she walked into the sparsely furnished room. Mikael got to his feet a little too quickly and his smile was a little too cheerful. Without a word Ursula walked over to the minibar and opened it. Empty, apart from two bottles of mineral water and a can of juice. In the bin she could just see the forbidden little plastic bottles. He hadn't even tried to hide them. Not enough to get him drunk. But even a little was too much.

Way too much.

Ursula looked at him and wanted to feel angry. What had she actually expected, though? There's a reason why the plus and minus poles are on opposite sides of a battery.

They're not supposed to meet.

Haraldsson was drunk.

It didn't happen often. His consumption of alcohol was usually modest, but to Jenny's surprise he had opened a bottle of wine with dinner and emptied it himself within two hours. Jenny had asked if something had happened and Haraldsson had mumbled something about a lot going on at work. What could he say? Jenny knew nothing about the lies he had spread. She knew nothing about his private surveillance of Axel Johansson's apartment block, and the consequences of his actions. She didn't know, and she was never going to know.

She would think he was an idiot.

Which he was.

A slightly tipsy idiot at the moment. He was sitting on the sofa flicking through the TV channels. The mute button on to avoid waking Jenny. They had had sex. Of course. His mind had been somewhere else altogether. It hadn't made any difference. Of course. And now she was asleep.

He needed a plan. He had been dealt a vicious blow by Hanser today, although he wasn't down for the count. He would show them that it wasn't possible to knockout Thomas Haraldsson. When he walked into work tomorrow, he would take his revenge. Show them all. Show Hanser. All he needed was a plan.

It was beginning to look more and more unlikely that he would be the one to catch Roger Eriksson's killer. At the moment he had more chance of winning a million on a scratch card. Without an actual card. He wouldn't be allowed anywhere near the investigation in future, Hanser had made sure of that. But Axel Johansson – there was still a chance there. As far as Haraldsson was aware, Riksmord had another suspect in custody. The principal of the boy's school. Axel Johansson hadn't been written off, as far as Haraldsson knew, but he had been given a lower priority.

Haraldsson was annoyed with himself because he hadn't brought home all the available information on Johansson. He also cursed the fact that he had been drinking, because otherwise he could have driven to the station to fetch it. Taking a cab there and back would be expensive and a lot of trouble, among other things. Under no circumstances did he want to bump into his colleagues in this state. He would have to gather all the information tomorrow. When he had perfected his plan.

Haraldsson knew that Torkel's team had spoken to Johansson's ex-girlfriend. He needed to know what she had said. Calling her or going to see her and questioning her was not an option. If he did that and Hanser got to hear about it, he would be in even more trouble. Hanser had been very clear – excessively clear – about the fact that if Haraldsson spent as much as one minute on the Roger

Eriksson case, she would arrest him for impeding the investigation. A joke, of course. Or rather, a warning: a way of demonstrating her power and putting Haraldsson in his place when he had made a little mistake for once. She was on his back straightaway. Bloody Hanser . . . Haraldsson took a deep breath.

Focus.

There was no point wasting time and energy cursing Hanser. He had to come up with a plan. A plan that would put her in her place. A plan that would prove which of them was the better police officer. Contacting Axel Johansson's ex-girlfriend was out of the question but someone from Riksmord had spoken to her, and even if Haraldsson no longer had access to anything connected with the investigation, there were others who did.

He picked up his mobile, searched for a number in the contacts list and pressed *Call*. It was almost midnight, but the phone was answered almost immediately.

Radjan Micic.

This was one of the advantages of having worked in the same place for a long time. You made friends. Friends for whom you sometimes did a little favour, and who were therefore prepared to help out when you needed it.

No funny stuff.

Nothing illegal, nothing like that.

Just a helping hand to make life easier. Writing a report for someone when they had to rush off to pick the kids up from nursery. Dropping by the state-run liquor store in the car on a Friday afternoon. Covering up, helping out. Little favours that made life easier for all concerned. Favours that meant you could ask a favour in return.

When Hanser took over the responsibility for trying to locate Axel Johansson, she gave the task to Radjan. This meant he had access to all the material relating to the missing caretaker. The conversation lasted less than two minutes. Radjan had been with the Västerås police almost as long as Haraldsson. He understood perfectly and would of course print out the interview with Johansson's

325

ex. It would be on Haraldsson's desk when he came in the following morning. Radjan really was an excellent colleague.

As Haraldsson put the phone down on the sofa beside him, a satisfied smile on his face, he discovered that Jenny was standing in the doorway, gazing at him sleepily.

'Who were you talking to?'

'Radjan.'

'At this time of night?'

'Yes.'

Jenny came and sat down beside him on the sofa, tucking her feet underneath her.

'What are you doing?'

'Watching TV.'

'What are you watching?'

'Nothing.'

Jenny rested her arm on the sofa and put her hand on his head. She started to stroke his hair as she nestled into his shoulder.

'Something's happened. Tell me.'

Haraldsson closed his eyes. Everything was spinning slightly. He felt as if he wanted to tell her. He wanted to tell her about work. About Hanser. Properly. Not just moaning and ridiculing. He wanted to tell her how scared he was. Scared that life was slipping through his fingers. Scared that he couldn't see himself in ten years' time. What he would be doing. Who he was. He wanted to tell her that the future scared him. That he was scared they would never have a child. Would their relationship survive that? Would Jenny leave him? He wanted to tell her that he loved her. He didn't say it often enough. There was so much he wanted to tell her, but he didn't really know how. So he just shook his head and leaned back with his eyes closed as her hand continued its caresses.

'Come to bed.' Jenny kissed his cheek. Haraldsson realised how tired he was. Tired and drunk.

They went to bed.

Close to each other. Jenny's arms around him. Holding him

tight. He could feel her gentle breathing on his neck. Closeness. It had been a long time. Sex was part of everyday life, but closeness . . . He realised how much he had missed it as sleep stole over him.

Those who are guilty run away.

One last lucid thought.

It is the guilty who run away.

There was a conclusion there. A pattern. It was there, but his alcohol-befuddled brain was unable to grasp it. Thomas Haraldsson fell asleep, into a deep and dreamless slumber.

Just after midnight Torkel finally managed to escape from the press conference. He had avoided answering specific questions on a possible link between the murders. He had ignored the person who wanted to know whether they had brought in any employee from Palmlövska High in connection with the murders, but he hoped he had still given the impression that the investigation was making steady progress, and that it was only a matter of time before the case was solved.

He walked quickly back to the hotel, hoping the kitchen wouldn't be closed. He was ravenous and intended to have a late supper in the small restaurant. When he got there he realised he wasn't the only one who'd had a bad day. Mikael was sitting in the bar. With a drink in front of him. Which wasn't good. Torkel was about to try to sneak out again when Mikael spotted him.

'Torkel!'

Torkel stopped and gave a feeble wave.

'Hi, Mikael.'

'Come and have a drink with me!'

'No, thanks. I've still got some work to do.'

Torkel tried to deflect him with a smile, making it as clear as possible that he wasn't interested, without being directly unpleasant. It didn't work. Mikael slid off the bar stool and headed towards Torkel in as straight a line as he could manage. Torkel just had time to think, *Fuck, he's drunk*, before Mikael reached him. He came and stood far too close. Torkel could smell his breath. Whisky and some sweeter kind of alcohol. Not only was he standing too close, his voice was too loud as well.

'Fucking hell, Torkel, I've messed things up. Big time.'

'I can see that.'

'You could have a word with her.'

'I don't think that's a good idea. This is between the two of you—'

'But she likes you. She listens to you.'

'Mikael, I really think you ought to go to bed.'

'Surely we can have a drink. Just one drink?'

Torkel shook his head firmly, frantically trying to work out how to get out of this. He had no desire to get any closer to Mikael. He already felt bad enough, and the very thought of getting to know the man better was terrifying. He suddenly understood the importance of Ursula's rules.

Always at work.

Never on home turf.

This was worse than home turf. But she was the one who had broken the rules. She was the one who had summoned her husband, the man who was now leaning against him, needing someone. Someone to share his feelings with.

'I've made such a fucking mess of things. I love her, you have to understand that. But she's complicated. Understand? I mean, you work with her. You know what she's like, don't you?'

Torkel decided to act. He would take Mikael up to Ursula's room and leave him there. That was the right thing to do. He put his hand under Mikael's arm and led him kindly but firmly out of the bar.

'Come on, I'll help you up to your room.'

Mikael cooperated. The lift was already waiting, so at least it didn't take long to get away from reception and the look on the face of the girl who was working there. Torkel pressed the button for the fourth floor. Is he going to wonder how I know Ursula's room number? He quickly dismissed the thought. They were colleagues, after all. Of course they knew each other's room number. Mikael looked at him.

'You're a good man. Ursula says lots of good things about you.'

'That's nice to know.'

'It was so bloody peculiar, calling me like that. I mean, when Ursula's at work, she's at work. She's got rules. If you're working, you're working. I never hear from her. That's the way it's always been. I'm fine with that.'

Mikael took a deep breath. Torkel didn't say anything.

'But then she rang yesterday and wanted me to come over. As quickly as I could. You understand?'

This was turning into one of the longest rides in a lift that Torkel had ever experienced. Only the second floor. Perhaps it would have been better to leave Mikael in the bar and just walk away after all.

'Things have been really difficult between us, you know. So I got the idea she wanted to tell me it's over, or something. Tell me she'd made up her mind. Why else would she ask me to come here, for fuck's sake? It's never happened before.'

'I don't know, Mikael. It's best if you talk to Ursula about this.'

'That's the way she is. *Bang*, and she's made a decision. Which has to be carried out right away. So what was I supposed to think?'

'I can't imagine she wants a divorce.'

They had reached the fourth floor at long last. Torkel quickly opened the glass door and walked out. Mikael stayed where he was.

'Maybe not, but that's what I thought. I mean, she didn't say anything. We had dinner and then she left me in the room. I asked her why she wanted me to come here and she just said she wanted to see me. But that's not true.'

'Come on.' Torkel waved at Mikael, who got himself out of the lift with some difficulty. Together they walked down the corridor.

'So I took a bottle from the minibar. I was nervous. I was sure she was going to leave me.'

Torkel didn't answer. What could he say? The needle was stuck on Mikael's record. When they reached the door Torkel knocked.

'I don't think she's there. She went out. She doesn't like to see me like this. But I've got the key.'

Mikael fumbled through his pockets and after what seemed like an eternity he produced the white key card and handed it over. Torkel saw that he had tears in his eyes when he met Mikael's gaze for a fraction of a second.

'Why else would she ask me to come here?'

'I don't know. I really haven't a clue,' Torkel lied. He opened the door. The room smelled of alcohol and Ursula, a combination Torkel had never experienced before. They went inside and Mikael flopped down on one of the two chairs in the corner. He looked upset.

'I've made such a fucking mess of things.'

Torkel contemplated the wreck in the armchair and felt sorry for him. Mikael was innocent. He and Ursula were guilty. Torkel wanted to leave, but at the same time he couldn't make himself walk away. For a moment he toyed with the idea of telling Mikael.

Telling him everything.

Explaining exactly why Mikael was sitting in the corner of a hotel room in Västerås, drunk.

That it was his, Torkel's, fault.

He was the one who was supposed to be punished.

Not Mikael.

Suddenly Ursula was standing in the doorway. She didn't say a word. Presumably she felt the same as Torkel: that there were many things she would like to say and do, and that none of them was appropriate at the moment. Silence was the only tune she could play.

Torkel gave her a brief nod and left.

Unaware that Torkel had left the building less than an hour ago, Billy was sitting with his feet on the desk in the small room he had more or less lived in while he was watching the films from the CCTV cameras. He was eating a chocolate biscuit to raise his blood-sugar levels. Worn out after a long day. He closed his eyes for a moment and just sat there taking in the sounds of the dark, deserted office. Apart from the gentle hum of the fans, he could hear the latest software from Stellar Phoenix Windows Data Recovery battling with Ragnar Groth's hard drive. The program was searching for deleted files, and the angry buzzing told him it was still working.

Billy knew there was something somewhere. There always was. The question was whether or not they were looking in the right place. Computers usually concealed more than people thought, which was why he was still searching. Most people were unaware of how much information still remains on the hard drive even after files have been deleted. When the user pressed *Delete* the file allocation system that governed the area of the hard drive in which information was stored did not remove the file itself, only the reference to it. This meant that the information was still there, deep inside the hard drive. When it came to Groth's computer, however, Billy was beginning to feel a certain scepticism. He had already gone through it twice – albeit with less effective programs – and found nothing of interest. Nor was there any indication that Groth had used the powerful logarithms that could permanently clear a hard drive – quite the opposite. Billy had found a large number of deleted emails and documents, which unfortunately had turned out to be of no interest whatsoever as far as the investigation was concerned.

Billy stretched. The software would finish searching within fifteen or twenty minutes. Not long enough to make a start on something else, too long just to sit around. He took a stroll around the room to get his circulation going, and for a second he toyed with the idea of going down to buy yet another bar of chocolate from the machine on the ground floor. He decided to resist. His sugar intake was already way too high, and he knew that if he had more chocolate now, he would want even more within a few hours.

He caught sight of one of the other monitors on the desk. It was showing a frozen image from the final sequence of Roger's movements. The boy was slightly turned away, heading towards the motel. At least, that's what they had assumed this morning. It no longer seemed quite so clear-cut. Billy reached for the keyboard and began to click through the images slowly. He watched the boy's final steps one frame at a time. The last thing to disappear was the right leg wearing a tennis shoe. The picture was empty now, apart from the rear window of the car behind which Roger had vanished, just visible in one corner of the screen.

Billy had an idea. He had assumed from the start that Roger had carried on walking, and so had searched for his appearance on another camera. But what if Roger had met someone, had an errand somewhere, then after a while turned around and came back? It wasn't beyond the bounds of probability. It was worth a try, at any rate, and it was far more useful than eating chocolate.

Billy settled down and began. He clicked back to the last frame in which Roger appeared and started from there. Increased the speed to 4x. Billy stared at the empty street. The time code rolled on: one minute, two, three. Billy increased the speed to 8x to save time. After thirteen minutes he saw the car behind which Roger had disappeared drive away, leaving the street completely empty. Billy carried on, 16x now. Soon two figures appeared, moving through the picture at sixteen times their normal speed. It looked quite funny. Billy stopped and rewound until he saw the two figures again. It was an elderly couple with a dog, walking in the opposite direction in relation to Roger. There was nothing to indicate that they were doing anything other than walking the dog. Even so, Billy made a note of the time and decided to ask Hanser to track them down. With a bit of luck they might have seen something. Billy restarted the tape. The minutes flew by, but nothing happened. Roger didn't come back.

Billy was suddenly struck by a thought: that car, the one that drove off approximately thirteen minutes after Roger had walked past – when had it arrived? With two clicks Billy was back at the point where Roger could again be seen in the picture. They had assumed that the car was parked at the roadside, like a dead object.

But that same car had been driven away by someone thirteen minutes later. Billy started to rewind and discovered that the car had reversed into the picture just six minutes before Roger appeared. Any tiredness Billy might have felt was swept away by the realisation that the car had been parked in close proximity to Roger for just nineteen minutes. Billy suddenly felt like an idiot. He had committed the cardinal sin of limiting the possible interpretations of the evidence in front of him. He had become trapped in searching for a particular pattern without leaving the door open to anything else. So far Roger had gone from one camera to another, moving on the whole time. And that was what Billy had continued to look for. Roger moving on. To the next camera.

Now that he had opened the door to other possibilities, he knew that there were other, highly credible scenarios. The car might not have been empty. It was possible that the person who had parked the car six minutes before Roger walked past had been sitting there the whole time. Billy could see only a part of the left side of the rear windscreen. It was impossible to tell whether anyone got out of the car or not, but he clicked back to the image of Roger again and restarted the film. Tried to tell himself he was watching it for the first time.

Without preconceptions.

Roger entered the picture from the right, walked a few steps then crossed the street. Billy stopped the film. Went back frame by frame. There! Roger suddenly turned his head slightly to the left, as if something had caught his attention. Then he continued across the street. Billy started the film again. Now that his tunnel vision was gone, it was equally possible to imagine that Roger walked behind the car and round to the doors on the passenger side.

Billy took a deep breath. No hasty conclusions. Check properly. Focus on the picture. On the car. It looked like a Volvo. Dark blue or black. Not an estate car, but a sedan. Not the new model, but perhaps 2002–2006. He would have to check up on that. But definitely a four-door Volvo sedan. Billy started to move forward frame by frame, focusing on the car. Just the car, nothing else. Fifty-seven seconds and six frames after Roger disappeared, Billy saw something he hadn't noticed before. The car shook slightly, briefly, as if a car door had been closed. It wasn't very clear and he might have been mistaken. But he could soon check.

Billy loaded the sequence into a simple program with image stabilisation software. He could assume that the fixed CCTV camera wasn't moving, so any possible movement had to come from the object in the picture. Billy quickly marked a couple of movement points on the metal edge of the rear windscreen above the wheel. At 00:57:06 these points definitely moved a couple of millimetres then stabilised at a slightly lower level. Someone opened a car door, got in and slammed it shut. The fact that the points stabilised at a lower level indicated that the car now contained more weight. Someone had got into the car. Presumably Roger.

Billy looked at the clock. Almost half past twelve. It was never too late to call Torkel. Torkel was more likely to be annoyed if he *didn't* ring. He picked up the phone and called him on speed dial. While he was waiting for an answer, he looked at the image on the screen. The new course of events would explain a number of things.

Roger wasn't picked up by any more cameras because he didn't walk any further.

He was in a dark-coloured Volvo.

Probably on the way to his death.

Lena Eriksson was sitting in the chair vacated by Billy some seven hours ago, looking around in surprise. There were a lot of people in the small room. She knew most of them already, apart from the young male officer who was doing something with a keyboard in front of two big blank computer screens.

So many police officers could mean only one thing.

Something had happened.

Something important.

She'd had that feeling as soon as they'd rung her doorbell, and it was growing stronger all the time. It was 06:45 when she dragged herself out of bed after the bell had been rung persistently and repeatedly for ages, and opened the door. The young female officer who had been to see her a few days earlier had introduced herself again, speaking quickly and eagerly.

They needed her help.

The whole situation – the early hour, the police officer's serious tone and concise request, the urgency with which she wanted Lena to accompany her, all of this erased days of broken sleep and fear. Lena's whole body was filled with unsettled energy.

They had driven through the grey, misty morning without a word. Parked underneath the police station in a car park Lena didn't even know existed. Walked up several flights of concrete stairs and in through a big steel door. The police officer moved quickly down the long corridors. They met some uniformed officers who seemed to be on the way out on patrol. They were laughing at something, and their cheerfulness seemed out of place.

Everything had happened so fast that Lena found it difficult to collate her impressions into a single picture. It was more like a series of separate, different images: the laughter, the corridors leading this way and that, the police officer who just kept on walking. One last turn and they appeared to have arrived. A number of people were standing there waiting for her. They greeted her, but Lena didn't really hear what they said, she was busy thinking that she would never find her way out of here. The one who seemed to be in charge, the one she had talked to about Leo Lundin what seemed like an eternity ago, placed a friendly hand on her shoulder.

'Thank you for coming. There's something we'd like to show you.'

They opened the door to the small room and led her inside. *This is how it feels when you're arrested*, she thought.

They say hello and bring you in here.

They say hello and then they expose what you've done.

She took a deep breath. One of the officers pulled out a chair for her and the youngest, quite a tall man, started fiddling with the keyboard on the desk in front of her.

'It's essential that what we tell you now remains within these four walls.'

It was the older one again. The boss. Torsten, was that his name? Lena nodded anyway. He went on.

'We now believe that Roger was picked up in a car. We would like to see if you recognise it.'

'You've got a picture of it?' Lena turned pale.

'Not much of it, unfortunately. Or very little, to be more accurate. Are you ready?'

With that the older man fell silent and nodded to the younger one at the computer. He pressed the space bar on the keyboard and suddenly the screen was filled with a picture of an empty street. A lawn by the side of the road, a smallish house, and up in one corner the reflection of what was probably the yellow glow of a street lamp.

'What am I supposed to be looking for?' Lena asked, somewhat confused.

'There.' The young man pointed to the lower left-hand corner of the picture. The rear windscreen of a car. A dark-coloured car. How the hell was she supposed to recognise it?

'It's a Volvo,' the young man went on. 'A 2002 to 2004 model. An S60.'

Lena stared at the picture and saw the car's indicator begin to flash just before it drove away and disappeared.

'Is that all?'

'Unfortunately, yes. Would you like to see it again?'

Lena nodded. The young policeman pressed a number of keys and the film jumped back to the beginning. Lena stared at the screen, desperately trying to find something. But it was just a part of a static image. A very small part. She waited for something else to happen, her body rigid with tension, but it was just the same street, the same car. The picture stopped moving and from the expectant faces around her Lena realised it was her turn to say something. She looked at them.

'I don't recognise it.'

They nodded. That was what they'd expected.

'Do you know anyone who owns a dark-coloured Volvo?'

'Maybe. It's a very common car, I assume, but I don't know . . . Not that I can think of.'

'Have you ever seen anyone give Roger a lift home in a car like that?'

'No.'

No one spoke. Lena could feel the excitement and expectation among the officers ebbing away, to be replaced by disappointment. She turned to Vanja.

'Where do these pictures come from?

'From a CCTV camera.'

'But where was it?'

'We can't tell you that.'

Lena nodded. They didn't trust her to keep quiet. So they weren't prepared to tell her. Her suspicions were confirmed when the boss spoke.

'It would compromise the investigation if any of this got out. I hope you understand.'

'I won't say anything.'

Lena turned back to the screen and the frozen image of the empty street.

'Is Roger on that film?'

Billy looked at Torkel, who gave a slight nod.

'Yes.'

'Can I see him?'

Billy looked at Torkel again and received another nod in response. He reached for the keyboard, rewound the film somewhat further then pressed play. After a few seconds Roger appeared from the right-hand side. Lena sat on the edge of her seat. She didn't even dare to blink, she was so afraid of missing something.

He was alive.

He was walking down the street.

With rapid, springy steps. He kept himself fit. Looked after his body. Was proud of it. And now it lay behind a stainless steel door in the mortuary, cold and sliced open. Her eyes filled with tears, but she didn't blink.

He was alive.

He suddenly turned his head to the left, crossed the road and disappeared behind the car.

Out of the picture.

Out of her life.

Gone.

It had happened so quickly.

Lena fought against an urge to touch the screen. Everything and everyone was silent and motionless in the room. The young officer approached her cautiously.

'Would you like to see it again?'

Lena shook her head and swallowed. Hoped her voice would hold.

'No, thank you, it's fine . . .'

The boss came over and gently laid a hand on her shoulder.

'Thank you for coming. We'll organise a lift home for you.'

With those words the meeting was over, and she soon found herself walking behind Vanja once more. They weren't in as much of a hurry now. Not as far as the police were concerned, anyway. It was different for Lena. Her anxiety had eased, replaced by the fury of realisation. The energy that came from certainty.

A Volvo S60.

A 2002–2004 model.

She knew exactly who owned a car like that.

They arrived at a desk with a uniformed officer sitting behind it. Vanja said something to him and he got up and grabbed his jacket. Lena shook her head. She could guess what the woman had said.

'I don't need a lift, thank you. If you could just show me the way out? I've got a few things to do in town.'

'Are you sure? It's no trouble.'

'Quite sure. But thank you.'

She shook hands with Vanja. The policeman hung up his jacket and led her down the corridor to the main doors.

A few things to do in town.

To say the least.

Well, one thing, anyway.

Vanja met up with the others in the conference room. Before she went in she could see that Torkel was looking unusually frustrated, pacing the room with his fists clenched. If she hadn't still been in a bad mood she would no doubt have thought he looked quite comical, circling the table where Sebastian and Billy were sitting. She pushed open the door. Sebastian stopped speaking when she came in. She refused to look him in the eye.

Her anger was not rational. It was Valdemar who had blabbed too much. He was the one who had ruined their evening. Who had invited Sebastian to join them, given him an advantage over her. Made him seem more important, ascribed far more significance to him than was actually the case. That was all down to Valdemar. But Sebastian had every intention of making full use of his newly acquired knowledge, she could feel it.

No, she *knew* it.

And she hated it.

She positioned herself next to the door and folded her arms. Torkel glanced at her. She looked tired. Fuck it, they were all tired. Worn out. Irritable. More than usual. Perhaps it wasn't all down to the Sebastian effect. This was an unusually tricky investigation.

Torkel nodded to Sebastian to continue.

'I said that if he reversed in because he knew there was a camera there, then it doesn't just mean that he's a master of forward planning and anticipation. It means he's bloody playing with us. In which case we should assume that even if we find the right car, we won't find any evidence.'

Vanja nodded reluctantly. That sounded reasonable.

'We can't be sure,' Billy replied. 'That he knew about the camera, I mean. It covers only one side of the street, which is a cul-de-sac. He could have turned in here . . . ' He got up, went over to the map on the wall and used the tip of his pen to illustrate the possible scenario. 'And reversed instead of turning around.'

Torkel stopped circling and looked at Billy and the map.

'So if he didn't know there was a camera there . . . If he'd reversed another two metres, we would have seen who was driving.'

'Yes.'

Torkel looked as if he couldn't believe his ears. Two metres! Were they two metres from solving this bloody case?

'Why the hell aren't we getting anywhere?'

Billy shrugged his shoulders. He was beginning to get used to Torkel's bad moods. If it had been about something he had done or failed to do, he would probably have reacted differently, but this wasn't about him, he was sure of it. It was more likely to be something to do with Ursula. At that moment she pushed open the door, carrying a cup of coffee and a bag from the local newsagent's.

'Sorry I'm late.' Ursula put down her things and pulled out a chair.

'How's Mikael?'

340

Was it Billy's imagination, or was Torkel's voice a little gentler? More sympathetic?

'He's gone home.'

Billy looked at Ursula with genuine amazement. Not that it was anything to do with him, but even so.

'I thought he only got here last night?'

'Yes.'

'So it was just a flying visit?'

'Yes.'

Torkel could tell from Ursula's tone of voice that this was the last he would hear about Mikael's visit, unless she herself brought it up later, which was unlikely. He watched her take a cheese roll and a yoghurt drink out of the plastic bag as she looked around the room.

'What have I missed?'

'I'll brief you later. Let's move on.'

Torkel waved to Billy, who went back to his seat and his papers.

'This isn't going to make you feel any better. I've checked the vehicle register. There are 216 black, dark blue or dark grey Volvo S60s, 2002 to 2004 model, in Västerås. If we include the surrounding areas such as Enköping, Sala, Eskilstuna and so on, we're up around the 500 mark.'

Torkel couldn't bring himself to respond. He merely clenched his fists a little more tightly. Sebastian looked up at Billy.

'How many of those are linked to Palmlövska High? If we cross-reference the vehicle register with parents and employees?'

Billy looked at Sebastian.

'We can't do that. Well, it would have to be done manually. Which would take quite some time.'

'In that case I think we should make a start. Everything so far has led us to that bloody school.' Billy thought Sebastian's suggestion was a good idea, but you didn't need a qualification in behavioural science to realise that the underlying irritation within the team could be traced back to Sebastian's involvement in their work. Billy had no intention of expressing any views on Sebastian's proposal until Torkel had made it known where he stood. But Torkel was nodding too.

'Good idea. But I want us to go through every single film, from every single camera, at the same time. I want that bloody car found!'

Billy sighed audibly when he heard this.

'That's not something I can do on my own.'

'No problem. I'll have a word with Hanser. Sebastian will help you in the meantime. It's time he did a bit of real detective work.'

For a second Sebastian considered telling Torkel to go to hell. Cross-referencing the vehicle register and running through CCTV films were the last things he wanted to do, but just as he was about to utter the harsh words, he stopped himself. He'd stuck it out for this long and he didn't intend to be driven out now. Not until the case was solved. Not until he'd got the address he wanted. It would be stupid to fall out with the one person who might be able to help him in his search for Anna Eriksson. The real reason why he was here. So instead Sebastian gave Billy a surprisingly big smile.

'Of course, Billy – you just tell me what to do and I'll do it.'

'Are you any good with computers?'

Sebastian shook his head.

Torkel stomped crossly round the room one more time. He'd tried to start a quarrel with his old friend, partly because he needed to give vent to a general feeling of irritation, and partly because he wanted to show Ursula that he wasn't letting Sebastian get away with everything. But even that hadn't worked. Sebastian got to his feet and patted Billy on the shoulder.

'Let's get started, then.'

Torkel marched out, still furious.

Lena hadn't gone straight there. The resolve she had felt at the police station had begun to falter after she had been out in the fresh air for a while. What if she was wrong? What if it wasn't the same car? Even worse, what if she was right? What would she do then?

She took a walk through the new shopping mall that had opened the previous autumn. The construction had gone on for several years, and sometimes the residents of Västerås had thought it would never be finished. Lena wandered aimlessly across the shiny stone floors, gazing into the huge, brightly lit shop windows. It was still early, the shops weren't open yet, and she was virtually alone inside the new jewel in the crown of Västerås. The stores were starting to advertise this year's summer fashions – that's what the posters claimed with great conviction – but Lena couldn't see any difference from the previous year's trends. And, in any case, nothing that was on display would look the same on her as it did on the stick-thin mannequins. Besides, she really did have other things to think about apart from trivial matters such as shopping. That little voice was back. The one she had more or less managed to suppress over the past few days.

Perhaps that was why it was now louder than ever.

It was you!

You know that now!

It was your fault!

She had to find out if the voice was right, she knew that. But it was so painful, so agonising even to go near that possibility. Especially now, when it seemed as if there was no chance of denying it any longer. The dark-coloured car on the film had made sure of that.

In a coffee shop in the middle of the mall a young girl was busy arranging freshly baked Danish pastries and cakes in the huge glass counter. There was a sweet smell of sugar, vanilla and cinnamon. A memory of another life, away from all the hurtful thoughts. Lena felt she needed to return to that life, if only for a little while. She managed to persuade the girl to sell her a Danish even though the coffee shop wasn't open yet. She chose an excessively large vanilla pastry with far too much sugar on it. The girl placed it in a paper bag and handed it to her. Lena thanked her and took a few steps towards the door before taking the pastry out of the bag. It was soft and still warm. That other life visited her for a second, and she greedily took a big bite. When the taste became reality and she felt the oversweet dough in her mouth, she suddenly felt sick.

How could she even be here? Window-shopping and eating. Standing there trying to enjoy something. Images of Roger came back to her.

His first smile.

His first steps.

School days, birthdays, football matches.

His final words: 'I'm going now . . . '

His final steps behind the car.

Lena threw the pastry into a garbage bin and set off. She had lost enough time. Ducking out, trying not to dig deeper into what she knew she had to find out.

Did she bear some of the responsibility for the terrible thing that had happened?

More than that.

Was she the guilty party?

That's what the little voice kept on insisting.

She scurried through the town. Her body wasn't used to such a speed. Her lungs were working hard, and she could feel the strain in her mouth. But she didn't slow down. She headed purposefully for the place she hated most of all.

The place that had been the beginning of the end for her and Roger.

The place that had made her feel so inferior, so utterly worthless.

Palmlövska High.

Lena found what she was looking for at the back of the school. First of all she had walked up and down in the big car park in front of the building without finding it, before taking a turn around the school in her frustration. She came across a smaller car park right next to the door of the cafeteria.

And there it was.

A dark blue Volvo.

Just as she had suspected.

Just as she had feared.

The feeling of nausea came back. The thoughts came crowding in again. This was the car he had got into. Her Roger. On that Friday which was so recent, but in some strange way seemed like an eternity ago. There was just one thing left to do. Lena went round to the back of the car and crouched down on the left-hand side. She didn't know whether the police had noticed – they hadn't mentioned it – but when the car on the screen had indicated and left the street, you could clearly see that the glass on the rear nearside light had been repaired with tape. Lena had seen it, anyway.

Roger had brought a letter home from school a few weeks ago: a dry, accusatory note explaining that both rear lights of the car had been found vandalised. A provisional repair had been carried out, but it was expected that the guilty party would own up and pay for the job to be done properly. She didn't know what had happened after that. She ran her fingers over the wide tape. As if she hoped that time would freeze, and nothing else would happen. Ever.

But it would. This was just the start. She knew that. She got up and took a few steps around the car. She touched the cold metal. Perhaps his fingers had also touched it here. Or here. She kept on moving. Tried to work out where his fingers might have touched the car. One of the doors, definitely. The front passenger door, probably. She tried it. Cold and locked. Lena leaned against the car and peered inside. Dark, plain upholstery. Nothing on the floor. A small amount of change in the little hollow between the seats. Nothing else.

She straightened up and realised to her surprise that all her anxiety had disappeared. The worst thing that could happen had already taken place.

Her guilt was confirmed.

Beyond all doubt.

Now she just felt empty inside. A chill was spreading through her body. As if that cold, concrete inner voice had finally become part of her.

It was her fault. There was no longer any defence against that realisation anywhere in her body. No warmth.

A part of Lena died the day Roger was snatched away from her. The other part died now.

She took out her mobile and keyed in a number. It rang a few times before she heard the male voice on the other end. She heard her own voice. It had the same icy chill as the whole of her insides.

'I saw something at the police station today. I saw your car. I know it was you.'

Cia Edlund hadn't had a dog for very long. She had never really thought of herself as a dog person. But on her birthday two years ago Rodolfo had turned up with an adorable, curly-haired puppy. A cocker spaniel bitch. Just like the dog in *The Lady and the Tramp*, Rodolfo had said with a big smile, his eyes shining as only his eyes could. It had been impossible for Cia to say no, particularly when Rodolfo, sensing her instinctive hesitation, had promised faithfully that he would help her.

'It won't just be your dog. It'll be ours, I promise. Our little baby ...'

Things hadn't quite turned out that way. Six months later, when Rodolfo's eyes shone less often and his visits were becoming less and less frequent, Cia knew that the dog was her responsibility, and hers alone. In spite of the fact that it had been named after Rodolfo's grandmother, Lucia Almira, a woman in Chile whom Cia had never met. They had planned to visit her as soon as they could afford it.

That hadn't happened either. So now Cia shared her bed with an animal named after a Chilean grandmother she was never going to meet.

The practical issues had quickly become her main problem. Cia worked long, irregular hours as a nurse, and Almira's walks had suffered as a result. Usually it was just a brief outing close to where they lived. She might get one walk in the middle of the night, the next in the afternoon the following day, depending on Cia's shift pattern. But today Cia had a day off and decided to take the opportunity to go for a really long walk. It would do both her and Almira good. They headed down the path towards the football ground, running alongside the forest and the illuminated exercise track.

When they reached the deserted football pitch Cia undid

Almira's lead, and the dog raced off into the undergrowth and the fir trees, barking excitedly. Cia could see Almira's tail wagging among the short, tangled bushes from time to time. She smiled to herself. For once she felt like a good dog owner.

Almira came hurtling back. She was never away for long, she always wanted to know exactly where her owner was. After making eye contact she would dash off again and, after a little while, come back. Cia frowned as she saw the dog emerge from the undergrowth. There was something dark around Almira's nose and mouth. Cia called her over, and Almira trotted up to her. Cia stiffened. It looked like blood. But the dog was perfectly happy. It couldn't be hers. Cia evaded her nuzzling kisses and put her lead back on.

'What have you found? Show me.'

After only fifteen minutes Sebastian was tired of staring at a monitor looking for dark-coloured Volvos. This was a masterclass in futility. Billy had tried to explain what they were going to do. Since they knew when the car Roger had got into drove away, they could *blah blah blah* work out approximately where it *blah blah blah* depending on which direction it had taken and *blah blah blah*. Sebastian had switched off. He glanced across at Billy, who was sitting a short distance away with a number of address lists he had just received from the principal's PA at Palmlövska High. Billy didn't look bored, he looked grimly determined. He glanced up at Sebastian, who was sitting there completely motionless.

'Is something not working?'

'No, no, it's working perfectly. How are you getting on?'

Billy smiled at him.

'I've hardly started. You carry on. There are plenty of cameras, believe me.'

Billy went back to his papers. Sebastian turned to the screen and sighed. The situation reminded him of the time when he had been a research assistant working with Professor Erlander thirty years ago, and he had been expected to collate the results of several thousand questionnaires. On that occasion he had paid some students to do the job for him and gone to the pub instead. This was a little more tricky.

'Did you get anywhere with that name I gave you? Anna Eriksson?'

'Sorry, I've had a few other things to do, but I haven't forgotten.'

'No rush, I just wondered.'

Sebastian saw Billy was looking at him with an encouraging expression, urging him to get on with the task. Might as well play along, he couldn't opt out at this early stage. Sebastian pressed F5 as Billy had shown him and wearily gazed at yet another colourless, boring back street somewhere in Västerås. The call that came in saved him from dying of boredom.

They arrived at the football ground in two cars, Vanja and Ursula in one, Torkel and Sebastian in the other. Torkel felt as if he was back at school, involved in some variation of boys versus girls. He had remained completely impersonal when Ursula stayed behind after the meeting to catch up on the developments of the past few hours, but she had still ignored him on the way down to the car park, and headed off towards her car without a word.

Two patrol cars were already on the scene. A uniformed officer met them as they arrived and accompanied them across the gravelled area. He looked tense, and seemed grateful that they were there.

'Some blood has been found. A lot of blood.'

'Who found it?' Ursula wanted to know. So far it was merely a forensic discovery, and therefore she was naturally the one who asked the questions.

'A lady called Cia Edlund. She was walking her dog. She's over there.' They crossed the football pitch and followed their uniformed colleague into the forest. After only a short distance the ground fell away steeply, and once you got down to the bottom you were no longer visible from the football pitch, Vanja noticed.

The path curved to the left and soon led to a small opening. Two people were waiting there: an officer who was fixing police tape to cordon off a large, rectangular area, and a woman of about twenty-five standing a short distance away with a cocker spaniel.

'That's the lady who found it. We haven't asked her too many questions, just as you requested.'

'I'd like to see the blood first,' Ursula replied, walking into the glade.

The officer pointed to a spot a few metres from the path.

'You can see it from here.'

Ursula stopped and gestured to indicate that the others should stay where they were. In front of her she could see last year's yellow grass lying flat and heavy on the ground. The fresh green blades were growing underneath, but they were shorter and provided only the slightest hint of green among the sea of pale yellow. What did, however, stand out in the limited colour palette were patches of dried, dark red blood. In the centre of the sporadically scattered patches she saw a large pool of coagulated blood.

'It looks like a slaughterhouse,' the officer who had set up the cordon couldn't help commenting.

'Perhaps it is,' Ursula said drily. She moved forward cautiously and crouched down in front of the pool. Most of the blood had dried up, but on the ground there were a number of small hollows resembling footprints that were filled with an almost jelly-like red substance. Was she imagining it or was there a strong smell of iron in the air? She nodded to the others.

'I'd like to run a quick analysis on this so that we don't waste time on some poor deer that lost its life. It will take a few minutes.' She opened her white bag and set to work. Torkel and Sebastian went over to the woman with the dog. She looked as if she'd been waiting for a long time for someone to come and listen to her story.

'It was Almira who found it. I think she might have drunk some of it . . .'

*

350

When Lena walked in through the door of her apartment and closed it behind her, the strain caught up with her. She sank down on the floor of the hallway. She couldn't walk another step. It was easier to maintain the mask when she was out and about, among other people. Shoulders back, gaze fixed straight ahead, keep on walking. Pretend. At home it was more difficult. Impossible. As she sat there in the middle of the floor amid shoes and plastic bags, she caught sight of an old school photograph of Roger, one she had put up ages ago. It was the first one she had bought, taken when he had just started school.

Roger was smiling at the camera in a blue polo shirt. Two teeth missing. It was a long time since she had seen the picture. She had hung it up when they moved into the apartment, but she had placed it slightly too close to the hat stand, so it ended up being hidden by padded jackets and winter clothes. As Roger grew older he had acquired more and more outdoor clothes that were bigger and bigger, and she had forgotten about the picture for a couple of years. It was wonderful to discover it now. Forgotten and hidden among all those coats and jackets for years. There would be no more clothes piling up to hide him now. He would sit there smiling his gap-toothed smile at her for as long as she lived. Mute. Never growing older. With his expression full of life.

The doorbell rang. Lena ignored it. The world could wait. These moments were more important.

When the man walked in she realised she had forgotten to lock the door. She looked at him. What seemed most strange to her was not the fact that he was standing there in her apartment. Even the desperation in his eyes was not altogether surprising. No, what was making the whole of her insides tremble was the realisation that her eyes, which had just been gazing at the smiling face of her seven-year-old son, were now contemplating the person who took his life.

Haraldsson was late. It wasn't at all like him to oversleep. He blamed the wine, and Jenny. The wine had made him sleep more deeply than usual, a dreamless sleep. And Jenny hadn't woken him before she left for the hospital. He had set the alarm but he must have switched it off instead of setting it to snooze. He had no memory of even hearing it ring. He had woken just after nine-thirty. At first he thought he would just throw on some clothes and dash off to work, but somehow the morning had passed in slow motion. By the time he had showered, had breakfast and dressed, an hour had gone by. He decided to walk to the station, and arrived dead on eleven.

Radjan had done as Haraldsson asked. There was a single folder on his desk when he sat down with a cup of coffee. He opened it eagerly. It contained three closely written sheets of A4. Haraldsson sat back in his chair with his coffee in one hand and the printout in the other. He began to read with great concentration.

After forty-five minutes he had read the interview with Linda Beckman three times. He put the folder to one side and turned to the computer. Keyed in Axel Johansson's details and began to scroll through the results. He had moved around quite a bit, good old Herr Johansson, and had obviously made the acquaintance of the police in every single place he had taken up residence.

Haraldsson glanced through the reports. Umeå, Sollefteå, Gävle, Helsingborg and a few minor offences here in Västerås. Disturbing the peace, pilfering, theft, sexual harassment ... Haraldsson suddenly stopped and went back. Sexual harassment in Sollefteå as well. Axel had never been convicted of this particular offence, but accusations had been made. Both preliminary investigations had been shelved due to a lack of evidence. Haraldsson went further back. Axel Johansson also figured in a rape case in Umeå. Eleven years ago. He had been at the same party as a girl who was brutally raped in the garden when she went out for a smoke. Everyone at the party had been questioned. Nobody had been charged. The case remained unsolved.

A thought from yesterday came back to Haraldsson.

Those who are guilty run away.

He allowed the thought to grow. Picked up the document

352

Radjan had copied for him. A brief note. Axel Johansson liked to be dominant in bed.

Those who are guilty run away.

A long shot. But bearing in mind that Haraldsson was approaching the reserves bench at breakneck speed, he might as well take a chance. He sat up and moved his fingers over the computer keyboard. First of all he checked when Axel Johansson had been living in Umeå, then he called up unsolved crimes from the same period. There were rather a lot. He discounted all those that were not of a sexual nature. Fewer, but still a lot. He carried on refining the search terms. First of all, rapes. Still a terrifyingly large number. Then women who had been attacked and raped. Far fewer. It was quite an unusual crime, in spite of everything. In most cases of rape the victim and the perpetrator knew each other, even if they had been acquainted for only a few hours. During the period when Axel Johansson had been living in Umeå, there had been five cases of women being attacked and raped. Three with exactly the same modus operandi.

Women who were on their own in lonely places. Lonely, though not totally isolated. People nearby. Presumably the fact that they could hear other people lulled the women into a false sense of security. They had felt brave enough to go a little further down the dark garden for a smoke, because they could hear the party through the open windows. They cut across the park because they could hear conversations at the bus stop behind the bushes. An illusion of security, as it turned out. The man in the three identical cases had approached the women from behind and brought them down. Pressed their faces into the ground, making it impossible for them to scream, then entered them from behind. All three carried through to their conclusion. A physically strong man. Afterwards he had disappeared. No doubt he had quickly and imperceptibly mixed with the people nearby. Walked the streets of the town like an ordinary person. The women hadn't even caught a glimpse of him. There were no descriptions, no witnesses.

Haraldsson repeated the procedure, this time in Sollefteå. First of all he checked on the dates between which Axel Johansson had lived there, then he looked at unsolved sexual offences. There were two rapes that were almost identical with those in Umeå. Lonely but not completely isolated spots. The attack coming from behind. The woman's face pressed into the ground. No description, no witnesses.

Haraldsson leaned back in his chair, breathing heavily. This was something big, he could feel it. He would have his revenge, with bells on. A serial rapist. Perhaps even worse than Niklas Lindgren, known as the 'Haga Man'. And Haraldsson was the one who had tracked him down. He could almost hear the chief superintendent's speech again.

Roger Eriksson and that psychologist was one thing, but this was big. Really big. This was the kind of case on which you could build a career. With trembling hands Haraldsson carried on clicking through the information. Gävle. One rape reported during the relatively short period when Johansson had been living there. Same MO.

Nothing during the years he spent in Helsingborg.

Haraldsson stopped. It was as if he had been out running and really got his speed up, then suddenly – dead stop. Oddly enough, he felt a wave of disappointment. Of course he ought to be glad that no woman had suffered the dreadful trauma of a rape, but it ruined his theories. And he was so close to finding definite confirmation of those theories. He checked again. Same depressing result. Axel Johansson had lived in Helsingborg for over two years, but not one single attack that fit the pattern had been reported during that time.

Haraldsson leaned back and finished off his coffee, which had gone cold. He thought things over. It didn't necessarily mean anything. Perhaps the crimes just hadn't been reported. Not all sexual assaults were reported. Far from it. Admittedly, most rapes involving a violent attack did end up in the hands of the police, but there were no guarantees.

He didn't really need Helsingborg. In almost all the previous attacks, DNA evidence had been secured.

But it was annoying.

It spoiled the symmetry of it all.

It was like drawing a dot-to-dot picture then missing out a couple of dots. You could still see what the picture represented, but your eye would always be drawn to those irritating places where the lines hadn't been completed. Annoying. Besides which, Haraldsson was certain that Axel Johansson hadn't stopped. Not for more than two years. Not when he had got away with it for so long.

Haraldsson got up and went to the staffroom to get another coffee. He had felt slow and dopey when he got to work, slightly hung-over in fact, but that feeling had quickly disappeared, replaced by a tingling, excited sense of anticipation. A feeling not unlike the excitement he had felt when he was a little boy, waiting for Santa Claus on Christmas Eve. All he had to do was crack Helsingborg.

Back at his desk he went into their own archive. He knew what he was looking for. And there it was: two rapes which matched Axel Johansson's MO. Both had taken place after he moved to Västerås.

So that just left Helsingborg.

He had the picture now. He could see what it was, but he still wanted to join up those last dots. He and Jenny had stayed in Helsingborg once. In the late 1990s. Before the bridge was built. A holiday in Skåne, with a trip across to Denmark. In those days the ferries ran a shuttle service back and forth. It only took ten minutes, as Haraldsson recalled. A different town, a different country. Ten minutes away. He found a number for the police in Helsingör, across the Sound in Denmark. Explained what he was doing, was passed on, was given another number, rang, was disconnected, rang again, was misunderstood, but eventually he got hold of a woman called Charlotte who was able to help him. Haraldsson's Danish was extremely limited, and after a few minutes of rephrasing and repetition they agreed to switch to English.

He knew the time frame.

He knew the MO.

It shouldn't take long.

And, indeed, it didn't. The Helsingör police had two unsolved incidents of rape involving violent attacks from that period. Haraldsson had to stop himself from punching the air. The case was international.

And it was solved.

All he had to do now was find Axel Johansson. But first he would go and see Hanser.

Hanser barely looked up from her desk when Haraldsson tapped on the open door and walked into her office.

'How's the foot?'

'Fine, thanks.'

He had no intention of playing her game. He wasn't going to allow himself to be provoked. Or cowed. He could allow her to have the upper hand for a few more seconds. Soon she would have to admit that he was a good police officer, in spite of his little mistake. Much better than she had ever been, or would ever be.

'You told me not to go near the Roger Eriksson investigation.'

'I did. And I sincerely hope you haven't.'

'Yes and no.' Haraldsson weighed his words carefully. He wanted to make the most of this moment. He wasn't going to reveal everything at once. He wanted to observe every step along the way as Hanser moved from uncomfortable disbelief to reluctant admiration.

'I took a closer look at Axel Johansson.'

Hanser didn't react: she continued to focus on the papers in front of her. Haraldsson moved a step closer. Lowered his voice. Spoke with greater intensity. Determined to arouse her interest.

'I had a feeling there was something about him. Something else, apart from the connection with Roger. A feeling . . . Call it intuition, if you like.'

'Mmm.'

She was pretending not to be interested. It might take a while longer, but soon enough she would be forced to react.

'It turned out I was right. He's a rapist. A serial rapist.'

Hanser looked up with an expression that could only be interpreted as a total lack of interest.

'Really?'

She didn't believe him. Didn't want to believe him. Soon she would have no alternative. Haraldsson walked right up to her desk and placed a simple summary of his day's work in front of her. Towns, times, relocations, victims.

'I've found a link which indicates that he has carried out rapes in Umeå, Sollefteå, Gävle, Helsingborg and here in Västerås over the past twelve years.'

Hanser glanced briefly at the list then gave Haraldsson her full attention for the first time.

'You are joking?'

'What? No, I mean of course we need a sample of his DNA, but I know I'm right.'

'The entire station knows you're right.'

'What? How come? I don't know where he is yet, but . . .'

'I do,' Hanser interrupted. Haraldsson was taken aback. The conversation had taken a completely unexpected turn. What did she mean?

'Do you?'

'Axel Johansson is in number three. Your colleague Radjan picked him up this morning.'

Haraldsson heard the words she spoke, but was incapable of processing the information. He simply stood there, his mouth literally hanging open.

Ursula had decided to put the failure of the previous day behind her and concentrate on what she was really good at: investigating the scene of a crime. Her simple test had quickly supplied the result she had expected, establishing beyond doubt that it was human blood they had found. This sharpened her concentration still further. She was now walking around getting an impression of the scene.

Taking her time.

It was a question of getting an overview at this stage, familiarising herself with the bigger picture before homing in on the details. Starting to analyse the clues, working out the most likely scenario. She could feel Torkel's eyes on the back of her neck but that didn't stress her out. She knew he was impressed. This was her moment. Not his. The others watched from a distance as she walked slowly back and forth inside the cordon, taking care not to compromise any evidence. After ten long minutes she went over to them. She was ready.

'It's difficult to comment on the amount of blood. It's soaked into the ground, and crows and other animals have probably been poking around in it, but it's definitely from a human being, and there's a lot of it. And look at this.' She walked over to one end of the cordon. Poked at the soft ground. Vanja, always the most alert, moved cautiously across and crouched down to get a proper look.

'Tyre tracks.'

'Probably a Pirelli P7. I recognise that zigzag strip down the centre. A car was parked here. It drove away over there.' Ursula pointed at the marks in the grass, leading to a narrow, churned-up forest track. She smiled at them with a certain amount of triumph in her expression.

'I would say that what we have here is a crime scene. The lab will need to confirm that it's Roger's blood, but I don't expect there are many other people in Västerås who have lost several litres recently.' She paused for dramatic effect, and gazed out over the glade.

'But he wasn't murdered here.'

'I thought you said this was the crime scene,' Torkel began.

'It is a crime scene. But it's not the scene of a murder. He was dragged here. Look.'

Ursula gingerly led the three of them along the path, back towards the football pitch. Past the cordon and further on.

'Try to keep to the side of the path. It's bad enough that we've walked along it once.' They carried on in silence and soon saw

358

what Ursula had found. Clear traces of blood in the pale yellow grass.

Torkel waved the uniformed officer over. 'We need to extend the cordon.'

Ursula took no notice and simply carried on past bushes and undergrowth, up the slope and onto the pitch.

'Someone dragged him. From over there.' She pointed at the pitch, and when they looked hard they could see faint marks in the grey gravel around the edge. Marks left by what could only have been a pair of heels.

They all stood motionless, weighed down by the seriousness of the moment: they had never been this close. There was a magic in the way an ordinary, boring spot could become charged with significance, just because they were seeing it through Ursula's eyes. Those small, almost invisible spots became blood, broken twigs became the impression of the dead body, and the dirty gravel was no longer merely chippings but the place where a young boy's life had been extinguished for good.

They were moving even more slowly now, keen to go on, but cautious. Their main concern was to avoid destroying any evidence, but they also wanted to hold onto that illuminating, liberating magic.

Torkel took out his phone and called Hanser. He needed more resources. The search area needed to be expanded significantly. Just as Hanser answered they reached the place where the almost invisible marks ended, to be replaced by a dark, circular stain that could mean only one thing. They were standing in the place where a sixteen-year-old boy had died. Where it all began, and where it all ended.

Torkel realised he was whispering as he told Hanser where they were.

Sebastian looked around. This was an important discovery. Not just a few random clues – an entire event. Now they needed to take the next step. Drag marks and traces of blood were one thing, but they had to read the significance, start to get inside the murderer's head. The scene of the crime was one of the most important components in a murder investigation. They knew quite a lot about Roger's final journey. But what did the scene tell them about the murderer?

'It's an odd place to shoot someone. In the middle of a football pitch,' Sebastian said after a while. Ursula nodded.

'Particularly with those apartment blocks over there.' She pointed to the three huge grey tower blocks on a hill not far away.

'This supports the theory that it wasn't planned.' Sebastian moved a few steps away from the dark patch, eager to go through the possibilities.

'Roger is shot here. Once he is lying dead, the murderer realises he has to remove the bullet. To do so he chooses a more secluded place. He goes for the closest spot – that choice doesn't tell us anything.'

The others nodded.

'We know that Roger was shot in the back, right? In that case, there are two alternatives. Either Roger knew he was in danger and was running away from it, or he was shot down without any idea there was a threat.'

'I think he knew,' Ursula said firmly. 'Definitely. He was running away.'

'I agree,' Vanja chipped in.

'What makes you think that?' Torkel asked.

'Look at the scene of the murder,' Ursula explained. 'We're down at one end of the pitch. If I felt threatened, I would run towards the forest. Particularly if someone was pointing a gun at me.'

Torkel looked around. Ursula was right. The rectangular football pitch lay before them. A large open car park ran along one of the longer sides, a tall fence with a road a dozen or so metres behind it and a field beyond that. The apartment blocks were opposite, on the other longer side. The shorter lengths of the pitch had a clubhouse on one end and forest on the other. It was logical that the forest would appear to offer the most protection, if you had to make a snap decision. Of course you could say that Roger would have been equally safe among the apartment blocks, but they were up on a hill, and resembled an impregnable fort more than a good hiding place. Besides which, the need to run uphill would mean losing speed.

Sebastian had been silently gazing at the surroundings, and he now raised his hand discreetly.

'Allow me to put forward a different theory.'

'There's a surprise,' Vanja said in a stage whisper. Sebastian pretended not to hear.

'I agree with Ursula and Vanja. *If* Roger saw the threat. In that case I'm sure he would have run towards the forest. But I don't see how he could have done that.' Sebastian paused. He had everyone's full attention.

'We are assuming that Roger came here by car. The car park is over there.' Sebastian pointed towards the clubhouse and car park, where several police cars now were.

A number of civilian cars turned in and parked. Men got out and were immediately stopped by the police. The press had found their way to the scene.

'Would Roger walk all this way with someone who was carrying a gun?' Sebastian went on.

'But there were tyre tracks in the forest as well,' Ursula piped up.

'You mean he wasn't on his way into the forest, he was on his way out?' Torkel wondered.

'It's possible,' Ursula replied.

'Possible but highly unlikely.' Sebastian shook his head. 'It's an inaccessible, remote, secluded place. Why would someone drive a car down there and park unless they were planning to harm Roger? We are in agreement that this was not the case, aren't we?'

The others nodded. Sebastian made a sweeping gesture.

'Look at this place. It's pretty isolated. A good place to drop someone off in secret, and aren't we quite close to Roger's home?'

'Yes, I think so. He must live somewhere behind those.' Vanja pointed in the direction of the apartment blocks. 'Half a kilometre, maybe.'

'So this is a pretty good short cut, wouldn't you say?' said Sebastian.

The others nodded again. Torkel looked at him. He scratched his cheek and realised he'd forgotten to shave this morning.

'What do you think? Someone gave Roger a lift here, and . . . ?'

Everyone's eyes were on Sebastian. Just the way he wanted it.

'Lisa said Roger was going to meet someone. The driver, who in the not-too-distant future will become the murderer, is waiting in the car and gives a quick beep on the horn when he sees Roger walking on the opposite side of the road. Roger crosses the street and after a conversation through the wound-down side window he gets into the Volvo, which drives off. As they are driving they have a discussion. They can't agree. The driver heads down to the car park by the football pitch and Roger gets out. Perhaps he has misjudged the situation and is feeling sure of victory. Perhaps he thinks the encounter has been unpleasant and hurries across the pitch towards home. Whichever of these is the truth, he cannot imagine what is happening behind his back. The driver thinks through the situation. Can't see any way out. Or, rather, he can see only one way out. He makes a quick decision without thinking it through, gets out of the car, opens the boot and takes out a gun. Roger is on his way across the football pitch, unaware that someone is aiming a gun at his back from the car park. The distance is not too great, particularly if you are used to a gun, perhaps for hunting or competitive shooting. The driver fires. Roger falls to the ground. The driver knows of course it will be possible to trace the bullet. He runs across the pitch, drags Roger into the shelter of the forest. Runs back, drives the car around, digs out the bullet, inflicts multiple stab wounds on the body, bundles it into the car and drives it to the dumping ground.'

Sebastian fell silent. The odd car passed by out on the road. A lone bird was singing in the forest. It was Torkel who broke the silence.

'You mentioned competitive shooting. Do you still think it's the principal?'

'It was just a theory. And now I'm going to let you get on with your forensic examination without me.' Sebastian set off towards the apartment blocks. Torkel looked at him.

'Where are you going?'

'I want to speak to Lena Eriksson, find out if Roger used this short cut. If he did, it backs up my theory and increases the chances that somebody might have seen him and the car here on another occasion.'

The others nodded. Sebastian stopped and turned around, waving one hand in an inviting gesture.

'Anyone want to come with me?'

No one volunteered.

Sebastian quickly found the narrow, well-trodden track leading up to the hill where the grey apartment blocks stood. The track soon joined a tarmac path that wound its way upwards between the buildings. Sebastian felt fairly sure that these apartments had been built when he was still a student at Palmlövska High, but he had never been this close to them. They were on the wrong side of town, besides which his parents had had an inbuilt middle-class aversion to rented apartments. The *right* sort of people lived in houses.

Behind him, down by the football pitch, he could see more police cars arriving. He knew they would be there for a long time. He had mixed feelings when it came to the forensic side of police work. Intellectually, he knew how important it was. It generated hard evidence that was usually crucial in court, and led to more convictions than his own specialty. The evidence he produced – if it could even be called evidence – was much softer. It could be called into question, twisted and contradicted, especially by a skil-ful defence lawyer. His evidence was more like a series of working hypotheses and theories about the dark impulses that drove people, more user friendly during the preliminary investigation than under the bright lights of the courtroom. But for Sebastian the evidence had never been the most important thing. He wasn't driven by the desire to contribute to a conviction. His aim was to get inside a perpetrator's head. The chance to predict a person's next move was his reward.

Once upon a time it had been all he thought about, all he longed for, and he realised now that he missed it. Over the past few days he had tasted that feeling again, even though he had barely been operating at half speed. It was something to do with the focus. For a second he almost forgot the grief and the endless pain. He stopped and tasted the realisation for a moment. Could he find his way back?

Find his motivation.

His obsession.

Shift his focus.

Of course not. Who was he trying to kid? It could never be like before.

Never.

The dreams would see to that.

Sebastian opened the glass doors leading into Lena's apartment block. In Stockholm there would have been a keypad requiring an entry code, but here you could just walk in. He couldn't remember which floor Lena lived on. The board in the entrance hall informed him that it was the third floor. He began to climb, his heavy footsteps echoing through the depressing, dirty white stairwell. When he reached the third floor landing he stopped dead. Strange. The door of Lena Eriksson's apartment was ajar. He moved forward. Rang the doorbell while at the same time cautiously pushing the door open with his foot and calling out.

'Hello?'

No reply. The door slowly swung open, and soon he could see the narrow hallway. Shoes on the floor, a brown chest of drawers with an untidy pile of junk mail on top.

'Hello? Anyone home?'

Sebastian walked in. On the left was a door leading to the toilet. Straight ahead was the living room with its IKEA furniture. The place stank of cigarette smoke. The blinds were drawn, which made the apartment dark, particularly with all the lights off.

Sebastian went into the living room and noticed an overturned chair and some broken china on the floor. He stopped, with a growing sense of unease. Something had happened here. Suddenly the silence in the apartment seemed ominous. He moved fast, into what he assumed must be the kitchen. Then he saw Lena. Lying on the linoleum floor. Bare feet, the soles facing towards him. One leg under the other. The kitchen table had tipped over.

Sebastian ran to Lena and bent over her. He could see the blood that had come from the back of her head. Her hair was sticky, and the blood had gathered in a round, shiny little pool beneath her like a halo of death. He felt at her white throat for some sign of a pulse, but the chill under his fingertips could mean only one thing. He was too late.

Sebastian straightened up and took out his mobile. He was about to ring Torkel when the phone started buzzing in his hand. He didn't recognise the number, but answered at once, sounding stressed.

'Hello!'

It was Billy. He sounded excited, and Sebastian didn't get the chance to tell him where he was or what he had just discovered.

'Have you spoken to Torkel?'

'No, but—'

'Palmlövska High owns a Volvo,' Billy said quickly. 'Or, at least, the foundation that runs the school has one. A dark blue S60, 2004. And it gets better . . .'

Sebastian took a few steps into the living room, away from the body. The situation seemed too bizarre to start discussing possible Volvos with Billy.

'Billy, listen to me.'

But Billy wasn't listening. He was talking. Rapidly and excitedly.

'I've the list of calls from the phone that sent those texts to Roger. Calls to Frank Clevén and Lena Eriksson were made from that same phone. Do you realise what that means?'

Sebastian took a deep breath and was about to interrupt Billy when he sensed something in Roger's room. Something that definitely shouldn't be there. He was hardly listening to Billy as he took the last few steps to the door of the boy's room.

'We can bring Groth in now! We've got him!' Sebastian could almost feel the triumph in Billy's voice.

'Hello, Sebastian, can you hear me? We can bring Groth in!'

'There's no need . . . He's here.'

Sebastian lowered the phone and stared at Ragnar Groth, who was hanging from the light fitting in Roger's room.

Ragnar Groth's dead eyes stared back.

They worked hard for the rest of the day. Made sure they were as quick and efficient as they could be without cutting corners. The day's events required inexorable focus. They had been waiting for a breakthrough for so long, and now it seemed they were within touching distance of the solution. Nothing must go wrong. Nothing. It was a difficult exercise. They needed time to consider what they knew, time for forensic tests to be carried out on what they had discovered, and yet at the same time the results were needed with lightning speed.

Torkel had tried to keep the press out of it for as long as possible. There was nothing to be gained from information about the scene of the murder or the two dead bodies in the apartment becoming public knowledge. But as in all complex investigations involving a large number of individuals, the news about Principal Ragnar Groth's death soon leaked out. This gave rise to wild speculation, particularly in the local newspaper, which seemed to have access to a well-informed source within the police, and soon it was impossible to wait any longer.

Torkel and Hanser called a press conference with the aim of restoring some semblance of peace and quiet in which to work. Torkel was usually very careful when he made a statement to the press, but after putting together a number of preliminary results and consulting with Ursula and Hanser, he had decided that they could risk promising an imminent breakthrough in the investigation. The room was packed with journalists when they arrived, and Torkel wasted little time on small talk.

Another man and a woman had been found dead.

The woman was closely related to Roger Eriksson and had been killed, in all probability by the man who had been found dead.

There were a number of indications to suggest that the man, who had previously figured in the investigation, had taken his own life after the woman's death.

Torkel did, however, make one thing very clear. The suspect was not the teenager who had been brought in for questioning at an earlier stage in the investigation. He was still in the clear. He stressed this point again before bringing his short presentation to a close.

It was like putting a dish of strawberry jam next to a nest of wasps. Eager hands shot into the air, questions came raining down. Everybody was talking without listening to what anybody else was saying: they were just demanding answers. Torkel was able to pick out the same questions, over and over again.

Was it true that the principal of Palmlövska High was involved?

Was he the man they had found?

Was the dead woman Roger's mother?

Torkel was struck by the special interplay between the two parties in the hot, crowded room. On one side were the journalists, who were actually just as well informed as those to whom they were addressing their questions. On the other side the police, whose real task was to provide official confirmation of what was already known. One side already knew the answers, the other already knew the questions.

It hadn't always been so obvious, but it was a long time since Torkel had been involved in an investigation where information didn't leak out. At least, that's what happened as soon as the information was passed beyond his own small team.

Torkel answered as evasively as possible and continued to refer stubbornly to the fact that the investigation was now at a sensitive stage. He was used to ducking and diving when it came to journalists' questions, which was likely why he was unpopular with them. Hanser found it more difficult to fend them off, which Torkel could understand. This was her town, her career, and in the end the desire to have them as friends rather than enemies became too much for her.

'I can confirm that certain indications do point towards the school,' she began before Torkel quickly thanked everyone, and led her out of the room. He could see that she was embarrassed, but she still tried to justify her lapse.

'They already knew anyway.'

'That's not the point. We decide what we give them, not the other way around. That's the principle. Now all hell will be let loose at the school.'

That was exactly what Torkel wanted to avoid. The school had, in fact, been given priority as a possible site where further clues might be found. One of the first things Torkel had done following Sebastian's dramatic discovery – after consulting with Billy and Ursula – was to widen the search area. Groth's house had turned up an almost suspicious lack of personal belongings, not to mention evidence. The car was registered to the foundation that ran Palmlövska High, so the idea of searching the school buildings seemed perfectly natural. It was the only place they knew of to which Groth had unrestricted access. Torkel quickly took the decision to send Ursula over there, once she had carried out a preliminary investigation of the new crime scene. But she wouldn't be going alone. Sebastian would go with her.

To Torkel's surprise, Ursula hadn't objected. The possibility of solving the case was far more important than her own ego when the pieces might fall into place so quickly, and Sebastian was the only one who knew the school well. Admittedly his knowledge was thirty years old, but even so ... Ursula had even invited him to sit in the front of the car.

They hadn't spoken on the way there.

There was a limit, after all.

*

Billy felt completely cut off from everything that was going on as he sat alone in the office. Torkel had asked him to track down the dark blue Volvo S60. It wasn't at the school, both Ursula and the principal's PA had confirmed that. Billy had sent out a call to all patrols then decided to go to Lena Eriksson's apartment anyway. He had done what he could, and wanted to form his own impression of the latest crime scene.

The station seemed emptier than usual, and Billy suspected that Torkel had commandeered most of the staff to cordon off the various crime scenes and the school. They had a number of places to analyse now: the football pitch, Lena's apartment, Groth's house again, and the school. Like a four-leaf clover of interesting places, but at the same time not all that easy to handle. Torkel had to prioritise which places they should process themselves and which they should hand over to the Västerås forensic technicians.

Billy was elated as he got in the car. For the first time in days he felt as if the solution to Roger's death was within reach. Everything seemed to be going their way at the moment. And that was set to continue. As Billy turned off towards Lena's apartment, he had a call from a patrol car reporting that the vehicle he was looking for was parked outside the building he was heading for. Thirty seconds later Billy was standing by the Volvo and rang Torkel to tell him. Torkel was inside Lena's apartment with Vanja, and had just found a set of Volvo keys in one of Groth's pockets.

Everything did indeed seem to be going their way at the moment.

For thirty minutes Ursula and Sebastian had been working their way through the school, and they were now standing in front of a dirty grey steel door in the basement. A door which neither the caretaker nor one of the secretaries, who had come down with them, seemed to know anything about. In Sebastian's day it had been a shelter, but now nobody seemed to know what the space behind the door was used for. None of the staff had been very helpful, and both the caretaker and the secretary wanted to check with the principal before they had any intention of helping open the door. Sebastian looked at them and remembered how anxious the staff had been around his own father. 'Anxious' hadn't really come close, in fact. Perhaps respect for authority – or rather fear – was impregnated in the walls. But enough was enough.

'Let me put it like this: Ragnar Groth couldn't give a shit whether you open this door or not. He doesn't care any more.'

That didn't help. The caretaker puffed himself up and suddenly maintained that he didn't have a key to this door, in any case. He'd never had one. The secretary nodded in agreement. Sebastian moved closer to them. There was a hint of doubt in the caretaker's eyes, he could see it. Ragnar Groth's power was in decline, they both knew it, and somehow this was giving the caretaker a spurt of energy. One last battle before the institution, which had always regarded itself as superior to most, fell.

Sebastian looked at the man and realised that at this moment he was closer to destroying his father's dream than he had ever been. Palmlövska High and its irreproachable reputation would never be the same after this, whether the principal was guilty or not. Sebastian knew it, and the man standing in front of him probably realised the same thing. Even though the caretaker didn't know what had happened to Groth, the interviews and the frequent visits from the police had told him something. What had been clean and pure would soon no longer be clean and pure. They looked at one another, locked into a mutual stare. For Sebastian it was no longer the school caretaker standing in front of him: it was the lies, the hypocrisy, everything his father's creation represented. Sebastian took a deep, energising breath and moved another step closer, ready to shake every single key out of every single pocket in the smaller man's clothing. That door was going to be opened. Ursula, who had rarely seen Sebastian looking so aggressive, stopped him.

'You can go.' She dismissed the staff with a wave of her hand then turned to Sebastian. 'We are police officers. Please bear that in mind. Behave yourself.'

Then she walked past him without another word. Sebastian

watched her, for once unable to come up with that spiteful retort he was usually so good at. But she was wrong. He wasn't a police officer. He was there for his own sake, no one else's. That was how it had begun, and that was how it would end. He would gladly help them to bring down Palmlövska High if he could, but then it would be over and he would move on. Go and look for a woman he had once slept with.

Nothing else.

Nothing more.

Ursula came back, still not speaking. She was carrying a tool-box, which she put down and opened. Dove into it and came up with a large electric drill. Three minutes later shards of metal were flying as she drilled around the lock. The two of them pushed the door open and peered into the room behind it, which looked like a neat and tidy office. No windows, of course, but it had white painted walls, soft lighting, and a large dark-coloured desk with a computer on it. Some stylish filing cabinets and an English leather chair in the centre. The pedantic tidiness immediately told Sebastian that they were in the right place. The furniture was arranged symmetrically and gave the room balance, while the position of the pens on the desk practically screamed the principal's name. Sebastian and Ursula looked at one another and actually smiled. The principal's little secret, whatever it might be, was revealed.

Ursula handed Sebastian a pair of latex gloves and led the way into the room. Sebastian thought it felt like one of those neat inter-rogation rooms he had seen when he and Lily visited the Stasi museum in the former East Germany. Stylish and civilised on the surface, but beneath the orderliness it vibrated with secrets and events that impregnated the walls. Secrets that were never meant to be known. The feeling was reinforced by the contradictory smell that met him and Ursula as they walked in: fresh lemon and dry stuffiness.

Carefully they made a start. Sebastian took the shiny, spotless filing cabinets, Ursula the desk. It wasn't long before Sebastian made the first discovery behind some files in the cabinet. He held up a pile of DVDs with brightly coloured pictures on them.

'*Real Men, Hard Cocks*. Volumes 2 and 3. I wonder what happened to Volume 1?'

Ursula smiled grimly.

'We've only just started. I expect you'll find it.'

Sebastian carried on sifting through the loose DVDs.

'*Bareback Mountain. Bears Jacking and Fucking*. There's not much variety.' He put them down and carried on going through the filing cabinet.

'Look at this.'

Ursula came over and peered into the drawer. Behind the files was a cardboard box belonging to a Samsung mobile phone. The box looked new. Ursula reached for it.

The examination of Lena Eriksson's apartment strengthened the theory Torkel and Vanja were working on. For some reason, Groth had confronted Lena at home. They had quarrelled. The deep wound on the back of Lena's head suggested that she had been pushed, or had fallen and hit the sharp edge of the kitchen table so hard that she had died of her injuries. They found nothing to suggest anything other than Ragnar Groth had then taken his own life. Vanja had even found a brief farewell note on Roger's desk. Written on a torn-off sheet of lined A4.

Forgive me, it said in blue pen.

After Ursula's preliminary investigation of the apartment, once she had gone off to Palmlövska High with Sebastian, Torkel organised the next stage of the procedure. The difficulty lay in preventing too much coming and going in the apartment, to avoid any forensic evidence being contaminated. It seemed as if the entire Västerås police force needed to call round for one reason or another, and Torkel soon stationed a well-built officer at the bottom of the stairs to make sure that only those who really did have legitimate business were allowed in.

They focused on the bodies first of all. Photographed them from every conceivable angle in order to send them off for an autopsy as soon as possible. Vanja found Lena's mobile phone in her handbag in the hallway, and it provided further clues to the course of events that had led to the tragedy.

Two hours after Lena had left the police station, where they had shown her pictures of a dark blue Volvo S60, she had made a call lasting just twenty-five seconds. To the man now hanging in her son's bedroom, the man who had access to a dark blue Volvo S60. Everything suggested that Lena had recognised the car, but for some reason had chosen not to tell the police.

The question was why. Why did she choose to contact Groth instead?

Vanja's immediate thought was that there must be a link between Lena and Groth that they didn't know about. When Ursula rang a moment later and told them that she and Sebastian had found a secret room at Palmlövska High that was turning out to be a veritable smörgåsbord of circumstantial evidence against Groth, Vanja realised she had been right.

Particularly damning was the prepaid phone, tucked away in its box in a filing cabinet. Its contacts list contained only three numbers.

One for Frank Clevén, one for Roger Eriksson, and one for Lena Eriksson. It was also the phone that had sent the pleading text messages to Roger just before his death. Vanja switched her mobile to speakerphone so that Torkel could hear the news too. Sebastian and Ursula had also found the school accounts and a whole load of gay porn. The four of them arranged to meet at the station in an hour.

Billy was slightly late, and the others had just started when he turned up. The conference room felt warmer, as if the past few hours had not only raised the temperature of the investigation but had also affected the air around them. Ursula nodded to him as he walked in.

'As I was saying, Palmlövska High really was Ragnar Groth's baby. He even did the accounts himself. Look at this.' Ursula took out some sheets of A4 and handed them out.

'We were looking for a link between Groth and Lena Eriksson. There were three entries in the accounts for the last few months that stuck out. "Personal expenditure". First of all two thousand kronor, then five thousand kronor twice the following month.'

Ursula paused. Everyone in the room suspected they knew where this was heading, but no one spoke, so she went on.

'I rang the bank. Lena Eriksson made deposits of almost exactly the same amount only a day or so later.'

Ursula had just irrefutably linked Lena Eriksson and Ragnar Groth.

'Blackmail?' Torkel left the question hanging in the air.

'Why else would he give her twelve thousand kronor?'

'Particularly in view of the fact that Groth sends a text to Roger at the same time, pleading for this to stop, whatever "this" might be' Vanja offered, pointing to the phone in its pristine box.

'The question is what was it that had to stop,' Billy said, feeling he wanted to join the game. 'There are a couple of options there.'

'We know Groth liked guys,' said Vanja, nodding at the porn films on the table. 'Perhaps Lena found out.'

'Would you pay twelve thousand kronor to stop people finding out that you watched gay porn on the computer?' Sebastian sounded sceptical, with good reason. 'I mean, he could just have thrown away the discs. Lena would had to have found out something a lot more incriminating for a blackmail scenario to work.'

'Like what?' Vanja wondered.

'I'm thinking about what Lisa told you. She said Roger had secrets . . . ' Sebastian left it there. Vanja knew at once what he was getting at. She sat up straight, her voice excited.

'And that he was meeting someone. Ragnar Groth?'

The others looked at Vanja and Sebastian. There was something in what they said, of course. They had all realised that the secret behind this tragedy must be a serious matter, if not utterly devastating for Ragnar Groth. An illicit sexual relationship with a sixteen-year-old student definitely fell into that category.

'If that was the case, that must have been what Lena found out. And instead of reporting him, she decided to exploit what she knew for her own ends.'

'We know she needed money. She even sold her story to the highest bidder, didn't she?' Vanja raised an eyebrow at Torkel, who went over to the whiteboard. He had the bit between his teeth now. His earlier irritation had been swept away. Along with his own private meltdown.

'Okay, let's run with this theory for a while.' He started to scrawl spiky, almost illegible notes on the board as he spoke. His hand-writing always got worse in direct proportion to his elation.

'One month before Roger Eriksson was murdered, Ragnar Groth began making payments to Lena. We are assuming this was to prevent her from revealing something. Correct? Perhaps her son was having an intimate relationship with him. What suggests that this was the case? Let's consider that for a second.' He looked encouragingly at his team, keen to hear their thoughts. Vanja went first.

'We know that Groth was homosexual. We know he sent text messages to Roger, wanting something to be interrupted or stopped. This suggests that they had something going on together. Lisa told us she thought Roger was meeting someone in secret.'

'Okay, hang on.' Torkel couldn't keep up with his notes. Vanja stopped speaking. When she saw something on the board that might possibly correspond to 'meeting' and 'secret', she carried on.

'We know that Groth was at the motel on the Friday evening, and that Roger was nearby. We know that Groth was in the habit of using the motel for sexual encounters. We also know that the car belonging to the school met Roger that evening, and that Roger in all probability got into the car. There are strong indications that the car took him to the football pitch.'

'I can tell you a bit about the Volvo if you like,' Billy added. 'We've made a number of interesting discoveries.'

Torkel nodded.

'Absolutely, carry on.'

'Unfortunately there were no visible traces of blood in the car, but I did find fingerprints belonging to Roger, Ragnar Groth and two other individuals. Roger's prints were on the passenger door and on the glove compartment. I also found a large roll of builder's plastic in the boot that could have been used to wrap the body. Ursula will need to look at the car after this meeting to see if she can find any traces of blood or DNA. It also had the right tyres: Pirelli P7.'

376

Billy stood up and produced a well-thumbed book with a red hard cover.

'I also found a driving log. The interesting thing is that a trip was logged on the Thursday before Roger disappeared, then the next is on the Monday after that weekend. But there is a discrepancy of seventeen kilometres between the two.'

'So someone used the car at some point between Friday and Monday morning and drove seventeen kilometres?' Torkel asked, frantically scribbling on the whiteboard at the same time.

'According to the logbook. It is possible to calculate the exact length of the journey, but that seventeen-kilometre trip is not entered into the log.'

Sebastian glanced at the map on the wall next to Torkel.

'It has to be more than seventeen kilometres between the school, the motel, the football pitch, Listakärr and back to the school, surely?'

Billy nodded.

'Yes, that is a problem, but as I said this is a driving log, so it's easy to manipulate the figures. At any rate, the car was definitely used.' Billy sat down. Torkel nodded.

'Good. Ursula will take a look at the car after we're done. There's one more thing we mustn't forget: Peter Westin, the school counsellor.'

Torkel wrote his name on the board.

'We know that Roger went to see him several times over the year. It seems likely that if anyone else found out about a possible relationship with Groth, it would have been Westin. Perhaps he even confronted Groth. That would explain why his notebook is missing. I mean, what do people talk to psychologists about?'

'I expect Sebastian knows,' Vanja replied with a grin. Everybody except Sebastian smiled. Instead he gazed at her for a while.

'Well, you've read my book, so you must know too.'

Torkel looked at both of them and shook his head.

'Could we stick to the matter in hand, please. It's reasonable to assume that if there was a secret sexual relationship between Roger and Groth, then Roger might have told Westin about it.'

'No, that's not right,' said Sebastian. 'Sorry. Roger wanted to fit in. Be one of the gang. To do that he needed money. He might have sold sexual services to Groth, but he would never have told Westin about it. That would be like killing the goose that laid the golden eggs.'

'Perhaps he was under some form of duress?' Ursula said.

'I don't think so. He left Lisa to go and meet someone.'

'However you look at things, I find it difficult to believe that Westin didn't die because of something he knew about Roger,' Ursula went on. 'I mean, there's nothing else. Particularly as his notebook is the only thing that's missing.'

There was a knock on the door and Hanser walked in. She was wearing a smart dark purple suit, which looked new. Torkel couldn't help feeling that she had bought the suit for the day when the case was solved. So that she would look good in the photographs. She was obviously preparing herself for the next press conference. Which meant she would be even more difficult to stop next time.

'Don't let me disturb you,' she said. 'I just wondered if I might sit in?'

Torkel nodded and gestured towards an empty chair at the end of the table. Hanser sat down carefully to avoid creasing her clothes.

'We're just going through possible scenarios,' Torkel went on, pointing to his illegible scrawl on the whiteboard.

'We now know that Ragnar Groth was secretly paying money to Lena Eriksson. Probably due to blackmail. Probably because Roger – voluntarily or under duress – was Groth's lover.' Hanser's expression sharpened and she leaned forward. 'The school's car has the right tyres, we have found fingerprints belonging to both Roger and the principal, and we know that it was on the street by the motel on the relevant evening. We haven't found any traces of blood yet, but we need to go over it again. We still believe that the murder was not planned, and that Groth and Roger drove off to the football pitch. While they were there, something went wrong. Groth shot Roger, then realised he had to get the bullet out. When we asked Lena Eriksson this morning whether she recognised the car, she lied to us. But she realised that Ragnar Groth had killed her son. She decided to put some real pressure on him this time, but Groth confronted her and things got out of hand.'

Torkel stopped in front on Hanser.

'Sounds reasonable to me.'

'It's a chain of circumstantial evidence, anyway. We need to find forensic evidence to back it up.'

Vanja and Billy nodded. There was always a special feeling at those moments when a possibility became a real probability. Now all they needed was a way to turn the probable into the provable.

Suddenly Sebastian began to clap his hands in a solo round of applause that echoed annoyingly around the room.

'Bravo. Perhaps you'd like me to keep quiet about the fact that there are a number of small matters that don't quite fit in with your fantastic theory? I mean, I wouldn't want to spoil the atmosphere.'

Vanja flashed an irritated look at Sebastian, leaning back in his chair wearing a supercilious expression.

'Bit late for that, don't you think?'

Sebastian gave her an exaggerated smile and waved his hand at the pile of DVDs on the table.

'Men. Real men. Grown men. Ragnar didn't like little boys. He liked muscles and big cocks. Look at Frank Clevén. A mature, macho man. Not some downy-haired sixteen-year-old. You are making the mistake of thinking that homosexuals don't have preferences. That as long as there's a cock, they're happy.'

'Although there are certain men who can't say no to sex. Regardless of any kind of preference. I mean, you know that better than most, don't you?' This was Ursula's contribution.

'For me it's not the sex, it's the conquest. That's a completely different matter.'

'Could we stick to the subject?' Torkel appealed to both of

them. 'That makes it kind of easier. You're right of course, Sebastian. We don't know if Groth and Roger really were having a sexual relationship.'

'There's another thing that bothers me in all this,' Sebastian went on. 'Ragnar's suicide.'

'What do you mean?'

'Look at our murderer. He may not have planned to murder Roger, but once it's happened he's prepared to go to any lengths to hide it. He even digs out the heart in order to remove the bullet.'

Sebastian stood up and started to walk around the room.

'When he feels threatened by Peter Westin, he eliminates him immediately. He has planted evidence in Leonard Lundin's garage, broken into Westin's office. Under extreme pressure he has always acted with great single-mindedness. All to avoid being caught. He's cold. Calculating. He doesn't get stressed. He certainly wouldn't hang himself in a boy's bedroom, and he would never, ever ask for forgiveness. Because he feels no regret.'

Sebastian stopped, and silence took over. Conflicting emotions: Sebastian's authority and argument versus the desire to have the solution within reach. Vanja was the first to speak.

'Okay, Sigmund Freud, just one small question. Let's say you're right. It's not Groth. It's a completely different murderer. Groth just happened to be at the motel. His car just happened to be parked on the street as Roger walked past. He was driving it. Roger was in the car. They went to the football pitch. But someone else murdered him. Is that your theory?' She sat back, her expression harsh but tinged with triumph. Sebastian stopped and gazed at her evenly.

'No, that's not my theory. I'm just telling you that it doesn't fit. We're missing something.' Torkel's phone rang. He apologised and took the call. Sebastian went back to his chair and sat down. Torkel listened for a while before speaking. His voice was firm, to say the least.

'Bring it here. Now.' He ended the call and turned to Hanser.

'Your forensic technicians have just found something new at Groth's house. They found the notebook belonging to Peter Westin in the wood-burning stove.'

Hanser smiled. They had Ragnar Groth now. Definitely.

Vanja couldn't help turning to Sebastian.

'How does that fit in with his psychological profile, Sebastian?'

Sebastian knew the answer. But he couldn't be bothered any more.

They'd already made up their minds.

Sebastian left the room.

Those who were still in there wanted it finished. He could understand that. This had been a complex case that had taken it out of them, and they were tired. On the surface, the solution was perfect. But the surface wasn't what mattered to Sebastian. He always strove to find the underlying connection. The clean answers. When everything he knew fitted together. When action, consequence, driving force and motive all said the same thing. Told the same story.

That never happened on the surface.

Why did he care? The circumstantial evidence was unassailable, and on a personal level he ought to be more than satisfied. He should, in fact, be ecstatic. The temple of knowledge his father had built up would be sullied, tarnished, dragged down from the gods and trampled underfoot by reality.

The early evening sun was shining in through the huge windows, and he took a few steps into the middle of the office full of busy police officers before looking back at Torkel and the others in the smaller room. They were busy gathering up their things. Westin's notebook in Ragnar Groth's stove. Most pages burned so that any possible evidence was missing, but the very fact that it had been found in Groth's house had convinced Hanser even more.

For Sebastian it was a discovery that blurred the picture still further. The Ragnar Groth he had met would never have been so careless. No chance. The man didn't even allow a pen or a sheet of paper to be out of alignment. It just didn't fit. He had glanced over at Ursula when he heard where the notebook had been found. She ought to be thinking the same thing as him. That was how well he knew her. Even though they always quarrelled about the details, they were both looking for the same thing: the depth. The pure equation. He had, indeed, seen the same doubt in her eyes as he was feeling, but for once she hadn't been her old self. Apparently she had taken some time off and gone for dinner with Mikael while she and Billy were searching the house. She hadn't searched that part of the house and assumed Billy had done it. Billy had misunderstood and thought she had already looked there.

Ursula didn't usually miss something so simple. Everyone in the room could see how embarrassed she was, and that was when Sebastian had made his decision. He was tired of this. If they were satisfied, then he would be too. They would drag Ragnar Groth's name through the mud, and the real murderer would get away with it.

Sebastian could live with both of those things.

So he had stood up and left the room.

Now he was looking back at them one last time. He put on his coat and set off. He had almost left the station when he heard a voice behind him. It was Billy. He looked around as he walked over to Sebastian. Lowered his voice a fraction.

'I had a bit of spare time yesterday.'

'That's nice.'

'I don't know what you want it for, but I dug out the address for that Anna Eriksson.'

Sebastian looked at Billy. He no longer knew what he felt. Suddenly she was close. From nowhere. Thirty years later. A woman he didn't know. But was he ready? Did he even want this?

'It hasn't really got anything to do with the investigation, has it?' Billy looked at him closely.

Sebastian didn't have the energy to lie. 'No, it hasn't.'

'In that case you know I can't give it to you.'

Sebastian nodded.

Suddenly Billy leaned forward and whispered to him. 'Storskärsgatan 2 in Stockholm.' He smiled and shook Sebastian by the hand. 'I enjoyed working with you.'

Sebastian nodded. But he had to be true to himself. Particularly now. When he had got what he came for in the first place.

'I wish I could say the same.'

Sebastian left. He decided that he would never come back.

Never.

The man who was not a murderer could hardly sit still. It was everywhere. On the internet, on TV, on the radio. It seemed as if the police had made a massive breakthrough. The high point was a short piece on the television news from the latest press conference. The female officer in charge was sitting there wearing a stylish suit, next to the inspector from Riksmord. She was relaxed and beaming, and her smile was so dazzling he almost thought she'd had her teeth whitened and wanted to show them off. The inspector from Riksmord didn't look much different: he was formal and serious as usual. The woman, who was apparently called Kerstin Hanser, according to a caption that appeared on the screen, said that the police now had a suspect for the murders. More details would be given when the forensic investigation had been completed, but they were so sure of their ground that they had decided to release the information now. The breakthrough had come with the two tragic deaths that morning, and the suspect was the man in his fifties, a resident of Västerås, who had taken his own life. They didn't say who it was. But everybody in the area knew anyway.

Particularly the man who was not a murderer.

Ragnar Groth, the principal of Palmlövska High.

He had picked up the rumour himself the previous day on a website called Flashback, which was absolutely packed with nasty gossip and speculation about everything and everybody. But there was also a surprising amount of accurate information. Under a thread entitled 'Ritual murder in Västerås' he had found an anonymous posting insisting that the principal of Palmlövska High had been taken in for questioning by the police. The man who was not a murderer had immediately phoned the school and asked to speak to the principal, but had been told he was out on official business for the rest of the day. The man who was not a murderer had made his excuses at work and scurried to his car. He had found out Ragnar Groth's address via directory enquiries and had quickly driven there. Parked the car some distance away and casually strolled past the two-storey house, as discreetly as possible, but the car sitting outside told him all he needed to know. Admittedly it was an unmarked car, but he recognised it.

It was the same car that had been outside Leonard Lundin's house a few days earlier.

The man who was not a murderer had suddenly felt hot all over. As if he had just found out that he had won the jackpot in the lottery and nobody else knew about it. The prize was his, and he could do whatever he wanted with it. As he stood there the door opened and a woman came out. He started walking so that she wouldn't notice him, but the woman was lost in thought and didn't see him. She seemed annoyed. He could see that by the way she slammed the car door. He carried on walking, but when her car had passed him he turned around and went back to his own car.

Ten minutes to fetch the notebook.

Ten minutes to get back here.

Only one police officer left inside the house.

It might work.

It had worked.

Sebastian was standing motionless outside his parents' house, which was in darkness. Gazing at it. The evening was chilly and he wasn't very warmly dressed, but he didn't care about the cold that came creeping over him. It suited the moment. So now it was time. To do what he had decided to do from the second he had arrived, but which the events of the past few days had prevented him from doing. Tomorrow he would leave. Clear off. Disappear. He had even managed to get the address that had led him into the investigation in the first place.

Storskärsgatan 12.

The answer could be there.

If he truly wanted to know what it was.

As he stood there he realised that there had actually been some positive aspects to everything that had happened. There were the letters and the immense possibility they opened up, and the case itself, working with Riksmord, had given him energy. There had been something else to occupy his days instead of the self-reproach and angst that had been his companions for far too long. Those feelings hadn't gone away, of course – the dream was still there every night and the scent of Sabine still woke him every morning – but the strength of his loss no longer crippled him. He had been able to touch the possibility of a different life. This was both frightening and tempting at the same time. There was something safe and secure about the life he had known for so long. However negative it might be, there was a comfort in the routine. It was an affiliation which he had somehow chosen himself, and which appealed to his innermost being.

The conviction that he didn't deserve happiness.

That he was damned.

He had known it ever since he was a child. It was as if the tsunami had merely confirmed it, in fact.

He turned to look at Clara's house. She had come out onto the steps and was standing there, staring at him. He ignored her. Perhaps he was at a critical moment in his life, after all. Something had definitely happened. He hadn't been with a woman since Beatrice. Hadn't even given it a thought. That had to mean something. He glanced at his watch: 19:20. The agent ought to be here now. They were supposed to meet at seven to get the contract signed so that he could catch the eight-thirty train to Stockholm. That was the plan. So why wasn't he here?

Sebastian marched crossly into the house and switched on the kitchen light. Called Peter Nylander, the agent, who apologised when he answered after a couple of rings: he was still busy with a viewing and wouldn't be able to come over until first thing tomorrow morning at the earliest.

Typical.

Another night in this fucking house.

So much for that critical moment in his life.

Torkel had taken off his jacket and shoes and collapsed on the soft hotel bed, exhausted. He had switched on the television, only to switch it off again when he saw the footage from the press conference. It wasn't just that he hated looking at himself, the whole case was bothering him. He closed his eyes and tried to rest for a while, but it was impossible. He couldn't escape the feeling of unease. The circumstantial evidence was strong, he had to admit that – after all, he was the one who had put it all together – but the irrefutable forensic evidence was missing. The evidence that would make him absolutely certain they were right.

He was most concerned about the lack of any traces of blood. Builder's plastic or no builder's plastic, blood was a difficult substance for a perpetrator to get rid of completely. An organic fluid so full of trace elements that only a microscopic amount was needed to leave evidence. Roger had bled profusely. And yet there were no traces of blood in the Volvo. Ursula felt the same, he knew. She had spent a couple of frustrating hours on the car after the meeting but had found nothing. If he knew her as well as he thought he did, she would still be there, going over it again. Missing the notebook at Ragnar Groth's house had been more than enough: she wasn't going to let anything go now until she had triple-checked it. But there had been no stopping Hanser, or even slowing her down, and she had managed to get the chief superintendent on her side. Torkel and Hanser had met him half an hour before the press conference, called by Hanser.

Torkel had begged for more time: surely one more day wouldn't make any difference? But he soon realised that the two people in front of him wanted to win now. As he frantically tried to persuade them to take a more cautious line it became clear that they were politicians rather than police officers. For them it was important to get the case cleared up so that they could move on in their careers without blotting their copybook. For him, the resolution was more than that. It was the truth. It was what the victims deserved, not something linked to his own career. In the end they had overruled him. He could have fought harder, he knew that, but he was tired, worn out, and he too just wanted to leave this case behind him. Not very good reasons, but that was the reality of the situation.

The decision wasn't his to make, in any case. It was the chief superintendent's. It wasn't the first time he'd had to make the best of things. It was something you got used to in an organisation like the police service. Otherwise you could end up like Sebastian, an impossible oddball whom nobody wanted to work with any more. Torkel reached for the remote control again, hoping the news was over, but before he had time to switch on the television there was a tentative knock on the door. He got up and opened it to find Ursula standing there. She looked tired too.

'Have you found something?'

She shook her head.

'The car shows zero as far as blood proteins and even albumen is concerned. It's just not there.'

Torkel nodded. They stood there for a while. Neither of them seemed to know what to say next.

'So we're going home tomorrow, then?' she said eventually.

'I guess so. Hanser is going to want to bring the case to a conclusion herself, and we're here at her request.'

Ursula nodded to show she understood and turned to leave. Torkel stopped her.

'Did you just come to tell me about the car?'

'Not really.' She looked at him. 'But that will have to do, I think. I don't really know what else to say.'

'Sebastian's gone, anyway.'

Ursula nodded.

'But everything else is a mess.'

'I know. I'm sorry about that.'

'I don't think you're the only one to blame, somehow.'

She looked at him. Took a step towards him and touched his hand.

'But I thought you knew me. I really did.'

'I think I do now.'

'No, I'll have to make things even clearer in future.'

Torkel laughed out loud.

'I think you made things perfectly clear. May I be so bold as to invite you in?'

'You could try.' She smiled at him and walked into the room. He locked the door behind her. She hung her bag and jacket on the back of the chair and went for a shower. Torkel took off his shirt and tidied the bed. That was how she liked it. First she took a shower, then it was his turn. Then he slid into bed beside her. That was the routine. That was the way she wanted it. Her rules.

Only at work.

Never on home turf.

No plans for the future.

And, thought Torkel, *she must have my unswerving loyalty.*

That was something he needed to add to the list.

388

Sebastian was finding it difficult to get to sleep. There was too much whirling around in his head. Too much had happened. At first he thought it was the Stockholm address that was haunting him, preventing him from winding down. Perhaps that wasn't so surprising: how could he sleep with such an incomprehensible opportunity or risk ahead of him? But it wasn't just the address. There was something else, something other than the possible consequences of a letter from the past. Another image. Much more current, much clearer. The image of a boy walking towards his death across a football pitch. A boy he couldn't get a handle on. Hadn't been able to from the start. That was the problem, he thought. He and the others had begun to focus on the periphery too quickly, rather than the centre. Axel Johansson, Ragnar Groth, Frank Clevén. It was logical. They were looking for a killer.

They had, however, forgotten the victim. Sebastian had a feeling that was where they had started to lose the coherence of the whole picture. Roger Eriksson. The young boy at the heart of the tragedy was still a mystery.

Sebastian got up and went into the kitchen. There were some bottles of mineral water in the fridge. He opened one and sat down at the kitchen table. He grabbed his bag and took out some paper, a pen, and the material he still had relating to the investigation. Files and papers he should have handed in. He'd forgotten he still had them, and he wasn't the type to return a few photocopies. He never had been. On the contrary, he preferred to have as much material as possible to hand, precisely for occasions such as this. He had always worked this way when he'd been in the job long ago, and he was glad he hadn't lost the habit of filling his bag. Unfortunately there wasn't much on Roger, apart from some documents they had taken from the two schools he had attended.

Sebastian put them to one side, opened up his pad, picked up his pen and began to think methodically. At the top he wrote:

changed schools

Sebastian tore off the page and put it right at the top of the table. He liked to work with key words on single sheets of paper. They helped his thoughts to flow smoothly. It was a matter of getting a feeling for the parts of the skeleton to which he had access, so that he could see how it might be possible to turn and twist them, to build on them. He carried on:

no friends

Roger's limited circle of friends was one of the problems for the police. He had too few companions, too few who knew anything about him. Lisa had only pretended to be his girlfriend, and even his childhood friend Johan had been slipping away from him. Roger was a lonely person. Lonely people were always the most difficult to get to grips with.

therapy sessions

With Peter Westin, who was dead. Probably to have someone to talk to. Which emphasised the point about how lonely Roger was even more strongly. Perhaps he also had something he needed to work through and talk about.

needed money

Selling booze and that whole business with Axel Johansson had turned out to be a distraction. But Roger was a boy prepared to go quite a long way for money. Money he needed in order to fit in. Particularly in his new school environment, the 'posh' confines of Palmlövska High.

The amoral attitude towards money seemed to be a family trait. The blackmail scenario, however, still seemed credible. Lena knew something about Ragnar Groth, and he had been willing to pay to keep it quiet. It had to be something that could damage the reputation of the school, because that was what he had lived for. Roger was the only link between Lena and Groth that Sebastian knew about. This led him to:

gay lover?

He quickly crossed it out.

It was this proposition that had bothered him the most when it came to the circumstantial evidence. It was the type of thinking that could become too dominant, and could end up influencing an entire investigation. Now he wanted to be able to move freely, not to lock himself into a particular point of view, to look at all the connections and contexts without overloading them with significance. The solution often lay in the minor details. He knew that, so instead he wrote:

secret lover – male / female

That line was too weak as well. It was based on a feeling Lisa had, something Vanja had picked up and pushed. A feeling he shared. But it could just as easily have been their subjective interpretation of the word 'secret'. If a person was hiding something, it probably had something to do with sex. Was there anything else to suggest that they were right, apart from a feeling? Yes there was, in fact. He wrote down the next heading:

'in the end he was only interested in money and sex'

That was what Johan had said to Vanja and him when they had

391

spoken to him at the campsite. Perhaps it was more important than Sebastian had first thought. According to Johan, that was the reason why he and Roger had drifted apart. It indicated an interest in sex on Roger's part that was so great that Johan had found it difficult to deal with. But who was Roger having sex with? Not Lisa. So who?

final conversation

This also bothered Sebastian. Roger's final conversation. When he had tried to get hold of Johan at home that Friday evening without success, why hadn't he tried Johan's mobile? For a while they had worked on the assumption that he hadn't had time, but now they had traced his final walk via the CCTV cameras, there was no longer anything to suggest that this was the case. On the contrary, Roger was walking through the town for quite a long time after the phone call to Johan's house, before he got in the car. So he had time. The most credible alternative was that his reason for calling Johan wasn't all that important. Perhaps leaving a message was enough. Perhaps.

Sebastian went and got another bottle of water out of the fridge. Was there anything he'd forgotten? Quite a lot, no doubt. He was starting to feel tired, frustrated at how difficult it was to get a handle on Roger. He knew he was missing something. He started flicking through the school documents, the yearbook, Roger's most recent reports. He found nothing apart from the fact that Roger's work had improved. Particularly in Beatrice's subjects. She seemed to be a good teacher. That was just about all he could find.

He got up, feeling that he needed some fresh air to clear his head and get some perspective on things. He knew how his thought process worked. Sometimes it took a while before he got the idea that turned some pieces of the puzzle the right way round. Sometimes it never came. As with all processes, there was no guarantee.

*

The agent arrived at eight-thirty. By that time Sebastian had packed his bag in frustration and been out for another walk. Still nothing. His thought process just kept sliding around in the same old pattern. Perhaps Roger's secret was impenetrable, at least with the information that Sebastian had.

The agent drove a big, shiny Mercedes, and wore a broad, far too cheerful smile and an impeccable jacket. Sebastian hated him on sight. He didn't even shake the outstretched hand.

'So you want to sell?'

'I want to get away from here as soon as possible. Just give me the contract and I'll sign. As I said on the phone.'

'Well, yes, but perhaps we should go through the details of the agreement anyway?'

'There's no need. You take a percentage of the final amount, I presume?'

'Yes . . .'

'So the higher the price, the more you get?'

'Exactly.'

'That's all I need to know. There's your incentive to get the best possible price. That's enough for me.' Sebastian nodded to the agent and picked up his pen, ready to sign on the dotted line. The agent looked at him with a degree of scepticism.

'I think I ought to take a look around first.'

'In that case I'll call someone else. Do you want me to sign, or not?'

The agent hesitated.

'What made you choose us?'

'You were the first agency in the phone book that had an answering machine that took messages. Okay? I'd like to sign now, please.'

The agent smiled smugly.

'I'm very happy to hear you say that. The thing is, these answering machines that just reel off the opening hours and ask the customer to call back are becoming more and more common. But I worked out that the customer just rings somebody else, in that case. Clever, eh?'

Sebastian assumed that the question was rhetorical. He certainly had no intention of confirming the agent's theory by telling him that was exactly what he had done.

'I mean, it's incredibly important to be accessible to the client. My mobile number will be in your folder,' the agent went on, without waiting for the answer that was never going to come. 'And you're welcome to call me at any time if you have any questions – evenings, weekends, any time at all. That's how I work.'

As if to prove how accessible he always was, the agent's phone rang before he had the chance to continue. Sebastian looked wearily at the man, wishing he'd never called him in the first place.

'Hi, darling. Well, yes, it is a little inconvenient ... but don't worry.' He moved away to speak with more privacy.

'Darling, you'll be fine. You can do it. Promise. I have to go now. Love you.'

He ended the call and turned to Sebastian with an apologetic smile.

'Sorry, that was my girlfriend. She's just on her way to a job interview, and she always gets so nervous beforehand.'

Sebastian stared at the man standing in front of him, the man about whom he already knew far too much. He started trying to think of some crushing remark that would shut him up. Preferably so vicious that the agent would never speak again. Then it came to him. The thing he had been waiting for.

The thought process.

The connection.

Who do you call?

Vasilios Koukouvinos thought it was a very odd trip. He had picked up the man with the bag outside his house. The man's conversation was strained. He wanted to go to Palmlövska High first, then off again straightaway. He didn't even want to get out of the cab. He just wanted to drive there. As quickly as possible.

Once they got there, the man asked Vasilios to set the trip odometer to zero, turn the car around and drive to the motel down by the E18, taking the shortest possible route. The man took out a map to show him where the motel was, but Vasilios reassured him he knew Västerås well. They drove in silence after that, but when Vasilios glanced across at the man from time to time, he noticed that he could hardly sit still. He seemed extremely agitated.

As they approached the motel the man changed his mind. He gave Vasilios the name of a street and wanted to go there instead. Spränggränd. Not only that, the man wanted Vasilios to drive in, reverse and park. When Vasilios had done this the man checked the trip odometer. It was showing just under six kilometres. The man gave Vasilios his credit card and asked him to wait for a few moments. Then he got out of the car and ran off in the direction of the motel.

Vasilios switched off the engine and got out for a smoke. He shook his head. If the man had wanted to go to the motel after all, Vasilios could have driven him there. He had taken only a few drags when the man came back, looking even more stressed if that was possible. Almost pale. In his hand he had something that looked like a school brochure. The cab driver recognised the picture. It was that toffee-nosed school they'd just left. Palmlövska High.

Vasilios got back in the car. This time the man wanted to drive out to the football pitch by the apartment blocks, then back to the school again.

He sat there staring at the odometer the whole time.

It was definitely a very odd trip.

A very odd seventeen-kilometre trip.

Sebastian should have realised. He, more than anyone, should have known. He had experienced it himself at first hand. The change, the strength and the power within her when you got to know her. The way you were swept along, wanting to see her again.

As Roger had been.

Roger had needed someone. Someone who was there for him. Someone who supported him when he changed schools. Someone he could call when he was nervous. When he'd been beaten up. Someone he loved. Roger had made a phone call.

But not to Johan.

To Beatrice.

When Sebastian ran to the motel, it was just a hunch. A feeling he got when the cab reversed and parked. A feeling that the motel was more important than he had thought. That Roger hadn't gone there by chance. He'd been there before. But not with Ragnar Groth. When Sebastian showed the woman on reception the school brochure, his suspicions had been confirmed.

Oh yes, she'd been there.

Several times.

She wasn't just a grower.

She was so much more than that.

Vanja and Torkel were sitting in the interview room, with Beatrice Strand opposite them. She was wearing the same dark green blouse and long skirt as the first time Vanja and Sebastian met her at Palmlövska High. But now she looked tired. Tired and pale. Her freckles stood out even more on her pale skin. Perhaps it was his imagination, but Sebastian, watching from the room next door, thought that even her thick red hair seemed to have lost some of its shine. Beatrice was clutching a tissue in one hand, although she made no effort to wipe away the tears slowly coursing down her cheeks.

'I should have told you.'

'It would certainly have made things easier.' Vanja sounded curt, annoyed, almost accusing. Beatrice looked at her as if struck by a terrible realisation.

'Would they still be alive? Lena and Ragnar? If I'd told you?'

The room fell silent. Torkel seemed to realise that Vanja was about to say yes so he gently placed one hand on her forearm. Vanja stopped herself.

'It's impossible to say, and there's no point in brooding about it.' Torkel's voice was steady, reassuring. 'Tell us about your relationship with Roger.'

Beatrice inhaled and held her breath for a moment, as if she was steeling herself against what was about to come out.

'I know you think it's highly inappropriate. I'm married and he was only sixteen, but he was very mature for his age, and ... it just happened.'

'When did it happen?'

'A few months after he started at the school. He needed someone, he didn't get much encouragement at home. And I ... I needed to feel needed. Loved. Does that sound terrible?'

'He was sixteen years old, and you were in a position of trust. How do you think it sounds?' Vanja again. Harsh.

397

Unnecessarily harsh.

Beatrice lowered her eyes, ashamed. She sat there with her hands on the table, clutching her tissue. They would lose her if Vanja didn't calm down. Beatrice would break down, and that would get them nowhere. Once again Torkel's hand rested lightly on Vanja's forearm. Sebastian decided to join in via the earpiece.

'Ask her why she needed to feel loved. She's married, after all.'

Vanja glanced at the mirror, her expression asking what that had to do with anything. Sebastian pressed the button and spoke to her again.

'Don't break her. Just ask. She wants to tell you.'

Vanja shrugged her shoulders and turned her attention back to Beatrice.

'What's the state of your marriage?'

'It's . . .' Beatrice looked up. Hesitated. Seemed to be searching for the word or words that would best describe her home situation. Her life. Eventually she found it.

'Loveless.'

'Why?'

'I don't know whether you're aware of this, but Ulf and I were divorced six years ago. We remarried about eighteen months ago.'

'Why did you get divorced?'

'I had a relationship with another man.'

'You were unfaithful?'

Beatrice nodded and looked down again. Embarrassed. It was obvious what the younger woman thought of her: she could hear it in her voice, see it in her eyes. Beatrice didn't blame her. Now that what she had done was spoken out loud, exposed in this bare room, it came across as deeply immoral. But at the time, caught in the middle of it all, she had experienced a love bordering on adoration. There was nothing else she could do. She had always known that it was wrong. In so many ways.

In every way.

But how could she reject the love she so badly needed, the love she couldn't get anywhere else?

'Ulf left you?'

'Yes. Me and Johan. He just walked out of the door, more or less. It must have been a year before we spoke to each other again.'

'But now he's forgiven you?'

Beatrice looked up att Vanja with an unusual clarity in her eyes. This was important. The young woman had to understand this.

'No. Ulf came back for Johan's sake. Our separation and the following year had a devastating effect on Johan. He was angry and confused. He stayed with me, and I was the one who had smashed the family to pieces. It was open warfare. We couldn't find a resolution. Most children cope when their parents split up. It can take time, but eventually things work out for the majority of them. Not for Johan. Not even when he was staying with Ulf every other week, or more often. He got the idea that nothing was any good unless the family was together. It grew into a kind of obsession. He got ill. Depressed. He had suicidal thoughts for a while. He started seeing a counsellor, but it didn't help. It was all about the family. The three of us, together. Just the way it used to be. The way it had always been.'

'So Ulf came back.'

'For Johan's sake. I'm grateful for that, but Ulf and I . . . It's not a marriage in the sense that you mean.'

Sebastian nodded to himself in the room next door. So he had been right when he felt as if Beatrice had seduced him and not vice versa. But it was worse than he thought. She must have gone through hell over the past few years. Living day after day with a man who overtly rejected her, who made it clear that he wanted nothing to do with her, and a son who blamed her for all the problems that had befallen the family. Presumably Beatrice was completely frozen out. Hardly surprising that she accepted love and affirmation wherever it was offered.

'How did Lena Eriksson find out about your relationship?' Torkel interjected. Beatrice had stopped crying. It felt good to talk to someone. She even thought the young woman opposite was looking at her with more sympathy. She would never defend Beatrice's actions, of course, but perhaps she could understand what had driven her.

'I don't know. All of a sudden she just knew. But instead of trying to stop it, she started trying to get money out of Ragnar and the school. That was how he found out.'

'And he paid up?'

'I think so. He valued the reputation of the school above everything. I would be allowed to work for the rest of the term. We'd already lost our caretaker halfway through the term, and if someone else went . . . it wouldn't look good. But he made me end the relationship with Roger, of course.'

'Did you end it?'

'Yes. Well, I tried. Roger refused to accept that it couldn't continue.'

'When was this?'

'About a month ago, I think.'

'But you saw him again that Friday?'

Beatrice nodded and took another deep breath. A little colour had returned to her cheeks. She might have done a terrible thing, and the people in this room were right to condemn her, but it was such a relief to talk about it. Tell them everything.

'He rang on Friday evening and wanted to meet up one last time. We needed to talk things through, he said.'

'And you agreed?'

'Yes. We arranged that I would wait for him in a particular place. I told Ulf and Johan I was going for a walk. I borrowed the school's car and met Roger. He was upset when he arrived: he'd been in a fight and his nose was bleeding.'

'Leonard Lundin.'

'Yes. We talked and I tried to explain. I drove him to the football ground. He was still refusing to accept that we couldn't see each other any more. He wept and pleaded and got angry. Said he felt abandoned.'

'What happened?'

'He got out of the car. Furious and upset. The last I saw of him, he was running across the pitch.'

'You didn't go after him?'

'No. I took the car back to school.'

Silence fell once more. A silence that Beatrice immediately interpreted as disbelief. They thought she was lying. Tears welled up in her eyes.

'I had nothing to do with his death. You have to believe me. I loved him. You can think what you like about that, but I loved him.'

Beatrice began to cry, hiding her face in her hands. Vanja and Torkel exchanged looks. Torkel gave a brief nod in the direction of the door, and they both got to their feet. Torkel said they would be back shortly, but it was doubtful if Beatrice heard him.

They had just opened the door when Beatrice stopped them.

'Is Sebastian here?'

Both Torkel and Vanja looked as if they must have misheard the weeping woman in the chair.

'Sebastian Bergman?'

Beatrice nodded through her tears.

'Why?' Vanja tried to remember whether Sebastian and Beatrice had even met. There was that time at the school, of course, and the day they called round to ask where Ulf and Johan were camping, but those were only brief occasions.

'I need to speak to him.'

'We'll see what we can do.'

'Please. I think he'll want to speak to me too.'

Torkel held open the door for Vanja and they went into the corridor.

A second later Sebastian emerged from the other room. He got straight to the point.

'She has nothing to do with the murders.'

'What makes you think that?' Torkel asked as the three of them walked down the corridor. 'You were the one who worked out that she was driving the car, and that she'd had a relationship with Roger.'

'I know, but I jumped to conclusions. I started with the premise that the person who was driving the car was also the murderer. But that isn't the case.'

'You don't know that.'

'Yes, I do. There is nothing in her story or her behaviour to indicate that she's lying.'

'That's not really enough to allow us to put her in the clear.'

'The forensic evidence in the car matches Beatrice's account of the evening. That's why we haven't found any traces of blood in the car.'

Vanja turned to Torkel.

'For once I have to agree with Sebastian.'

Torkel nodded. He was of the same opinion. Beatrice had sounded highly credible. Unfortunately. Vanja was thinking along the same lines. She couldn't suppress an air of both fatigue and disappointment.

'That means there's another car. So we're back to square one yet again – how many times is that?'

'Not necessarily,' said Sebastian. All three of them stopped. 'If you deceive someone, that means someone is deceived. What do we know about her husband?'

Haraldsson was in shock.

It was impossible to describe his current state in any other way.

His plan.

His revenge.

Destroyed.

He was sitting alone in the staffroom with a cup of rapidly cooling coffee in front of him as he tried to work out how it could have gone so wrong. He must have said more to Radjan when he rang him than he could recall. He must have babbled. About how those who are guilty run away, and how there was more to Axel Johansson than just bootlegging. Perhaps it was nothing to do with Roger Eriksson and Peter Westin, but there was definitely something. The booze talking.

Too much, apparently.

Radjan had not only copied the file, he had also read it with fresh eyes. Read it, and just like Haraldsson he had searched for all the available information on Axel Johansson. Radjan Micic was not a bad police officer. It hadn't taken him long to reach the same conclusion that Haraldsson would draw several hours later. Other officers in Gävle and Sollefteå had noticed the similarities between the various rapes, as had colleagues in Västerås, suspecting that the same perpetrator was involved, but without a name to bounce the information off, that wasn't much help.

Haraldsson had a name, and he had given it to Radjan.

Radjan who, Haraldsson now realised, had a considerably wider network of contacts in town than he had. The word around the station was that it had taken fifteen minutes from the time when Radjan and his colleague Elovsson left the station until they had an address. They had picked up Axel Johansson at ten-thirty. Just about the same time that Haraldsson had set off for the station. When it became clear that they were going to take a sample of

DNA, Johansson had confessed. Just like that. And to more rapes than they had on record. He denied, however, having anything to do with the murders of Roger Eriksson and Peter Westin. He even had an alibi for the time of Roger's murder, which given the current circumstances appeared valid. Even so, it had been a good morning for the Västerås police.

Fifteen cases of rape had been cleared up.

By Micic and Elovsson.

Rumour had it that they would be seeing the chief superintendent later that afternoon. Haraldsson could feel his eyes burning, and he pressed his fingers against them. Hard. Held back the tears. Colours appeared in the darkness. Flashing lights. He wanted to sink deeper. Away from reality. Hide behind his eyelids. Footsteps approached and stopped by his table. Haraldsson lowered his hands and gazed blearily at the figure standing beside him.

'Come with me,' Hanser said tersely.

Haraldsson followed her obediently.

They had gathered in the conference room again, all five of them. Billy and Ursula had spent the morning putting all the information relating to the investigation back up on the wall. There was a general feeling of sluggishness in the room. For a while they had thought – or had wanted to convince themselves – that they were done. That everything had been cleared up. It was as if they had just won a long-distance race, only to be told that they had to run another ten kilometres. They didn't really have the strength.

'Ulf and Beatrice Strand separated six years ago, and remarried eighteen months ago,' said Billy, who had put together as much information as he could find on Beatrice's husband in the time available.

Vanja sighed. Sebastian glanced at her and quickly realised that the sigh had nothing to do with boredom or lack of interest. It was an expression, if not of sympathy, then a certain empathy with an act of self-sacrifice that had in many ways led to a wasted life, or so it seemed.

'There are two complaints against Ulf Strand in our records,' Billy went on. 'Threatening behaviour and assault. Both from 2004, both made by one Birger Franzén, who at that time was in a relationship with Beatrice Strand.'

'Was he the one she had an affair with?' As soon as she heard the sound of her own voice Vanja knew her question was totally irrelevant, and had been prompted only by curiosity. She also knew she wouldn't get an answer. She was right.

'It doesn't say. It just says they were in a relationship but not living together at the time of the complaints.'

'And what happened?' Torkel asked impatiently. He wanted to move on, get out there, get this finished.

'The first one resulted in a fine and a suspended sentence, the second in a restraining order. Preventing him from going anywhere near Franzén, not Beatrice and Johan,' Billy clarified.

'So he's the jealous type.' Sebastian leaned back in his chair. 'The fact that his wife was going to bed with his son's best friend might just have upset him a little bit.'

Torkel turned back to Billy.

'Go on.'

'He has a gun licence.'

'Any guns?'

'A Unique T66 Match is registered in his name.'

'Twenty-two calibre,' Ursula said, stating a fact rather than asking a question. Billy still nodded to confirm the point.

'Yep.'

'Anything else?'

'That's more or less it. He works as a systems administrator for a recruitment company and drives a 2008 Renault Mégane.'

Torkel got to his feet.

'Okay, let's go and have a chat with Ulf Strand.'

Vanja, Ursula and Sebastian pushed back their chairs and stood up. Billy stayed where he was. When they returned with Strand they would want all the available material ready and waiting. That was his job. The four of them were about to leave when there was a knock on the door and Hanser poked her head in.

'Could you spare a moment?' She walked in without waiting for an answer.

'We're just on our way out.' Torkel couldn't quite manage to suppress the irritation in his voice. Hanser heard it and chose to ignore it.

'Anything new in the Roger Eriksson case?'

'We're just going to pick up Ulf Strand. Beatrice's husband.'

'Just as well I got here in time, then. I've been talking to the chief superintendent, and—'

Torkel broke in.

'He must be very pleased. I heard about Axel Johansson. Congratulations.'

Torkel gestured towards the door, indicating that they could talk as they walked. Hanser didn't budge.

'Thank you. He is pleased, but not as pleased as he could be.'

Torkel knew where this was going, and suspected he knew why. His suspicions were immediately confirmed.

'We made a pretty big thing of saying the case had been cleared up yesterday.'

'That's not my fault. Yesterday there was a great deal to suggest that it was Ragnar Groth, but on closer scrutiny the evidence didn't hold up. These things happen.'

'He's rather annoyed because you brought in Beatrice Strand without informing us. He wants a representative of the Västerås police present if and when you make an arrest.'

'I am under no obligation to inform him about what I or my team do.' Torkel's voice hardened. He wasn't one for marking his territory, but nor was he prepared to listen to this crap just because the chief superintendent was pissed off after a PR cock-up.

'If he has something to say about my job, why doesn't he come here himself?'

Hanser shrugged her shoulders.

'He sent me.'

Torkel realised he was just shooting the messenger. He gritted his teeth and quickly thought through the situation. What was there to be gained, and what did he have to lose?

'Okay. Fine. We'll take someone with us.'

'We've got a demonstration about a youth club that's got slightly out of hand and an accident on the E18, so we're a bit short of manpower in the station at the moment.'

'I've no intention of waiting, if that's what you mean. There are limits.'

'No, there's no need to wait. I just wanted to explain why I'm sending this particular officer with you.'

Torkel thought he saw a fleeting expression of sympathy before Hanser nodded in the direction of the open-plan office. Torkel followed her gaze. He turned back with an expression that suggested he had just been the victim of a practical joke.

'You can't be serious!'

At that precise moment Haraldsson leaned against a desk and knocked a pot full of pens flying.

The unmarked police cars parked roughly twenty metres from the yellow house and all five of the people inside got out. Haraldsson had sat on his own in the back of one car, with Torkel and Vanja in the front. As they'd left the station he had attempted some small talk, but he soon realised that no one was interested, so he shut up.

They crossed the street, with Haraldsson, Vanja and Torkel slightly ahead of Ursula and Sebastian. The residential area was quiet and peaceful in the afternoon sun. Somewhere in the distance they could hear the sound of a lawnmower. Sebastian knew nothing about gardening, but wasn't April a bit early to be cutting the grass? An enthusiast, presumably.

The group approached the Strands' drive. When they had picked up Beatrice at the school she had said that Ulf was usually home when Johan got back in the afternoons. The recruitment company said he'd left for the day. This seemed to fit: the family's Renault Mégane was outside the garage.

Vanja walked over to the car and crouched down by the back wheel. Her eyes were shining with anticipation as she turned to face the others.

'Pirelli.'

Ursula quickly went over. She took out her camera, squatted down and photographed the tyre.

'P7. Good match.'

She took out a small knife and began to scrape off mud and dirt that was stuck in the tread. Vanja got up and moved behind the car. She tried the boot. It wasn't locked. She glanced at Torkel, who nodded. Vanja opened the boot. Torkel came over and together they looked down into what was virtually an empty space. The sides were black, and without the right equipment it was impossible to determine whether there were any bloodstains on them or not. The bottom was lined with a plastic mat.

A new plastic mat.

Torkel leaned over and lifted it up. Underneath were two covered compartments, presumably housing the spare tyre, warning triangle, fuses and other uninteresting items. The covering itself, however, was far from uninteresting. It was made of needle felt. Grey needle felt. At least, the outside edges were grey. A large, dark red stain had spread outwards from the centre. Both Vanja and Torkel had seen dried blood often enough to be aware immediately of what they were looking at. If they had any doubts, the smell helped to confirm their suspicions. They slammed the boot shut.

Sebastian saw the grim expression on their faces. They had found something.

Something vital.

They were in the right place at last. Sebastian quickly turned to face the house. He thought he had seen a movement at the upstairs window out of the corner of his eye. He fixed his gaze on the window. Nothing. Everything was quiet.

'Sebastian . . .'

408

Torkel called them over. Sebastian gave the upstairs window one final glance before turning his attention to Torkel.

The man who was not a murderer had seen them walk up the drive and stop by the car. He knew it. He'd known it all along. The car was his Achilles heel.

The day after that fateful Friday he had toyed with the idea of scrapping it, but had decided it against it. How would he explain that? Why scrap a perfectly usable car? It would have looked very suspicious. Instead he did what he could. Washed and scrubbed, bought a new mat for the boot and advertised the car for sale. Two people had been to look at it, but no one had made an offer yet. He had ordered new lids for the two compartments at the bottom of the boot and was waiting for them to arrive. They would be here next week.

Too late.

The police were here.

By the car.

Two women crouching by the back wheel. Had he left traces? Presumably. The man who was not a murderer swore to himself. He could have done something about that. New tyres. Nothing odd about that. But now?

Too late.

There was only one thing to do. Go out and confess. Take his punishment. Perhaps they would understand. Understand, but not forgive.

Never forgive.

No one forgave him. Forgiveness demanded not only confession, but also regret, and he still felt not a trace of regret.

He had done what he had to do.

For as long as possible.

But now it was over.

'We know he has access to a gun, so be very careful.' Torkel had gathered them all around him and was speaking in a low voice, almost whispering. 'Stay close to the walls. Vanja, you take the back.'

They all nodded, their expressions serious. Vanja drew her gun as she disappeared down the side of the house, crouching slightly.

'Ursula, take this side in case he climbs out of a window and tries to get away via next door's garden. Sebastian, you stay in the background.'

Sebastian had no problem following this particular instruction. This aspect of police work did not interest him in the least. He knew this was what the others had been looking forward to ever since they first heard about the missing sixteen year old by the name of Roger Eriksson, but the arrest itself meant nothing to him.

To him the journey was everything. The destination nothing.

Torkel turned to Haraldsson.

'You and I will go and ring the doorbell. I want you to draw your gun, but stand to one side with the gun lowered. We don't want to frighten him. Understand?'

Haraldsson nodded. The adrenaline was pumping. This was serious. This was for real. He was going to catch Roger Eriksson's murderer. Not on his own, but still. He was there. He was part of it. There was a rushing sound in his ears as he drew his gun and walked towards the front door with Torkel.

They had gone only a few steps when the saw the doorhandle slowly being pushed downwards. Torkel drew his gun with lightning speed and aimed at the door. Haraldsson glanced at Torkel, realised that the order to keep his weapon lowered no longer applied, and also took aim. The door opened slowly.

'I'm coming out,' a voice said.

A male voice.

'Slowly! And keep your hands where I can see them!' Torkel stopped four or five metres away from the door. Haraldsson did the same. They saw a shoe-clad foot appear in the gap between the door and the frame, then push the door open. Ulf Strand stepped out with both hands up.

'I presume it's me you're looking for.'

'Stop right there!'

Ulf obeyed. He gazed calmly at the police officers as they approached him with their guns at the ready. Ursula and Vanja reappeared round the front of the house. They too were armed.

'Turn around!'

Ulf turned around and stared into the untidy hallway. Torkel gestured to Haraldsson to stay where he was, then approached Ulf.

'Down on your knees!' Ulf did as he was told. The rough stones on the step dug into his knees. Torkel moved towards him and placed one hand on the back of Ulf's neck, then quickly searched him with the other hand.

'It was me. I killed him.'

Torkel finished the search and pulled Ulf Strand to his feet. The other officers put their guns away.

'It was me. I killed him,' Ulf repeated as soon as he made eye contact.

'Yes, I heard you.' Torkel nodded to Haraldsson, who came forward with a pair of handcuffs.

'Hands behind your back, please.'

Ulf's expression was almost pleading as he looked at Torkel.

'Would it be possible for me not to wear those? It would be nice to leave here in a normal way. So that Johan doesn't have to see me as . . . a criminal.'

'Is he at home? Johan?'

'Yes. He's in his room. Upstairs.'

Even if the boy hadn't yet seen or heard what had happened, he was bound to come out of his room eventually. He shouldn't have to find an empty house. He would need someone to talk to. Torkel called Vanja over.

'Stay here with the boy.'

'No problem.'

Torkel turned back to Ulf.

'Okay, let's go.'

411

Ulf turned his head and called into the house. 'Johan, I'm just going with the police for a little while. Mum will be home soon!'

No reply. Torkel grabbed hold of one arm. Haraldsson put away the handcuffs and moved around the other side. With Ulf Strand between them they walked towards the car. Sebastian joined them.

'How long have you known?' he said.

Ulf squinted into the afternoon sun as he looked at Sebastian with a genuinely puzzled expression.

'How long have I known what?'

'That your wife was having a sexual relationship with Roger Eriksson.'

Sebastian saw Ulf's eyes open wide for a second in total surprise. Shock and disbelief chased across his face. Before he managed to get his features under control, Ulf quickly looked down at his feet.

'Erm ... for a while.'

Sebastian stopped dead. His entire body stiffened. He realised what he had just seen: a man taken by surprise. Completely. Utterly. A man who hadn't had a clue what his wife and his son's best friend had been up to, until Sebastian told him. He turned to the others.

'This isn't right.'

Torkel stopped. So did Ulf Strand and Haraldsson. Ulf's eyes were still fixed on the ground.

'What did you say?'

'He hasn't got a fucking clue!' Sebastian walked over to Torkel.

'What? What the hell are you talking about?'

Sebastian realised the implication of his words the moment he uttered them.

'It wasn't him.'

Before anyone had time to react they heard a shot, followed by a scream. Sebastian turned to Ulf and saw Haraldsson clutch his chest and fall to the ground.

'Gun!'

Ursula hurled herself forward and with a single movement

412

dragged the profusely bleeding Haraldsson behind the parked Renault. To safety. Torkel reacted equally fast, shoving Ulf Strand out of the way as he crouched down and followed him. Out of range. In just a few seconds they were off the drive. Seconds that Sebastian made use of, to cast a quick glance over his shoulder. The barrel of a rifle was jutting out from the upstairs window. Behind it he could see a young, pale face.

'Sebastian!' yelled Torkel. Sebastian knew that the others had acted instinctively, and that years of training meant that they were out of danger. He was still standing in the middle of the drive. In full view. He looked up at the window again and saw the barrel of the rifle move slightly to the left.

Towards him.

He took off.

He ran towards the house and the open door. After a couple of steps he heard the crack of a bullet as it hit the stone path behind him. He put on a spurt. Someone appeared in the doorway in front of him. Vanja. With her gun in her hand.

'What's going on?'

Sebastian was pretty sure he was close enough to the house for the angle to make it impossible to hit him from the upstairs window, but he had no intention of risking it by stopping to update Vanja. He threw himself into the safety of the hallway. Vanja was beside him in a second.

'Sebastian. What's going on?'

Sebastian was gasping for breath. His heart was racing. His pulse was pounding in his ears. Not from the exertion, but he must have used up a year's ration of adrenaline in the past fifteen seconds.

'He's up there,' Sebastian replied breathlessly. 'With a rifle.'

'Who is?'

'Johan. He shot Haraldsson.'

They heard footsteps from above. Vanja spun around and pointed her gun at the staircase. No one appeared. The footsteps stopped.

'Are you sure?'

'I saw him.'

'Why would he shoot Haraldsson?'

Sebastian shrugged and took out his mobile, his hands trembling. He keyed in a number. Engaged. He cancelled the call, tried again. Still busy. He assumed Torkel was calling for back-up.

Armed back-up.

He tried to gather his thoughts.

What did he know?

There was a teenager upstairs who had just shot a police officer. A teenager who, according to his mother, had been mentally unstable in the past. It might have been an impulsive action when he saw them taking his father away from him. Perhaps he was involved in the murder of Roger Eriksson in some way, and now he felt as if his whole world was falling apart.

Sebastian set off towards the stairs. Vanja placed a hand on his chest to stop him.

'Where are you going?'

'Upstairs. I have to talk to him.'

'No, you don't. We wait for back-up.'

Sebastian took a deep breath.

'He's sixteen years old. He's scared. He's shut in his room. If he sees an entire fucking armed response team turn up and thinks there's no way out, he's going to turn that gun on himself.'

Sebastian looked at Vanja, his expression serious.

'I don't want that on my conscience. Do you?'

Vanja met his eyes. They stood there in silence. Sebastian could see Vanja weighing the arguments against one another.

For and against.

Sense and sensibility.

He gazed at her, wondering how he was going to persuade her if she refused to let him go upstairs. It would be difficult, but he had to do something. He was certain that if someone didn't make contact with Johan soon, the boy would die. That just couldn't be allowed to happen. To his great relief Vanja nodded and stepped aside. Sebastian walked past her.

'Call Torkel and tell him what I'm doing. Tell them to wait.'

Vanja nodded. Sebastian took a deep breath, grabbed hold of the banister and placed his foot on the first step.

'Good luck.' Vanja touched his arm.

'Thank you.'

Sebastian started up the stairs, moving slowly.

At the top a small landing led off to the left. Four doors. Two on the right, one on the left and one straight ahead at the end. The white painted walls were adorned with framed posters, photographs and a child's drawings, arranged in no discernible order. On the floor was a red runner a few centimetres narrower than the landing. It was dusty. Sebastian looked at the closed doors and thought things over. The staircase turned ninety degrees to the left. The front door was on the same side as Johan's window. So that should mean that the door at the end of the landing would lead him to Johan. Sebastian crept towards it.

'Johan?'

Silence. Sebastian pressed himself against the wall on the right-hand side, uncomfortable with the idea of standing directly in front of the door. He had no idea whether a bullet from a Unique T66 Match was capable of passing through an internal door, but nor did he have any desire to find out.

'Johan, it's me. Sebastian.' He knocked tentatively on the door. 'Do you remember me?'

'Go away,' he heard faintly from inside the room. Sebastian breathed out. Contact. An important first step. Now it was a matter of taking the second step. He had to get inside that room.

'I want to talk to you. Would that be possible?'

No reply.

'I think it would be a good idea if we had a little chat. I mean, I'm not even a police officer, remember. I'm a psychologist.'

In the silence that followed Sebastian could hear sirens approaching in the distance. He swore silently. What the fuck were they doing? The boy would just get more stressed. Sebastian had to get into that room.

415

Now.

He moved across to the left and placed his hand lightly on the doorhandle. It felt cold to the touch. Sebastian realised he was sweating. He wiped his forehead with the other hand.

'I just want to talk to you. Nothing else. I promise.'

No reply. The sirens were getting closer. They must be in the street now. Sebastian raised his voice.

'Can you hear me?'

'Just go away!' Johan's voice sounded resigned rather than threatening. Subdued. Was he crying? Was he on the point of giving up? Sebastian took a deep breath.

'I'm opening the door now.' He pushed down the handle. No visible reaction from inside. The door opened outwards, so Sebastian opened it just a centimetre, then stopped.

'I'm going to open the door all the way now, and then I'm coming in. Is that okay?' Once again Sebastian's words were met with nothing but silence. He inserted his index finger in the gap and gently pulled the door wide open while still standing to one side. Protected by the wall. He closed his eyes. Focus.

Then he stepped forward and stood in the middle of the doorway, his hands clearly visible.

Johan was sitting on the floor under the window with the gun in his hands. He turned to face Sebastian with an expression that suggested his appearance in the doorway was a complete surprise.

Confused.

In shock.

And, therefore, dangerous. Sebastian remained motionless. He looked at Johan with sympathy. He looked so small. So vulnerable. The skin on his face was pale and sweaty. There were dark rings around his eyes, which looked sunken and bloodshot. Lack of sleep, perhaps. Whatever had happened, whatever Johan had done, it had persecuted him. Hunted him down to this point, where there was no longer any way back. The risk was that the pressure would be too great. That the thin surface keeping him in the real world would crack. Sebastian could see how tense the boy

416

was. His jaws were working beneath the pale cheeks. Johan suddenly seemed to lose all interest in Sebastian and turned his attention back to the window and what was going on outside.

From his position in the doorway Sebastian saw an ambulance draw up, along with yet more police cars. Activity everywhere. He could see Torkel speaking to an officer from what must be the local armed response team. Johan lifted the rifle off his knee and pointed it at Sebastian.

'Tell them to go away.'

'I can't do that.'

'I just want them to leave me alone.'

'They're not going anywhere. You shot a police officer.'

Johan blinked hard and a tear ran down his cheek. Sebastian took another step into the room. Johan twitched and raised the gun. Sebastian stopped, holding out his hands in a calming, non-threatening gesture. Johan's gaze darted ominously around the room.

'I'm just going to sit down here.'

Sebastian stepped to the side and slid down onto the floor with his back against the wall, next to the open door. Johan didn't take his eyes off him, but he did lower the rifle.

'Would you like to tell me what happened?'

Johan shook his head, then turned and studied the activity out in the street once more.

'Are they going to come and get me?'

'Not while I'm here.' Sebastian stretched his legs out in front of him, moving slowly. 'And I've got all the time in the world.'

Johan nodded. Sebastian thought he saw his shoulders drop a fraction. Was he beginning to relax? It seemed so. But the boy's head was still twitching like a baby bird's as he tried to see everything that was going on outside, and the rifle was still pointing straight at Sebastian.

'We try to protect the things we love. That's only natural. I can see that you really love your dad.'

No reaction from the boy. Perhaps he was concentrating so hard

417

on the activity in the street that he didn't even hear. Perhaps he just wasn't listening. Sebastian fell silent. They both sat there. From the open window Sebastian could hear a stretcher being wheeled across the tarmac, then the rear doors of the ambulance slammed shut. Haraldsson was in good hands. Muted voices. Footsteps. A car starting up and driving away. The lawnmower still humming away somewhere in the distance, where life was still comprehensible, still manageable.

'I tried to protect those I loved. But I failed.'

Perhaps it was something about the tone of voice. Perhaps it was that things had quietened down outside and were no longer demanding his attention, but Johan turned to face Sebastian.

'What happened?'

'They died. My wife and daughter.'

'How?'

'They drowned. In the tsunami – do you remember that?'

Johan nodded. Sebastian didn't take his eyes off the boy.

'I would do absolutely anything to get them back. So that we could be a family again.'

As Sebastian had hoped, it looked as if his words had struck a chord deep inside the boy. This was something he could relate to. Family. The sense of loss when it was no longer there. Beatrice had talked about how Johan's sorrow had made him ill. The family. The image of the perfect family. Sebastian was beginning to suspect just how far Johan would go to stop anyone spoiling that image.

Johan didn't speak. Sebastian was feeling uncomfortable. Cautiously he drew up his knees and rested his forearms on them. Much better. Johan didn't react to the movement. They carried on sitting there like that.

Opposite one another.

In silence.

Johan was chewing on his lower lip, a preoccupied look on his face. He glanced out of the window with unseeing eyes, as if nothing out there was of any interest to him now.

418

'I never meant to kill Roger.'

Sebastian made out the words with some difficulty. Johan was speaking quietly through clenched teeth. Sebastian closed his eyes briefly. So that was it. He had suspected it when it became clear that Ulf had no motive, but he hadn't wanted to believe it. The tragedy was great enough as it was.

'I told Lena, his mum, so that she could stop it. But nothing happened. It just carried on.'

'Roger and your mother?'

Johan carried on staring out of the window, his gaze fixed on a point outside. Somewhere else.

'Mum met somebody else once. Before. Did you know that?'

'Yes. Birger Franzén.'

'Dad left us.'

Sebastian waited. Nothing else came. It was as if Johan was counting on the fact that Sebastian could work out the rest for himself.

'You were afraid he'd leave you again.'

'He would have. This was worse.'

Johan sounded absolutely certain, and Sebastian couldn't contradict him, even if he'd wanted to.

The age difference.

The relationship between teacher and student.

Her son's best friend.

This betrayal would undoubtedly have been perceived as greater. Much more difficult to forgive. Particularly for a man like Ulf. A man who hadn't even begun to forgive her for the last time.

'How did you find out they were seeing one another?'

'I saw them kissing once. I knew he was seeing someone. He used to talk a lot about . . . what they did. But I . . .'

Johan didn't finish the sentence. Not out loud, anyway. Sebastian watched the boy shaking his head, as if he was continuing the discussion inside his head.

Sebastian waited.

The process was under way. Now the boy had started to open

up like this, it would take a great deal for him to shut down again. He wanted to tell someone. Secrets were a heavy burden. If they were combined with guilt, they could destroy a person. Sebastian was fairly sure that Johan was beginning to feel a sense of relief. He thought he could detect a physical change in the boy. His shoulders had dropped still further. His jaw was no longer so tightly clamped shut. His back, which had been straight and tense, was more relaxed.

So Sebastian waited.

It almost seemed as if Johan had forgotten that Sebastian was in the room. But then he began to speak again. As if he were running a film in his head and narrating what he was seeing.

'He phoned. Here. Mum answered. Dad was at work. I realised they were going to meet up. Mum was going to go for a walk.' Johan almost spat out the last few words. 'I knew where they were. What they were doing.'

The words came faster now. His voice was louder. His eyes were still fixed on a place where only Johan could go. As if he were there, as if . . .

He is waiting by the football pitch. Hidden in the trees on the edge of the forest. He knows where she usually drops him off. Roger told him. Before he knew that Johan knew. He sees the school's S60 approaching the car park. It stops, but no one gets out. He doesn't even want to think about what they might be doing in there. The rifle he brought from home is lying on the ground, and he nudges it with his foot. After a while he sees the car's interior light go on as someone gets out. It's Roger. Johan thinks he hears him say something, but he can't make out what it is. Roger walks quickly across the pitch. Coming towards him. Moving fast. Johan gets to his feet and picks up the rifle. Roger is heading for the path that will take him home when Johan calls his name. Roger stops. Peers in the direction of the trees. Johan steps out, sees Roger shake his head when he catches sight of him. Not pleased. Not surprised. Not scared. It's as if Johan is just a problem that he could do without right now. Johan takes a few steps onto the pitch. It looks as if Roger has been crying. Does he notice the rifle, hanging down by Johan's right leg? He doesn't mention it, anyway. He asks what Johan wants. Johan explains exactly what he wants. He wants Roger to stop going to bed with his mother. He wants Roger never to come anywhere near their house again. He wants Roger to stay as far away from Johan and his family as possible. He raises the gun in order to give weight to his words. But Roger's reaction is completely different from what Johan had expected or hoped for. He starts yelling.

That everything is just crap anyway.

That everything, his whole fucking life, has gone to hell.

That Johan is a fucking idiot.

That he can't deal with him right now.

He starts crying. Then he walks away. Away from Johan. But he can't do that. Not now. Not like this. He hasn't promised that things will change. He hasn't promised to stop. He hasn't promised anything. It seems as if Roger doesn't understand the seriousness of the situation. How important this is. Johan has to make him understand. But in order to make him understand, he has to make him listen first of all. In order to make him listen, he has to make him stop. Johan raises the gun. Shouts at Roger, tells him to stop. Watches him carry on walking. Shouts again. Roger gives him the finger over his shoulder.

Johan pulls the trigger.

'I just wanted to make him listen.' Johan turned to Sebastian, his cheeks wet, his energy spent. His hands no longer had the strength or the will to hold the gun and it slid to the floor in front of him. 'I just wanted to make him listen.'

His body began to shake with deep sobs. It was like a convulsion. The boy was almost doubled over, his forehead touching his legs. Sebastian shuffled slowly across the floor to the trembling wreck. Gently he picked up the rifle and moved it to one side.

Then he put his arms around Johan and gave him the only things he could give him at that moment.

Time and closeness.

421

Vanja was worried. Impatient. Almost half an hour had passed since Sebastian had gone upstairs. She had heard him talking to Johan through the closed door, but once he had gone into the room she had heard nothing apart from subdued murmuring. The odd scrape as someone changed position. She assumed that this was a good sign. No screams.

No agitated voices.

And, above all, no more shots had been fired.

Haraldsson was on his way to hospital, or perhaps he was already there by now. The bullet had entered just below the shoulderblade on the left-hand side and passed straight through. He had lost a great deal of blood and needed surgery, but initial reports indicated that his injuries were not life threatening.

Vanja had remained in constant telephone contact with Torkel on the outside. Six police cars were in position. Twelve armed response officers had thrown a ring of steel around the house. But Torkel was keeping them outside. Uniformed officers had cordoned off the entire area. Curious neighbours were gathering on street corners, along with journalists and photographers who were doing their best to get closer. Vanja looked at her watch again. What was actually going on up there? She hoped she wouldn't end up regretting her decision to let Sebastian go.

Then she heard footsteps. Footsteps nearing the stairs. She drew her gun and adopted the correct stance at the foot of the staircase. Ready for anything.

They came down side by side, Sebastian and Johan. Sebastian had his arm around the boy, who looked much smaller and younger than his sixteen years. Sebastian appeared to be more or less carrying him down. Vanja put her gun away and spoke to Torkel.

*

Once Johan had been handed over and driven away, Sebastian turned his back on everything that was going on in the street and re-entered the house. His heart was heavy as he walked into the living room, moved some laundry on the sofa and sat down. He leaned against the rough fabric, put his feet up on the coffee table and closed his eyes. During the time when he had been working with the police he had seldom allowed cases, perpetrators or victims to stay on his mind. They were simply problems to be solved, tools to be made use of, obstacles to be overcome. In the end everything and everyone existed only to provide him with a challenge.

To prove how clever he was.

To feed his ego.

Once they had fulfilled their function, he forgot about them and moved on. He found the ensuing legal process just as uninteresting as the actual arrest. So why were the Strands still with him? A young perpetrator. A family in ruins. Tragic, yes, but nothing he hadn't seen before. Nothing he intended to carry around with him for any length of time.

He was finished with the case.

He was finished with Västerås.

He knew exactly what he needed in order to be able to let go of the Strands.

Sex.

He needed sex.

Have sex, get the house sold, go back to Stockholm. That was the plan.

Would he go to Storskärsgatan 12? Would he try to get in touch with his son or daughter? The way he felt at the moment, probably not, but he had no intention of making any definite decisions until he was feeling better.

After he'd had sex.

After he'd sold the house.

After he'd left Västerås.

Sebastian felt the cushions sag as someone sat down beside

423

him. He opened his eyes. Vanja was perched right on the edge. Spine erect. Hands clasped on her knees. Alert. The complete opposite of Sebastian, who was lying there sprawled on the sofa. It was as if she wanted to mark as great a distinction between them as possible.

'What did he say?'

'Johan?'

'Yes.'

'That he killed Roger.'

'Did he say why?'

'He was afraid his father would leave him again. It just happened.'

Vanja frowned, her expression sceptical.

'Twenty-two stab wounds and dumped in a bog? It doesn't sound like an accident.'

'His father helped with all that somehow. You need to talk to him. The boy didn't kill Westin either.'

Vanja seemed satisfied. She stood up and headed for the hallway. When she reached the door she stopped and turned around to face Sebastian. He met her gaze with a questioning look.

'You've slept with her, haven't you?'

'What?'

'His mother. Beatrice. You've slept with her.'

It wasn't a question this time, so Sebastian didn't answer. There was no need. As always, silence provided the best confirmation.

Was that a flicker of disappointment he saw on his soon-to-be ex-colleague's face?

'When you went upstairs because you thought the boy might harm himself, I thought that maybe, just maybe, you weren't a complete shit.'

Sebastian knew where this conversation was going. He'd been here before. Other women. Other contexts. Other words. Same conclusion.

'Obviously I was wrong.'

Vanja walked away. He watched her go. Stayed where he was. Didn't speak. What was there to say?

She was right, after all.

Ulf Strand was sitting on the chair that had been occupied by his wife just a few hours earlier. He appeared to be calm and collected. Polite, almost considerate. The first thing he asked when Vanja and Torkel walked into the interview room and sat down opposite was how Johan was. Once he had been reassured that the boy was being taken care of and that Beatrice was with him, he asked after Haraldsson. Vanja and Torkel informed him that Haraldsson was out of danger, then they switched on the tape recorder and asked Ulf to start from the beginning. From the moment he first found out that Roger was dead.

'Johan called me at work that evening. He was crying, he was absolutely beside himself. He said something terrible had happened at the football club.'

'So you drove down there?'

'Yes.'

'What happened when you got there?'

Ulf straightened up in the chair.

'Roger was dead. Johan was falling apart, so I tried to calm him down as best I could, then I got him into the car.' Vanja noticed that there was not a trace of emotion in Ulf's voice. It was as if he were giving a lecture to colleagues and clients: keen to come across as formal, his voice well modulated.

'Then I took care of Roger.'

'Took care of him in what way?' asked Torkel.

'I dragged him out of sight. Down into the forest. I realised it would be possible to trace the bullet, so I had to get it out.'

'And how did you do that?'

'I went back to the car and fetched a knife.'

Ulf stopped and swallowed hard. *Not surprising*, thought Sebastian from his position in the room next door. So far Ulf had not played an active role, apart from moving the body. But he hadn't harmed it. From now on things would begin to get difficult.

Ulf asked for a glass of water. Torkel fetched one. Ulf took two, three gulps. He put down the glass and wiped his mouth with the back of his hand.

'You fetched a knife from the car. What happened next?' Vanja was pushing him. Ulf's voice was noticeably weaker when he spoke.

'I used it to hack out the bullet.'

Vanja opened the folder in front of her on the desk. She leafed through several A4 photographs of the young, mutilated body. She seemed to be searching for something. *Playing to the gallery*, thought Sebastian. She knew everything she needed to know to conduct this interview without having to consult any papers or records. She just wanted Ulf to catch a glimpse of what he had done.

Not that he had forgotten.

Not that he would ever forget.

Vanja pretended to find the piece of paper she was pretending to look for.

'There were twenty-two stab wounds to Roger's body when we found him.'

Ulf was struggling to tear his gaze away from the terrible photographs that now lay spread out all over the desk around Vanja's folder. The classic car-crash dilemma: you don't want to look, but you just can't help it.

'I . . . I thought I could make it look as if he'd been stabbed to death. Some kind of ritual murder, perhaps. The act of a madman, I don't know.' Ulf managed to lift his eyes and looked directly at Vanja. 'I just wanted to hide the fact that he'd been shot, that's all.'

'Okay, and when you'd stabbed him twenty-two times and cut out his heart, what did you do then?'

'I drove Johan home.'

'And where was Beatrice?'

'I don't know. She wasn't at home, anyway. Johan must have been in shock or something. He fell asleep in the car on the way

426

home. I took him upstairs and got him to bed.' Ulf fell silent. He seemed to be caught in the moment. It occurred to him that this was probably the last thing that had any vestige of normality about it: a father tucking in his sleeping son. Everything since then had been one long battle. To keep quiet. Hold things together.

'Go on.'

'I went back to the forest and moved the body. I thought I would put it somewhere that a sixteen-year-old couldn't possibly take it. To make sure no one would suspect Johan.'

Sebastian sat up in his chair and pressed the button on his head-set. Through the window he could see Vanja pay attention as she heard the humming in her ear.

'He didn't know that Beatrice and Roger were screwing, so why did he think Johan shot his friend?'

Vanja gave a brief nod. Good question. She turned her full attention back to Ulf.

'One thing I don't understand: if you didn't know about the relationship between your wife and Roger, then why did you think Johan had shot him?'

'There was no reason. It was an accident. A game that went wrong. They were out getting in some shooting practice and he was careless. That's what he said.'

Ulf looked from Vanja to Torkel with renewed intensity, as if he had believed until now that his son had been guilty of lying at worst, as if he had suddenly realised that Johan was not innocent. That it hadn't been an accident. Or not just an accident, in any case.

'What will happen to Johan?' Genuine anxiety and solicitude in his voice.

'He's over fifteen, so he's reached the age of criminal responsibility,' Torkel said matter-of-factly.

'What does that mean?'

'That he'll face prosecution.'

'Tell us about Peter Westin.' Vanja changed tack, eager to get things tied up.

'He's a psychologist.'

'We know that. We want to know why he's dead. What did you think Roger had told him that was so dangerous he couldn't be allowed to live?'

Ulf looked completely bewildered.

'Roger?'

'Yes, Peter Westin was Roger's counsellor. Didn't you know?'

'No. He's Johan's psychologist. Has been for several years. Since the divorce. Johan was in a real mess after ... well, after all this business. With Roger. Understandably. So he went to see Peter. Afterwards. I didn't know what he'd said. I asked him, but he couldn't really remember. I realised he hadn't confessed to anything, because otherwise the police would have come knocking, but he might have talked about things that would enable Peter to put two and two together at a later stage and work out what had happened. I couldn't take the risk.'

Vanja gathered up the photos. They knew all they needed to know. Now it was up to the court. Because of his young age, Johan would probably get off lightly. Ulf, on the other hand ... It would be a long time before the Strand family was together again.

Vanja was reaching across to switch off the tape recorder when Torkel stopped her. There was one question left to ask: one that had been troubling him ever since he had learned what had actually happened.

'Why didn't you call the police? Your son rings to tell you that he's shot his friend by accident. Why didn't you just call the police?'

Ulf met Torkel's curious gaze. This was simple. If Torkel was also a father, he would understand.

'Johan didn't want me to. He was petrified. If I'd called the police, I would have been letting him down. I'd done that once already. When I left. This time I had to help him.'

'Four people are dead, you're going to end up in prison and he's completely traumatised. In what way were you helping him?'

'I failed, I admit that. I failed. But I did everything in my power. I just wanted to be a really good father.'

'A good father?' The dubious tone of Torkel's voice was met by a gaze that radiated absolute conviction.

'I wasn't around for some of the most important years. But I don't believe it's ever too late to be a good father.'

Ulf Strand was taken away. He would be charged later that evening. The job was over. Sebastian sat in the room next door, watching as Torkel and Vanja gathered up their things. They were chatting happily about going home. Vanja was hoping to catch a late train that evening, unless Billy was planning to drive back to Stockholm. Torkel would be staying on for a day or two, as would Ursula. Torkel would tie up all the loose ends, while Ursula would go through Strand's house to make sure all the angles were covered when it came to the forensic evidence. The last thing Sebastian heard before the door closed behind them was Torkel expressing the hope that there would be time for them to have dinner together before Vanja left.

There was a lightness about them. In their voices, their movements. Relief. Good had triumphed. Mission accomplished. Time to ride off into the sunset with a song on their lips.

Sebastian didn't feel like singing. He didn't feel like celebrating. He didn't even feel like having sex any longer.

He could only think about two things:

Storskärsgatan 12, and Ulf's voice: 'I don't believe it's ever too late to be a good father.'

The strange thing was that Sebastian realised he had already decided, more or less. Not expressly, not consciously, but deep down inside he was pretty sure that he wouldn't go looking for Anna Eriksson and/or her child when he got back to Stockholm. Pretty sure, and happy with the decision his subconscious had made on his behalf.

He couldn't see the positive aspect.

What it could give him.

What it might lead to.

Anna would never be another Lily. The child would never be

429

another Sabine. And they were the ones he missed. They were the ones he wanted back. They were the only ones he cared about. Lily and Sabine.

But, in spite of himself, Ulf's words had touched something within him. Not what he said, but the way that he said it.

The certainty.

The conviction. As if it was an incontrovertible fact. A universal truth.

It's never too late to be a good father.

Sebastian had a son or a daughter. He had a child who, in all probability, was still alive. There was someone out there who was half made up of him.

Who was his.

It's never too late to be a good father.

Those simple words posed difficult questions.

Was he really going to let yet another child slip through his fingers?

Could he do that?

Did he want to?

Sebastian was becoming more and more convinced that the answer to all three questions was 'no'.

The train that would take Sebastian back to Stockholm would be leaving in an hour. It had been almost three days since he had walked out of the police station with Ulf's words still ringing in his ears and headed back to his parents' house. He had had no further contact with Torkel or Ursula, even though he knew they were staying in town for a few days. He didn't know whether they were still around. The investigation was over. No one seemed to feel the need to keep in touch outside work. Fine by Sebastian. He'd got what he came for.

Two days ago the agent had returned and they had done everything necessary so that the house could be sold. In the evening Sebastian had dug out the piece of paper with the name and phone number of the woman who had been reading her book on the train to Västerås: an encounter that seemed like an eternity ago.

She had been dubious when he called. He apologised. Explained that he had been up to his neck in work. That murder investigation she had perhaps heard about. The dead teenager from Palmlövska High. Exactly as he had expected, she had been curious and agreed to meet up the following day. Yesterday. They had ended the evening at his house. He hadn't managed to get rid of her until this morning. She wanted to see him again. He made no promises. If he didn't call her, then she would call him, she said with a smile. He wouldn't get away, not now she knew where he lived. Three hours later Sebastian had taken everything he wanted from the house, locked the door and walked away, never to return.

Now he was standing in a place he never thought he would visit. To tell the truth, he had sworn never to come here. Never to visit him again. Now they were both lying there. In the churchyard. His parents' grave.

The funeral flowers had wilted. The grave looked shabby. Sebastian wondered why no one had taken away the dead wreaths, the floral arrangements that had been knocked over and half eaten by deer. Was there a form he had to sign in order to get the church to tend to it? He certainly wasn't going to look after it. He wouldn't have done it even if he'd been living in Västerås. As things stood, it was completely out of the question.

The red granite gravestone depicted a sun rising, or possibly setting, behind two majestic pine trees. The inscription read BERGMAN FAMILY PLOT, and beneath that was the name of his father: TURE BERGMAN. Esther's name hadn't yet been added. The grave would be allowed to settle properly before they moved the stone to add a new inscription. Six months, Sebastian had heard somewhere.

Ture had died in 1988. She had been alone for twenty-two years. His mother. Sebastian wondered whether she had ever considered coming to see him. Reaching out to him. If she had done, would he have taken her hand?

Probably not.

Sebastian was standing a few metres from the neglected grave.

Irresolute. He was surrounded by stillness. The spring sun warmed his back through his coat. A lone bird was singing in one of the birch trees planted here and there among the graves. A woman and a man cycled past along the path. She was laughing at something. Bubbling, sparkling laughter that seemed misplaced as it rose into the clear blue sky. What was he doing here? He really had no desire to get any closer to the grave than this. At the same time there was something doubly tragic in the fact that his mother's final resting place looked like a compost heap, when she had been such a tidy person.

Sebastian stepped up to the grave and crouched down. Clumsily he started gathering up the wilted flowers.

'I bet you never thought this would happen, Mum. I bet you never thought I'd come.'

The sound of his own voice surprised him. Confused him. He had never thought of himself as the kind of person who would end up crouching down and tidying a grave while talking to his dead mother. What on earth had happened to him?

It was something to do with those numbers.

1988.

Twenty-two years.

Alone. Birthdays, weekdays, Christmas, holidays. Even with friends around, alone in the silence of that big house most of the time. Plenty of time to think.

About what had been.

About how things had turned out.

Her pride greater than her longing.

The fear of being rejected stronger than her need for love.

The mother of a son she never heard from. Grandmother for a few short years to a child she never got to see. Sebastian gave up on his inept attempt at tidying and got to his feet. He reached into his pocket for his wallet and took out the photograph of Sabine and Lily that had been on the piano in his parents' house.

'You never got to see her. I made sure of that.' His right hand tightened on the wallet. He could tell that the tears were not far

432

away. The grief. Definitely not for his father. Not for his mother, either, even if he was able to feel a certain sorrow when he thought about how meaningless their conflict seemed in relation to the consequences it had had. He wasn't even weeping for Lily and Sabine. He was weeping for himself. For the realisation.

'Do you remember what you said the last time we saw each other? You said that God had left me. That he had taken his hand away from me.'

Sebastian looked at the picture of his dead wife and his dead child, at the unfinished gravestone in the churchyard in the town where he had grown up, where no one knew him, no one asked after him, no one missed him. A state of affairs that was true of every town. Sebastian wiped his cheeks with the back of his left hand.

'You were right.'

Storskärsgatan 12.

He had ended up there after all. Outside the imposing functionalist building. Sebastian knew nothing about architecture, nor did he have any interest in learning more, but he did know that the buildings to the west of Gärdet were examples of functionalism.

He knew that Anna Eriksson lived in the apartment block in front of him. Anna Eriksson, the mother of his child.

Hopefully.

Really?

Sebastian had been back in Stockholm for almost a week now. He had walked past Storskärsgatan 12 every single day. Sometimes several times. So far he hadn't been inside. The closest he had come was to peer through the main entrance to see if he could catch a glimpse of the list of residents that was on the wall in the entrance hall. Anna Eriksson lived on the third floor.

Should he?

Shouldn't he?

Sebastian had been wrestling with this issue ever since he got home. In Västerås it had all seemed more abstract, somehow: a mind game. He could weigh up the pros and cons. Make a decision. Change his mind. Change his mind again. Without any consequences.

Now he was here. The decision he made might be irrevocable.

Turn and walk away. Or not.

Make himself known. Or not.

He kept on changing his mind. Several times a day. The arguments were the same as those he had gone over and over in Västerås. Nothing new occurred to him. No fresh insights. He cursed his indecisiveness.

Sometimes he walked over to Gärdet convinced that he was

going to march straight in, walk up the stairs and ring the door-bell. But then he didn't even turn into Storskärsgatan.

On other occasions, when he had no intention of making him-self known, he would end up standing outside the dark wooden door for hours. It was as if someone else was directing his actions. As if he had no real say in what he did. But he hadn't been inside the building. Not yet.

Today, however, he was going to do it. He could feel it in his bones. He had managed to hold a steady course. He had left his apartment on Grev Magnigatan and headed along Storgatan. Turned right onto Narvavägen and up towards Karlaplan, past the Fältöversten shopping mall, then across Valhallavägen and he was there. No more than a fifteen-minute walk. And Anna Eriksson lived there. He wondered whether she had been living there when the child was younger. If so, they might have seen each other in the shopping mall. His child and the child's mother might have stood in front of him in the queue for the deli counter in Sabis. These thoughts filled Sebastian's mind as he stood in the street looking at Storskärsgatan 12.

Twilight was beginning to fall. It had been a beautiful spring day in Stockholm. You could almost feel the warmth of early summer.

Today he would make himself known.

Today he would speak to her.

He had made up his mind.

He crossed the street and headed towards the main door. Just as he was wondering how he was going to get inside, a woman in her thirties emerged from the lift in the foyer and came towards the door. He took this as a sign that he really was meant to meet Anna Eriksson today.

He got there just as the woman stepped out onto the pavement, and grabbed the door as it began to close behind her.

'Thanks, that was good timing.'

The woman barely glanced at him. Sebastian went inside and the door closed behind him with a heavy thud. He looked at the list of residents again, even though he knew what it said.

Third floor.

He thought about taking the lift, which travelled up through the centre of the building through a black metal cage, but decided against it. He needed all the time he could get. His heart was beating faster and faster, and his palms were sweaty. He was nervous. That didn't happen very often.

Slowly he began to walk up the stairs.

There were two doors on the third floor. He could see Eriksson and another name on one of them. A moment to gather his thoughts. He closed his eyes. Took a couple of deep breaths. Then he stepped forward and rang the bell. Nothing happened. Sebastian felt almost relieved. No one home. He had tried, but no one had opened the door. He had been wrong. They weren't meant to meet, he and Anna Eriksson. Not today, at any rate. Sebastian was just about to turn away and head back down the stairs when he heard footsteps inside the apartment, and the next moment the door opened.

A woman a few years younger than Sebastian was looking at him. She had dark, shoulder-length hair and blue eyes. High cheekbones. Narrow lips. Sebastian didn't even recognise her now she was standing in front of him. He had no recollection whatsoever of going to bed with this woman who was drying her hands on a red checked tea towel and looking at him with an enquiring expression.

'Hi, are you . . . ' Sebastian lost the thread. Didn't know where to start. His mind had gone blank. Even though a thousand thoughts were whirling around. The woman stood there staring at him, not saying a word.

'Anna Eriksson?' Sebastian managed at last. The woman nodded.

'My name is Sebasti—'

'I know who you are,' the woman interrupted him. Sebastian was completely taken aback.

'Do you?'

'Yes. What are you doing here?'

436

Sebastian didn't know what to say. He had pictured this meeting so many times since he had read the letters. But now events had taken a completely different turn from the way he had imagined. He had expected her to be almost shocked, perhaps even sway slightly. It would be a total surprise. A ghost from thirty years ago was standing outside her door. He would have to provide proof of his identity in order for her to believe him. Nothing like this encounter with a woman who tucked a corner of the tea towel into the waistband of her trousers, then stared at him with a challenging look in her eye.

'I . . .' Sebastian broke off. He had gone through this in his mind as well. He might as well stick to the plan. Start from the beginning.

'My mother died, and when I was clearing out her house I found some letters.'

The woman remained silent but nodded. She obviously knew which letters he was referring to.

'It said in the letters that you were pregnant. With my child. I just came to find out if that was true, and if so, what happened.'

'Come in.'

The woman stepped aside and Sebastian walked into the narrow hallway. Anna closed the door behind him, and he bent down to undo his shoelaces.

'There's no need for that. You won't be staying.'

Sebastian straightened up. 'Oh?'

'I wanted you out of the stairwell. It echoes.' Anna positioned herself directly opposite him and folded her arms.

'It's true. I was pregnant and I looked for you, but I didn't find you. And to be perfectly honest, I stopped looking a very long time ago.'

'I realise you're angry, but—'

'I'm not angry.'

'I never got the letters. I didn't know anything about it.'

They both fell silent. Stood there facing one another. For a moment Sebastian wondered what would have happened if he had

437

known. All those years ago. If he had gone back to Anna Eriksson and become a father. What would his life with this woman have been like? It was ridiculous even to think about it, of course. It was pointless to speculate about a possible future, an alternative present. Besides which, he would never have gone back to her, even if he had received the letters. Back then. Not the old Sebastian.

'I saw you maybe ... fifteen years ago.' Anna's voice was calm. 'When you helped to catch that serial killer.'

'Hinde. Ninety-six.'

'I saw you on TV. If I'd still wanted to get in touch, I'm sure I could have tracked you down then.'

Sebastian absorbed this information for a moment.

'But I do have a child?'

'No. I have a daughter. My husband has a daughter. You do not. Not here and not with me, anyway.'

'So she doesn't know that ...'

'He's not her father?' said Anna. 'No. He knows, of course. But she doesn't, and if you tell her you will destroy everything.'

Sebastian nodded, looking down at the floor. He wasn't altogether surprised. This was one of the scenarios he had played out in his mind. That the child didn't know it had a different father. He would shatter a happy family. He had done it before when he had slept with married women and had perhaps not always been as discreet as he might have been, but this was a different matter.

'Sebastian ...'

He looked up. Anna had unfolded her arms and was looking at him with an expression that demanded his full attention.

'You really would destroy everything. For all of us. She loves us. She loves her father. If she found out now that we've been lying to her all these years ... I don't think we'd get through it.'

'But if she is mine, then ...' A feeble final attempt. Doomed from the start.

'She isn't. Maybe she was. For a while. She could have been, if you'd come back. But now she isn't.'

Sebastian nodded. He could see the logic in what she was

saying. What would be the point? What would he get out of it? It almost seemed as if Anna could read his mind.

'What can you give her? A total stranger turns up after thirty years and says he's her father. What's that going to achieve, apart from destroying our family?'

Sebastian nodded and moved towards the door.

'I'll go.'

As he was about to open the door, Anna touched his upper arm. He turned to face her.

'I know my daughter well. You would destroy our family, and she would end up hating you.'

Sebastian nodded.

He understood.

He left the apartment and the other life that could have been, could have become his. Anna closed the door behind him and he stood there at the top of the stairs.

That was it, then.

Done.

He had a daughter. A daughter he would never see. Never get to know. All the tension that had been building up for so long ebbed away, and he felt utterly exhausted. His legs almost buckled. He moved over to the stairs leading up to the next floor and sat down.

Stared into space.

Empty.

Completely empty.

Far away he heard the dull thud of the outside door closing three flights down. He wondered how he was going to get home. It wasn't far, but at the moment it seemed like an insurmountable obstacle.

It took a few seconds before he registered that the lift on his left had begun to move. He stood up. If the lift stopped here, he would travel down in it. At least that would be a first step on the long journey home to his empty apartment.

He was in luck. The lift stopped at the third floor. Sebastian really didn't want to see anyone. Not even to exchange meaning-less smiles in the doorway of a lift. As the person inside the lift pulled back the metal door, Sebastian moved a couple of steps fur-ther up. The person emerged and Sebastian caught a glimpse of her through the grille above the cage.

There was something.

Familiar.

Extremely familiar.

'Hi Mum, it's me,' he heard. Vanja. She left the door open as she kicked off her shoes, and Sebastian was just able to see Anna before Vanja closed the door behind her.

He remembered now. The names. On the door. He had been so focused on Eriksson that he hadn't even registered the other name.

Lithner.

Vanja Lithner.

Vanja was his daughter.

Nothing could have prepared him for this information.

Nothing.

Sebastian felt his legs give way, and he had to sit down.

It was a long time before he got up again.

ACKNOWLEDGEMENTS

We would like to thank everyone at Norstedts; they have been positive and supportive ever since our very first meeting, giving us confidence and making our work even more enjoyable.

Special thanks to Eva, Susanna, Peter and Linda.

We would also like to thank the company Tre Vänner, particularly Jonas, Tomas, Johan and William for allowing us to try out our wings with their blessing.

A big thank you to our families, who have heard so much about Sebastian Bergman over the past year that it has probably bordered on torture.

Hans would like to thank Sixten, Alice and Ebba: you're absolutely fantastic. And Lotta, truly the 'Queen of fucking everything'.

Micke would like to say to Astrid, Caesar, William and Vanessa: you're the best thing that's ever happened to me.

Need more Swedish crime fiction?

SHE'S NEVER COMING BACK

Hans Koppel

'Excitement from the first page to the last . . . nail-biting'
DAST magazine

When Ylva, a loving mother and wife, fails to come home from work,
her husband is not initially suspicious. But as time passes, he becomes
frantic with worry. And by the time he finally contacts the police,
he is almost hysterical. Given the mysterious circumstances
of her disappearance, he becomes the number one suspect.

But what no one knows is that she's being held hostage
in the cellar of the house opposite her own.

A camera is rigged against her own house and Ylva can only watch her
family on the screen. They cannot see her – and they most certainly
cannot hear her scream . . .

This is the story that has obsessed readers across Scandinavia.
She's Never Coming Back is a thrilling, unforgettable page-turner
that does not loosen its grip from the first page to the last.

'A masterpiece'
Boktipsaren magazine